BEST SERVED COLD

BEST SERVED COLD

HILLY BARMBY

This edition produced in Great Britain in 2023

by Hobeck Books Limited, 24 Brookside Business Park, Stone, Staffordshire
ST15 0RZ

www.hobeck.net

A CIP catalogue for this book is available from the British Library.

ISBN 978-1-915-817-26-6 (pbk)

ISBN 978-1-915-817-25-9 (ebook)

Cover design by Jayne Mapp Design

Printed and bound in Great Britain

Are you a thriller seeker?

Hobeck Books is an independent publisher of crime, thrillers and suspense fiction and we have one aim – to bring you the books you want to read.

For more details about our books, our authors and our plans, plus the chance to download free novellas, sign up for our newsletter at **www.hobeck.net**.

You can also find us on Twitter **@hobeckbooks** or on Facebook **www.facebook.com/hobeckbooks10**.

To my mum and dad (who have now both passed on), as they never wanted me to let go of my dreams and told me to do whatever I wanted with my life.

I did, but I wish they were here to see it.

And, to all the dogs who like avocados.

Chapter One

IT MAY BE my eighth book launch, yet a cocktail of anxiety and exhilaration still makes me queasy. The launch is in my local Brighton Just One More Chapter bookstore at three this afternoon. Which gives me time to walk along the beachfront, padding over the pebbles in my bare feet, swinging my high heels by my side and listening to the sibilant waves sloshing up the shingle. The sea is gunmetal grey and blends seamlessly with the sky. As it's mid-November, the air is chilled but fresh.

Breathe, now. Breathe. I should try to get a handle on such emotions, except it gets to me every time. My feet numb, I sit on the steps leading up to the promenade and slip into my shoes. It takes a moment, and then I get chronic pins and needles. *Ouch and double ouch!* Brushing the sand from my coat, I can tell the salt air has made my face and hair sticky. I hope no one notices.

The bouquet arrived this morning. Twelve long-stemmed red roses. A pretty card tucked into the leafy-green foliage, but nothing on it except a kiss. They've arrived early morning for every book launch, and I still have no idea who is sending them to me. At first, it was cute. A secret admirer? A fairy-tale fan?

But in the dark of the night, the kiss changes to X marks the spot. It's not cute anymore and I try not to be surly as I take them. Who the hell is it? Own up or ship out!

I walk back up towards the bookstore, and when I push through the glass door into the shop, I spot the table with my books placed on it. The usual stand of best-sellers has been shunted to a different position, so the first thing anyone will see when entering after three will be me, sitting at my table, pen raised in anticipation. Well, that's the crux, isn't it? Will anyone come to see (and hopefully buy) the latest Lily Maye book? Don't get me wrong, I'm not a J. K. Rowling, but I do have a hardcore group of fans. I'm an illustrator, and the book I will be signing is a compilation of fairy tales: ten Grimm and ten Hans Christian Andersen. These are not the Disney versions. Most people don't realise the original stories were too dark and scary for kids. Thinking about it, they are pretty dark and scary for adults too!

Three chairs are tucked behind the table. One for me, one for Mary, my publisher, and one for Mr Hudson, an academic researcher in folklore, here to tell us of the origins of the fairy tales in my book. About thirty fold-up chairs are placed in front of us, and I wonder if they will be filled.

By five past three, people are milling about, getting seated and chatting in low voices. More are coming in, looking a little guilty for being five minutes late. So very *English*! Hopefully, this means today will not be a washout, as I sometimes fear. These people are often enthusiasts, and some are grannies searching for unique Christmas presents for the grandkids. Illustrated books with full-colour plates are not cheap, and I'm always thankful I get a few free copies to give to my nearest and dearest. Otherwise, I probably couldn't afford it all.

Mary clears her throat. That is the signal for everyone to stop. She always begins by singing the praises of the book's quality and saying how brilliant my illustrations are. Whoop-whoop! Mr Hudson takes over after a while. I'm scanning the room, and the audience seems enthralled, listening intently as he dissects the provenance of the original tales.

'Fairy tales are much older than previously thought,' he says. His voice is deep and resonant, booming across the space. I spot a few souls nodding and smiling.

'Stories such as "Beauty and the Beast" and "Rumpelstilt-skin" can be traced back thousands of years to prehistoric times, with one tale originating from the bronze age. While these types of stories were first written down in the seventeenth and eighteenth centuries, the researchers found they originated significantly earlier. Both tales can be securely traced back to the emergence of the major western Indo-European subfamilies as distinct lineages between 2,500 and 6,000 years ago.'

There are a few oohs and aahs at this point. Even though I know all this stuff, it is still an incredible fact that most people are not aware of. I suspect many believe the tales exist only as Disney animations, with a few musical numbers thrown in.

Then I see a woman tucked at the back in the corner. She's hidden by others in bulky coats and the odd bobble hat they haven't taken off. Leaning forward, her face becomes clearer. It's like I've been jabbed with a cattle prod. I feel a snap of recognition as I look at her, although I can't place her. *What the hell?* Why is my hair standing on end? The voice next to me is a burble of sounds. It feels as if I am underwater in a fast-flowing river. I need my ears to pop. A hard nudge in my ribs brings me back. Mr Hudson has stopped talking, and Mary gives me a sharp look.

'Lily, *dear?*' She is in her late fifties, although exceedingly well turned out. Smart, slim, wearing modern glasses and a designer suit. Her mind is as sharp as the look she is giving me. What did I miss? 'So, where *do* you get your inspiration from?'

Even her teeth look sharp. I realise we are at the question part of the session. I must have zoned out. Glancing about, I catch an enquiring look from a woman in the front row. I focus on her.

'I've always had a rich imagination,' I start. 'Painting from nature seemed so instinctive to me, and over the years, I've combined that love with painting what's not seen, the wild and the fey.' The woman at the back of the room shifts position, and I can see her more clearly. Red-gold hair. There is another stab of recognition, and my words stumble, although I pick up again. 'I use multi-media, so in a way, a lot of my work has to evolve as I go along.'

'So, are you saying,' says another voice from somewhere in the middle, 'you don't work out what you want beforehand? You create a painting as you go along?'

'That's a good question.' I think for a moment. Every launch has a different set of queries. 'I have a pencil sketch that I work into, and usually I overlay some colours on it, but mostly I get going on it, starting with watercolours and then building up from there.'

There are more questions, and when no more hands are raised, Mary says, 'Right. Anyone who would like a signed copy, please line up here. Can you all be aware Lily doesn't have time to write an essay for you all, so can you try to keep any inscription brief? Thanks.' Laughter ripples around the room, though Mary isn't joking. She never jokes. You wouldn't believe what people want you to write as their dedication to someone. Downright scary, sometimes.

I smile as expected at each person who stands with the book outstretched for that pretty little signature I had to practise getting *just right*. I know people are shy, and this is when they ask their questions, so the bodies in front of me dwindle at a snail's pace until there's only one woman left. My arm is aching, and I long to set the pen down and have a cup of coffee. I look up. It's her. *It's that woman.* She's beautiful. Eyes the colour of recycled glass, lightly freckled face and thick tawny hair cut in a short bob. Her clothes are stylish, and she looks polished and sophisticated. Why can't I recall her?

'Hi,' she breathes. Her voice is husky. 'I can't believe I'm here and getting a signed copy of your new book. I've been a fan of your work for years. I have all your books.'

'That's really nice to know,' I say. 'I'm sorry. Have we met before? You look familiar.'

There's a long pause, and her lovely face freezes for a nano-second. 'I have copies of all your previous books. You've signed every one of them. So, yeah. We have kind of met before.'

A wave of embarrassment washes over me. That must be it. What a jerk I am, yet that reaction to her still seems over the top. 'I'm so sorry. Of course. Sometimes I get so nervous I don't see what's in front of me, or in this case, who. I didn't mean to be rude or anything.'

'Don't worry. I'm sure it must be quite stressful, and how can you be expected to remember everyone who is clamouring for a book? We must be a blur of faces, hands and blank pages.'

'I should, especially someone who has all of my books.'

'You are so talented.' Her smile takes a moment to reach her eyes. 'I was brought up on such tales from a little kid. Your illustrations capture everything I saw in my imagination. I suppose you could say I'm your number one fan—'

She must have seen my face fall and laughs. 'I didn't mean in a deranged Annie Wilkes sort of way.' She grins at me. 'I'm presuming you have read Stephen King's *Misery*, or that would be meaningless.'

'Yeah, I've read it. A long time ago, though "number one fan" definitely has different connotations since that book.'

'Clearly, and I didn't mean to scare you, simply show you my appreciation.' She plays with the front cover of the book laid in front of her, although she doesn't open it. I'm about to inquire if she's ever sent me roses when she asks, 'So, Grimm and Andersen. Which do you prefer?'

'Andersen is lighter, I suppose you could say *frothier*, but I adore the Grimm tales. So dark and sometimes rather appalling, as Mr Hudson pointed out! Not that you'll find them in this book, I might add. These are the tamer versions, though the originals are something else.'

'Like what, for instance?'

I hesitate as these stories certainly *are* grim. 'Do you really want to know, as most of them are truly ghastly?'

'Now, how can I refuse that? I'm intrigued, so please go on.'

'Okay.' I pause again. Should I be saying this? Mary said to keep the interactions short, but she appears to be the last person waiting in line, so I plough on. 'In the original "Sleeping Beauty", after her father lays her out, she is raped by a king, who is angry his endeavour to wake her failed. She bears two kids, one of whom saves her. In the meantime, this king has married someone else, and when he hears of the miraculous awakening of his "one true love", he burns his actual wife alive, so he is unhindered in his quest to get to the princess.' I raise an eyebrow at her. 'Nice, eh?'

She seems pretty shocked. 'Yes, you're right. *Ghastly*. I didn't realise they were quite that bad! Mind you, my favourite is "The Little Goose Girl", especially the part when the false princess describes her own fate. You must know this one?' But now there's another look on her face, as if she is staring into my soul, and that comment is *personal*. Then her expression changes, and she's smiling gaily at me again.

I nod. 'Of course. She says a false princess should be put naked in a barrel with nails punched through from the outside and then dragged along by two white horses from street to street until she is dead.'

'I like the fact the false princess gets her comeuppance. It's only right, after all.' Once more, by the way she is staring at me, I feel her words are somehow personal, but I have no idea why. Rolling her eyes, she says, 'I was never into the soppy Disney stories. I prefer these, as they are deep down and dirty.'

'Exactly what I was thinking earlier.'

'Then we are on the same page...' She laughs, though there's a strange undercurrent to the sound that I can't quite put my finger on. I see movement behind her. An elderly lady has cleared her throat and is peering past this woman at me.

'I'm so sorry, someone is waiting behind you. Would you like a special inscription or just the scrawl?' I am aware that she is staring intently at me. It's as though her eyes are lit from behind, glowing emeralds. This woman is unsettling me, and I want her to go.

'Oh, please can you put, "For Mama Anna and baby Lara. Always in our thoughts." That would be great.'

I find that a bit unnerving, as it's not the usual request. It sounds too... mortal. As if Mama Anna and baby Lara are... No, don't go there.

'And do you want me to put your name, too?' I can see my hand shaking slightly. I put it down to a long afternoon, and it has nothing to do with this ephemeral woman in front of me.

She pauses. 'No, only what I said.' I write and then wait a moment to allow the ink to dry.

'There we go,' I say as I hand it to her. I'm not sure what else to say.

'Thanks. I look forward to the next one.' Her voice is soft as she steps away.

'I will remember you, don't worry,' I call at her receding back.

'Oh,' and it's a murmur now, 'I think you can *count* on that.'

The hairs on the back of my neck rise.

As the woman behind her pushes forward, I glimpse her hugging the book, bowed over it as she slips out of the door. My head feels like a snow globe that has just been shaken, full of glittery flakes. That was plain weird.

The elderly lady wants an inscription for Joshua. Standard stuff, and thank *goodness* for that!

'She was a bit odd, wasn't she?' The woman nods over her shoulder. 'I wonder who she was talking about?'

'I wondered, too, but I suppose it's not our business.' I must have unintentionally come across as curt, as the old lady huffs. I smile up at her. 'There you go.'

'Thank you,' she says with a rigid smile as she takes the book.

I'm glad we are nearing the end of this session, as my neck is aching, and I'm beginning to get a fatigue headache. At five-thirty, we start to clear up. Mr Hudson is chatting animatedly with an elderly lady by the counter, and Mary is bustling about, whistling cheerfully. That's a good sign the launch has been a great success. If not, smoke and fire would be razing this book-store to the ground.

Mary does a little excited wave. 'I've checked the numbers online, and you're doing well.'

'Brilliant!'

Hallelujah for that!

Chapter Two

ALICE

THE EVENING LIGHT is rather glowering as my best mate Alice comes to drag me back out into the real world. Everyone should have a friend like Alice; someone quirky, who isn't one to 'toe the line' and keeps me on my toes.

'Whoa, babe!' she calls as she heads up to the main doors. 'It's right bloody cold.' She blows on her fingertips.

I stare up into the sky, billowing with pewter-tipped clouds, as I slide into my coat and sling my bag over my shoulder. Maybe it will snow? Now that would be a magical end to an afternoon of spells and enchantments. And peculiar fey women.

'Thank God you're here.' I motion behind me. 'I think I got writer's cramp in there. Mary always tells people not to ask for too much, but I still get the ones with an inscription at least a page long!' I grin at her. 'I know. Moan, moan, *moan*.'

'Oh!' Alice postures with her hand limply at her forehead. 'The trials of being a famous artist!'

'Yeah, right.' I put on my woolly beanie hat. It's not flattering, but it is warm.

Alice tugs on my arm. 'Did the roses arrive today?'

'Yep.' I shrug. 'I stuffed them into the juice jug—'

'Like normal then? I'm sure there's nothing sinister about it all. Someone just likes to wish you well—'

'If you know,' I eye Alice,' who this person is, then this is the time to tell me. It's now bordering on creepy.'

'I think it's sweet,' she mumbles, avoiding my stare. 'Anyway, sorry I couldn't make it this time.' Alice pulls me into a firm hug. Her tight braids smell of coconut oil, and today she has them pulled back under a brightly coloured headband.

'You've been to all the others, which I appreciate no end. I know you couldn't swap shifts, and also, I didn't want you to.'

'Yeah, though the boss lady could have been a bit more accommodating.' She's rubbing at her neck, so I know she's tired from working a day shift at her bar.

'I believe she has accommodated you enough recently, what with sneaking off to festivals while pretending to have the flu...' I know I shouldn't poke her about this, but she can be so badly behaved! Maybe I'm jealous, as I can't afford to be naughty anymore.

'I didn't feel well when I came back, so I wasn't really lying—'

'I think that's called a three-day hangover.' I have to let her off the hook. 'Anyway, talking of accommodating, where are we off to?'

Alice stops at the crossing near the clock tower, and I watch her face scrunch. It's an expression she always does, which I have nick-named her 'thinking face'.

'It's your day, so you should choose. Which one of the numerous Brighton pubs shall we visit tonight?' She tugs her scarf tighter about her neck, but it catches in one of her long dangly earrings. I free her but my fingers are icy. She jumps when I touch her neck and I notice her legs are jiggling. She's covered in goosebumps. As she's black, she never goes a ghastly bluey-pink colour, as I do.

'I wouldn't mind an indulgent little something at the Vitalist. And if you're cold, I hate to point this out, but it is November and maybe wearing a mini skirt and bare legs isn't the way to go?'

'I didn't have time to change. And anyway,' she winks at me, 'I rock mini-skirts, so it's worth it.'

I eye the reams of leg she waggles at me. 'Can I also point out that I hate you?'

Giggling as she links arms with me (possibly to leach the warmth from my body), she pulls me against the flow of people heading up West Street. Dodging through the snarled-up traffic, we turn left down Duke Street.

'I presume', said Alice, 'you had a good time today?'

'Once I'd crushed my nerves, I had a ball. I met my number one fan—'

'Ugh!' Alice squints at me, and neon lights from shop windows play across the sharp planes of her face. 'I hope she's not going to break your ankles and all that?'

'She seemed nice, though I got the feeling she was a little lost.'

'Well, as long as she paid upfront, it doesn't matter. You'll never see her again—'

'All heart, Alice, eh? And she told me I will see her at my next book launch, as she said she's been to all the previous ones. I did kind of recognise her. I wrote an inscription, though it sounded quite sad.'

'What was it?'

'For Mama Anna and baby Lara. Always in our thoughts.' I tilt my head to look at Alice. 'That sounds to me as if they might not be with us anymore. What do you think?'

'If they are dead or whatever, why is this woman getting them a book of old fairy tales? Sounds a bit weird to me.'

'And me. Ooh,' I point, 'look at the Christmas window in England at Home. I love all the stuff in there. I know I don't need anything, but I definitely want most of it.'

'There's consumerism and capitalism in one sentence. Apart from the fact that it's not even December, and therefore they should not have their bloody Christmas window up yet. You'd better hope you get a big, fat royalties cheque then.' We're practically sprinting now, and I marvel at Alice's ability to run in such high heels. 'Come on,' she wheezes, and I see her breath huff in the air. 'I'm freezing my nipples off here.'

'I hope it's not too busy. I don't want to stand, as my feet are killing me.'

She slows the pace. 'Er, haven't you been sat down all afternoon?'

'So? I'm still knackered. I'm worried my wrist will be too limp to hold a glass!'

'That will never happen, as we well know.' She grins at me. 'And let's not forget that you are ambidextrous, so you can use the other hand.'

The Vitalist is an eccentric place, painted a deep charcoal grey with iconic nineteenth-century lettering and gold-painted details on the windows. It's also in a central position in Brighton, where you can head off in any direction afterwards and be within walking distance of all the hot spots in the city. I'm pondering where we might go later.

Luck is on our side, or maybe it's because it's early Saturday evening and that in-between time when most people are getting ready for their night out and not actually out.

'Quick,' Alice waves her hand as we bustle in, 'let's grab that table over there. I don't want to be too near the door as you always get blasts of air as punters come in.'

We dash for the small round table and ease ourselves onto the dark blue banquette seating that runs along the lengths of the massive windows. The polished wooden flooring squeaks as if we are stamping on rodents under our high heels. Hauling off our jackets and bags, we pile them to the side of us.

Alice adjusts her headband. 'What do you want, Miss Famous?'

'Listen, I'll get these as I fancy one of those, oh, what are they called again?' I reach for the red and black menu and peer at the drinks list. It's extensive, and most of the names are a right mouthful. 'Ah! Here it is. A Salted Caramel Espresso Martini. What about you? Fancy one of those? My treat, and then we share after that.'

'Sounds good to me.'

I walk to the copper-topped bar and order. When I pay, I'm told the drinks will be brought to our table. Now that's service. I always like it here. There's a mad gold DJ booth for those nights when the place is thumping out dance music and the place is packed with gyrating students. It's funny – when we're here with the students, they make us feel old, and we're only in our late twenties. How can so few years make such a difference in our perspectives? Do they look at us and think we're old too? Are we already dancing like their mums around a handbag? I have seen this and was horrified. Or are they jealous of our maturity and sophistication? Maybe we don't need to know...

The lights above us are an eclectic mix of pendant lamps with soft and subtle flame effect bulbs. Deep twilight has seeped into night, and the pavement outside is bathed in the glow of streetlights. The scurrying crowds have hunkered down into jackets, heads lowered against the cold, intent on their journeys. I think maybe Christmas *is* in the air, and people can smell it. All pine needles, wood-burning and roasting meat. Or perhaps that's just in here?

I ask, 'Are we eating, or do you want to go somewhere else?'

'Here is fine for me. I don't fancy going back out into the cold. We might not get a table at this time.' Alice tweaks the menu from my hand. 'Anyway, I have a hankering for their smoked ribs and maybe that charred corn on the cob we had last time. If you get the nachos, we can share?'

The two drinks are deposited in front of us, and I nod my thanks to the lithe young barmaid. They are beautifully presented and should be for that price. And they are far too small. I need to remind myself to sip demurely. We grab the chance and order our food before it gets too busy.

'So,' says Alice, 'many people there today? Are you going to be able to buy me that Porsche for my next birthday, then?'

'I think you might be able to count on a bicycle if you're lucky.' I finish the terribly tiny glass of expensive sweet yummi-ness. 'Mary seemed happy, and that's good enough for me. When she's not happy, it's like being with a bad-tempered dragon. I'm fearful she might toast me with her breath alone.'

'Are there nice-tempered dragons, then?' She giggles. 'I mean, of anybody, *you* should know.'

'Ugh! Not this again.' This is a perennial joke. I illustrate magical things, so I must be the fount of all knowledge on them. 'I presume so. There's good and bad in every species, isn't there?'

'Not true.' She waggles a finger at me. 'You only get nice dolphins, and please don't tell me otherwise, or you'll be worse than when Harry told me Santa wasn't real.'

'All dolphins are wonderful,' I lie to her. 'Even the ones who aren't!'

Her eyes are slits. 'You're a mean bugger, Lily.'

I slither off my seat and hitch my skirt down. 'I'll get a bottle of Rioja in before our food arrives. That caramel whatsit barely touched the sides. It's getting pretty crowded in here, and I'm parched.'

As I stand at the bar with my card waving about as if I'm using some sort of semaphore (which, of course, I am), I spot the woman I was talking to at the book launch sitting at the far end of the bar. It's quite a jolt to see her there. She looks up and catches me staring. I'm unsure what to do. So, I flutter my fingertips at her and mouth 'hi', and I'm disconcerted when she tugs her bag and coat free and comes towards me.

'I am *so sorry*,' she says. 'I didn't know you were in here. It looks as though I'm stalking you. I'll finish my drink and go.'

I'm flummoxed, as I wasn't expecting such a reaction. 'Why on earth should you have to go?' Although part of me wishes she would. Now, why is that?

She brushes a lock of tawny gold hair from her forehead. 'It's an invasion of your privacy. You're off the clock now and are out enjoying yourself.' She peers back down the bar just as the barman takes her half-finished drink and sloshes the remains into the sink. 'Oh!' She laughs, and her laugh is musical. 'That's that, then. Well,' she turns back to me, 'it's been a pleasure to meet you, er, Miss Maye—'

I can't be that mean. Can I? *Oh, shite!* 'Please call me Lily, and I'd like you to join us. It's my fault your drink has been binned.'

Shaking her head, she gently touches my shoulder. 'No, it's mine for leaving it unattended on the bar. My mistake.'

'No, I insist. I'm with my friend, Alice. I'm sorry, I didn't catch your name?'

'Rose. My name is Rose.' She extends her hand, and I shake it automatically, although I'm thrown for a moment.

'How incredible. My middle name is Rose.'

'Really? Lily Rose? What a lovely name. My middle name is Briar. God alone knows what my parents were thinking. As I said, I was brought up with endless fairy tales. I suspect they were a bit obsessed.'

'Rose Briar is a beautiful name. I'm jealous now. Briar Rose is one of the names for the original Sleeping Beauty, isn't it?'

'So that makes me Beauty Sleeping, does it?' She pulls a face. 'As I said, my parents were a bit off the wall.'

I indicate down the bar to the missing glass. 'What were you drinking?'

'A table red, nothing fancy. But only if you insist.'

'I do.' I order her drink, and then she follows me back to where Alice has been watching us. I'm suddenly struck by the thought that Alice might be pissed off by my inviting this stranger to our table.

'Alice, this is Rose. I met her at the book launch today. She's my number one fan.' I hope Alice is astute enough not to blurt out anything derogatory. 'I just got her drink thrown away, so I've invited her over.'

I see a momentary wariness before Alice smiles and slides over. 'So,' she raises an eyebrow, 'I'm stuck between two beautiful flowers, am I?'

Rose drops her coat and bag on the seat and eases herself next to Alice. 'But only one of us has *thorns*.'

Alice looks a little taken aback. 'Sorry? *What?*'

Rose laughs. 'We were discussing our middle names, and mine is Briar. Lucky my surname isn't Barb or Prickle, or it would be a bit of a coup!'

Alice covers her mouth as she sniggers. 'That's really funny.'

'Hmm, only sometimes. I hope you don't mind me barging in on you both. I'll have the one drink and then leave you in peace.'

I make a decision and hope Alice is on board. 'We've ordered food,' I say, 'and it would be lovely if you could join us?' After all, she is a fan and I'm nothing without the people who reach into their pockets to buy my books. I simply had a funny moment earlier. Probably tired.

'Are you sure? I think I've already come over as a stalker, and I don't want to outstay my welcome.'

'Alice?' I turn to her. 'You don't mind, do you?'

Alice makes room for her on the table. 'No, you're very welcome, Rose.'

It's awkward initially, though after a couple of glasses of red, we are relaxing. Rose orders the Smokey BBQ ribs and a side salad. The food comes fast, and we tuck in.

'Well,' I start, 'you all know what I do, so, Rose? Can I ask you what you do?'

'I work in health care.' She nods. 'Mental health.'

'I take my hat off to you, then,' I say. 'I would find that very tricky.'

'Are you like a psychiatrist?' Alice pours the remains of the bottle equally into our glasses.

'No. I'm more of a consultant.'

'I don't know,' I muse, 'how you manage not to take it all home with you. Do you have to deal with terrible things?'

There's a look on Rose's face I can't fathom, as if she's looking inwards. 'Suicide attempts, loss of family, rage. And yes, sometimes you can't help but take it home. We're trained not to, although it can be hard.'

'Rather you than me, then.' I raise my glass. 'Here's to never having to experience any of that.'

'Yep,' Alice clinks her glass to mine, and Rose takes a sip of her wine. Her eyes are veiled, and I wonder what she's seen or heard in her line of work. I guess I shouldn't ask at this stage.

Alice continues, 'I'm thinking of doing a plumbing course.' This is pretty left-field for her, and I try not to splutter guacamole over the table. 'I've been talking to Janet, who works in the same bar as me. We're putting out feelers to see if there's a niche for us, and it looks as if there is. We're going to make a website, get business cards and advertise in all the local shops as well as getting an ad into the Yellow Pages.'

'Plumbing?' This comes out as a squeak. 'You're saying you are going to ditch the heels and false nails and get into overalls, so you clamber under people's sinks and tinker with their toilets?'

'Yeah, why not?'

'I thought you loved working in the bar?'

'Things change, Lily.'

'I think,' says Rose with a thoughtful expression, 'it's a great idea.'

'See?' snorts Alice, 'First customer right there. I'm designing a logo as we speak.' She eyes me. 'Yeah, I know. I'm finally putting my degree to some good use!'

'I didn't say anything.'

'You didn't have to. Anyway, we've come up with our new company name, which we think is pretty cool if we say so ourselves.'

'And that is...?' I say.

'Leaky Women Enterprises,' says Alice with a straight face, and I don't know whether we're supposed to laugh at this point.

Alice cocks her head to one side. 'You think it's a joke, but we're serious.'

I try not to snigger.

'Well,' Rose's grin is wide, 'it's a name you won't forget in a hurry, and if it makes people laugh and they then remember you, it might just work in your favour.'

I'm trying to get my head around this. 'Would people really want to call you with a name like that? It conjures up all sorts of things...'

Alice snorts again. 'We're not aiming at *people*, per se, as they are not our target market.'

'You mean you're aiming at other "leaky women"?' I smile at her.

Rose chuckles. 'I'd definitely call you.'

'I'm serious about this. There are loads of women out there who don't want men coming into their houses for all sorts of reasons. We'd be filling that spot.'

'Joking aside,' says Rose, 'I wholeheartedly agree. I'd rest easier if I knew I had women entering my private space. No misunderstandings or miscommunication.'

'Point taken,' I say.

The food is delicious, as usual, and we have another bottle of wine. I find Rose easy to chat with, and we laugh a lot. I am still trying to understand why I reacted the way I did earlier.

'We should do this again,' says Alice. 'What do you think, Rose?'

'I'd love that. Thanks.' Rose turns to me. 'If you're okay with that too, Lily?'

'Yes.' I nod, although I'm a bit startled. I would like to have discussed this first. 'Would you like my phone number, as well as Alice's?'

'That would be great. I've just moved to this area, and you know how that can be, feeling lonely in such a bustling and cosmopolitan city.'

'Where were you before?' Alice leans forward as I also give Rose my number. 'I can detect a slight accent, though I'm not sure where from.'

Rose's eyes narrow. 'I'm from a small town near Bristol. I've spent the last few years trying to escape from my... past. If that makes sense? People judge you if you have a strong accent.'

'My sister's in Bristol. You might have even bumped into her and never known.'

'It's possible, but we'll never know, will we?'

'Bristol?' Alice frowns. 'I would have pegged you as more

northern, not western. I'm usually good with accents.' She tilts her head and peers at Rose. 'Especially as I'm from the north.'

I, too, would have said she was from the north. There is something familiar about her cadence. A specific rhythmical pattern I've heard before. I shake my head, as it makes me feel like I'm poking at a wobbly tooth.

'Rose?' I look at her. 'Do you mind me asking who Mama Anna and baby Lara are?'

'*Anna!*' It's as though I've thrown a bucket of dead fish over her. Very rotting, extremely dead fish. I can see out of the corner of my eye that Alice has frozen.

'I'm sorry, I didn't mean to pry...' I should have known better than to broach that at this juncture. We were having such a lovely time, and now I've ruined it. How stupid of me!

'Anna is, *was*, my sister, but she died. Lara was her daughter.' Rose laughs shakily. 'You must think I'm very strange getting a signed book for them, except now it's become a ritual.'

'I feel like a complete idiot,' I say. 'I didn't mean to upset you in any way—'

'It's my choice to be upset or not. Were their deaths anything to do with *you*?' Her eyes are green lasers.

'Er, no, all I meant—' My cheeks are hot, and I feel out of my depth.

'Hey!' Alice has her hand in front of her as if she's a referee. 'I'm sure Lily didn't mean to distress you, Rose. It was only a question, and she didn't know...'

'Yes, of course.' Rose looks close to tears, and she draws in a deep breath. 'I'm obviously still working on issues to do with...' She struggles. 'I'm sorry. I didn't mean to upset you either, Lily. It caught me by surprise.'

'You didn't upset me, and I promise not to mention her again.'

'No. No, that's fine. As I said, I was caught by surprise.' She pushes her hair back from her face. 'Anyway, you were bound to be curious as to what my inscription meant. It was such a sad time for us all. To lose them both.'

'Again, I'm sorry—'

'No need to be, Lily. Well, I think this is my cue to go.' Rose stands suddenly and smiles, although I note it doesn't reach her eyes. 'I've had a lovely time, and it would be great to see you both again, though no pressure.' She gathers her coat and bag. There's a lot of bustling, which I take to mean she's hiding her emotions. 'Oh, and this is on me. To say thank you to you both for being so welcoming.'

'I can't allow that,' I say, and I also rise, but she waves a hand. 'It'll be my pleasure. So, Lily,' she nods at me, 'Alice, adieu.' She pays at the bar, her back to us.

'I'm so sorry,' I call, although she doesn't turn around or acknowledge my words as she walks to the door, where she is swallowed by the dark and restless night. I don't know what to make of this evening. I sit down with a bump.

'She's really nice,' says Alice as she tips the last of the Rioja into our glasses.

'Is that because she paid for dinner?'

'That helps, but no, I liked her. She's got a wonderful sense of humour.' Alice raises her glass and peers into it as if it's a crystal ball. 'Although that last bit was freaky.'

'Yes, it was, and note to self: engage brain before opening mouth.'

'That wasn't your fault. How were you to know what was going on?'

'I should have guessed, especially as we kind of hit on it earlier.'

'Well, she pulled herself together as she left, so that's something. I mean, poor thing, losing her sister and her niece. Ugh, horrible!'

'I know, I can't even contemplate it. It sounds like they may have died together. You know, a car crash or a fire or something? I wonder how it happened—'

'Oh God, Lily! Please don't ask her if we see her again!'

'Look, I know I ballsed it up earlier, but I'm not so stupid to do it again.'

'Here's hoping. You know,' says Alice, 'I think I must have seen her at one of your book launches. There's something really familiar about her.'

'See? I told you. So, you think we should meet her again?' I am definitely in two minds here, but I'll go whichever way Alice does.

'Absolutely. She seems really nice.'

Decision made.

Chapter Three

It seems natural for the three of us to meet up again. This time, it's early morning, and we are all bright-eyed and bushy-tailed, as they say. We are sitting inside café Moa at one of their sturdy wooden tables. I love the Caribbean feel of the bright orange and yellow lettering and stylised sun on the front signage, although the decor is solid farmhouse inside. Wooden panels that could do with a lick of varnish, white painted walls, brick-work, and shiny, dented wooden floors. There are black and white photos adorning the walls; the ubiquitous Brighton Pier and one I particularly like of the Beatles pre-beads and beard stage. I wouldn't mind it on my wall at home, as it reminds me of my parents, of happier days.

It's Rose's first time here, and Alice and I believe she's in for a treat. Apart from the fact that we should have asked if she's a vegetarian. Then it'll be a disaster, as the big old farmhouse breakfast they serve here is meat, meat and more meat, with added hash browns. Which probably have meat in.

Rose is perusing the menu, but I will have what I always have. Since I discovered this café, I have not wavered in my breakfast choice. Only the farmhouse will hit the spot. Bacon, sausage, mushrooms, two eggs, hash-browns, beans and tomatoes and then toast. With butter.

I phoned Rose at stupid o'clock to tell her where to go but had to add, 'If you are worried about your figure, it's best to avoid this place, and if you do make it through the doors, wear something that can be loosened.' Mind you, she is one of those women that could wear a black bin bag and make it look haute couture.

Rose snaps the menu shut and leans back in her chair. 'I actually thought you were joking this morning.' She looks aghast at a passing plate as it is manoeuvred to a nearby table. The waitress has trouble carrying it. 'Good God. How do you two eat so much and still look so slim?'

'Father's genes,' says Alice. 'At least I hope so.'

'The rest of the week down the gym.' I cross my eyes and grin. 'But it's worth every scrummy mouthful.'

The waitress shimmies over and we order. I'm relieved that Rose chooses the same as me.

'I'm sorry,' says Rose, 'about how I reacted last time I saw you... When you mentioned Anna and Lara.'

'No, you have nothing to apologise for. It was my fault for blundering around like a bull in the proverbial china shop.'

'Enough said,' says Rose and smiles.

We sit and stare around us, people watching, but the silence is comfortable, not strained.

'Okay,' says Alice. She moves stuff off the table. 'The breakfast of champions is here.'

While we are stuffing down our breakfast, Alice asks the question I've been dreading.

'So, Lily the Pink. How did your last date go?'

I put down my knife and fork and have a swig of tea. 'Please don't even go there, especially when I'm eating. It's the same as watching a horror movie. You tend not to do it mid-dinner.' I was hoping Alice wouldn't bring this topic up, especially in front of a new friend.

'That good, eh?'

'Lily the Pink?' Rose looks confused.

Alice laughs. 'My grandparents always played this song about Lily the Pink, from way back when.' She starts to sing, and I want to cover my ears. 'Let's drink a drink, a drink, to Lily the Pink, the Pink, the Pink, for saving all the human race. For she invented medicinal compound, most efficacious for *something*, *something*. I can never remember the last bit. I loved it, really funky, and when I met Lily, the rest is history.'

Rose nods. 'I seem to remember hearing that song.'

'Not sung like that,' I add.

Alice raises an eyebrow at me in mock indignation. 'Are you saying I can't sing?'

'Der! Yes!'

'Oh! Right.'

'Aren't you seeing anyone then?' Rose looks perplexed. 'I would have thought you'd be married, possibly with kids. Not to pry or anything.'

'Nope. I was in a relationship a few years ago. When that went south for the winter, it's been a little rocky. I'm twenty-nine, and it shouldn't be that hard. Except it is. The good old days of finding a nice bloke in your local bar seem to be a myth nowadays. They are more likely to spike your drink.'

'Okay,' says Alice. 'What did this last idiot say to you then?'

I dab at my mouth with the paper napkin. 'He said, and I quote, "You're too pretty to have a job. You should be at home having someone take care of you". He then enlightened me that he didn't mind providing for me in exchange for "companionship". I told him I didn't need his money, and I definitely didn't want any of his company. He said I probably wouldn't get a better offer! I mean, what the *hell*?' I crunch into my toast.

Rose shakes her head. 'That's awful.' She looks down. 'I went to see a professor at my college to get help with some of the work in his class, and he said to me, "Do you have rape fantasies?" I was only eighteen or so. I bolted from his room and changed course.'

Alice nods, but her jaw twitches where she's grinding her teeth. 'Funny how we have to modify our behaviour, and they just get away with it.' She eyes me knowingly. 'At least mostly get away with it.' She's aware of what happened to me.

'Yes,' I say, feeling jarred. 'I've had an experience similar to that.' It awakens my memories. *Harry*.

Alice taps the table with a rainbow-painted nail. 'Janet, who you remember is one of the Leaky Women I'm going into business with, well I think her one tops it. One bloke she had dinner with said, "You know, I can't decide who you look more like, a blow-up Japanese sex doll or a sexy version of Sid from Ice Age". Can you believe it? Some of them must be aspiring comedians, because I can't fathom how they can ever believe they would get anything, let alone laid, after a comment like that!'

'Sexy Sid? Oh my God!' I know I'm making snorkelling noises, but I can't help it. 'I can't get that image out of my head. Thanks, Alice.'

Rose intervenes. 'Not changing the subject or anything, but are you on any dating apps?' She makes a face. 'I'm on OkCupid. It sounds a bit crap, but it is officially, according to them, the best dating site there is.'

'Are you saying you're single too?' I waggle an eyebrow at her. 'I find that hard to believe, though I rather think the more attractive and educated you are, the more the nice men keep running.'

'Or they've been snapped up already,' nods Alice.

'Yes,' I agree. 'We then get left with the ones who have egos the size of the moon and are as thick as two short planks.'

'Oh yes. The planks are delightful, aren't they?' laughs Rose.

'So, you're saying OkCupid works?' Alice turns and looks squarely at me. 'Then we need to get Miss Lily the Pink set up. Right now. Here, give us your mobile.' She snaps her fingers as if that's going to induce me to give it to her.

'If you think I'm going to set you free with my potential love life, you've got another think coming!'

'No, really. It'd be great.' Rose is reaching out now as well. Hit on two fronts, I buckle, and they hunch like witches around a cauldron over my phone and make the sorts of sounds I suspect witches make when cooking up a spell.

'*When shall we three meet again?*' I cackle.

'How about next week?' says Alice.

'No, I meant, "When shall we three meet again, in thunder, lightning, or in rain?" It's a joke...'

'Probably in the rain then, all things considered.' Alice winks at me.

'You are an utter sod!' I try to tug the phone back, but they are as tenacious as the limpets on the underwater struts of the old Brighton pier. 'What the hell have you put about me? Please don't say I love football or cricket or that I'm up for ale trails. I can't abide men in sandals and socks and wearing their mum's hand-knitted sweaters.'

'So shallow,' says Alice.

'Too right!' I say.

'Damn,' smirks Rose, with a theatrical hand over her mouth. 'How did we get it so wrong?'

Alice is flicking through my photos. 'This one.' She shows a photo she took of me back in the summer. I look relaxed and refreshed, even sun-kissed, with my hair down and minimal make-up. That dress suits me. Red to go with my dark brown hair and tan. I look almost Mediterranean. I nod. 'Yeah, I'm happy with that one.'

'Don't worry.' Alice hands the phone back to Rose. 'It's all truthful, above board, and very boring, yada, yada, yada.'

'Am I boring then?' I'm not sure if I should feel insulted.

'Don't be ridiculous. It's the chance to reinvent yourself as someone who loves skydiving, swimming with sharks and eating scary, dangerous sushi stuff. You know, the fishy bit that if they get it wrong, can kill you dead.'

'Why on earth would I do that? Start with complete lies?' I'm a bit uncomfortable. It's like we're scrabbling through my underwear drawer in front of strangers.

'Because you can?' Alice grimaces at me. 'Because all of us have started with the truth and got nowhere, so we might as well hedge our bets once in a while.'

'No.' I feel very emphatic about this. 'I'll try this Cupid site, but I start by being me and only me.'

'Ugh, spoilsport. Okay,' says Alice, 'we've put that you are a twenty-nine-year-old children's book illustrator who loves to drink red wine with friends at the weekend. You like visiting National Trust houses and gardens, museums and art galleries. Your favourite books are Jane Austen and Tolkien – make of that what you will. As to your favourite film, this year must include the remake of *Dune*, and you adore the dark Scandi series on Netflix. Your ultimate snack is a crunchy fresh apple with a lump of cheddar, and your favourite song currently is Adele's "Easy on Me". You prefer spring out of all the seasons and love walking in the countryside.' Alice looks across at me while I take all this in. 'How does that sound?'

I shrug. 'That sounds like me.'

'So,' says Rose, 'are we going with that?'

'I suppose so,' I say and try not to bite my lip as they sort out the last requirements.

'All right.' Alice looks as if she's the cat who got the cream. 'You've been uploaded and are pending acceptance. You have to let us vet who you might go on a date with. It's only fair.'

'Yeah,' says Rose, 'let us vet them for you. The least we can do. Especially as I feel responsible as I suggested it.'

'Did you tell the truth, Rose? When you applied to join?'

Rose tilts her head. 'As best I could. I've had a few nice dinners, some stimulating chats and a couple of... sleepovers.' she looks down quickly. 'It was great, although none of them, as yet, have been contenders. I'd prefer an adult relationship with another adult. They appear to be quite hard to find in the male species. I sometimes feel men are like children set free in an unsupervised sweetshop. They have to stuff everything in their mouths all at once.'

I believe there's a clue in her words there. It looks as though Rose hasn't had a good time with the men in her life either. I can sympathise.

I nod. 'Well, at least one of us is in a happy relationship. Alice has been with Matt for ages, so there's still hope for us. Decent men do exist.'

Alice frowns at me. 'I'm not sharing him, no matter how much you grovel.'

'Your Matt is safe with you.'

'Are you saying you wouldn't then?'

'Oh, do shut up!'

'Hey, moving on,' says Rose. 'You said you were in a relationship before. Do you mind me asking what went wrong?'

I think for a moment and see Alice twitch. 'What went wrong? Hmmm. You know, I'm not sure anything went wrong.' Rose may have her secrets she doesn't wish to divulge, but so do I. What went wrong? I don't want to dredge this all up. Harry is Alice's cousin, and quite frankly, she was as upset as I was at the time. 'We met at college and grew apart. We ended up being two completely different people from who we were, so it didn't make sense to carry on pretending we were. He moved to the States, and I do believe he's happy there.' Is he? Is he happy? We say 'hi' to each other on Facebook every Christmas and birthday, the usual platitudes. Realising I lie to him almost every time we talk, it occurs to me he could be doing the same. So what does that say? Alice chats with him all the time, though she doesn't tell me what they talk about. I suppose it's better this way.

Rose jerks me back with her next question. 'What was his name?'

'Harry.' I find it hard to say his name out loud.

'I knew a Harry once.' There's a dreamy sound to Rose's voice. 'He was a complete and utter *shit*, and if he'd fallen off a cliff, I would have clapped!'

'Didn't like him much then?' Alice's eyes are wide.

'Oh no. We all loved him dearly, but as I said, he was a shit.' I'm shocked by her vehemence, and I can see the same etched on Alice's face. I don't know how to respond to that. What the hell did *her* Harry do to make her feel this way? Who is 'we'? Dare I ask her? Maybe I don't honestly want to know. I don't always feel so bright and chipper thinking about *my* Harry, either! There was a time I, too, might have clapped if someone had shoved him out of a twentieth-floor window somewhere.

Harry. *My Harry*.

At nineteen, I was accepted into a prestigious art school in central London to do an illustration course. Many find it a shock to leave the nest, but I couldn't wait. I was so ready to have autonomy over my life, what time I came home and with whom, when I could eat and what, to explore and wander around the hidden places in London and know my parents couldn't worry about me, as they wouldn't know. The only person who could worry about me was me. And I wasn't about to let that get in the way of my new life.

A deposit had been put down on a tiny bedsit near Tavistock Square in a large, Victorian multiple-occupancy building. When my parents moved me and my boxes of an odd assortment of clothes, art equipment, old toys and new cooking utensils, they stood forlorn in the tiny space between the single bed and the table, worry written across their faces as they stared about them.

'It's very small,' said my dad. As a big-boned man, he could barely turn around.

'Yes, well,' said my mum, 'it has all she needs. See? She has a fridge, a Baby Belling stove—'

'That looks like it's older than me!' my dad huffed.

'—and she's got a sink, a worktable, and a wardrobe.' I knew she was trying to make my dad see it all in a good light, though she didn't sound convinced.

'It's perfect,' I crowed.

'Where are the toilet and bathroom?' My dad hadn't been there when Mum and I came to London a couple of months before to look for a place for me. I adamantly didn't want to go into halls of residence or share a house with other students. No, I stated, I needed a place of my own.

'The toilet is down the hall,' said my mum, 'and the bathroom is two flights up.' Her voice wavered. 'She'll be fine, I'm sure.' Although she didn't sound sure, again, I let it go.

'Listen,' I said. 'It's within walking distance to my art school, so I won't have to pay for buses or trains. It's central, so I can get to most parts of London on foot. And more importantly, get home again. It's a nice area, too.' I gestured around me. 'All in all, it's the best result I could have wished for. Isn't it? And it doesn't cost the earth.' I was being a bit too challenging, but I needed them to know I'd be fine here. They still thought of me as a child, and that was a view I had to change.

It was a Friday, which meant I'd have the rest of the weekend to settle in. We'd already been out for lunch in a cafe around the corner, and now it was time for them to go home. *Without me.* For the first time in their lives. And mine. Satisfied there was a launderette close by, along with a small supermarket, a weekly fruit and veg market, and to clinch it, at least for *them*, a post office, there was nothing much more to discuss. It was as if they were stuck to the carpet, which was ironic, as it had been sticky when we first saw it. The previous week, me, my mum and my younger sister, Sophie, drove up here to clean the carpet. We discovered it wasn't shit brown; it was mushroom pink and fluffy under all that grime. The curtains were then taken down and washed, and I had them and a new set of nets in one of the boxes. It was amazing how the colours changed when things were washed. They, too, had gone from russet to a bright orange after a hot wash cycle. We'd scrubbed the walls and paintwork, cleaned the grime-smeared windows, and finally, we had to tackle the fridge, which had been switched off with a packet of peas still left inside. It stank like the Devil's fart. Gagging, we cleaned it as best we could, sanitised it and then took the trays and wire shelves we couldn't do home in a bag to sterilise. Those bits were also in a box somewhere.

Mum said, 'The fact they were willing to rent it out in that condition is awful. You would think they'd get a cleaner in, at the very least!'

'It's fine,' I smiled as I opened the door into the communal passageway. 'Listen, I have my mobile, and I can call you any time, and you can call me...' I hesitated. 'But not tonight. I need to do this on my own, okay?'

They inched forward. It was torturous, though we were getting there gradually.

'If you need anything at all, you let us know.' Mum pulled me into a tight embrace. 'We love you, Lily. Just be careful now.' She stepped over the lintel.

'Give Sophie my love.' I let my dad enfold me in a big bear hug.

'She'll miss you, you know,' he said.

'And I'll miss her. I'll be popping home soon enough. She probably won't even notice I'm gone.'

My dad patted my back. 'Well,' he said, 'better catch the last bit of light to get home. You know I hate driving at dusk.'

I kissed them both, saw them to the main front door and watched as they linked arms and crept towards the car parked nearby. They turned a final time and waved. I had to blink to stop any tears. As I shut the door, I had one moment of nervousness, and then I crushed it. There was no room for fear in my life, as it was now opening out, and I had to grab every experience I could from this day onward.

When I had finally sorted through the most necessary things in the boxes, eaten the rather soggy sandwich, and iced doughnut I'd bought earlier, nipped to the loo (making sure I didn't shut myself out, which would not be a good move on my first day), and cleaned my teeth, I checked the lock. This was my first time alone in a big city. Streetlight shone through my window as I switched off the lamp by my bed. Lights from a world I had never encountered before shone on things I didn't know about. I had to get up at least twice in the night and double-check the lock. Listening to cats shrieking and howling in a garden nearby, I lay in the semi-dark and wondered what the next few months would bring.

They would bring Harry. And I would meet him in a way that I could never envision. *Ever.*

Poring over my drawing board, day after day, I would sometimes surface and see him. *Harry*. I watched him from afar,
feeling too inadequate to compete with the other girls for his
affection. I was far too unsophisticated to even aspire to be part
of the in-crowd to which he belonged. One girl was even dating
her tutor from her Art Foundation course, and he was nearly
thirty! Harry was the attractive 'rough' northerner with dark
curly hair and startlingly blue eyes. He was permanently
surrounded by a bevvy of admiring, slim, professionally made-
up, coiffured and well-dressed beauties, while I was in jeans,
second-hand sweaters and Chinese slippers. What was even
worse was that I hadn't even mastered the art of foundation and
went about with a natural, healthy rosy glow that, looking back,
must have made me look about thirteen. Even now, I cringe at
the photos of me at that time.

I managed to skulk on the edge of all the different factions
for a year, working flat-out on the briefs we were given and
attending every lecture. My mind was a supernova, bursting
with information, ideas spiralling out that I believed were so
bright they could be seen from outer space. I couldn't wait to get
to my drawing board every morning to explore these new
concepts and then to return to my bedsit, to sit at my desk and
draw and doodle and research until my eyeballs felt as if they
had been dipped in salt. It took a while to realise the others on
my course were not quite so dedicated.

'Lily? You are called Lily, aren't you?' Jenny, a girl from
Liverpool, asked one day.

'Er, yes.'

'Have you really been to all the lectures so far? Someone
told me that, except I didn't believe them.'

'Well, yes. I thought that was part of the deal here?'

'God, no. The deal...' she made the little bunny ears with

her fingers, 'is to have as much fun as possible and live your life to the max.'

'Ah! It is?' I said. 'Don't we need the accreditation at the end of our degree course? You know? To get our degree?'

'Never thought of that.' Jenny looked mildly perplexed. 'I suppose you're right.' She spun on her heel. 'See you at the next lecture, then.' Of course, I didn't see her, as she was off having fun. I had to wrap my head around this. It occurred to me that a degree course was at least two things. A place to get a degree and, conversely, a space to meet people, get drunk, take drugs, have sex and most definitely hacksaw off the shackles of childhood.

And what was I doing in my spare time so far? Reading fantasy books and watching Netflix. Alone. I wasn't sure how this had happened, given that my life goal was to be a free and independent woman. Okay, I was working hard but was I living my life to the max? It was great fantasising about being able to do what I wanted but it was a lot harder to go out and do it. Turns out, I'm quite shy. This next year would have to change, except I needed to figure out how to go about it.

All of us were aware over time of a particular tutor. Hugh Penfold. Initially, there were just the rumours.

'Have you heard? Hugh's broken up with his wife?'

'Really?' we all said. 'How sad.'

'Have you heard Hugh's been accused of hitting his wife...?'

'No way,' we said. 'What a douchebag!'

'Have you heard? Hugh's got a drinking problem?'

'That's for sure...'

You knew not to enter the main auditorium where we did our critiques in any close proximity to the man. It was as if he had a miasma of alcohol hanging around him; you could smell it sweating out of his pores, his breath reeking like he'd gargled in tequila and had chomped on an ashtray of old cigarette butts. Add to that the mood swings, alternately letching at the pert young things in the class or berating them, depending on the state of his relationship at home. At some point, every girl had done 'the corridor dance' with him. You took a step one way, and he did the same, so you couldn't get past him, and you ended up dodging back and forth. And always with an awful drooling look on his face. It was embarrassing at best and downright nasty at worst. The other tutors must have been aware, though no one did anything about him. If there was a line to be crossed, he was well over it, and everyone knew.

We huddled at lunchtime around a table. 'They all seem to laugh it off or sweep it under the carpet!'

'That man has a serious problem!' We all sighed in unison. 'You don't know where you are with him...'

'I'm quite frightened of him. He's pretty unstable.' Lots of nodding.

'Why hasn't he been dismissed yet?' said one girl. 'It's disgusting!'

'They look after their own,' said another girl. 'Close ranks.'

'Ain't that the truth!'

'The "Me too" movement is still going strong.' We all nodded. 'Maybe we should do something about him ourselves?'

'Like what?' We looked at each other. 'What exactly could we say?'

So it was fortuitous that at the second-year party to welcome the new first years, a ghastly thing happened that meant I met Harry properly. *Hurrah for ghastly things!*

As the party was being held in the school's main building, most of us carried on working at our desks until we thought we should join the revelry. I knew the in-crowd girls had gone to the toilets to change and touch up their make-up. I remained until the lights were switched off and followed the others into the canteen. It had been set up very prettily, with decorations and soft lights instead of the harsh neons that usually lit the room. Tables groaned under bottles of wine and tins of beers cockled in ice. Other tables had bowls of crisps and dips. We'd all chipped in for this, and it was then subsidised by the school. I noted that the first-year students were glued to the walls, nervous and excited, while the second years drifted around, exuding an urban sophistication. Tutors were hovering to ensure any merrymaking didn't get out of hand, though Hugh Penfold had possibly been imbibing more than he should have. As usual.

He sort of lurched towards me. 'Hello, Lily,' he slurred. 'Having a nice time?'

'I got here about a minute ago,' I said, 'so I'm working on it.' I could smell the alcohol on his breath, combined with the usual off-putting tang of old fags. Not particularly inviting, was it?

'Jer want a drink then?' He tottered over to a table and poured a hefty slug of wine into a plastic cup, splashing it over the table and down himself. 'Here we go. Get jer chops around that.'

Taking the over-filled cup, I was trying to work out how to politely get away from him when I felt something on my bum. It appeared to be his hand. I took a step back, assuming it had been an accident.

'I love the work you do, Lily.' He took a step towards me. 'You have a unique style, and I predict,' he got a little closer, 'that you will do very well out in the big bad world.' He leered into my face. Maybe he thought he was charm personified, but a drunk lecturer who was nigh on twenty-five years older than me was not on my 'to-do' list.

I felt like saying the *big bad world* was here in this canteen, standing only inches from me, especially when he reached for my face. I ducked, and he caught some of my hair in his cuff link. It hurt as I yanked it free, and I think I tugged a tuft of hair out. '*Ouch!*'

'Whatsermatter?'

'Thanks for the drink,' I waved it at him, 'but that doesn't give you the right to touch me. You hurt me.'

'Oh, don't be like that.' He brandished an admonishing finger at me. 'Come on, Lily. Lovely, *lovely* Lily. I've been watching you. Don't you worry about all these boys. You need a real man.' He thumped his chest, as a big male chimp might do. This sudden image in my mind made me sputter out laughing.

'Here.' He grabbed hold of my arm, and his fingers dug into my flesh. 'What's so funny then? You think this is funny, do you? Well, it'll be funny when your grades go down—'

The import of his words sunk in. 'Are you threatening me?' I tried to pull away, but his grip tightened.

'Threatening you? Now, why should you say such a horrible thing? No, no, Lily. I'm simply advising you of what would be a good move on your behalf...'

'And what, exactly, would that be?' I hoped I was wrong.

'You know, don't you, lovely Lily?'

'Are you saying what I think you're saying?'

'And what's that?'

'Are you saying if I don't—' I gulped, '—do what you want with you, I'll get crap grades?'

He laughed, making the hairs on the back of my neck ping up. 'Not *crap*, so much as not as good as you might have got. You scratch my back, so to speak, and I'll scratch yours, but in a more *biblical* way, if you get my drift?' He started to pull me towards him as if he was reeling in a plump trout.

Christ-on-a-bike! Had I got that right? Was he expecting me

to shag him in exchange for not giving me a rubbish grade? *Sod that!*

'Get off me!' My breath caught in my throat as I lashed out at him.

'It's not a good idea to try to punch your tutor.' His face was sweaty and laced with throbbing purple veins. I hoped he'd have a heart attack and keel over right there, right *then!*

'Well, I don't think it's a good idea to solicit your female students for sex!' I heard the hiss in my voice as if I couldn't unclamp my jaw. 'Get your fucking hands off me—'

'You do know, *sir*,' a voice came from behind him, 'that I'm recording this, and I can have it on social media and YouTube quicker than you can say 'dirty old letch'. If you get *my* meaning?'

Hugh whirled and nearly fell over, steadying himself on the table, which rocked alarmingly. 'What the *fuck?*'

Harry stood with his phone in his outstretched hand. 'Smile for the camera, *sir*.'

Hugh tried to snatch it, but Harry was younger and not half as pissed. 'Don't think so.' He held out his other hand to me. 'Come on, Lily. I think we have a better place to be than here.'

I prised Hugh's fingers off my arm, dumped the plastic cup back on the table, grabbed Harry's hand, and we fled down the main corridor and into one of the side studios, giggling like children.

Hugh Penfold's anger followed us, bouncing off the walls as we ran. '*Oy!* Come back here, you *little shits!*'

Harry kicked the door shut. 'No more of that!'

'Thanks, Harry. I appreciate what you did.' I reluctantly let go of his hand, but he took it back.

'I can still upload this if you want me to?' He took a step closer and stared into my eyes. 'These guys shouldn't be allowed to abuse their positions of power over us.'

'Us?' I raised my eyebrows.

'Okay, *women* then. But remember, we're not exempt either. Pretty young men like me have our fair share of advances too.'

I didn't know whether he was joking, although thinking about it, probably not.

'Can you send it to me, and then we can both have a copy? You know, just in case.' I sucked on my lips, a bad habit, I know. 'I don't mean for blackmail or whatever—'

'I know what you mean. His word against yours will always be tricky unless you have evidence.'

I nodded. 'I wonder what would have happened if you hadn't come along?'

'It might have been ugly—'

'He certainly was—'

'You'd have most likely kneed him in the nuts?'

'I hope I would have...' But would I have done that? I felt I had no control, as if the whole course of my life might have been hanging on what I did next. I felt nauseous. 'He *was* asking what I thought he was asking, wasn't he?'

'You think you might have misinterpreted what he said?'

'Did I?'

'Nah! And I've got it all filmed.' He hesitated. 'Perhaps you should make a formal complaint? Thinking about it. He could easily do this again...' Harry frowned. 'Or he might have been doing this for years to vulnerable students. Sex for grades or whatever.'

'Ugh! I can't get that out of my head now.' I shook it, hoping to dislodge the horrible images playing out in my mind. 'Do girls fall for that? Do they feel they have to shag the tutor to get the grades they deserve—'

'Or maybe don't deserve?'

'That's shit!' I shook my head again. 'And there's me thinking we are in the enlightened twenty-first century! Mind you, we were only talking about the "Me too" movement the other day. Entitled old men trying to get what they want through coercion.'

'Listen,' said Harry. 'I'll go with you to the principal as I was a witness. This should be stopped dead in its tracks.'

'*You* might get flak from this!'

'It's the right thing to do. A united front, eh?'

'Are you sure, Harry?'

'Yeah, we'll both go in tomorrow.' He paused and scuffed the floor with his boot. 'I think we should go and have a drink now. I've got a nasty taste in my mouth.'

'Yeah, strangely, so have I. I didn't even get to drink my drink, and considering this is a party, we're lagging behind.'

'Well then,' Harry held out his elbow, and I linked arms with him, 'let's go, my lady.'

'Why, thank you, kind sir.' As we passed the other students, laughing and mucking about, I felt as though I was walking on air. Their faces said it all. I was on the arm of the coolest guy in the group, even if it was for the oddest, no, *creepiest* of reasons. I didn't care. Just for one night, *I* was cool, too, and I pushed Hugh Penfold from my mind.

Typical. Why on earth did Rose have to have a Harry? How bloody weird and ironic is that? I don't want or need to remember him. I'm moving on with my life.

Chapter Four

THE FOLLOWING SATURDAY NIGHT, *we three witches* have all met again, and yes, it's raining. It is the end of November, after all. I have invited Alice and Rose to my flat, so I had to do a deep clean. I can't bear the thought that I should ever be caught with a grimy bathroom sink or a hob covered in splots of old food. I can be a little anal in my cleaning, so I must tell myself when enough is enough, but I'm still polishing the light bulbs when there's a buzz from the main front door.

I live on Lewes Road, not far from The Level, which is one of the largest public open spaces in central Brighton. I own a one-bedroom, first-floor flat, so my bicycle is hung on hooks in the main hallway, much to the annoyance of the other people in the house. I've been here for over a year, leaving the world of rent for the so-called security of a mortgage. I know I'm lucky, as many women my age would never be able to have one, although sometimes it worries me. At least when you rent, you can move on to somewhere else. A mortgage can be a bit of an albatross around the neck, still kicking and pecking at you. There's a smidgeon of guilt also pecking at me, as I left Alice back in that rented flat, and although she tried not to show it, I know she felt I'd let her down, as we came here together.

Opening the door, a squall of wind showers us all and Alice's umbrella is blown inside out.

'Quick, come in before we are swept away.' I wave inside, and they pile through the door. We clop up the wooden stairs and into my flat. Alice hangs her coat on the rack and skips ahead, whipping out a bottle of red wine from her copious hippy-themed bag and placing it on the Moroccan mosaic table I picked up from the sizeable Moroccan shop across the street. I'd like to pretend I got it on my travels, but that's never going to work with anyone passing the shop as they walk up my road. I have an eclectic look, though that's due to insufficient money to get a decent style going. Most of my stuff has been picked up over time, and none of it matches. I kind of prefer it, as it's more organic. At least, that's what I tell myself.

Alice ducks through the doorway into my long galley kitchen. The door is conspicuously missing, and I didn't bother to ask the original owners where it went, as it makes the place feel less closed in. I can hear clinks and rummaging sounds, so she must be looking for glasses.

'Sorry about the mess,' I lie, and I hear Alice snort in the kitchen. It's what *she* does.

'I bet you were polishing the lightbulbs before we came,' she laughs. I can feel heat hurtle up my neck, and now my cheeks are burning. How did she know that? Has she got a hidden Nanny-Cam set up in here? I close my eyes. She knows me. It's what *I* do, but I wonder what Rose thinks of me now? Does she think I'm terribly anal?

Alice pops her head through a strange, perfectly round hole in the kitchen wall. It reminds me of peering into a goldfish bowl and is another weird legacy of the previous owners. 'Lily here is a bit OCD when it comes to cleaning. Mind you, I know why.'

She makes a face at me, and I can feel a second surge of embarrassment, and I hope Rose hasn't noticed.

'Better that,' says Rose, 'than a friend of mine who had things growing in her flat, and I don't mean only on the food. The carpet was spongey, and the walls had some dangerous-looking black stuff all over them. And she never washed up. It was disgusting.' She takes a bottle from her bag and hands it to me. We may want a lie-in tomorrow morning.

'Eauaugh!' Alice swings back into the room with the glasses. 'Yuckety-yuck! I lived in a shared house like that in London with...er...' She pauses. 'Lily? Where's the bottle opener?' I realise what she was about to say. With Harry. She lived with Harry in a student house, and that's why I'm OCD about cleaning. I'm still trying to forget!

'It should be in the usual drawer; if not, it's hung on the rack by the cooker.'

'I can't find it.'

'It's there. In front of you.' I point as I push past her, go to the fridge and give her the eye. *No Harry*, I mouth at her. 'I've just finished making guacamole and hummus, and I have loads of tortilla chips and other dips.' I tweak the opener from the drying rack and hold it out to Alice. 'Here we go.' It still has the cork in it from the last bottle we opened. 'Make yourselves comfortable.'

Bustling about in the kitchen, taking dishes from the fridge and emptying crispy things into bowls, I hear the satisfying pop of a cork being pulled. As I head back in, I see Rose has left her jacket over the back of my computer chair and has put her full glass of wine on my work desk, where there is not only my iMac but one of my latest paintings. A watercolour that has already taken me over ten hours to paint, and it still needs to be finished. It's my own fault. I should have put it away safely, so I wrestle with myself; do I ask her to move her glass out of sheer paranoia or stamp on my fear as if it's a deadly Brazilian wandering spider? I've never come across one, and quite frankly, I never want to. But if the glass gets knocked over, I will be very, *very* upset. I have to heave in a deep breath, and then I take the glass Alice has offered me. She always overfills, so she doesn't have to get up so many times for a refill. This often leads to wine stains and mishaps. I'm hoping it doesn't lead to one now, and I wonder how some people can be so heedless of what's around them.

I fill the table with bowls of crisps and snacks and wrestle the cork out of another bottle of wine. Well, there are three of us, and it needs to breathe. I place plates and serviettes next to it all. 'Help yourselves.'

'Lovely flat,' says Rose, and I sigh in relief as she takes her glass and sits on the sofa that backs onto my work area. 'Do you own it?'

'Yep. I am deeply ensconced in the world of the mortgage. I'm hoping it was the right decision, as I feel a little trapped now. I can't ever afford to miss a payment, and as you know, I don't exactly have a normal job.'

'Still,' says Alice, 'a flat in Brighton is an investment no matter the economic situation.' I mentally wince, as this is still a tender point between us. I watch her ladle dips and tortillas onto a plate. She tucks three olives into her mouth and chews, spitting the stones into a small terracotta bowl. I can't believe she's thirty, as she acts like a teenager. Oh, God! Was that my mother in my head?

'And what about you, Alice?' Rose gestures at her. 'Owner or renter?'

Alice returns to the sofa. 'Rent, although I hope to change that in due course, Leaky Women notwithstanding.'

I'm happy to hear this. I always felt I'd left Alice in the lurch, even after her boyfriend Matt moved in. I was never sure if it was through necessity or because they genuinely wanted to live together. I'm still trying to figure it out.

'You, Rose?' I'm curious.

'Rent. I've always had the hankering to travel, and I'd like to be able to drop everything and go. I don't know where yet, but I'll know when I get there.'

'That sounds nice. I think a part of me is jealous.'

'Oh, come on.' Alice crows loudly, and I think the wine is winning. 'You've got a great job, a lovely flat in a blinding town. I don't think for a minute you'd give it all up to go back-packing around Romania?'

'I meant a stint being pampered in a posh, luxury island retreat like the Maldives.'

'Maybe', says Rose, 'Lily feels she needs the whole package. Talking of which, how has OkCupid gone? Any contenders?'

I think that this is a bit obvious. How 'needs the whole package' can lead on from 'back-packing around Romania' is quite mystifying. It's a clunky way to get me to talk about any prospective blokes, but perhaps she is taking responsibility for bulldozing me into it. Rose again leaves the wine glass cockled on the arm of the sofa while she loads up with food, and I feel a rankle of annoyance.

'You know,' now, pulling all this into focus, there's definitely apprehension, or maybe it's excitement, 'I haven't looked.' I eye that glass and wonder if we will make it through the evening without a significant spill. Ah, this is familiar. I'm spotlighting side issues, so I don't have to face the real situation, although I'm not going to be let off the hook so easily.

'Let's do it.' Rose is snapping her fingers for me to give her my phone, then she must have seen the look on my face. 'Sorry, I don't mean to be pushy...'

I lever myself out of my armchair and retrieve it from the

sideboard. 'Listen, I'm just rusty and a little bit scared, I suppose.'

Rose and Alice again have their heads together, humming and hawing over my potential dates.

'Ooh, here we go,' says Rose. 'What do you think of him, Alice?'

'Appears to tick all the boxes...' Alice glances at me from beneath her lashes. 'Ale lover, hand-knitted sweaters, lives at home with mum—' She sniggers. 'No, really, he looks good. In person and on paper.'

My heart does a small somersault as they pass my phone back to me. I stare at the photo on my screen and then read his description.

There's no denying he's cute. A bit unshaven, a mop of blond hair, not so much hippie as surfer-dude style. He's got dimples where he's smiling, and he's in a round-neck, long-sleeve top over jeans and boots. I spot a silver bracelet and chain, though no rings. I don't want nylon slacks, beige loafers or V-neck tops with pockets. Yep! I am that shallow.

I read what he's put up out loud. 'He's on this site because he's looking for a meaningful relationship, and he's not into one-night stands.'

'That's a tick then,' nods Alice.

'He's got a degree in engineering and is working in industry—'

'So,' says Rose, 'not on Benefit Street.' She makes a face. 'Sorry, but it can make a difference if you know you are on a more equal footing.'

'Too true.' Alice stuffs more olives into her mouth and then licks her fingers. 'Although I want to experience what it's like to be a *kept woman* at least once in my life.'

'I don't think it's all it's cut out to be,' says Rose. 'Dependent on a man? For everything? Not sure about that.'

'Who says it has to be a man?' Alice has a saucy smirk on her face. 'Eh?'

'Okay,' I continue. 'It seems he's passionate about anti-hunting and Greenpeace. Now that's a positive for a start. And', I wave the phone at them, 'he loves going to art galleries and walks around parks.'

'How old is he?' Rose grins. 'Toy-boy or daddy figure?'

'Thirty-two.'

'Sounds good to me.' Rose nods.

'Anything about what he eats?' Alice points at our empty plates. 'Veggie or vegan?'

I scan through a bit more. 'No, says here he is open to veggie influences but is a meat-eater. Anyone offended by that should not bother contacting him.'

'Result!' crows Alice. 'What's his name again?'

'Jack. Jack Kelly.' There's something about him I find engaging; along with a ruggedness, there's also a sweetness or a vulnerability. He could be a Viking, gardener, chef, or hopefully all of that.

'Are you going for it then?' Alice looks like a child approaching Christmas. Her face is lit up. Although, that might be the wine.

'Oh, do…' smiles Rose. 'I think he's a real contender.'

'I just might.' I tuck the phone away. 'Now, I want to move to another subject. After all, our lives are not only about men, are they?'

Silence greets me until we all burst out laughing.

Jack Kelly? Yes, he has potential but am I ready to get back into the world of dating again?

My mind wanders back in time. It could have gone so many different ways.

There was a right old hoo-ha when Harry and I showed the principal the video of Hugh Penfold at the party.

'We can't accuse an upstanding member of this faculty of gross misconduct,' said the principal. 'We have to be absolutely sure.'

'Er,' said Harry, 'I think we are all absolutely sure, and we've shown you what he did. It's there for anyone to see—'

'Yes, but,' said the principal, 'Hugh has been teaching here for over twenty years—'

'What's that got to do with it?' Harry's fists balled. 'Are you saying you're not going to do anything about this?'

'No, no.' The principal held up his hands. 'Only that we have to proceed with utmost caution. We don't want to ruin a young man's life, now do we?'

'Hold on.' I stood up. Considering I was the injured party, I hadn't said a word so far, and it seemed to be all about the 'men'. 'So it's okay for him,' I launched in, 'to potentially ruin mine? He, very blatantly and in full and crisp colour, asked me for sex so I would get my grade. Are you saying teachers here can *rape* their students whenever they want to?'

The principal looked as if he was about to pop. 'Don't be ridiculous. Who said anything about rape—'

'Then what do you call this?' I was beginning to shout. 'Demanding sex in exchange for a grade I would have got anyway? If you ask any other tutors here, they'll tell you I'm an excellent student.'

'Okay,' said Harry. 'We'll upload this into YouTube and ask if anyone else has experienced the same, eh? Maybe you'll have a whole gamut of women over these last twenty years he's been teaching here come out of the woodwork. Won't that be a great advertisement for the school? What do you think, *sir*?'

'Now, now.' The principal was turning a deep puce. 'Let's not be hasty—'

'No.' I pointed at Harry's phone. 'I think Harry's right. Let everyone else see this. It's sexual harassment, and we can take it to the police, too.'

'The police? There's no need to involve the police, now is there? The man was clearly drunk—'

'Hang on.' I now thought I might pop. 'So what you're saying is all young people in your care have to take that into account? Oh, he was drunk, so I must excuse his terrible behaviour?'

Harry was practically yelling now. 'That's like saying someone was so drunk, they didn't mean to kill that family while they were driving!'

'It's not like that at all!' spluttered the principal.

I used the voice I adopted when talking to little kids. 'You have a sexual predator in your faculty.' He took a hasty step backwards, 'So you either fire the man *right now*, or I go to the police *right now*.'

'Well.' The principal steepled his fingers. 'Put like that...'

Hugh Penfold was dismissed on the spot. Harry and I waited, with trepidation for any fall-out, although we felt he'd slunk off into the shadows with his tail between his legs. Or so we thought.

There was a pub near the school where tutors and students from across the faculty hung out and discussed art and design until the sheer amount of beer turned them from discussions to arguments. There always seemed to be a lot of finger-waggling and spit. I'd been there the year before a couple of times. Harry invited me to go with him a few days later.

'We have to celebrate our win,' he said. 'We got that slime bucket out, and we should feel good about that.'

'I do feel good, although I wonder what would have happened if you hadn't been there to film it.'

'As I said, it would have got ugly.'

I sighed. 'What I'm trying to say is, would I have done it? This is all I've ever wanted, to come to this art school and get my degree. And he was threatening to take that all away from me.'

'I reckon you would have definitely kneed him in the balls.'

'I'm not so sure, although I'd like to think I might have.' I knew it was a moot point, yet it haunted me. Would I have done just about anything to get my degree? Even that? It didn't bear thinking about.

The pub was called The Enterprise, and many Trekkie jokes abounded every time you entered.

'Beam me up, Scotty,' I said, and Harry rolled his eyes. 'It's got to be done, surely?'

'Not every single time!'

'Oh, I think every single time.'

The pub was packed, with far too many squashed around the tables, playing pool or darts or trying to catch the harassed bartender's eye. There was an underlying scent of sweat and testosterone.

'Go and sit with Alice and her lot over there, and I'll get the drinks in. Oh, by the way, Alice is my cousin. She's in the year above on the graphics course. Er, what would you like?'

'A pint of cider?'

'Any particular kind?'

'The one made from apples?'

'Nuff said.'

I scanned the pub. 'Sorry, who is Alice?'

'That black girl over there with Amy and Lauren.'

Harry grinned and fought his way to the bar. I turned and

negotiated to where Alice was sitting with Amy and Lauren, who were on my course. It wasn't as though I didn't know them. It was more I wasn't *one of them*. They shuffled over for me and looked up expectantly.

'Hi, I'm Lily.' I did some sort of stupid wave.

'We know, so sit down. Come on, spill the beans then,' said Alice. 'We all know about it.'

I squeezed in next to Alice.

'Good riddance,' said Amy, sitting by Alice. 'He was creep personified.' Sleek as an otter, she fluttered her eyelashes and simpered prettily. I felt Amy was far savvier than she let on and knew how to manipulate any situation. Clever girls are not supposed to look like her.

'Yeah,' Lauren joined in. 'I heard he's done this before, and I mean loads of times. Good on yer, Lily.' Now Lauren was more badass. Backcombed black hair, kohl ringed eyes and blood-red mouth gave you the impression she might either bite you in the neck or leap up to start singing with a voice that sounded as if she'd smoked forty Gauloises cigarettes a day.

'Yeah,' said Amy. 'Lucky you had Harry there to save you.'

Alice frowned. 'I watched the video, and from what I saw, Lily was saving herself, and no disrespect to Harry. I know he filmed it all, but Lily stuck up for herself. I mean, she belted the prick one!'

'All I meant,' said Amy, 'was thank God Harry had the foresight to film it.' She pursed her plump lips. 'Although we do tend to film absolutely everything.'

'And then some,' I butted in.

Lauren said, 'More like, thank God for technology. My mum told me last night you didn't stand a chance in her day. Your word against theirs. *Bastards, the lot of them.*'

'I know,' I said. 'My mum told me my nan and granddad had

phones, but you could only use them as phones. No filming, no texting, no Instagram or Twitter. Nothing. Imagine that.'

'They used their phones *as phones*? How funny is that?' Amy giggled. Then I remembered another girl on the course saying, 'I wonder if she keeps her piranha teeth in a glass of water by her bed at night'. All the girls on the course had seen what damage this pretty little thing had done over the last year. The number of relationships she had ruined. We all knew who to be wary of.

'At least the principal did the right thing,' said Alice. 'Although that might be because of the overwhelming evidence Penfold was a letching old pervert.'

'You think then,' I said, 'without that, he might have let it go? It certainly looked as if he was willing to sweep it all under the carpet.'

'Course!' Lauren leaned over Amy to speak to me. 'That's what they do. All the old boys togevver. They protect each other. This is exactly what the "Me too" stuff is about.' Her eyes were luminous.

'You've only got to look at the news, at politics – they're all at it,' said Alice, and then she swallowed the last of her pint in a gulp. 'Even the bloody monarchy is corrupt and dirty. Hiding all their rotten eggs under a barrel or whatever that saying is.' She turned and hollered across the pub. 'Oy! Harry! Mine's a Stella and make it snappy!'

A grunted shout came from the bar.

I nodded. Yeah, hiding all their rotten eggs under a barrel sounded about right to me.

It took Harry quite a while to return with the drinks clutched between his outstretched fingers, and the three girls were in full flow by then. I listened to them raptly, joining in every so often. It felt good.

'Orright, ladies?' As Harry lowered the glasses, hunching

over my shoulder, something rammed into us. The pints were tipped over the table and sloshed into my lap. There were squeals and screeches of indignation. As I stumbled upright, I felt a hand grab my hair and yank me upwards. I yelped in pain and tried to twist to see who my attacker was.

'Get off her, you *fucktard*!' Harry was grappling with whoever was holding me, and the girls were shouting and screaming. The table got knocked over, glass shattered, and all I could see were frightened and angry faces; I heard words called, lots of swearing and people struggling.

Alice yelled, 'Watch out, Harry!' There was further scuffling and the sound of more things breaking.

Whoever had my hair thumped into me, and we both fell heavily onto the upended table. The breath was knocked out of me, and I struggled to drag in air. A dead weight was on top of me, and my leg was twisted beneath me. Little spirals of white light were at the corner of my vision. Oh, God! I wasn't going to pass out, was I? It kind of went dark for a bit.

'Lily? *Lily?*' Harry's voice was in my ear, and I could feel hands dragging me upright. 'Can you hear me, Lily? Are you okay?'

'What the hell happened? I feel as if I've been kicked by a bad-tempered mule.'

'A bad-tempered tutor, more like.' Harry came into focus. His face was creased into a worried frown, but what was strange to me was that red stuff was leaking from his hairline down his forehead. 'That was Hugh Penfold. Seems he wasn't too pleased with us "ratting" on him. We've called the police and an ambulance—'

'Who is the ambulance for?' I searched about me, looking to see who else had been injured. 'You?' I peered at his blood-daubed face.

'Well, not exactly,' said Harry. 'That'd be you.'

'Me? I'm fine—' I tried to stand but fell back with a yelp. 'Oh!'

'Exactly. Hold still and wait for the medics to suss out how you are.'

Another voice chimed in. 'What a *prick*! God,' said Alice, 'I hope he gets banged up good and proper!' She was on the other side of me. 'Don't worry, Lily. We've got you.'

Sirens were wailing outside, and there seemed to be a lot of movement.

'Let us in, now,' said a deep, authoritarian voice. '*Oy!* You lot, I said *move!*' A paramedic leaned over me and checked me over. 'Hmm.' He sucked on his teeth. 'We need to get you to emergencies.'

I was loaded onto a trolley and wheeled out. Harry and Alice remained by my side.

'Only one of you can be in the ambulance,' said the deep voice.

'You go, Harry.' Alice motioned at him. 'You need to get your head seen to—'

'Oy, what are you saying here?' He laughed, though I saw him wince.

'Shut it!' Alice kissed his cheek and patted my arm. 'You're both hurt. Let me know how she is.' She nodded at me. 'I'll see you in a bit, Lily the Pink.'

'Don't worry,' shouted Lauren, 'we filmed the whole lot. Gonna give it to the police now.'

Amy materialised at her side. 'You'd think he'd have learned his lesson by now. Of course we'd film it all. I mean, what a DER-brain!'

The bruise down my leg was magnificent, and my ankle swelled to the size of a melon. The cut on my forehead where I'd head-butted the table looked nasty, and I prayed it wouldn't scar. The doctor took photos as evidence, yet I reasoned it wasn't essential if the girls had filmed it all. When I came out in a wheelchair, I said this to Harry, who replied, 'It'll be the cherry on the top. Any jury faced with what he did to you can't help but throw the bloody book at him.'

'You mean it might go to court?'

'Of course it will. This is assault.' He fingered at a bruise on his cheek that was beginning to bloom, and I noticed butterfly stitches creeping across his head into his hairline.

'You got clobbered too.' I pointed to his face. 'You won't get into any trouble, will you?'

'Self-defence, or at least, I was trying to defend you.'

I smiled at him. 'Thanks for that.'

'Sorry to intrude.' A voice emanated from above us. 'We need to take your statements now.' A massive boulder of a policeman appeared in front of us. 'Would you follow me, please?'

Harry wheeled me into the proffered room.

'Now,' said the policeman, 'what happened?'

Two hours later, we were released. No charges pending, but don't leave town or something like that. The wheelchair had been replaced with crutches, although negotiating them posed a problem. The painkillers I'd been given had made my head float off, and I was having trouble concentrating.

'I'll take you home and make sure you're settled, then I'll go back to mine. If that's all right with you?'

'Lovely, jubbly,' I grinned as Harry hailed a taxi.

Poor Harry had to lump and bump me up the steps to the main door of my house and then manoeuvre me into my bedsit. By then, it was past two in the morning.

'Nice place, Lily.' He stared about him. 'You live here alone?'

'Independence and liberty. And snug.' I thought for a moment. 'Am I rambling?'

'No, you're fine.' He helped me into bed, put a glass of water on the edge of the TV table, as I could lean out and reach it from there, and placed the pot of painkillers beside it. Then he leaned down and kissed me on my cheek. 'It's been a rollercoaster in the few days since I met you, Lily Maye, but it's been fun. I mean, apart from us being beaten up and all that. Listen, have you got a spare key, because I can lock you in and then come back tomorrow to make sure you're okay? How does that sound?'

'Come back for breakfast. I have muesli.' I pointed out where my spare keys were for the main door and my room.

'Well, that's an offer I can't refuse.' He chuckled, and then I heard the click as the door locked and footsteps receding down the hall.

———

Why are the memories of Harry surfacing now? It's bloody disconcerting, and I don't like it. It feels as though something in my mind is trying desperately to sabotage my future happiness. I need whatever it is to well and truly *sod off*!

Chapter Five

AFTER A RESTLESS NIGHT, I decide I'll send a message to Jack and see where it leads. I will start by asking some random questions, and I wonder if he will answer me or if I'm not his type. I stare at the photo Alice chose. How do I come across to a stranger? More to the point, a strange man? I'm above average height although not as tall as Alice. I suppose I'm quite sporty, with broad shoulders and slim hips. Will he find me attractive? As attractive as I find him? I hope so.

I think about all the questions I can ask him, although maybe starting with 'have you any bizarre talents or quirks' is not the way to go. This may not be taken in the vein it is meant, and I may end up going down routes I hadn't envisioned. Better not mention eyebrow dancing or limbo skating, let alone anything to do with bondage and gimps!

So, start again. I will ask three questions. Do I mention religion at this point? Could he be a Druid or a Scientologist? Neither of which sounds tempting to me. How about, 'what is an accomplishment you are most proud of?' Followed by, 'do you work to live, or live to work?' And the third will be, 'what three words would your closest friends use to describe you?'

I don't want to sit and wait, so I busy myself clearing my desk ready to start my morning's work.

I hear the 'ping' as his answers come through.

'Hey, Lily. Nice to hear from you. In answer to your first question: I have saved the life of someone who tried to take their own life. The second is easy: I work to live as I believe we only have this one life and why waste it working yourself to the bone and then you die? Not to be pessimistic about stuff, as many don't make it past retirement. The third question is trickier. Three words? I had to ask a mate for this. So: loyal, caring and trustworthy. I sound as if I'm a pet dog, don't I? I would have preferred: manly, strong and capable. But hey! So now I have some questions for you.

1. What motivates you to get out of bed in the morning?
2. What is your favourite type of holiday?
3. What was it about my profile that made you want to contact me?'

Glad he has responded, I wait a bit to reply, as I don't want to come across as needy. Re-reading his answers, I smile to myself. I like what he's written here. Dare I say he comes across as normal? I mean, in a good way. I need normal, all things considered.

I have to think hard about his questions to me.

'Okay, so to get out of bed, I need to know I am doing something. That I have work to complete, friends to meet or a new walk to experience. I hate the idea of letting what time I have slip through my fingers. As you said, we don't know how much time we have left. None of us are getting out of here alive, and you can't spend your life waiting for retirement. Even if you make it, your health might be compromised, or you can no longer do anything you want to. My favourite holiday is going somewhere that offers a bit of everything. I adore the beach, although I don't wish to spend two weeks roasting on one. I love seeing unusual things, visiting ancient sites or slipping down unknown alleys in cities and seeing if there's a tiny restaurant serving Mama's authentic local dishes. You get the picture. And the third? The photo of you is attractive, but more importantly, you appear to have the same sort of hobbies as I do, for want of a better word. I like that you are anti-hunting and you are into walks and visiting art galleries. It's no good liking a face or body and then discovering you are incompatible. And you're not vegetarian. I want to be, except I keep finding bacon in my fridge. Those are my answers. I've tried to be as truthful as possible because I never want to start something with someone based on lies.'

I press 'send' and close my eyes. I mustn't pin my hopes on him. Just because he comes across well on paper doesn't mean he'd be the same in real life. Does it?

The questions continue as we build up a 3D picture of each other. He asks me if I'm religious, and after saying 'no', I ask him the same. He says English Protestantism is not religious, as it's so fluffy. I agree, and there are laughing emojis. I find out his ultimate snack is a marmalade sandwich on thick farmhouse bread, made with real butter, never spread. His favourite holiday is finding an Airbnb in a foreign city, preferably in the old quarter, and then going exploring. That's what I'd want to do too. He doesn't have any brothers or sisters, and he likes the fact I have a younger sister. He asks where I live, and I reply, Brighton. He's in London, so that's easy, as trains run from Victoria station to

Brighton and take less than an hour. Then it depends on where-abouts he lives as to how much longer it will take. If we get that far. It's exciting and fresh and makes my head whirl. I have butterflies in my stomach and it's been an age since anyone stirred me like this.

It's gone one when we say goodnight. We have interests in common, not precisely the same, but workable. Very workable. I don't want someone identical, for where would be the fun in that? As I drift off to sleep, I hope Jack will ask to meet me.

It's then I have the dream. I'm in a dark corridor, and a woman is crying, no, screaming, but I can't catch what she's saying, although, from how she hurls the words, I know it is abuse. She is masked by shadows, yet somehow I know her. I turn and see Harry, and the look on his face makes me wake with such a start I can barely breathe.

To say I'm a bit jaded the following day is an understatement. I feel as if I've been put through a juicer and come out all shredded and sucked dry. One part of me is anticipating a message from Jack, and another is worrying about what that dream meant. I know where it has come from. It's a morphed dream sequence of *Psycho Jo*. Harry's ex. At least, that's what Alice called her. I thought I'd managed to blot her from my mind, but I suppose the possibility of meeting a new guy has made the memory resurface. To remind me not to trust or give my heart away carelessly. It's like a firewall.

I need to shake these weird feelings off and get on with plan-ning my next commission. My publisher has approached me with a story from a new author, who is Polish and has a different take on kids' stories. Again, this tale is dark and mysterious, and after a discussion with him, we have decided how to proceed. In the New Year, I will paint two colour plates, and then we will discuss if they are what is intended or if we need to modify the style, colours or general impressions. I now have to finish the last illustrations for my latest book and take them to Mary before Christmas. Then I can crack on in earnest.

As I sit at my desk, I stop myself from peering for messages on my phone by hiding it under one of the cushions on the sofa. We are hurtling towards Christmas, as December 1st is on Tuesday. That is the day we are allowed to put up the decorations and play Noddy Holder. Sometimes, it makes my head spin. Already, the adverts on TV are yelling at us to buy this product or to consume that, making sure we all know we can't possibly have a good time without it all. I itch to nip to the local supermarket to get a bottle of Baileys and a turkey crown. I am susceptible to indoctrination, I realise, and must be vigilant not to have hidden stashes of Brussels sprouts and walnuts in my store cupboard before December 23rd.

I hear a beep from under the cushion and nearly trip over myself trying to grab the phone.

'Want to meet up? Coffee/lunch/dinner/film? I can be in Brighton at a time suited to you?'

I put the coffee percolator on and rummage for some biscuits. I find some digestives at the back of a cupboard. Munching on a biscuit and sipping at a coffee, I write back, aware my hands are shaking but unsure if it's to do with the coffee or sheer excitement.

'How about lunch on the beach this Saturday? There's a great Mexican restaurant that's practically on the pebbles, but they have an inside area too. The food is good and not expensive. The views from upstairs are lovely as the windows look out over the sea. How does that sound?'

He's there immediately.

'Perfect. Shall I meet you at the restaurant or at the station? You can be the one with a big placard with my name on it.'

I reply straight away too. 'I can meet you at the station. After all, I know what you look like. Unless you uploaded someone else's photo, then we'd be a little stuck!' There was a recent film about this, where the guy put a mate's photo up. It was meant to be a comedy, and it ended happily ever after, although I think that in reality, this would be tricky. It shouldn't be about the looks, but we all know it is, initially.

'What you see is what you get. I'll text through train times, and we can arrange when to meet. Back in a bit, then x.'

There's a kiss at the end. I roll my eyes at myself. How old am I? Twenty-nine going on fourteen? The message comes through that he can arrive at 12.38 at Brighton station. Now all I have to do is get through my week. I send a message to Alice and Rose that I have a date. Yes, I'm definitely fourteen.

Alice and Rose are quick to respond, demanding details, and a little bit of me is loath to hand it all over to them on a plate. I'm being mean, but I don't give them the restaurant name where we hope to go. I want to have something for myself, as it feels like three of us are going on this date. I don't think Jack signed up for a *hydra!*

And yet more memories are surfacing. Is this because I feel I might have a chance with Jack? Are they warnings? No, I chide myself. I should be cautious. I don't know him, although that will hopefully change next Saturday. I will not blow it right at the start with unfounded misgivings. I will be open to this.

. . .

Harry came around the following day. By then, I could truly feel the extent of my injuries, and there didn't seem to be enough of the Co-codamol tablets left in that little orange pot. The previous night was a bit hazy, although I seemed to remember Hugh Penfold had me by the hair in the pub. My neck felt as if I'd been under a meat tenderiser.

'Are you decent?' The key rattled in the lock.

'Yes,' I called back.

Cold air entered with him as he wrestled off his coat. He clutched a bag, and I wasn't sure if it was the bag or Harry that smelt so good. I hoped it was the bag.

'Much as muesli was so enticing, I thought I'd come prepared. I have two coffees and two Danish pastries. They're still warm from the oven.'

'Ooh! Give me, give me.' I held out my hand.

'Plates?'

I waved towards a small cupboard on the wall, and we were soon eating and slurping at the coffee.

'Thanks so much for this, Harry.' I didn't know if it was the effect of the painkillers, but I felt pretty confident, which was a bit of a first for me.

'You're welcome. By the way, Alice sends her love. And, back to the nitty-gritty. How are *you* feeling today?'

Licking my fingers, I pulled back the duvet and showed him the discolouration spreading down most of my thigh and my pumpkin-sized ankle. 'I would say it looks worse than it is, but I'd be lying. It hurts, and I mean really, *really* hurts. And I think I might have lost some of my hair.'

'It looks dreadful. Don't worry, Lily. He'll get what's coming to him.' He stood, wrenched open the fridge door and rummaged through the cupboard. 'Okay. I'm going to go and get some supplies in for you, and we can spend the day watching films or listening to music or whatever you want.' He turned abruptly. 'Or not? Sorry, didn't mean to assume or anything?'

'I'd appreciate some help with food and things, though you don't have to stay with me.' I looked away. 'Unless you want to stay with me.' I tried to sound flippant, 'No worries, either way.'

'Of course I'll stay with you. I'll be back in a mo.'

All I can say is, 'thank God for Netflix', as we spent that day and the day after nestled into my duvet, binge-watching series, eating crap and talking about the weirdest stuff. We didn't even share a kiss, yet it was terrific.

Of course, as the bruises faded and my ankle resumed its usual size, the Netflix sessions turned into something else. Many a time, a film finished, and neither of us had a clue what it was about. Harry wasn't my first boyfriend, yet I hoped he would be my last. All the sexual experiences I'd had so far now seemed adolescent fumbling and gropings. It felt easy with Harry, as I'd always imagined sex should be. And we talked about everything, art, politics, religion and history, though we never broached the future. I suppose it was because we were so young – the future was shining brightly in front of us, and we didn't need to discuss it. In my mind, we would be together until we were grey and wrinkly and knew each other inside out. Until our teeth and hair fell out. Until we died in each other's arms. *How naive!*

Without even realising it, I had become part of the in-crowd. I cut my hair short, dyed it deep burgundy, started to wear retro clothes bought from various trendy markets and fitted in seamlessly. Apart from the feeling that I was a fake and *they* would all see through the façade to the painfully shy little girl inside. But *they* never seemingly did. I'm not sure if Harry did, either. It occurred to me maybe all of us were doing this, reinventing ourselves in the image we wanted to be, not as the pimply, gangly, unsophisticated kids we'd all been at home. That made me feel better. We were all forcing ourselves out of our chrysalises, slowly unfolding our wings, ready to show off our dazzling colours, transitioning into the beautiful butterflies we longed to be.

That's my theory, and I'm sticking to it.

At some point, Hugh Penfold's case was sent to court. As witnesses, all the students present who had seen the assault in the pub were in the front seats. We wore our best clothes and tried not to be intimidated by the austerity of the courtroom. The principal was sitting at the back, face grave, with a couple of the other tutors from our school. What were they expecting? Clemency? A clean slate? No shit on their shoes?

When the judge entered, we all stood. A woman judge, and for that I was grateful. The press were stationed in the top gallery, and the jurors in their benches down one side. They were sworn in on either the Bible or the Quran.

It was pretty cut and dried after that. The list of offences was read out: sexual harassment, intimidation and Grievous Bodily Harm. GBH. The film Harry took of Hugh intimidating me at the party was shown, quickly followed by Lauren's film when Hugh attacked us in the pub. Seeing myself on the screen like that was horrifying, as I hadn't seen the footage until this moment. It was a brutal attack, and watching it now from the outside, so to speak, I hoped the judge would lock the bastard up for ever and a day. I also saw how Harry had been injured. He'd taken a blow meant for me. I didn't think I could love Harry more, but I did that day. Harry and Alice also looked shocked, and Alice turned her face away at the end, even though she'd been there that night.

There was absolutely no wriggle room. It was blatantly

evident Hugh was guilty, although I wondered if he might still deny it all. Head in the sand. *Anyone can see that it wasn't me.* I thought at that point it was done. Except it wasn't, was it?

I was called as a witness and had to go through it all again, aware of everyone's eyes on me. Feeling judged. Was any of this my fault? Would I be the one to be condemned? Images of my injuries were blown up huge on the screen, and photos were passed along the row of jurors for them to um and ah over. I could see some of my friends wince when they saw them and mutter under their breath. Harry was called, as were Alice and Lauren. They all swore to tell the truth, the whole truth and nothing but... except it was all there to see in glorious colour. It wasn't as if we would differ from the filmed evidence.

Hugh was called then. He'd been watching and listening from a glass-fronted area in the middle of the courtroom. A prison guard stood at his back. His eyes slid to mine, and I felt queasy. 'No comment,' was all he said.

When Hugh was finally asked how he would plead, he said, 'Guilty.' His face was granite, his jaw grinding, and he stared forward through the whole proceedings, never looking at me or Harry again. A wave of relief swept over me, then a woman in one of the seats at the back put her head in her hands, and I saw her shoulders heave. This poor woman must be his wife. Was she relieved or saddened?

The jury was led out to deliberate. They quickly filed back in and stated that, yes, Hugh Penfold was definitely guilty. The judge nodded solemnly and sorted through some paperwork.

'I sentence Hugh Penfold to five years imprisonment and a fine of twenty thousand pounds.'

There. Now it was done.

Did Hugh Penfold do five years, or was he let out for good behaviour? I won't bother to check. The most important thing was that the court case was so high profile, appearing in newspapers and the news channels; it also helped to change the culture in the school. And for that alone, I was proud. It turned out other women had come forward to accuse Hugh Penfold of sexual misconduct and worse. This evidence was not allowed to be part of the court case and was suppressed until after the trial when it all came out. It was a bit of a scandal the school tried to weather as best it could. Things had to change, and I felt I was a part of that change.

Why on earth is Harry popping into my mind, left, right and centre? What? The mention of another Harry can send me off on a tangent like this? God help me! I need to get a handle on this, having at long last made contact with the first possibly non-weird bloke in ages. There have been so many stomach-curdling, arrogant, clingy wackos so far since I broke up with Harry; I can't afford to lose my shit at this point. My head must be clear if I have any chance with Jack. Just saying his name out loud makes me shiver in anticipation. *Jack Kelly*. What will he be like? And more to the point, I hope he likes me.

Chapter Six

TOAST AND TEA are all I can manage this morning, as anything heavier might make me throw up. Today I will meet Jack Kelly. I roll his name around on my tongue to taste it. *Jack Kelly*. I shouldn't have nerves such as this for a first date, especially as the last few have been so disastrous, yet I'm hoping this time it will work. It's not so much that I think Jack could be *the one*; more like, at least, we might start off on the same page. In one of my previous encounters, the man had obviously chosen a ten-year-old photo (I'm being complimentary here), and then he enlightened me that 'women always get their way by using sex'. I'm not sure what I expected to happen after such a comment. Perhaps he thought I might fall face-first onto his dick, and the fact we were in a café *be damned*! To say I couldn't get out of there fast enough is an understatement. He seemed surprised as I raced out the door, so maybe this initial gambit had worked for him before. Can't see it myself, but it takes all sorts.

I agonise over what to wear. The only picture he's seen of me was summer and soft focus. Now it's mid-winter, which means red runny noses and chapped lips. Not a good look, and not to mention resembling a hamster with all the scarves, gloves and coats. I wonder if he will be able to recognise me, and maybe waving a placard with his name on it isn't such a bad idea now. I choose a pair of bootleg jeans and a long-sleeved black sweater over a T-shirt. And team them with low-heeled boots.

I lurk close enough to the barriers to see who is pushing through but not so close I appear too eager and, conversely, so I have leeway to run should the need arise. I spot Jack at the exact moment he sees me. Wearing jeans and boots, a dark leather jacket over a hoodie and with his hands stuffed into his pockets, he looks like a young Chris Hemsworth. That's good enough for me! I hope his first impression of me is as favourable. He grins and waves as he sticks his ticket in to get through the barrier. I start to move forward, and we meet in the middle.

He peers at me. 'Lily?' He holds out his hand, and I shake it. 'At least I hope you are, or you're going to think I'm a nutter.'

'Hi, Jack.' I seem to be still holding his hand, which is warm and a bit rough, as if he does manual labour. I pull away and say, 'Good journey? Sorry, that sounds so crass.'

'No, it's what people say who have just met up. And I will say back, "thank you, Lily. It was a delightful journey, indeed". Okay?'

I laugh and peer down at my boots. 'Yeah, that's better.'

'It's very nice to finally meet you, Lily. So? Where are we going again?'

I peek up at him, aware he is taller than me. That's a plus to start with. 'Do you still want to go to the Mexican place?'

He nods. 'That'd be great. But I'd prefer indoors if poss. It was a bit parky on the train. I'll follow you, as I don't know Brighton.' I have to blink a few times. There's something about his accent. I can't quite put my finger on it, except that I've heard it before. Neither this nor that, though still *something* recognisable, and in that recognition, I get a strange fleeting feeling of loss.

'Are you from here?' he asks.

I shake my head, but that's more to knock out these odd feelings. 'No, I'm from a town called Edenbridge. It's not too far away.' I nod at him. 'You?'

'A small village near Cheshire. And like most people, I got out years ago.'

Ah! That must be it. Every slight northern accent reminds me of Harry... Best not to start thinking of him just as I'm meeting Jack.

Heading out, we push against the flow of people and walk down Queen's Road. Our pace is slow as he is looking about, and then he steps on my heel.

'Sorry, but I've just seen the view and wasn't watching where I was going!' He turns to me. 'I still have that feeling like when you're a kid, and you see the sea for the first time. Too long cooped up in the big city. I'm so glad it's a nice day. I mean, the colour of the sea is beautiful, especially against that sky.'

It's not as if I need reminding, though seeing it through someone else's eyes is great. And to know he can appreciate the same feelings I have. After all, colour is my life. 'That's one of the reasons I love it here. I can easily walk to the sea from my place and either go towards the main drag or along the wilder part of the coast. The city is big enough to feel like a city but small enough to walk from one end to the other.' I laugh. 'Sorry, didn't know you were on a tourist excursion, did you?'

'It makes me want to visit more.' He smiles, and his eyes crinkle at the corner. They are such an intense blue, although I'm not sure if they are simply reflecting the sky above. 'And we both have to stop saying "sorry" so much. Agreed?'

I nod.

We wander down the slope to the beachfront. We are close

but not touching as we dodge the crowds. Bars, restaurants and
tourist traps abound, and we browse a little through the artists'
quarter. There's some excellent stuff here, though I can't afford
to be frivolous, especially as I have decided to pay for the meal
for the both of us. The sun is warm on my face, and people are
snarling up the winding walkway as usual. A man on a bike
zigzags his way through the crowd, and I marvel he doesn't clip
anyone. There are kids licking ice creams, and even the thought
makes me shiver. Being British, everyone is sitting at the wooden
benches outside the pubs, snuggled into hoods and coats but
hands around a cold pint. I don't think even a light blizzard
could stop us.

Spotting the restaurant, I scan to see how crowded it is.

'What do you think? Want to try inside?'

'Sure. Looks great.'

Some of the tables out front are occupied with hardy souls. I
steer Jack to the main entrance as a waitress bobs out, carrying
four bottles of a Mexican beer and a hearty platter of nachos.

'I'll be with you in a minute,' she calls over her shoulder.

As she returns, she barely slows her pace. I ask, 'Is there any
space upstairs?'

'For two? We have a table by the window. Follow me,
please.'

We clip-clop up the wooden staircase with a carved pome-
granate on the post, passing the open kitchen where the chef, a
tall, thin blonde woman, is pink-faced, cooking in a fug of smoke
and steam. It smells delicious and authentic, although she
doesn't look particularly Mexican.

Upstairs is painted white, with wooden accessories,
including old-fashioned farm tools, hung on the walls. The
windows are semi-circular and look out over the front courtyard
and walkway, across the pebbles to the stretch of sea and horizon. We are shown to the last remaining table, and I'm pleased

as we have a perfect view. The rusty remains of the West Pier crumble into the sea to the right of us, and the more vibrant though somewhat tacky Brighton Pier is to our left. I want his first impressions to be good ones.

'I like this place.' Jack smiles at me as we are handed menus. 'Wine or beer?'

'Wine, for me.'

We both look down at the wine list and select a bottle of Campo Viejo Reserva 2015. At the same time, we order quesadillas and a salad to share. I listen to the waitress as she clomps down the wooden staircase.

There's a lull as we look at anything except each other. Jack clears his throat.

'Is this a favourite haunt of yours?'

'Yep. The food is always cooked fresh, and the prices are affordable. If you can get a table in the summer, you can simply watch the world rollerblade by and the kids playing on the beach.' I indicate out of the window. 'And this is such a great view, even in winter.'

'It certainly is.'

'Where do you normally go? Do you stay in London, or do you go further out?'

'Local pubs and then out to eat when I have time. I mean, nothing is cheap in London, though you can still find places that don't need a second mortgage to be able to pay for it.'

'Well,' I shrug, 'the fact Brighton is called "London-by-the-sea" says it all. Still, we also have our private little places that only Brightonians know about.'

Settling back in his chair, he stares at me. 'I'd like to see a few of those. It's not as if I'm bored of London, but as they say, a change is as good as a rest.' Peering out the window, he sighs. 'And even though I love English beaches, I hardly ever get the chance to be on one.'

'Do you prefer our beaches to, say, Mediterranean ones?'

'Yeah, I do. Endless blue sky and golden sand? How boring. I prefer glowering skies, crashing waves and the myriad colours of pebbles.'

'So do I.' I wonder if, one day, he might want to come swimming as the sun struggles to breach the horizon. I've done that a few times in the summer months, which is exhilarating. Cold but exhilarating! Or will this be our first and only date?

He changes tack. 'I'm interested to know what's your accomplishment *you're* most proud of?'

The wine is placed on the table with a small pot of olives. I think about Jack's question as he fills our glasses. It's not an Alice measure.

'I think the fact that I secured my first children's book commission before my mum died. She got to see the finished book and passed a month later.'

'I'm sorry to hear about your mum. That's a lovely story and she must have been so proud of you.'

'She was. I hope she still is.'

'She must have been young.' He sounds sad.

'Yeah, she was only fifty-two. An aggressive cancer. One minute she was here, strong as an ox, and then the next, she was gone. Still can't believe it.' I need to change the subject, as I know I will cry. The pain has worsened over the last six years, not lessened, as I suppose the realisation that I will never see her again has finally hit home. And then what happened straight after, which I know I haven't processed properly. That crushing pain. That imagined guilt.

'That's dreadful. Dare I ask about your dad?'

'He's in a grandad flat at my sister's, although he's not exactly grandad material as he's only fifty-eight. They live in Bristol. I think he's out on the town more than she is.'

'Top bloke. Who is your publisher? Or do you have many?'

'My main one is New Renaissance Books, but I have worked for a number now.'

'Woo, New Renaissance Books? Patrons of the arts?'

'That's them,' I nod. 'It all has to be tasteful, traditional. And very, *very* nice.'

'So, no rabid rats or axe-wielding badgers, then?'

'I think the MD would have to be overthrown before that ever happens. What about you? You work in engineering. What does that entail?'

'A respectable job that can be very repetitive and sometimes tedious, which pays the rent and allows me to have fun.'

'Mum and dad? I know you don't have any brothers or sisters...' I see something in his eyes, a reflection, but it doesn't seem to be of anything here in this room. Have I upset him?'

'Sorry.' He sucks on his bottom lip. 'I always wished for a brother, you know, someone to play with. As to Mum and Dad, they both died in a car accident when I was twenty-six.'

'Oh, God! I'm so sorry—'

'You didn't know. It was a shock at the time, but I've compartmentalised it. It still hurts, of course, though I can deal with it better now.'

I know all about that, except he's lost both parents simultaneously. What must that feel like? *Quick!* What can we talk about now? 'Okay, changing the subject, what is your most bizarre talent or quirk?' I close my eyes briefly. Should have thought that through a bit more and saved it for at least the third or fourth date. Maybe we won't get that far now. Me and my big mouth! Still, if it takes his mind off the dreadful death of his parents, then job done.

His eyes roll upward to the left, and I feel he is really thinking about this. 'Talent? Hmmm. What can I do? Not sure if this fits the bill but here goes. My body is classed medically as an ultra-rapid metaboliser. This basically means my liver produces very active enzymes, breaking down drugs before they can have any effect. I haven't taken many drugs in my life, though when it has been needed, the doctors had to give me a much higher dose for the drugs to work properly.'

I'm taken aback, and it must show. 'Wow! That must have been tricky on occasions?' I think. 'So, if you take painkillers, they don't work?'

'Nope. Just pain all the way, as I've been told not to mess with opioids or whatever in case I destroy vital organs. I can't self-medicate for this reason. I have to be in a safe situation with medically trained staff. It can get pretty annoying.'

'I've never heard of anything like that.'

'No worries. Just means I have to be especially careful.'

Our plates of food arrive. The salad is fresh and crispy, and the quesadillas are toasted and smell deliciously cheesy.

'What about you? Talent or quirk?'

It's now my turn to consider. 'I can write with both hands at the same time, and they are identical.'

'What? Crazy! That must have come in handy for school?'

'Not really, as it has to be the same words. I can't do two different sets of words, or I think my head would explode.'

'No shit!' he mumbles, and we both laugh.

Jack's body is an ultra-rapid metaboliser? Drugs don't work on him? The mention of drugs pings me back. Drugs. Hmm...

My bedsit was snug for one and became very intimate for two, and Harry and I were beginning to trip over each other. The months passed, and we were midway through our second year. We regularly returned to Harry's place in his multiple shared house in Hackney and crashed at mine when it got too much. Poor Alice had to live there permanently, and I sometimes wondered how she managed it. It wasn't the place so much as the people in it. I know we were all students but *really*! It made me wonder if some of them had been brought up by feral dogs.

Everyone in the household heaved a collective sigh of relief when Mad Scottish Jane decided to take her miniature Doberman, Buddha, and herself back to Glasgow. Jane had doted so much on Buddha, they'd even shared the same dog food, taking turns to eat a spoonful from the tin.

Harry and I had just made it through the front door when we saw Jane sitting at the bottom of the stairs, and she was holding the spoon out for him to lick. She then stabbed it back into the tin for another mouthful, which she ate with gusto.

'Should you be eating that stuff?' I unthinkingly asked the two of them and was greeted by a withering look, either from Jane or, more likely, Buddha.

'What's good enough fer me is good enough fer Buddha,' Jane snapped back and proceeded to ram another spoonful into Buddha's mouth. She then licked the spoon. The thought of where *he'd* recently been licking made me gag. Was that one of the spoons we all shared? Oh, yuck!

Later that day, Harry and I sat with Alice in the communal living room on the badly sprung sofa, eating Pot Noodles as no one wanted to venture into the kitchen for long. I had always thought it was an unwritten rule that if you lived with other people, you shared the chores, washed up after yourself, cleaned the communal areas in turn, and a real *biggie*, you kept your music down after midnight. It appeared the others in this house had never heard of this. Well, what a shocker! The kitchen was so filthy, we'd all stopped using it. Nagging wasn't working and seemed to have the opposite effect, as did going on strike, as neither Jane nor their other flatmate, Big Tone, noticed. The plates would pile up, the floor would suck you down, and the heavy rock blared continuously.

'Who thought it was a good idea to share with her?' I motioned at Harry and Alice.

'Er, she was here first.' Alice looked rueful. 'We moved in with her and Big Tone.'

'Anyway,' said Harry, 'she'll be gone in a few days—'

'You mean in a few very, *very* long days,' Alice put her head in her hands and made a groaning sound.

'Then,' continued Harry, 'we must be cautious who we choose to replace her. (Famous last words!)

'Harry?' I said.

'Yes, Lily?'

'I don't mean to be rude or anything, but I honestly don't like it here. It's kind of strange and unnatural. I think I must have lived a truly sheltered life.'

'What?' He drained his Pot Noodle and grinned at me. 'Not brought up with people who eat dog food with their dog? Is that not normal where you come from?'

'More like, not brought up with people who use the same spoon as the dog. I seem to remember horrible tales of worms and stuff.' I thought for a moment. 'We should make sure we clean the utensils well. And I mean *really* well!'

'Hear, hear,' said Alice. 'I know someone said that if you get worms, it keeps you thin, though I think using this method isn't the way to go.'

'Weight loss by worms.' Harry made a face. 'It has a certain ring to it.'

'That's so gross,' I said. 'Can we change the subject now?'

Big Tone, tall, with huge hands and feet and a large, shaved rectangular head, was the other flatmate, and lived in the small back room of the shared house. He had at least three degrees under his belt and was likely the most intelligent person we knew. A perennial student who never wanted to engage with real life, jobs and mortgages. I could understand that. He also did gardening in the backyard, and at the far end I noticed a different variety of plants growing tall and strong.

'Tone?' I queried one day. 'Are those dope plants in the garden?' I had spent a while examining the leaves and then looked them up on Google.

'Absolutely,' he beamed. 'Picked up all the seeds at a party I went to last year. Marvellous, aren't they?'

'Aren't they illegal?'

'Only in some people's minds.'

'Um, I think that covers the police, the government, any law enforcement group—'

'Yeah? And?'

'Then why are you growing them? What if someone notices?'

'Lily.' Big Tone lowered his voice, bent down and looked pityingly at me. 'This is *Hackney*. It's taken for granted we grow our own. Have you not noticed what is in everyone else's gardens? And in all the window boxes?'

I sucked on my teeth for a moment. 'Ah!' I rushed upstairs and hung out of Harry's bedroom window. It all came into focus, and now I saw marijuana being grown in any space available all along the row of terraces. There even seemed to be a small plant struggling for life in a Wellington boot.

Now Big Tone was a quiet, unassuming man who constantly thought about the state of the world and, terrified by his conclusions, turned to whatever could console him. There's a lot of stuff out there that can be used to numb the mind, and he seemingly had access to all of it.

This time, Alice, Harry and I were sitting on Harry's bed,

watching Netflix, though our focus was patchy as we were talking about Big Tone.

'I can't understand how someone so intelligent can be so frightened all the time,' said Alice.

Harry clambered off the bed to butter some more bread. We were now making toasted sandwiches in Harry's bedroom as the mess in the kitchen was crawling out of the door down the hallway.

'I think,' said Harry, 'his coping mechanism is to take a disproportionate amount of illegal substances, so reality takes a step away from him—'

'Dearest God!' I turned to Alice. 'I think by now reality is running so fast in the opposite direction, he'd be hard pushed to ever catch up!'

'Ha, ha, ha!' Alice laughed so much she nearly fell off the bed.

'Yeah, well,' said Harry, 'unfortunately, he doesn't take any one substance by itself, does he? He's on uppers, downers and inside-outers!'

'And let's not even mention the huge dope plants in the back garden...' I rolled my eyes at them.

'Ha!' said Alice. 'Lily, you are so innocent!'

'Isn't it illegal?'

'No worries. They're great, aren't they?' said Alice. 'They're pretty big now, and I sit in their shade and read. He told me his next idea is to paint lots of ping-pong balls red and gently hang them all over the bushes, so if any busybody was suspicious, they would assume they were tomato plants.'

I persisted. 'But it's all illegal! We can go to jail for drug offences, can't we?'

'Only if we're caught doing it.' Alice looked perplexed.

'Oh! That's okay, then.'

'Lily,' Harry held out his hands and shook his head 'come on. We're not exactly some Mexican cartel, now, are we?'

It was possibly at this point I realised I might, indeed, be a little bit innocent in the ways of the world.

Relationships are tricky. Both past and present, it appears.

Possibly spending time in that shared house with Harry and Alice was where my need to clean first started. There's nothing like the thought of getting worms to galvanise you into becoming OCD about cleaning! That was Alice's hypothesis, anyway.

As to the six-foot dope plants in the garden, I hoped we'd never get busted, and my parents find out their daughter lived in a drug den. We nearly did, when Jane moved out and Bernie moved in. So much for being careful who they chose to live with next.

Chapter Seven

GOODNIGHT, LADIES

IT FEELS EASIER to chat with Jack now, and the flow back and forth is fluid. We have a margarita to finish the meal. Time has crept away from us. The light outside leaches until the sky merges with the sea. The thinnest silver line, a thread, separates them now.

'I love winter afternoons,' I say.

'I thought you said your favourite season was spring?'

At least now I know he read my details.

'It is. Look at that view and those wonderful, washed-out colours.'

'Yes, it is gorgeous,' he says, though I notice he is not looking out the window but is staring straight at me. A tickle of appre-hension slides down my back. Is he expecting to come back to my place? *Am I expecting him to come back?* I'm not sure I want this, although part of me does. Oh, contradictions galore.

He continues, 'Shall we go for another drink? You can show me some of the sites a normal tourist doesn't get to see.' He reaches for my hand. 'Listen, don't worry. I mean just another drink, as I don't want this afternoon to end, then I'll be back on the train to London. I don't want to rush things with you.'

'Okay. It's just I'm very rusty at this. I've been out of the game for quite a while.' Six years, I want to shout. *Six bloody long years* full of creeps and weirdos!

'We all have baggage, Lily, but it's got to be water under the bridge, or we never move on.'

'Thanks, I needed to hear that.' I wave for the bill. 'This is on me, as you paid to get here. If that's all right?'

'Indeed, it is. I'm not some macho bloke who can't or won't let a woman pay. Everything's equal in my book.' He grins. 'And I appreciate it. The next drinks are on me, though, and no quibbling.'

Gathering our stuff, I glance out of the window. There's a figure who has ducked behind one of the old-quaint fishing huts, and for one second, I think it is Rose. I stumble, but he reaches out to hold me up.

'Oopsy,' I say. 'A bit too much wine. I should be careful what I have next.' That couldn't have been Rose, surely? Is she checking up on me? Making sure nothing untoward happens to me – as she so aptly put it, it's her fault I'm here in the first place. I need to ask her, although now isn't the time. I'm stepping with care behind Jack down the stairs (as I don't want to trip and send us both crashing down) and then the cold outside hits us at the exact time as the realisation. Oh, stupid me. I didn't tell either Rose or Alice where we were going, so it must have been a trick of the light.

I haul my scarf tighter around my neck. 'Brr. Blimey, that's cold!'

Jack puts his arm around me, and I don't resist. We huddle into each other and walk against the ever-increasing wind along the beachfront, turning to go through the underpass that takes us back to West Street.

'I was here a few weeks ago,' I say, 'as I had a launch for my latest fairy tale book. I get so nervous beforehand I have a blow across the beach to settle me. I even take off my shoes and walk barefoot to feel, I mean really feel, what I'm walking on.'

'To connect yourself?'

I like the way he understood without me having to explain more. 'Yes, that's it. Sometimes I feel a little disconnected, so it's a restorative of some sort.'

'I get that, although my go-to restorative might be a good quality whisky.'

'I get that, too. Except it would be red wine for me.'

Pulling him up a street, I lead him down the side roads, off the beaten track, down Zion Gardens and up around into Kew Street.

'It's nice getting off the main drag,' Jack says. 'What's the name of the place we're going to?'

'The Mulberry Tree. It's just up here in North Gardens.' And close to the station. I need my options open.

The pub comes into view, painted grey with black window frames and doors. A chalkboard is set outside, advertising tasty morsels to eat. Straggly winter plants survive in pots on either side of a bench by the inset board displaying the opening times. There are hints of blue and purple.

'Come and have a look at this.' I tug him by the arm to the other side of the street, where the façade is clearer to see. A graffiti image of a heavily tattooed Amy Winehouse picks up on the blues and purples, even though the main image is black and white.

'That's special.' Jack looks down. 'I couldn't believe it when she died, and you know what I felt more than anything? Anger.' He makes a sound that reminds me of Alice when she does her snorts. 'Anger that someone so talented and beautiful could die in that way. She was younger than you are now. Imagine that.

Such a waste. It hit me hard. I still listen to her albums, and it makes me sad.' He glances at me. There must be a look on my face because his changes in that second from deeply troubled to laughing. 'Sorry, and I know we said we wouldn't use that word. I didn't mean to bring you down.'

He takes my elbow, and we push in through the door. A semi-circular opening in a wall divides two large rooms to allow customers in both to access the bar. The colour scheme has followed us in; the walls are a smoky grey, and the beams and wooden details are black with tiny fairy lights strung along them. It has an olde-worlde look about it. A black-painted cast-iron Victorian fireplace is unlit, though it looks the part. Next to it are bookcases filled with books and games.

'I've been told,' I say, 'most of these are travel books from all over the world.' I can't get close enough to see the titles. I spot a group in the corner playing cards. It's good to see most punters are enjoying their drop of ale without needing to be fixated on their phones.

'God forbid,' I breathe. 'Unbelievable, there are people in here talking to each other!'

'I know. What is the world coming to?'

He heads towards the bar. 'Loads of great ales, although I was thinking of a whisky. Fancy one?'

'Okay. You choose as I don't know a good whisky from toilet cleaner.'

Jack raises his eyebrows. 'I've never tried toilet cleaner, so I wouldn't know either. You can trust my choice.' He orders two Jack Daniels. 'If you're not a whisky aficionado, then I think a JD is best. It's a bourbon. We can destroy its soul by adding coke if you don't like it.' I like his sense of humour, as it's nearly as asinine as my own!

Clutching our glasses, we find an empty table at one corner and squeeze past punters playing a board game.

It's a struggle to strip off coats and scarves in the confined space, and my make-up must be running by now. Hot, cold, hot, cold. But Jack is watching the other people in the bar and doesn't seem to notice. It's getting closer to *crunch* time. Do I invite him back to mine or usher him towards the London train with a demure kiss on the cheek? What is he expecting? I'm so rusty at this, I must creak.

I remember something I wanted to ask him.

'Jack? You said your greatest achievement was saving some-one's life. I mean, did you stop someone jumping off a bridge or —' I see the look on his face morph into a mask of rage and pain. I rear back. 'I'm so sorry, I thought—'

'*That was the worst fucking night of my life!*' He shakes his head as if to dislodge an image there. It may be a trick of the light, but his eyes are practically black.

'I'm sorry—'

'I found her in the bath. Lying there in bloodied water. I thought she was already dead.'

A terrible image of a pale girl immersed in red is in my head. 'Oh God, I—'

'I got her out and bound the wounds as best I could. I nearly lost her a couple of times that night in the hospital.'

I remain silent this time, unable to risk my voice while he is focused on another time and place.

He closes his eyes briefly and then looks at me. 'As I said, the worst day of my life.' He laughs but it is shaky. 'And also the best, if you see what I mean. She lived through that.'

'That's good to hear,' I venture, still wary of pushing him too far.

'Yes, it is.' He nods. 'She recovered well.' There's an odd glint in his eyes. Then he smiles and blows out of the side of his mouth, and there is Jack again. *My Jack.*

'Aaagh!' He rubs his hands through his hair. 'Sorry. You

caught me by surprise. It was such a big thing for me, and I try not to think about it. It's not your fault, Lily. I did tell you about it, and I should have expected you to ask at some point.'

'Listen, the main thing is she's all right now. And that's a massive win, isn't it?'

He closes his eyes for a second. 'It is.'

We both take a swig of our drinks to let a little time pass between us.

'Okay.' He points at me. 'My turn. I wondered why you're not writing your own kids' stories.'

At last, I'm on safer ground. 'That's because most people think writing a kids' story is easy when in fact, it's one of the hardest things you can do. Every word has to be considered, every sentiment, the cadence, the rhythm. Anyway, the writers who can do it are unbelievably good at it and hats off to them.'

'Do you think you need to be a mother or maybe a primary school teacher to do it?'

'That's a fair point, as an awful lot of the picture book writers are exactly that. Just being good at words isn't enough. You have to understand the whole package. You have to understand how kids tick.'

'Do you want kids?' He shakes his head slightly. 'Sorry, way too personal. Scrap that and forget I said it.'

I consider for a moment. 'No, it's all right. I'm still young, so I'm not going to rush into anything. But if I end up in a steady relationship with a guy who wants kids with me, then that will be a different matter.' Well, he did ask, didn't he? It's not as if I'm insinuating it will be with him. I have to crush the memories that are bubbling to the surface. I don't want or need to look at them right now. It's still too painful.

'Fair do's.'

We chat for a while until we have both got to a certain point when conversation Peters out. We are suddenly as bashful as teenagers.

He clears his throat. 'As I said, Lily. I'm not going to put you on the spot. The next train to Victoria leaves in about twenty minutes. I'll be on it.'

I nod, not wanting to risk my voice, as along with creaks, I might squeak.

Jack continues, 'I've had a great time, and I need to say I'd love to see you again, although I understand if you don't feel the same way.' He holds up his hand as I open my mouth. 'No, you don't need to say anything now. Think about it and get back to me if you want to meet again.' He swallows the remainder of his glass, so I feel obliged to neck the rest of mine, too, as it looks as though we are leaving. Right now.

'Are you okay getting home?' He's shrugging into his jacket.

'Yeah, it's not far from here, and I go up the back routes.'

'Well, be careful then.'

'Always.'

I follow him as he weaves past the crowded tables and out into the street. The air nips at me like a nasty little dog. I can feel my eyelashes freezing.

'Shall I—' Suddenly, he leans forward and kisses me gently on my cheek. I have a flash of memory. Of Harry kissing my cheek that first time in my bedsit.

'I'll get off now. Thanks for a great afternoon, Lily.'

'I had a great time too,' I say, and then I watch him stride away, hands in pockets and hunched into his jacket, towards the station road. He doesn't turn back.

It feels odd when I close my front door. There's been a subtle shift in my little world. I make a hot chocolate and hope the wine and whisky will ensure a good night's sleep, except I know

I will be thinking about that sweet kiss on my cheek and re-running everything we said and talked about as if it was a mini-series on TV.

There are messages on my phone from Alice and Rose asking the same thing. Did I have a good time, and what is Jack like?

I reply the same to them both. *He's everything he said he was and more. Goodnight, ladies.*

I love living alone, although that might be due to my experiences with other people's flatmates. I don't count Alice in all this, as she's more like my second sister, but living with her and Harry in their shared house has made me appreciate my own space. Another memory drifts into my mind, and I can't help laughing, although at the time I was terrified, truly believing I would spend years banged up in a filthy jail for drug possession.

'So,' I began. Alice and I sat on her bed with the door firmly shut.

'Yep,' agreed Alice.

'Maybe you all need to think through your interviewing techniques?' I still couldn't believe it.

'That might be an idea.' Alice grimaced. 'We should have a questionnaire at the least, as we seem to allow anyone off the street to come and live with us.'

We were talking about Bernie, who had moved into Scottish Jane's old room. He was a graduate student, like Big Tone, who worked in the local petrol station. And he loved to drink. Which might be an understatement. He loved to drink a lot.

'Admittedly,' said Alice, 'he was one of the few applicants

who showed he could pay the rent. That had to be something, didn't it?'

'Well, what's he really like? Because what I've seen so far is quite scary.'

'I know. He's kind of similar to a tiny tornado when he's drunk,' said Alice. 'He gets pretty aggressive, and you're right; Bernie can be scary.'

'Who on earth liked him enough to let him move in?' I didn't wish to criticise as it wasn't even my place. But...

'It was bizarre. He seemed to get on with Harry and Big Tone like a house of fire.'

'That's what I'm worried about.' I nodded downstairs. 'He tends to stick things on the hob and wander aimlessly off. I'm hoping he doesn't burn the house down.'

'Yeah, with us all in it. And,' Alice rolled her eyes, 'his mates? I mean, does he always have to invite the whole pub around after it closes? I came home from work yesterday to find at least half a dozen guys in the kitchen doing hot knives!' She glanced down. 'Actually, some of them are hot!'

'What are you like, Alice?'

She stuck her tongue out at me.

'Talking of work.' I was aware that Alice was giving me the eye. 'I'm just wondering, that's all.'

Alice had decided to work part-time and had nipped up the road and got herself a job waitressing in a local, less than salubrious bar. In my mind, the bar work was overtaking her coursework. She knew how I felt. That I believed she was potentially throwing her degree down the toilet.

'I know you get bored easily,' I started, 'but surely, as this is your final year, you should be working all out now? Concentrating on getting a good grade?'

Alice snorted and looked away from me. 'I'm happy pulling

pints, having a bit of banter with the customers and smelling of French fries.'

'What? Really?'

Alice stood up and headed for the door. 'Why not? Are you saying it's not a worthy job?'

'Of course not. It's just that you've spent nearly three years aiming to get that piece of paper, and it feels as if you're tossing it away.'

'You let me be the judge of that.'

I sighed. 'I'm not judging, and maybe next year, when I've graduated, I'll be asking for a job in your bar too.' That wasn't a joke. We all knew so many of us graduated, and so few entered the field of work we were trained for. Thinking back to what that girl Jenny had told me, that college was about having 'fun and learning about life', I wondered if she'd been right all along.

Alice tilted her head to stare at me. 'Not so sure about that, but fancy a coffee? I have a hidden stash of Columbian in the cupboard.'

'Sounds good to me.'

'I'm sure Bernie will be fine,' said Alice. Again, famous last words!

It was only a few days later, and it had to be me, didn't it? Harry and I had stayed at the house, as it was closer to where we were that night than my bedsit.

The knocking on the front door had the quality of sound that meant whoever was banging on it wasn't going anywhere any time soon. I'd waited to see if any other flatmates would get up to answer it, yet the house remained silent. As it was early Saturday morning, I knew everyone was tucked under their duvets with a pillow over their heads. As Harry was.

'Oh, God!' I hauled on my leggings and a sweater and

traipsed downstairs. The banging made the frosted glass window rattle. 'All right!' I called. 'I'm coming.'

As I yanked open the door, I wished I hadn't. A policeman in full uniform was standing on the doorstep.

'Hello?' I squeaked.

'Good morning, Miss.' He bent slightly at the waist to address me. 'Do you live here?'

'No.'

He frowned. 'Right, then. Can you at least tell me if Bernard Swales lives here?'

I thought for a moment. A copper on the doorstep didn't bode well, yet was that anything to do with me? Should I lie to save Bernie's scrawny little hide? 'Yes. He does.'

'May I come in, please, and could you direct me to his room?'

I let him slide past me and pointed up the stairs. 'Second door to the left.'

'Thank you, Miss.' His footsteps thumped up the stairs. As I shut the door, a vision of red ping-pong balls flashed into my mind. Didn't Bernie's room overlook the garden? *Oh, shite!*

Slinking up the stairs, I tapped on Big Tone's door. Nothing. I tapped again harder and heard a grunt from within.

'Tone!' Again, a sound that didn't appear to be happy. *'Tone!'*

The door flung open, and Big Tone glared down at me. A very grubby dressing gown was tied loosely around him. *'What?'*

'There's a copper in Bernie's room.' I whispered, trying to get across the enormity of this with my strategic waggling of eyebrows.

'Good. I hope he locks the stupid bugger up.' Tone was swinging the door shut, but I stuck my foot in the gap.

Lowering my voice further, 'His room overlooks the garden?' More eyebrow semaphore.

'And?' Tone was edging my foot out of the way.

'The plants? In the back garden?'

All movement stopped.

'*Shite!*' he said. 'Hang on.' Diving back into his room, he reappeared with a set of clippers and large gardening gloves. Handing me the clippers, he slipped on the gloves. I averted my gaze from his dressing gown, now slipping off his shoulders. I didn't wish to find out what he was, or more pertinently, wasn't wearing underneath it. We crept down the stairs, through the stinky kitchen and out into the patch of ground masquerading as a garden. Peering up, I could see the silhouette of the policeman, and I hoped he had his back to us.

'You clip them,' hissed Tone, 'and I'll drag them over there. If the pig up there can't see them, he won't come down, will he?'

'They're not even mine,' I whimpered. 'Why am I doing this?'

'You're an accessory to the crime.' He waved a gloved hand. 'Get on with it, then.'

Crawling over to the first plant, I clipped it at its base. As it fell, the ping-pong balls cascaded across the mud and tiles, plinking and plonking.

'Shhh!' Tone ran around and retrieved the balls, then grabbed the plant, which was at least six feet tall, and hauled it to the wall.

Un-hitching all the red balls, I placed them in a pile, and keeping a wary eye on the window above us, I clipped all the other plants down. At the end, when they were piled in a frothy green heap by the back door, I heaved a sigh of relief.

'Bit of a shame to cut them all at once,' said Tone, 'but I'll get it all dried.' He grinned at me. 'I'll give you some later, you know, to say thanks.'

'I don't smoke—'

'All the more for me, then.'

'I'm going back to bed.' When I was halfway up the stairs, Bernie's door opened, and the policeman ushered Bernie out.

'There's no need to be like that, sir.' He didn't look happy, and no wonder, as Bernie was calling him all manner of names, none of which were complimentary. I waited until they'd both passed me and then went to Harry's room.

'What's happening?' He'd managed to surface.

'Oh, nothing much. I think Bernie's been arrested, and Big Tone and I have just cut down all the dope plants in the garden.' I yawned and slid under the duvet.

It must have finally sunk in. 'Do what?' Harry sat upright in bed, and the duvet went with him. 'How did I sleep through that?'

'I don't know, but if you're awake now, mine's a tea.'

It transpired Bernie had smashed up his ex-girlfriend's new bloke's car. With a sledgehammer. His ex and her bloke had stood watching out of the living room window and, of course, filming it.

'That would do it,' said Harry. 'Don't you love technology?'

'And,' said Alice, 'I met her new fella the other day. She popped round to give Bernie some stuff he'd left at her flat, and he was with her—'

'I suppose for backup?' Harry raised an eyebrow.

'Yeah, I suppose so, but the thing was, he looked exactly the same as Bernie.' She nodded. 'And I mean exactly. Like a twin.'

'How weird is that?' said Harry.

'Not really,' I said. 'She obviously has a type that looks like Bernie, except she found one with a sunnier personality.'

At least Jack looks nothing like Harry... In fact, they are polar opposites. While it is true I haven't found a Harry look-a-like, am I now purposefully going for a man who could never remind me of him? Do I hate Harry that much? This is something I don't want to investigate, so maybe my subconscious mind is giving me a kick up the arse as it dredges up all these memories!

As to today, I wish I hadn't asked Jack about his greatest accomplishment, but I wasn't to know how he'd react. That was hard to listen to. As he said, he'd told me about it, and he should have expected me to ask at some point. Still, it was freaky. I don't know what I'd have done if I'd been in the same situation. Who was she? An ex-girlfriend? Was that why he was so upset? Could it be she tried to kill herself because of him? Maybe his anger hadn't been directed at me but at himself? Did he feel guilty...?

I have to stop myself. Making up stories to fit a narrative I know nothing about is not only stupid but potentially dangerous.

Chapter Eight

FRIDAY, 11 DECEMBER - PROBLEMS?

It's now Friday evening, and I'm meeting Jack tomorrow morning. He'll be going back sometime Sunday, depending on how it all goes, which means he'll be staying over at mine. Maybe this weekend, we'll do 'the dirty'. I certainly hope so. I have cleaned the flat, and there's not a surface that hasn't been scrubbed or polished.

Christmas is creeping closer and closer, with all the pressures that go with it. Should I go to my sister Sophie's and stay with her, her husband Bob, their little boy Mike and my dad? I'm not sure if my dad has a new girlfriend, and at this stage, I don't want to know. He deserves happiness, but there's a clod of emotion in my gut that mourns for Mum, and I wonder how he can let go of her so fast. Maybe as you get older, especially after what happened to Mum, you understand time is precious, and you may not have as much as you thought. Best not to squander it. I should heed my own advice then.

'So,' says Alice, sitting on my sofa beside me and drinking tea, as I want a clear head in the morning, 'do you think he might be Mr Right, then?'

'It's way too early for anything like that,' I say, but she raises an eyebrow at me, and I buckle. That's all it takes. God! I'm such a push-over. 'Okay, from everything I know about him, he's, well, I don't want to say perfect because that'd jinx it, but he's right up there.' I wonder in an idle part of me if I might spend Christmas with Jack. It's a naughty thought. He has no immediate family left to spend Christmas with... What a terrible thing to contemplate. Unless he hangs out with his cousins as Alice used to do with Harry. Sometimes cousins can be as close as siblings, but he hasn't mentioned any other near family. Although that means nothing, as I've only just met him. We don't reveal everything about our lives all at once. Most of us ease into full disclosure.

'I know you've been texting, but have you been '*sexting*'?' Alice sticks out her tongue lasciviously.

'Oy! Even if we have, which we haven't, that's none of your business. And I'm not a *teenager*.'

'Just getting a picture here.' As she reaches for another biscuit, I marvel how she can pack away so many calories and still remain that slim.

I need to get her off this subject. 'How's Matt?'

Her face falls, and I wonder if I've now steered us into rockier waters. There's been an underlying uneasiness when I've asked about him recently. I hope to God they are not breaking up.

'I haven't seen much of him in the past couple of weeks. We've got different shifts, except I'm beginning to wonder if it's more than that.'

'What do you mean?'

'I'm not sure if he's carrying on with another girl.' She purses her lips. 'Or even another boy.'

'No way, Alice.' I shake my head. 'He adores you. He wouldn't do anything like that?'

'Oh, really? We all know about the men who would never do anything like that, don't we, Lily?' She tilts her head to one side and stares at me. I know she's alluding to Harry, but I won't be goaded. Not tonight.

'I'm sure it's fine, and if you're worried, talk to him.'

'Hmm, he's not the most talkative of souls, is he?'

Monosyllabic is the word I link with Matt, but he sure is cute. 'Not particularly, but you can try.'

'Yeah, I suppose.' She shakes herself. 'Okay, moving on. Where are you off to tomorrow?'

'I was thinking of a walk along the Undercliff towards Rottingdean and then dinner at the Marina? Oh, I don't know. I'll play it by ear.'

'Or somewhere in Kemptown? It should be a place he wouldn't find by himself. You don't want to go down the route of all the tired tourist bars and restaurants along the main drag from the station. So many people from out of town think that's what Brighton is.'

'In some ways, I don't mind, as it keeps them out of our secret little places, and they can remain ours.'

'You're right. I think we have to be a bit possessive, or it'll all be swallowed up by rich Londoners popping down for the weekend.' Alice twitches. 'Jack's a Londoner, isn't he? Sorry, I didn't mean *him*.'

'I don't think he's a rich Londoner. Not exactly a Russian oligarch, is he?'

'No. I presume not. Anyway, where's Rose tonight? I'm sure as the instigator of all this, she'd want to be in the know?' She stops and looks at my face. 'What?'

I suck on my teeth, which I know is a bad habit that drives Alice bonkers. 'I just wanted *us* tonight. It's always been us... and now there's Rose, and somehow, we're all best mates and hanging out all the time, and it's fun and, and...' I pause for a moment. 'And sometimes I feel I don't know her at all, yet she's entrenched in our lives, in my life. Oh, God!' I put my face in my hands and then run my fingers through my hair. 'Does any of that make sense?'

Alice nods before reaching for another biscuit. 'Yeah. We've gone from nought to sixty in seconds. And now you don't know how to slow down.'

'That's it exactly. I mean, I know she was the one who picked Jack out of the jumble of possible dates, so am I meant to feel beholden to her? Do I have to tell her everything we're up to?'

Alice looks puzzled. 'No, although I'm sure she'd still like to know. She's lovely, Lily, and she'd be really happy if you include her. I don't see what the problem is.'

'You think I have a problem with her?'

'I'm not saying that, but you do seem to be a bit funny about her.' Alice takes her mug into the kitchen and swishes it out. There seems to be a lot of clattering and this usually means she's annoyed. 'Listen, I've got to go as I've also got an early shift tomorrow, and wouldn't it be amazing if I turned up for once without a hangover?'

'Yes, that would be amazing!'

Chapter Nine

SATURDAY, 12 DECEMBER - FRIENDS AND LOVERS?

ARRIVING a little late at the station, I see Jack lounging by the donated pop-up piano. It says 'Play Me' in Vaudeville gold lettering, and someone is sitting on the stool, tinkling the ivories, as they say, but whoever it is seems to be bashing that old piano to within an inch of its life. It's magnificent! Can Jack play a musical instrument? That's something I haven't asked him yet and it reinforces how much I don't know about him. I certainly can't, and judging by my and my sister's efforts as kids learning the violin, musicality does not run in my family.

Shifting position, he spots me and walks over. 'Thought for a moment you'd got cold feet.' I know it's meant as a joke, but it stings a bit.

'I didn't mean to be late.' I glance at my watch. I'm only ten minutes after our agreed meeting time. 'There's some sort of parade along the main street, and I got tangled up with everyone.'

Pulling me into a gentle hug, he leans and whispers in my ear. 'I was worried, and I know you're not late.' Pulling apart, he picks up a hold-all. 'What have you got planned for us?'

'I thought we'd take your stuff to mine, and I can show you my flat—'

'Ah! The inner sanctum, eh?'

'Something like that. Then, a walk along the Undercliff towards a little town called Rottingdean.'

'Now that conjures up some strange images in my head...'

'It was a place the more affluent visitor went to get away from dodgy old Brighton.'

'Dodgy old Brighton?'

'Yeah, Brighton was the town of dirty weekends away with your mistress.'

'You mean a bit scuzzy?'

'Hell, yeah. But Rottingdean had people like the painter Edward Burne-Jones and his nephew Rudyard Kipling. They lived there and made it way more up-market.' I grin. 'Oops! Done it again. Hereby endeth the tourist info for today.'

'No, I like it when you tell me stuff I don't know anything about. Please don't stop.'

'Okay, but let me know if I get boring, and I'll shut up.

'I don't think you can be boring if you tried.'

'Oh, trust me, I can. Right. I'm going to take you down the side roads, so we can get away from the tourists.'

'I like the sound of that.'

I lead him down Trafalgar Street under the arch. We keep walking until we turn left onto St. George's Place and pass St. Peter's Church, a powerful building with stained glass windows, spires and turrets and clean looking stonework.

'Wow!' says Jack, shading his eyes against the sun's glare. 'That's really gothic!'

'It is. Shame it's got scaffolding on it, but it's been freshly sand-blasted.' We scoot across a slice of green lawn and start to head up Lewes Road. The Level is to the left of us, enclosed by tall elms, now stark and leafless.

'What's that weird clacking sound?' Jack stops.

'That's an urban park called The Level. There's a skatepark in there. It's all been renovated and updated and is pretty gorgeous.'

'Come on. Let's have a look.'

The skatepark has kids flying on their boards up and down and over incredible ramps. They are all wearing some sort of uniform of baggy trousers, sweatshirts and back-to-front caps. The whole place is graffitied, but it's tasteful, not some of the deplorable scrawls I've seen on the sides of buildings here. That makes me mad, or maybe I'm getting old? I wouldn't mind if the 'artists' had put one iota of thought or talent into them.

'There's a new pavilion and café with a kiddie play park over there.' I wave indiscriminately. 'And some nice bits of grass to have picnics on in the summer. There's even a sensory garden—'

'A what?'

'It's a space where everyone can go and stimulate all their senses at once, but it's also somewhere that autistic people in the area like to go. It was designed with them in mind. A place to feel safe.'

'So, what does it involve?'

'Things to touch, plants to sniff, water to play with, sounds in the air. That kind of stuff.'

'Cool place. How far is the sea from here?'

'About a ten-minute walk over there.' This time I wave behind me.

'I'm usually good with directions.' He turns around a couple of times. 'Okay, now I've got it.'

Passing the turning to Elm Grove, we are silent at the crossing. I'm feeling a little fizzy inside at the thought of him in my home. I haven't had a man back to mine in ages. It's terrifying and electrifying at the same time. Traffic is all over the place, and it takes an age for the little green man to pop up and get us across.

'Here we are.' Clumping up the steps to the main door, we enter the communal hallway and squeeze past my bike. The pedals are at shoulder height as it is hung on the wall. They often catch the unwary.

'Bet that gets annoying on occasions?' Jack flicks a wheel, and it spins.

'I expect my neighbours find it annoying, but as it's mine, I can't complain.'

Jack reddens. 'Oh, shite! Sorry.'

'Ah, ah! No sorry's to be allowed. You know the rules.'

'I do. Come on, you know I'm itching to see your flat.'

As we enter, I sniff. I hope he can't smell the furniture polish or disinfectant. 'Hang your jacket here,' I show him the coat hook, 'and I'll make us a hot drink before we go out.'

Having hung his jacket and deposited his bag, he follows me into the living room.

'Why have you got a strange hole in your wall?'

'I have no idea, but I like it. You can peer out at your mates when they're not expecting it.'

'And make faces at them?'

'Yep.' I indicate the kitchen. 'Tea or coffee? I have black, green and herb teas or ground Columbian coffee.'

'Coffee, please.' He goes to the window, which by anyone's standards is big, and peers out. 'Great view of the Labour Club.'

I don't know if that is a derogatory statement or not.

'Watching the punters is entertaining.' I fill the percolator and pop it on the stove. 'Many a time, the old codgers have come out, and they're all singing or falling over and showing their knickers. Or there's a big fight in the street.' I sigh. 'Alice and I have always wanted to join, as it looks as if they have great fun. I don't think we're their demographic, though.'

'Who is Alice?'

'My best friend. We've been mates for years, go way back together.'

'Will I get to meet her?'

'At some point, but I want you to myself for a little bit before I have to share you with my friends.' I waggle my eyebrows at him, then turn back into the kitchen and fumble with the percolator.

'Nuff said.'

Filling mugs, I put sugar and milk on the table. 'Not sure how you like your coffee.'

Slopping in a good amount of milk, he ladles in two teaspoons of sugar. 'Sweet tooth.'

My work area is behind the sofa, so he spots it as he turns. He peers at the large wooden table, although I have tucked my latest illustrations into an A3 portfolio and tidied my equipment away. I'm not taking any risks, and there's nothing to see.

'Are you going to give me the grand tour?'

'This is the living room. This is where I work,' I smile at him, 'and that's the kitchen.' I walk down a narrow corridor. 'The bedroom is in here,' I open the door, and he squeezes through. 'It's not huge, but I don't need much space.'

Jack nods, 'Nice.' Again, he goes to the window and flicks the gauzy curtain back. 'Great view. Is this yours?' He points. 'This roof terrace?'

'Yeah. I had it decked a while back to spread the weight out, as I was worried I might crash through into the neighbour below.'

'Good idea.' He raises an eyebrow. 'It happens on roofs that aren't built to bear weight.'

Neither one of us looks at the bed. It is the elephant in the room.

'The bathroom is here.' I head out of the bedroom and he

trots after me. 'As you can see, it's big enough that you can clean your teeth, sit on the loo and still wash your feet in the bath, all at the same time. I think the word they used was "bijou".'

'I think it's cute... cuddly even. Is this the door to the roof terrace?' He tries the handle. It's locked.

'The key is on a piece of string nailed to the wall. I lose keys all the time, so I literally have to nail them somewhere.'

Outside, it's a bright winter morning, the sun low on the horizon, and rays of light hazy through the branches of the trees in the gardens opposite.

'What's below us?' Jack indicates his feet.

'We're on top of my neighbour in the ground floor flat. It's his living room, but even so, I try not to bang about up here.'

Jack is peering over the railing. 'He's got a great garden. So many nooks and crannies.'

'Last summer, he invited me down for a barbeque and it was easier to hop down the side here,' I show him, 'than to go via the front door. Mind you, it's a scramble getting back up.'

'Yeah. Looks it.'

Even though my terrace is barely big enough for the table, four chairs and a small terracotta chiminea, it has the illusion of space because it overlooks all the gardens along my row of terraces and the ones facing us. Potted plants are nestled against the wall to the side, which acts as a bulwark against any blustery winds. The plants have that dejected winter look about them. I have a bright orange throw draped over a trellis, although it's a bit faded. Maybe I should take it in now to protect it, but I adore a splash of cheerful colour when I have a mug of tea in the morning.

'This is lovely,' says Jack. 'An outside space in London pushes a property price sky-high. Even ones half this size.'

'Half this size? Wow, that'd make it really small. This is great. It's easy maintenance, which is what I wanted. I'm not an avid gardener, although I'd like to be one day. What about you, Jack?'

'If I had space, I'd plant some veg. Nothing fancy, you know – tomatoes and peppers, maybe some chillies.'

We sit at the table.

'You've got squirrels!' Jack points at some agile little devil doing hi-jinks on someone's shed roof. 'You're so lucky.'

'And foxes. They come with their cubs.' I drain the last of my coffee. 'And we also have gulls, and they never shut up. Quite often, right at the crack of dawn, when it's still dark, a couple of them sit and chat on the neighbour's roof up there.' I point to their spot. 'Back and forth. Squawk, squawk, squawk. Some people hate them, but I love them. They're crazy.'

'I'd rather them to our rats and grubby pigeons in London.'

'Right.' I look at my watch. 'We'd better be off if we want to get along the Undercliff. It's quite a walk.'

Having turned up Elm Grove and then switched right almost immediately up Islingword Road, the slight incline makes me unwrap my scarf and tuck my gloves in my pocket, although I know I'll need them for when we hit the beach. The wind can be harsh and unforgiving along the Undercliff Walk. We keep walking up until we come to the pathways that snake past the famous Brighton Pepper Pot.

'You know,' says Jack, staring at the building in front of us, 'this is one funky looking structure. Wow! Someone had some serious ideas of grandeur. Oh man, look at all those columns. I bet you're going to tell me some amazing snippet of information about it now, huh?'

I could tell him that no one is sure about its original function. There's some blather about it being a water tower or a vent for the sewers that run below it. I know that in the late eighteen hundreds, it was used to print and publish a local newspaper, the *Brighton Daily Mail*. I won't say this because I don't want him to think me a 'know-it-all', even if I am.

I shake my head. 'Nope. Not a clue apart from its name. The Pepper Pot, because with the cupola and that green metal urn on top, well, it speaks for itself.'

Jack laughs, and there's something familiar about it, except I can't put my finger on why.

'Come on,' I say and hurry down the road that leads to Queen's Park.

We scout around the edge and then head down to see what might be splashing around in the lake. It needs to be cleared, as the weeds have a stranglehold on most other plant life. The water reflects the steel blue of the sky.

'There are often terrapins in this lake, though I think the herons that sometimes end up here have gobbled them.'

'This is like something from one of your fairy tales. The herons are eating the terrapins? In England? The south of England at that? No way. This is so strange.'

'But nice?' I say.

'Yep. Strange but nice.'

The next road is long and downhill, and we chat until we reach Madeira Drive. The sea is dazzling in front of us. To our right, we can see Brighton Pier and the fairground rides going through their motions. A faint sound of shrieking drifts in the air. To our left, as we walk, are huge graffitied walls.

'Brighton does a lovely line in graffiti.' Jack peers at the artwork. 'If this was in London, it'd be painted over with rubbish fast.'

'It's controlled along here by the Council. The artists are allowed to put up their designs, and they're proud of their work. They put a lot of care and effort into each one. They're not those horrible tags that ruin everything.'

'Brighton has a lot going for it.' Shielding his eyes, he points. 'Is that the Marina coming up?'

'Yes, but we're going to skirt it. You see, this,' I pull him up a slope and shimmy around a barrier, 'is the Undercliff walk. We just have to get past the supermarket delivery areas.'

Jack must think my idea of a romantic walk is crap until we get to where the posh Marina houses back onto a waterway. They all have jetties and boats tied to them that must cost more than my flat and annual wage put together. And then some. As we walk, the scenery changes and becomes wilder. Tiny birds with sharp cries wheel overhead and appear to be nesting in small holes in the chalk cliff that towers above us. Out to sea, dark-hued cormorants perch on wooden stakes that barely crest the outgoing tide and look as if they are shadows of themselves. Jagged rocks are rising from the waves. Spume and sea mist hang in the air, and everything glistens. On some beaches, pools are already visible. Jack bounds down the slimy, mottled concrete steps so he can peer into one.

'There are those tiny shrimp things and a crab. My first pool in nearly twenty years, and I get one with shrimps and a crab. Perfect.'

'Not as perfect as the slab of chocolate cake waiting for us in the cafe up there.'

'Chocolate cake? Did you say chocolate cake?'

'Oh God, you're not diabetic, are you?'

'No way. It's simply that I love chocolate cake.' He frowns. 'Homemade or shop-bought?'

I gasp in mock horror. 'Homemade, of course! Look, there's the café. Come on, I'm freezing...' I was going to use Alice's colourful quote about 'nipples', but maybe I should be a bit more ladylike.

The waves here are washing up and down across the shingle on this patch of beach, sucking and sloshing, and the wind is getting to that biting stage. I tighten my scarf and stick my gloved hands in my pockets. The gulls are in force here and are warding the rails and tables. Tilting their heads, their beady yellow eyes watch us with intent.

'Beware of the gulls,' I say. 'They are cheeky buggers and will nick the food out of your mouth, given half a chance.'

'If they try to nick my cake, I will brain them with a pebble!' He looks over towards the café. 'That's sweet, that is.'

I've always loved the undulating edge of the café's roof and the ubiquitous red and white striped awning. The place was completely renovated a few years back, for which I'm eternally grateful, as along with the modern building (instead of the old shack you were frightened might fall down on you), they now have toilets. It's a long walk in the cold, topped with a drink, and I was perpetually worried I might not make it home in time.

A few hardy dog walkers are throwing stuff for their hounds on the beach, and we can hear the dogs yelp and bark their enthusiasm.

'I've always wanted a dog,' says Jack. 'Trouble is, it's not fair to have one in London unless you can give it the attention it needs, and I don't have time for the recommended amount of walks they advise.'

'What about a small breed? One you can put in your pocket and forget about?'

'I don't really like little dogs. They tend to yap and bite everyone viciously.' He stares at the dogs with their wagging tails. 'And they still need walks.'

'How about a cat?'

'Not really a cat person. And anyway, I live in a high rise flat, which again is not fair on an animal.' He turns to me. 'What about you?'

'Both, if I could. I don't lean either way.'

One mother with a stroller jogs at a decent rate along the

walkway past the tables and chairs set outside. Steps go down to
the pebbles or up the cliff behind us to reach the village of
Ovingdean.

Standing outside the kiosk, we peruse the cakes as we order
two mugs of coffee. None of your posh foreign muck here. It is
powdered Nescafé, and if you don't like that, you can lump it!
At least, that's what it says on the chalkboard behind the woman
serving. It is handed to us in giant workmen's mugs.

'Along with the chocolate cake,' I say, 'there's also a date and
walnut to die for.'

'We could share?' Jack blows on his hands.

'Then we'll do that.'

Sitting at a table, we munch our cake and gaze out at the sea.

'Sometimes,' I say, 'when I'm here, I'm hard-pressed to
believe a city is just over there. That's what I love about this
spot.'

'As I said, it certainly has a lot going for it. This is great.' He
pauses. 'I bet it's packed in the summer?'

'Only with locals. Everyone from the villages above piles
down with their lilos, barbecues, umbrellas and beach balls. It's
a happy place to be.'

'I hope I get to see it then.'

I nearly choke on my slab of cake. That must mean Jack is
thinking about *the future*. Something I can't allow myself to do,
all things considered.

'I know.' Jack swivels so he can see my face. 'I know I go on
about wanting to come back here, and maybe that worries you?'

'No. Of course not. It makes me... happy.' I smile at him.
'That you like it here.'

'It's not simply here, though, is it? It's you I'd be coming to
visit. The scenery is an added delight.'

I have to look down.

'Have I frightened you, Lily?'

'Not at all.' I can't quite look him in the eye, so I gaze at the waves crawling hungrily up and down the shingle. 'It's been a long time, Jack, since I felt able to... well, have faith in someone again. We've only just met, and I hope we're both having fun?' I turn to him. 'We are having fun, aren't we?'

'Yes. We are.' Then he says the worst possible thing he could say. 'You can trust me, Lily.'

'That's nice to know.'

I think for a moment. *Trust.* Such a small word for such a vast, messy, chaotic concept.

───────

Trust? Yeah, I remember what that was like. This next memory hurts. It has teeth and nails and it rips at me. It was the first time my trust was broken. And I've never forgotten it, that feeling of betrayal, of loss, as it has become an integral part of me now. It was a lesson that had to be learned.

I don't know whose idea it was to have a Masquerade Ball, probably Alice's, but it was jumped on like fleas on a dog. My twenty-first birthday was in February, and Alice's twenty-second was in April, so it was decided we'd have it mid-March. Seemed logical. A person has each 'birthday' only once in their lives. While that may be essentially true, the big ones, the eighteenth and twenty-first birthdays, are the ones we want to celebrate. They had to be memorable, and I wanted this one to fulfil all my dreams and wishes. It had to be a party to be remembered for the rest of my life. A masquerade... now didn't that sound wonderful?

Hunting through all the markets and second-hand stores around London, I found a nineteen twenties style gold lamé dress, which I teamed with strappy gold sandals. Somehow, I imagined myself as if I'd stepped out of the pages of *The Great Gatsby*. Alice looked amazing in some sort of belly dancer's outfit of reds and golds that shimmered and tinkled and left little to the imagination.

Sitting at a large table in Alice's room, we were getting the party organised and making our masks. Beads and paints and feathers were littered across the table, as it was the only one big enough for all three of us to work on and not to crack elbows and get in each other's way.

'We have to ensure everyone wears a mask,' said Alice, 'else it won't work.'

'We can't be that pedantic, can we?' I stopped painting and stared at her. 'Otherwise, we might have to turn our friends away if they haven't made an effort.'

Alice frowned. 'Then they should have. Why come to a Masquerade Ball and not be masqueraded?'

'We could have a spare set of simple masks to hand,' said Harry, 'then we won't have to turn anyone away.' Indicating the bottles on the table, he continued, 'We could paint them gold and put a bit of detail on. Just in case.'

I thought for a moment. 'Only for our friends, though. I mean, I know we said Big Tone and Bernie could bring friends, though we don't want Bernie to invite the whole pub. You know what he's like.'

'Yeah,' said Harry. 'We'll have to go over that again with him, as I don't think he was listening.'

'Does he ever?' Alice asked, then suddenly shouted, 'Ouch, ouch and *bloody ouch!*' Scraping off a blob of hot glue, she waved her finger at us. 'This is dangerous work.'

'Er,' I said, 'I don't mean to be presumptuous, but has anyone met any of Big Tone's friends?'

'I'm not worried about Tone,' said Harry. 'Anyone he invites to the party will be tucked with him in his room.'

'Mustn't forget the invitations!' I said. 'I can design the invites and—'

'And everything else.' Alice sighed. 'Not to be rude, but we know you are a control freak who believes the rest of us cannot possibly do anything right—'

'Too true and no offence taken.'

'You *have* to let us do something, Lily.'

'I do?'

'I can organise the drinks,' said Harry, 'and Alice the food—'

'No.' Alice waved an admonishing finger. 'I want to do drinks. Let me do the drinks. I'm good at drinks.'

'We know you are.' Harry made a face at Alice. 'Good at drinking them.'

'All right.' I held up my hand. 'Harry can do the nibbles then?'

Harry placed his hand over his heart. 'I'll make you proud, Lily. Now let's see. I'll make a list like Lily does. So, peanuts and, um, er...'

I knew they were kidding, but this was my *big* birthday, and I wanted it all to be perfect. Who wouldn't?

It all started out as it should.

'Wow!' said Harry, eyeing us. 'Don't you two scrub up nicely?'

'I should bloody well hope so,' huffed Alice. 'The amount of time and effort it took for us to get here.'

We were indeed backcombed, painted, moisturised, perfumed, shaved and polished.

Harry whistled. 'All I can say is, it was worth it.'

'You look pretty good yourself.' I hugged Harry. He was in a tight, black suit, long black boots and a white shirt with a large, winged collar. His curly hair was slicked back. His black mask was swirled with diamanté jewels that glittered in the light, and he appeared to be wearing Alice's blood-red lipstick and matching nail polish.

Tonight was going to be my first real ball. Now I knew how the young ladies who were *coming out* in a Jane Austen book felt. You could say you were an adult at eighteen, allowed to vote, smoke and drink, let alone have sex, but I believed I'd still been a kid at eighteen. Now I was officially an adult, and I felt it. There was a fizzing deep inside.

A music system was set up at the end of the living room, where a friend of Alice's, headphones askew, was banging out some great tunes, and people were dancing. A folding table under the main bay window was laden with bowls and plates of easy finger food-type snacks.

'I hope that's enough.' Harry looked worried. 'You know what our lot are like. They don't eat for weeks and then fill up anywhere there's free food.'

'Let them, then. They'll stop when there's no more to eat.' I patted my stomach, aware I couldn't eat anything, or I might bust the seams of my dress, which I think Alice had spray-painted onto me.

'And we didn't promise them a banquet, did we?' Alice raised an eyebrow. 'Please tell me we didn't?'

'Of course not.'

'The main thing is the booze,' said Harry.

'I think we're all right there, then,' I said. A black bin had been filled with ice cubes, and quantities of tins and beer bottles now nestled in the sludge. It squatted in the corner of the kitchen. Bottles of red, white and rosé were clustered on the main counter. Alice's family had chipped in with mine to supply the drinks.

Hand-made paper decorations were pinned to the walls in the living room, along with a large dangling 'Happy Birthday' sign. It glowed iridescently in the light.

Soon, pretty young lithe things in masks adorned with most of the beads from the bead shop and a few pilfered budgie feathers were cruising through into our house. We decided to leave the door ajar as the constant bell ringing drove us nuts. Harry kept watch for a while, heading off people passing in the street who stumbled through the door. Then he got bored and wandered off to raid the black bin. Initially, I was too nervous to drink much and worried that I would spend half of the night queuing for the loo.

The pile of masks on the stand by the front door dwindled, though most of our friends had made an effort. In fact, I was stunned by the ingenuity of some of our masked guests. Most had gone out of their way to dress up. The masks ranged from petite ones that barely covered the eyes to full facial ones adorned with ostrich feathers and strings of dangling beads. There were friends I recognised instantly, though many were so gilded and painted, I was hard-pressed to suss out who they were. It was great, as we didn't know who we were talking to most of the time. There was even a plague doctor guy who seemed to be wrapped around Alice.

'Harry? Who is that with Alice? I mean, that's one scary costume.' I stared in trepidation at the beaked mask and black ankle-length coat. He had the full kit of gloves, boots and a wide-brimmed hat. I had no idea what he looked like under all that. I hoped Alice did, as he had his hand on her bum and was twirling a cane in front of her. I think he was whispering to her down the long length of the beak. She laughed and snuggled closer to him. Way to go, Alice.

Harry swivelled and grinned. 'I think he's one of the guys she works with. Looks as if they're getting on okay.'

'And then some.' Catching her eye, I waved and grinned. She gave me a saucy wink. Tonight was to be the best ever.

Amy and Lauren arrived in masks and gowns to rival any Venetian ball. Those costumes must have cost a bomb. I felt as if I was the bride who'd been outdone by the groom's mother.

'Let's get this party started,' trilled Amy. 'Now *we're* here.'

Before I could respond in a notable fashion, Lauren handed me a poorly wrapped present.

'Happy birthday, Lily. Not good on the presentation, babe, but I hope you enjoy the sentiment.'

'Thanks.' My initial pique melted away as I ripped off the sparkly paper. It was a photo of Hugh Penfold, except it had been upgraded in Photoshop to include an array of added bits and bobs that made me laugh aloud.

'Brilliant. Thanks, Lauren.'

'Shh, you're not supposed to know who we are!'

'I'm going to put it safely upstairs. Help yourselves to drinks.'

They waved bags. 'We have our own. Where do we put them?'

'The kitchen is through there. We have a big black bin filled with ice cubes for beer. Wine is on the side.'

Someone had brought a bottle of syrupy red stuff no one recognised. It would, inevitably, be the last bottle to be drunk, along with the bottle of Limoncello that had sat sadly at the back of the cupboard since the year before.

Nipping upstairs, I unlocked Harry's door and placed the present on his bed, next to the gifts I'd been given so far.

The night progressed. I eventually had a few glasses of Cava. After all, it was my *big* birthday. That led onto at least a couple of tequila slammers with Alice and her new fella, who was introduced as Matt.

'Burble, burble, burble...' Matt said.

'Pardon?' Alice poked him. 'You need to take the beak off. We can't understand a word you're saying.'

Matt took off the hat and tipped the mask back. The long beak looked very odd, sticking up from the top of his head. He was adorable. Was he with Alice? Questions needed to be asked.

'I said, you have a Tequila topped up with Champagne, then you put your hand over it like this... and then bang it hard on the table and drink it in one go.' We watched as he slugged the drink back, and then we did the same. What a hit!

'Yum, yum,' I said and held out my glass for more. 'Happy birthday to us.' I clinked glasses with Alice. Then I even tried a bit of that red stuff but instantly regretted it.

I turned as there seemed to be an altercation behind me.

'Oy,' said Harry, 'who the hell are you? You can't just walk in off the street and start nicking our beer!'

'I'm a mate of, um, hang on a minute... he lives here...' The man clicked his fingers. 'Oh yeah. Billy.'

'Apart from the fact there's no Billy here, it's actually a private birthday party.'

'I'm okay with that. Happy birthday, mate.'

'Not mine. It's two girls.' Harry grimaced at the man. 'I bet you also don't know who they are?'

'Woah, no need to be aggressive. 'Course I know. They're Betty and Boo.' He laughed and looked unsteady. 'Don't be a knob, sonny, and let me get a beer.'

'I'm not the one being a knob! And don't ever call me *sonny*!' Harry squared up to the man in front of him, though I didn't like Harry's chances as the bloke was a lot taller and muscled. It made me feel quite nauseous to think there might be a punch-up in our kitchen.

Harry snarled, 'When you come to a party, you generally know the people, and you bring something with you. If not, then you're a gate crasher. So, if you don't mind, *piss off*!'

Bernie pushed in through the throng, now watching. 'You can't chuck out one of me mates.'

'He doesn't even know who you are!' Harry raised his hands. 'Ask him.'

'Stuart?' Bernie peered up at the man. 'Who am I again?'

'I shouldn't have to remind you,' said the man, sniggering. 'You should know who you are by now.'

Alice slithered in. 'He called you Billy. A close friend, is he?'

'*Billy?*' Bernie glared at the man. 'Fuck me, Stuart, I've been drinking with you for three years now, and you can't get my name right?' He nodded down the hall. 'Piss off and take the others with you.'

'Others?' I looked about me. 'Oh no. Did you invite the pub?'

'Bernie?' Harry shook his head. 'Remember we asked you specifically not to do that?'

'Oh yeah. Soz.'

'Listen,' said Alice. 'If anyone turns up with a bottle of something, they can stay, but they get shown the door if not. How does that sound?'

'Fine by me,' I said. 'Harry?'

'Okay.' He made sure the men left. I could hear a lot of grumbling receding down the hall. When he came back, he grabbed a bottle of Cava and waved it at us. 'Need a top-up? It's the last one.'

I held out my glass. It was amazing how small it was. One

minute it was full of lovely bubbly stuff, and the next, it was empty. How extraordinary.

'Having a good time?' Amy's mask barely covered any part of her face. No mistaking her. 'You look like you are.'

Not sure what she meant by that, I laughed and told her, 'Well, it is my birthday party, so I hope I am.'

'Am I right in thinking you, Alice and Harry live here?'

'No, just Harry and Alice. I have my own place.'

'Aaah!' she smiled. 'That's interesting to know.'

'Is it?' I couldn't for the life of me work out what was so interesting about that.

At some point in the evening, I felt a tug on my elbow. 'You and Alice,' said Matt, 'need to go into the living room.' He had the plague doctor's mask pulled up onto his forehead again.

'Why's that?'

'Just do it? Please?'

In the living room, I stood next to Alice. 'What's going on?'

'Buggered if I know.' Alice sounded a little drunk.

All of a sudden, the lights went out, and a shadowy figure carrying something on fire shambled in.

'Happy birthday, Alice and Lily,' chorused the group around us. 'Blow out the candles.'

The shambling figure was Harry, trying not to catch fire or drop the cake, adorned with far too many candles to be safe. Giggling and holding hands, Alice and I blew out all the candles.

'Make a wish,' shouted someone. I already knew what my wish would be, as I'd been thinking long and hard about it for the previous months. It's not good to squander a wish. You don't get them often, and I've never seen a real shooting star, so it had to be right.

My wish is to spend the rest of my life with Harry. I thought for a moment. *Do you mind if I add something? Could you make that happily with Harry? Better to be safe, not sorry.*

I don't know what Alice wished for, but I wonder if hers went all to shit as mine did. Almost immediately!

Handed a large knife, which probably wasn't a good idea as we were pretty drunk, Alice and I carved the cake into odd-sized and shaped lumps, and Lauren placed them on napkins and handed them out. Maybe having a large slab of creamy, choco-latey delight on top of those Tequilas also wasn't a good idea.

Dropping the remains of the cake on the table, I ran upstairs and was eternally grateful no one was in the bathroom as I threw up into the toilet bowl.

A light tap on the door startled me awake, and a voice slid through the keyhole. 'Lily? Are you okay?'

'Yeah, I don't think that cake did me any favours.' I threw up again. 'Sorry.'

'Right,' said Harry. 'I'll leave you in peace. I'll be downstairs when you're, er, feeling better.'

Hogging the bathroom for as long as I could, I had to emerge as the banging and swearing got too much for me to handle.

'It's my birthday, sorry,' I mumbled, but I did feel a little better. Possibly needed another drink. Passing Big Tone's door, I realised it was slightly ajar. Soft voices and giggling wafted out, along with the heady scent of weed. Stumbling downstairs and into the kitchen, I grabbed a tinny from the bottom of the slush in the bin and started to chat to anyone I could chat to. Masks were coming off, and sweaty faces appeared. There seemed to be a lot of the paper decorations that had been pinned to the walls now on the floor, stuck to the soles of shoes and being walked through the puddles of ice, beer and God knows what on the kitchen floor. I'd cleaned the kitchen a couple of days previously. Got down on my hands and knees to find the places that had never seen the light of day. Shouldn't have bothered.

Chapter Ten

TRUST. SUCH A LITTLE WORD.

DRIFTING FROM CONVERSATION TO CONVERSATION, I finally found myself dozing on the sofa. An arm was draped around my neck, but it suddenly tugged from me. Jolting awake, I turned and saw Harry next to me. He moved a can of Stella into that hand. His other arm was wrapped around someone else. Hang on... *what?* Leaning forward, it was as if a bolt of electricity had passed through me. Was this what it felt like to be tasered? The other person was *Amy*.

'Harry? What are you doing?' Strange things were fluttering in my chest.

His face was slack. 'I dunno. Wha' am I doin'?' He swivelled. 'Hello, Amy? Phoar, you look right lovely tonight.' His head lolled onto her shoulder, and I watched, as if it was in slow motion, as she turned to face him. Then he kissed her. *Right. In. Front. Of. Me.* My boyfriend kissed my so-called friend, right in front of me.

'Harry? *Harry!*' I tugged on his arm. 'What are you doing?'

Amy's face materialised in front of me. '*Oh!* Lily! Sorry,' though her face didn't show any guilt, quite the opposite. 'Bit drunk.' She kept her hand on his chest under his jacket.

'*Sod off, Amy.*' It's incredible how fast you can sober up when you need to!

It was like watching a pantomime. Amy's face morphed into mock remorse. 'Oh, dear! Will do.' She levered herself upright and tottered over in her four-inch stilettos to where Lauren was glaring at her. 'Hey, Lauren. Think we need to go.'

'No shit!' Lauren made a face at me and shook her head. 'Sorry, Lily. Hope you still had a great party.'

'Anyway,' said Amy, 'they've run out of anything good to drink.'

The look on my face must have spoken volumes as Lauren hurriedly tugged Amy out into the hall. I heard the front door slam.

A great party? Hope I still had a great party? *Like fuck I had!*

'What the hell is going on?' Alice plumped herself next to me on the sofa. Her plague doctor was swigging anything he could find out of discarded cans left about.

'Ask Harry.' I stood up. 'I'm going to bed.'

'Can I come to bed, too?' Harry waved at me.

'Not with me.'

'I don't understand,' said Alice. 'What did Harry do?'

'Snogged Amy while I was sat on the other side of him.'

'I didn't do anyfing wrong,' said Harry. 'Did I?'

Alice groaned and put her head in her hands. 'Oh, for God's sake, Harry. Not again. You utter knob!'

'*Fuck you, Alice.*' He climbed unsteadily to his feet. 'And you, Lily. I didn't do anyfing, and now I'm going out. Remember, it's *my* bed.'

It was as though a wave of cold air washed over me. Why would he go out? Was he going to follow *her*?

'Come on, Lily. You can sleep with me tonight.' Alice guided me by my elbow to her room. I followed her almost blindly.

'Hang on.' I held out my hand, now aware of how much I was shaking. 'What about Mr Plague?'

'Much as I adore him, by the time he's drinking other people's ash and fag butts from old beer cans, I've sort of gone off the boil.'

'Okay.' As I sat on the edge of her bed, she helped me out of my gold dress and strappy shoes. She then wrestled a T-shirt over my head.

'Why did Harry do that to me, Alice?' My breath was coming in stutters.

'Because he's a drunken bonehead, that's why.'

'But to do it right next to me. He chose a can of Stella and *bitchface* Amy over me.'

'As I said, a drunken idiot. I know he's my cousin and generally a nice guy, but men can be douchebags when they've drunk too much, and I don't think I've seen Harry this drunk before.'

'Should I go and talk to him?' I started to stand, but Alice pushed me back onto the bed.

'Absolutely not. You're both drunk, and you won't talk. You'll yell and say stuff you'll regret in the morning. Anyway, it's not up to you to go to him. He's in the wrong, and he should come grovelling on his knees to you.' She patted the mattress. 'Get into bed. I'm going to look for him. I'll be back in a bit. Don't worry. I'll sort him out.' Rummaging in her wardrobe, she emerged with a long coat. She grimaced. 'Probably not a good idea to go out in only a belly dancer's costume. Some people might get the wrong idea.'

I remembered something. 'You said, "not again". To Harry. What did you mean by that?'

'Oh, shite!' Alice had one arm in the coat. 'I didn't mean to say that—'

'Okay but what did you mean? Has Harry done this before? With someone else?'

'Listen, Lily. Harry's an all right bloke, except if he's mashed. It's not often but he can do stupid stuff when he's drunk, you know?'

'So, he has then.' I bit down hard on my lip.

'He had this girlfriend – well, I thought of her as more of a stalker. She had her claws in him since they were kids and wasn't about to let him go. I kinda showed him what she was really like, and he didn't take that well. He got seriously pissed, sent her a wanky 'Dear John' text and then that same night, she spotted him snogging her best mate down the pub...'

'That's awful.' I dragged Alice's duvet up about my ears. 'What an utter cockwomble!'

Alice hauled on the coat and buttoned it up. 'It's partly my fault. She was his first love and I ruined it. But she was a cow—'

'Yeah but,' I gulped in a breath, 'he didn't even give her a bit of time to get over him. Poor girl—'

'Don't feel sorry for her, Lily. She was bad news all round—'

'But still! The same night?'

'All I can say is he was young and really upset about what he found out about her. You know that saying, "the first cut is the deepest". And it sure was.'

'Ugh! My head hurts. I don't know what to think.'

'Listen, I'll go and find him and drag him back. You try and get some sleep. Okay?'

'Thanks, Alice.' As I lay there, a part of me wondered what would have happened if I hadn't been there, sitting next to him? Would it have gone further than a kiss? Did it that other time? Or, conversely, if I'd kissed some stray bloke next to him? What if I'd got so bladdered I didn't know what I was doing or didn't care? Would he have called me a 'slut' and broken up with me? Or would he have realised the terrible vagaries of alcohol? We'd have an adult discussion, then kiss and make up? Hmmm. Could I be that adult? Especially as this wasn't the first time. When a wave of nausea washed over me, I stumbled to the bathroom and threw up. Again. Maybe I wasn't as 'adult' as I thought I was.

I think Alice came in quite a while later, so late it was early morning, as a pre-dawn haze was filtering under her curtains.

'Did you find him?'

'Eventually.' She slid into bed. 'He was haranguing the homeless guys on the High Street and had a few altercations with some lamp posts. He's home now, and I really hope he wakes up with a banging head.'

'Not as much as I do.'

As Alice switched off the side-lamp, I crawled out of bed. 'I have to go and see him. I've got to sort this out.'

'No. You don't. Trust me, it's a very bad idea.'

'I feel like shit.'

'I know you do. I'm so sorry, Lily.'

'This was meant to be the best birthday ever. The one I'd remember for all my life. And now I will but for all the wrong reasons.' What had my wish been? *Stupid me!*

Alice crept out of the room at some ungodly hour, having only snatched a couple of hours sleep. I stretched across the whole bed and went back to sleep, though I knew I had to brave the kitchen soon, as I was starving. It was that point of either eat as much fat, sugar and carbohydrate as possible or be sick.

My ordinary clothes were still tucked in Harry's room, and I wondered if I could sneak in and grab them, then I thought better of it. No good would come from arguing on an empty stomach. At least I had supplies of make-up remover and eye drops in a bag in the bathroom. I wouldn't have to brave this new world with yesterday's smeared and tear-stained foundation still on. Slipping on the gold lamé dress, a baggy sweater and a pair of Alice's socks, I padded my way downstairs.

Although I had prayed for a full-fried breakfast to be waiting for me, all I could find was muesli and tepid milk, which only just stayed down. Looking about, I noticed something strange. All the glasses, bowls and plates from last night had been washed up and put away, the cans crushed and put in their recycling box, the bottles swished out and lined up along the work surface by the sink. And miracle upon miracle, the floor was no longer sticky. Where had this cleaning fairy materialised from, and why hadn't they ever been here before?

Clutching a mug of tea, I ventured into the living room. A prone body lay on the sofa with a towel draped over it. It was Bernie, who hadn't made it back to his own room. Another body was sprawled in one of the easy chairs, snoring lightly, so at least I knew he was still alive.

Alice was standing on a wooden chair, grunting and swearing as she tried to pull a pin from the wall. The 'Happy Birthday' sign was already rolled up on the floor, and the last decorations were in heaps next to it.

'I was coming in to help,' I said.

'Good,' said Alice. 'Pass me the screwdriver on the table there. I can't get this last pin out.'

As I handed it over, I said, 'Did I help?'

'You were marvellous.'

'Have you seen Harry this morning?'

'Not yet, and I don't particularly want to.'

'Should I—'

'Nope.' Alice clambered off the chair. Dark circles ringed her eyes. Not surprising after running around most of the night after us. 'We're going to pick up two coffees and some jammy doughnuts and go to Clissold Park.'

'You're inviting me to a cemetery? Wow, Alice. You know how to show a girl a good time.'

Clissold Park was our 'go-to' place when we were feeling down. Not because it was a cemetery but because it was one of the few places near us in London where, at the heart of it, you couldn't hear traffic, wailing sirens or voices. Only bird song. And there were squirrels. It was a wistful place, not creepy at all, as no one had been buried there for decades.

'It'll do us both good to have a breath of fresh air.'

I pointed at the gold lamé dress. 'I'm not dressed for the cemetery.'

'You can borrow some of my stuff.'

We always followed the same route, reading the inscriptions on the headstones, saddened by the endless lists of babies that barely made it past a year old, enjoying the noise of Hackney slipping from us until there was silence. Sitting with our backs against a large tomb, we drank our coffees and ate our doughnuts. I searched the trees for squirrels, but this time, none showed up. *Selfish little shits!*

'Am I making a mountain out of a molehill?'

'That depends on what you thought your relationship was about. If you thought you were his girlfriend and it was an exclusive relationship, then no.' Alice put her arm around my shoulders. I was shivering and trying not to cry. 'But if Harry told you that you were in an open relationship and you could do whatever with whoever, then yes.'

'I thought we were exclusive. But after what you told me last night, I don't know what to think.'

'I shouldn't have blurted that out to you. It wasn't fair. He'd hate me if he knew I'd told you.'

'It's okay. I won't dob you in it.'

'Thanks. But still, words will have to be spoken.'

By the time we got back, windblown and pink-cheeked, Harry was eating a Pot Noodle in the kitchen. He looked dreadful, for which I was eternally grateful. He didn't meet my eye, and the look Alice gave him could have curdled milk.

'I'm going upstairs to get my stuff,' I said. 'Then I'm off back to my place.'

There was still no response from Harry, and I could physically feel my heart breaking. Could hear it cracking. Why didn't he at least say 'sorry'? One tiny word that meant so much. *The bastard!*

Trust. The dictionary definition is: firm belief in the reliability, truth, or ability of someone or something. I trusted Harry implicitly. He let me down, and not just that one time. Now I don't know if I can trust Jack, but I hope I can and I'm willing to find out. How utterly sad something from your past can so easily affect your future. I mean *my future*. This is not an abstract concept. It is my life. Right now.

Thank God I have Alice. She is my rock in a swirling ocean of mile-high waves. I know I've clung to her in the days when I've felt as if I was drowning on dry land. When Psycho Jo attacked me, she was there. When my mum died, she was there. When I broke up with Harry, she was there. When I lost the baby, she was there.

I wonder if I have ever been there for her in the same way? I hope so.

Chapter Eleven

READY OR NOT?

THE WIND COMING across the channel is picking up, and I wonder if it might rain or even snow. It will be a harder trek back to my flat, as we are both tired and cold. We'll have to stop en route somewhere for something to eat. But, for now, we've had two delicious cakes and not-so-delicious mugs of coffee (that are definitely not Colombian), and we are ready to start moving.

'I think,' I say, stretching, 'if we stay longer, we will be found frozen to death in our bucket seats.'

'Where are you taking me now?' Jack didn't bring gloves and is blowing on his hands. I give him one of mine.

'Are you sure?'

'It might help. Now. We could go for dinner in one of the restaurants in the Marina?' I wind my scarf tighter around my neck. 'Or a beachfront cafe? Or local in Kemptown?'

Jack and I walk back along the Undercliff, arms linked, one bare hand in a pocket. The birds are still screeching above us and whirling into the honeycomb rock cliff to nest.

'I have loads of pubs, bars and restaurants near me in

London. I don't have a beach and a sea, even if it is only a channel.'

'Beachfront it is. Then I vote we go to a place called the WalkAbout Café. It's halfway between here and home.'

It's late afternoon by the time we stand staring at the sand-filled volleyball court. There are a few people, fit-looking, stripped off, bopping a ball back and forth and grunting. The pier can be spotted in the distance, and again, the screams are pretty audible from people on the rides. If it's so frightening, why do we do stuff like that? And we all do, don't we? We love to be scared shitless. Is it because the fear is controlled? Because it has a time limit? A simulation of a near-death experience is just that. It's not real.

The tables and chairs are arrayed on weathered decking for the best view over the sea, which is changing colour by the minute, although it's far too chilly to sit out. Inside the main building, it resembles the underside of a large wooden hull, with curved booths reminiscent of an American diner and a sleek bowed wood ceiling. There is a vast picture window, so you can see what's going on outside from the comfort of being inside. It's all painted white, with black chalkboards at intervals with their 'Specials' and mainstays. It appears they are proud of serving organic food, local meats and craft beers. The stools are chunky blocks of wood with padded covers.

I scan the menu. 'Do you want a snack or something substantial?'

'Hm, I'll go for the homemade soup of the day and the sour-dough baguette.'

'I'll go for that too. Do you fancy sharing a mini mezze?'

'Great.'

We order our food and two mixed-fruit smoothies and slip into one of the booths.

'Ugh,' I say as I unwind my scarf. 'I think I'm now at the

stage where I can start to feel my nose. It must be as red as Rudolph's!'

'It may be a bit pink,' says Jack, 'but it's still adorable.'

I smile. 'As long as I don't have frostbite yet.'

'Done all your Christmas shopping yet?' His eyes twinkle.

'Prezzies, yes. I did all my family last week. Food, not yet. I'll wait until Tuesday morning to do a Crimbo jaunt to Sainsbury's. I've discovered through trial and error that Tuesday mornings are a weird dead time with very few customers. Knowing my luck, it'll be rammed to the gunnels when I go.'

'Sod's Law. And, rule number one is, never tell anyone, or it will not go to plan.'

I roll my eyes. 'Yep, doubly damned. I don't have a car, so I'll walk there and get a taxi back.'

'You don't have a car?'

'I work from home, and the parking in Brighton is extortionate. I bike to local places and it's much easier to catch a bus or train for anything further afield. I've found it's way less hassle.'

'Ah, yes. I saw your dangerously situated bike. But you can drive?'

'Yeah, my dad made sure of that before I left home. He said it was one of the most important skills I could have. That independence was priceless.'

'Wise man, your dad.'

'He is.'

When the food arrives, the soup is delicious, and the bread, well, the bread reminds me of Harry. *Damn!*

I scrape the last bit of soup out. 'So, where do you live in London?'

'Hackney.' Mopping the soup bowl with his bread, he doesn't look up.

'I used to live in Hackney. Small world,' I say.

'Which part?'

'Near Ridley Road market. Do you know it?'

'Yeah, I live up near Dalston. I get my fruit and veg there all the time. Small world indeed. When did you move down here then?'

'About six years ago, give or take.'

'Work-related?'

'Not really, as my main publisher is based in London. It was more personal.'

'Relationship?'

'Yep.' I nod, not wishing to pursue this further. 'Isn't it always?'

'Usually.' He leans back and stretches. 'Do you mind me asking if it was amicable? You don't have to answer if you don't want to.'

'Amicable?' I laugh, although I know it is not a happy sound. 'Not really, no. I caught him shagging someone else when he thought I was out.'

'Oh, nice!' Jack sucks on his teeth. 'I can understand if that leaves you with *trust* issues, Lily.'

'It was a long time ago. I'm getting on an even keel about it all.' Oh, God! Trust? Yeah, I have trust issues.

'Let me know if you are feeling insecure about anything. I don't want us to get off on the wrong footing in any way. I'll be there for you, no matter what.'

'I appreciate that, Jack.' I reach out to touch his hand. 'I really do.' I don't wish to put it to the test.

'Did you move down alone or with mates? I mean, it must have been hard after that happened to you?'

'I came down with my friend Alice, as she wanted a change at the same time. We got a flat together, and then, later, I decided I should try for my own place. Simply to get on the property ladder.'

'What happened to Alice? Is she here in Brighton? I know you still see her, as you spoke about her earlier.'

'She's in our old flat, but her boyfriend moved in when I left.'

'So, it all turned out for the best?'

'Looks like it. At least, I hope so.' Although now I can't say for sure. If she breaks up with Matt, then she'll have to go through all the references and checking to make sure her next flatmate isn't a mad Scottish Jane, a drug-fuelled Tone or a drunken Bernie and all the others waiting out there, ready to cause havoc in our home lives.

I don't want to think about Harry, but he's in my mind as if he is an omen of what might come. But that won't happen to me again. Hit twice by lightning? No. I must trust Jack. I cannot let the past affect my future. My 'now'.

Three days later. That's when I finally got a message asking if Harry could come over to my bedsit to talk it all through. Three bloody miserable days and godawful nights. My bedsit was scrubbed and polished. I mean, what else could I do except mope about, eat utter crap and clean like a devil? Alice had popped by with supplies of chocolate and a welcome shoulder, though I knew she didn't want to be caught in the middle between us.

That day, Harry came in and stood in the centre of the room, looking about him as though he'd never seen the place before. He didn't take off his jacket. I could only imagine what that meant.

'Do you want a tea?' I was desperately holding my shit

together, although I wanted to either brain him with a frying pan or hug him and never let go.

'Thanks, yes... a tea.' He sat tentatively on the edge of the bed. 'Lily?'

'Yes, Harry?' I ensured I had my back to him as I put teabags in our mugs.

His voice shook. 'It was just a kiss, or so Alice told me. I can't take it back, though I need to let you know it wouldn't have gone further. I am so sorry. I have no defence, except I was unbelievably drunk, but as Alice told me, that's not an excuse either.' He sniffed and I wondered if he was crying.

'No. It isn't,' I said quietly. I'd gone over this in my head, around and around. Should I mention that I knew about that other kiss? Okay, you could say that it was after they'd broken up, but she'd barely received that awful text before he was off with his tongue down someone else's throat. Alice had said they were kids and there were mitigating circumstances, in the fact she was a cow. Did that make it more acceptable? Anyway, if I said something, he'd know that Alice had let it all slip and I didn't want to cause a family rift. Wow! My head still hurt.

'I barely remember anything after talking to you when you were... in the bathroom.'

'Throwing up.'

'Yes. I didn't mean to do anything like that. It has no bearing on what we have—'

'What do we have, Harry?' I had to turn to look at him. I had to see his eyes. They were wet. *What, exactly, do we have?*

'We have everything.' I heard him swallow. 'At least we did. Before I fucked it all up.' Wiping his face with his sleeve, he gazed up at me. 'Can you forgive me, Lily?'

'Yes, I can forgive you, you stupid twat! I love you, Harry.' There. I'd said it and said it out loud.

Harry took a deep breath, then half grinned. 'I love you too, Lily.'

'Harry?' I still had to say it. 'If you ever do anything like this again, that will be it. You understand me?'

'I promise I will never, ever do this again.'

Oh, promises, promises. I suppose Harry kind of kept his word because what he did was much, much worse.

I feel as though my worlds, past and present, are connecting somehow. Is all this coming up because I didn't give myself time to grieve over Harry? Was I so angry with him, *with them,* I bottled it all up and suppressed it in the far reaches of my mind? Stuck all that emotion in a box and put chains around it. Had it fermented so much the *bloody* lid had finally blown off?

Chapter Twelve

HARRY BE DAMNED!

JACK and I both realise at the same time we need to get home. We chit-chatted through lunch and gazed out of the window as the winter evening rolled in across the beach, obscuring the sea and the courtyard outside. The volleyball players have long since donned sweaters and jackets and packed up, and no one is braving the outdoor tables.

Paying up, we stomp out to keep warm along Madeira Drive to the Old Steine. It's freezing now, and our breath puffs out as wispy plumes in the air. Up, up, up along Grand Parade and Richmond Place to where we walked past The Level this morning. It feels an age ago.

Ripping off our jackets before we even make it through the front door, we are like animals, hands pawing, tugging at clothes, belts, buckles, buttons and hooks. Our mouths are joined. Then our bodies. There are inevitably awkward moments, elbows that knock, bits of body in the way, a movement that is not so graceful, but it doesn't matter. Familiarity comes with time, and we haven't had that luxury yet. Depleted and satiated, we lie back, pulling the covers over our nakedness, suddenly self-conscious.

At least the central heating came on earlier this afternoon, or it would be glacial in here.

Moonlight pours in through the window and lights us in silver. Hugging the duvet to cover my breasts, I focus. There's a big scar across his left shoulder. I touch it, and he jumps.

'Sorry—'

'No worries.' He pulls the duvet up. 'It's what I call my old war wound. I cut some nerves a few years back, so it's strangely ticklish.'

'How did it happen?'

'Bicycle accident. It was long ago, and I don't like talking about it much. My fault, you know?'

I think back to what he told me. 'You said your body was an ultra-rapid something or other?'

'Metaboliser. Yeah.'

'Then that must have hurt?'

'It hurt like hell. Still does.'

'Yeah, I understand. Okay, changing the subject then, do you fancy something to eat and maybe a glass of wine?' I sit up.

'Always.' Jack has his face turned from me as he pulls on his pants and trousers. 'Got any cheese? I am a bit peckish for some reason.' He laughs again, and I wince. Who has a similar laugh? I wish I could place it.

'I'll get a plate of food sorted while I open a bottle.' I also shrug back into my clothes. Are there protocols nowadays about nudity?

'Great,' Jack says, and now he's pulling his top on. I would've liked to see him properly, but maybe that's something for tomorrow.

In the kitchen, the cork comes out with a satisfying pop, and I rummage in the fridge for the variety of cheeses and hams I have bought for this evening. The posh crackers are in the cupboard, so I take them out, though I'm unsure if he wants any salad. I pop my head out of the kitchen, but he's in the bathroom. I decide *I* want some salad, so I plate up lettuce, cherry tomatoes and cucumbers, and I've got bottles of pickles, relish and mayonnaise. That should be more than enough to start with. It's all on the table when he comes in.

'Brilliant, I'm starving.' He lays into the food as if he hasn't eaten in a week. The bottle is empty in less than half an hour, so we run, giggling like children, back into the bedroom and strip off our clothes again. This time it is slower, and we don't clack our teeth and dig into our ribs quite so much. I could get to like this. Yes, I could, and Harry *be damned*.

Chapter Thirteen

I WAKE to the smell of percolating coffee. I yawn and stretch. This is the first time in over six years someone else has made me coffee in the morning. No one has ever got this far. I must remember to thank Rose for her choice.

Jack is fully dressed when he leans around the bedroom door. 'I fancy a croissant with the coffee. Do you mind if I nip out and get a couple from that French baker's I spotted across the street?'

'I can go if you want. I should have got something in. I didn't think.' I'm levering myself out of bed.

'That's fine. I'd prefer them fresh, and I'm already dressed, and it'll only take a moment. Can I borrow your keys?'

'Yep, hung up on the wall by the door.'

He turns to leave then darts back to kiss me quickly on the lips. 'I'll only be a mo. Why not have a shower? I can reheat the coffee if it gets a bit cold.'

'Okay.' He darts out again, and I hear the click of the door. Ambling into the bathroom, I shower and wash my hair while listening for his return. I dress in fresh clothes and towel-dry my hair. The coffee will definitely have to be heated up. Has he got stuck in the usual Sunday queue?

Flicking the curtain, I'm relieved to see him coming out of the baker's. He looks up at my window, and I wave at him. He grins up at me.

I'm already decanting the coffee into mugs to pop in the microwave when he comes in.

'Seems there's a lot of people who want croissants down this street,' he calls over to me as he shrugs out of his jacket. 'The baker's was packed! Great range of stuff. Very arty-farty.'

'Well, it is a French patisserie, so everything will be exquisite, tiny and very expensive.'

'That's why I had to get two croissants each. I hope you have butter.'

'In the fridge, and there's also *Bonne Maman* strawberry jam.'

'Couldn't be better than that.' He nods down the hallway. 'I know it's bloody cold, but could we have breakfast on the terrace? I love being outdoors, and I rarely get the chance when I'm home in London.'

'It's what I normally do, come rain, shine, snow, even hail.' I smile. 'I put the summer brolly up until it's either sodden or blown away.'

Hauling on our outdoor gear, we bustle out onto the tiny roof terrace and sit at the table, the steam from the coffee curling seductively into the air. The croissants are flaky and soft in the centre.

'It's beautiful here, Lily. You are lucky to have this,' he sweeps his hand up and down the neighbour's gardens, 'right on your doorstep. It's practically like living in a large village, not a city.'

'I do love it here.'

'What are the chances of seeing any foxes?'

Shrugging, I hold out my hands. 'A watched-for fox will never be seen. You might be lucky, although I rarely spot them at this time of the morning.'

'Then I need to be here at the time when I might see one.' Jack leans back in the chair, stares across the many gardens and sighs. 'Yeah, I do like this.'

When we have washed up and put the mugs and plates away, Jack nods at my worktable.

'Can you show me some of your work?'

'Yeah, sure.' I have a plan chest that butts up against my desk. My latest work is in a portfolio in the top drawer. I pull it out and lay the work out. 'The author is Romanian. The story is quite off-the-wall, so my problem is how to convey his ideas but not scare the prospective buyers, which are the parents.' I make a face. 'And that also includes the publishers. As I said, they don't want it too scary.'

'They're bloody excellent.' Jack nods. 'I wish I had a talent like that.'

'As an engineer, your work is essential. That's a major talent in its own right.'

'I suppose you could say that.'

'So, what are you working on now?'

His eyes narrow. 'Oh, a bit of this and a bit of that. It's pretty boring, and I don't want to bring my work into this.' He indicates me and then himself. Which is strange, as he's just brought my work into it.

'Maybe I won't find it boring?'

'Trust me, you would.'

'I hope it's not because I'm a... woman, is it?' I laugh. 'We can handle physics and maths as well as the guys, you know.'

There's a strange expression on his face. 'That was meant as a joke?'

'Yeah, yeah, okay.' Blowing out the side of his mouth, he says, 'It's nothing to do with your imagined competence and understanding. It's more I'm bored to tears by my work and want to get away from it at the weekend.'

'Okay,' I nod. 'I understand. But,' I raise a finger, 'I want you to know I am interested in what you do.'

'Thanks. And I appreciate it.' Glancing down at his watch, he says, 'Listen, Lily. I should really get off now. I know I didn't want to talk about work, but there are some things I need to get done before Monday. It'll take me a while to get home, so I need to be heading out.'

'*Oh!*' I must have sounded shocked because he tugs me into a tight bear hug and kisses the top of my head.

'You smell lovely,' he murmurs. 'I'm not leaving because I want to. I'm going because I need to. I'd like to come down again, Lily. Are you all right with that?'

'Yes, of course, I am.' I look down at my socks. They have stars on them. 'I just didn't want it to end so quickly. I suppose I hoped you'd be able to stay a little longer.'

'I will next time, I promise.' He pulls my head up and kisses me lingeringly on the lips. Even though the central heating is chuffing out warmth, it feels chilly when I hear the front door close and his footsteps clattering down the communal staircase. I stop myself from rushing to the window to watch him walk away. It's not even midday yet.

What do I do now? Facebook Alice and Rose and admit he legged it after breakfast? Albeit quite late in the morning? That sounds suspiciously as if it's a one-night stand. At least he bought me breakfast. He could have snuck out at first light. A quick *shag*! Was that all I was to him? I realise I'm not friends with Rose on Facebook. I need to find her and send a request.

A text pings through. *I had a great time with you, Lily. So sorry (!) I had to rush off. I promise I'll make it up to you in ways that will make your eyes sparkle. (!!!) Let's plan for next week. I make it the 19th. I don't know what you intend to do for Christmas but are you around then?*

I write back that although I'm not sure what I'm doing for Christmas, I will still be here for that Saturday. I tell him I have a meeting scheduled for the following Monday at my publishers. I need to hand over my work for this next book.

Looking forward to it. And he finishes with lots of kisses.

———

It doesn't take a lot. I'm fazed by Jack leaving so soon, and my mind automatically slips back to Harry.

After a rocky start following the 'Amy' incident, Harry and I seemed to find our rhythm again. I suppose he could feel a hesitancy on my part. I still didn't know the answer to 'what if I'd not been there?' True, I loved him, but did I trust him? I had to, didn't I? Else why be together? There were moments I found it hard, until I focused on that day in my bedsit. I remembered the look on his face.

As to Amy, I avoided her as best I could at school and was polite if I had to cross paths with her, even though in my heart of hearts, I longed to lump her one! She simpered at first, tried to goad me after that and then finally ignored me. I often wondered if she'd hoped to break us up that night. Maybe the 'interesting' thing was when I'd told her I didn't live in the house. Had she intended to sneak upstairs with Harry and expect I'd not be bothered by a locked door? That I'd just go home to my place? Without my boyfriend? The thing was, had we both given out mixed messages? I didn't know until Alice pointed out that Amy had a track record of smashing relationships and then walking away.

Alice grimaced. 'We should call her motorway pile-up Amy.'

'I suppose I got off lucky then?' I shrugged. 'Mind you, I wouldn't be particularly sad if she got hit by a runaway truck.'

'*Miaow!*' laughed Alice. 'Hark at you, Miss Blasé!'

This experience had shown me that I had to question my reality from time to time. Which made me feel old.

The days sped into months, and time flew past us. I know we had enjoyed being the usual student stereotypes, yet now, as we hit our final year, reality had come sharply into focus. What was the point of doing a three-year degree show if you didn't bother working on getting the best grade you could? We both upped our game, and maybe there was even a little gentle competition between us.

Alice had graduated the year before with a respectable degree in Graphic Design, but instead of sending her CV to potential design studios, she remained working in her bar.

'Why?' I asked. 'I don't understand. You worked so hard for your certificate.'

'Those three years gave me more than just a piece of paper, Lily. I might want to use it in the future, but I like working in a bar. It suits me, and I get great tips 'cos I'm cute. I don't have any deadlines hanging over me. I leave work at work. Oh, and the guys are hot, too.' She grinned. 'Come on, Miss Lily the Pink. You can't knock it.'

Harry and I were spending quite a bit of time at my bedsit, as the need for privacy outweighed the use of the amenities at the shared house. Harry ostensibly said it was because flatmates tended to either walk in on us or bang on the door until we answered, just to ask a dumb question, like did we have any Branston Pickle in our cupboard? Although I began to believe he knew the flatmates freaked me out and was trying to make amends for his 'indiscretion'.

Then Harry caught me by surprise. The last days of May had raced past, and our degree show was in less than a week. We were both stressed, city hot, and walking home from the launderette, clutching two big bags of freshly laundered clothes and sheets. I was alternately moaning about wanting a washing machine and wanting to kill his flatmates. This was slowly becoming my perennial cry. Part of me wondered what would happen once we'd completed our course. We'd been together for nearly two years as students. Was it about to change as we entered the world of jobs and wages? And what would happen if one of us got work and the other didn't?

'Listen, Lily,' he said. 'It's not rocket science. If we rent a place together, it'd be much cheaper, and we would make sure there's a washing machine and, God forbid, an accessible toilet and bathroom that doesn't have a bath with other people's accumulated grime around it. And, there would be way less to and fro.' He stared expectantly at me. 'What do you think?'

I wasn't sure if I'd heard him correctly. 'Are you saying you want us to move in together?'

'That's what I thought I'd said.'

'And we never have to see your flatmates again? I mean, except Alice, of course.'

'Of course.'

I stopped walking, and he bumped into me. This was a big deal. The adjustment from hanging out at each other's places to living together. Was it only due to the savings, or did it mean something more? I had to be cool about it all. 'Okay, but where? And when?'

'I've been scouting places out, and Stoke Newington is a good place to start. We already know the whole area. As it hasn't got a handy tube station nearby, it's cheaper, and it's fairly easy to navigate to most parts of town on bikes—'

'Bikes? I haven't ridden a bike since I was about ten!'

'You'll pick it up again. It's as easy as riding a bi...' He smirked. 'Sorry, fell into that one.'

'Really, Harry?'

'It has to be after our show. So, what do you say?'

'Yes?'

Looking back, and I am doing a lot of that, I realise what a wonderful life Harry and I had together. So why did it end again? Oh yes. *Because he cheated on me when I was at the lowest point in my life.* For one golden moment in time, I was completely happy. I can nearly taste it on my tongue again, but I'm fearful it will turn to ash as it did last time.

I don't intend to bring up more unpleasant memories, yet if they come freely, I won't stop them. This might be the answer. If I block them, I could miss whatever it is holding me back, but if they come to me unhindered, I have an opportunity to sort out part of my life I've shored over without resolving.

Well, that's the idea, anyway.

I wish I could compartmentalise my thoughts. Keep the ones about Harry segregated from Jack. I don't want them to become meshed in case I project perceptions about Harry onto Jack and then mess it all up.

Chapter Fourteen

CHRISTMAS FOOD SHOPPING can be either fun or a downright nuisance, and I have a bit of both this morning. I know my Christmas shopping list is in a back pocket of my jeans, but do I bother to get it out? Do I heck! I simply barge my wobbly wheeled trolley down every aisle, the same as everyone else is doing, and plop anything that takes my fancy into it. There seems to be too much of one thing or not half enough of another. Do I get stuff for two? I mean Christmassy stuff. I know Jack will be here on Saturday and I have my supplies sorted for the weekend, although I wonder if I'll see him after that. Christmas Eve will be on the Thursday after this coming weekend. Plenty of time to get back down here. Will we spend Christmas together, or is it far too soon? We may have only been seeing each other for a couple of weeks, although it has been pretty whirlwind. That in itself is scary. Do I have a commitment phobia? No. I have bad memories that make me doubt stuff. Anyone who'd gone through what I did would be reticent about a new relationship, but that doesn't mean I'm not going to give it my all. If I feel Jack is into me, then the feeling is reciprocated.

After calling a taxi, I wait out at the front of the supermarket for over ten minutes, with my reusable bags spilling at my feet. Will my mince pies be smashed and my parsnips bruised when I get home? Probably, as they usually are. It's frosty today, and I forgot to bring my gloves. I'll be glad to get home.

Piling the bags into the taxi's boot, we drive the short hop to my road. The taxi driver knows the ropes and goes further up, so he can turn and be on the right side of the road for me to unpack and get my bags to the top of the steps. I tip generously.

'Thanks. Happy Christmas,' I call, and he gives me a thumbs up. I know I will have forgotten something and will have to go out again in the week, and, when I've accidentally eaten or drunk my Christmas stash, to replenish what I've had.

Alice and Rose are coming around this Friday. I decide to put my Christmas decorations up before they come over. December 18th is a good time to start being sparkly and merry. Jack will be here on the 19th. They've been texting like mad and asking questions. I didn't say he'd left after breakfast, and I don't know whether I should. Let's see what this next weekend brings. I try to answer them as best I can.

How did it go? It was great, really romantic.

Did he look the same as you remembered? Absolutely. In fact, even more gorgeous!

Will you see him again? Yes. He's coming next week.

There are lots of heart and smiley face emojis.

Hauling the bags two-by-two up the stairs to my flat door, I'm exhausted when I stumble into my hallway. I kick off my shoes and slide into my moccasin slippers.

'Oh, yeah, baby!' Flinging open the cupboards, I jiggle things around so I can fit in the extra bottles of gin, rum and sherry. The wine bottles are placed in a wooden rack by the side of the fridge, which is now groaning under the sheer mass of tonic waters, cheeses, hams and salad. I'm deciding what I'll make for Alice and Rose. A buffet-type thing or a pre-Christmas dinner, complete with bruised parsnips?

Then I focus. There's a bowl in the sink, one of my cereal bowls. Now that's weird. I have such OCD about cleaning that I never leave home without washing everything I've used. I may still have it out in the dish rack, but I always remember to wash it up in the first place. So how did I miss this? Ah! I must be so wrapped up thinking about Jack I blipped over it. It takes a moment to realise I had toast this morning... hang on... That can't be right? No, I distinctly remember having toast. Except I can't have had toast. Else why would this bowl be here? My head hurts. Stress must be getting the better of me. The dead-line for my book is next Monday, and the spectre of Christmas is looming. That's it. I had toast yesterday, but my days are getting mixed and muddled up.

This afternoon I discover something I really can't account for, and now I feel quite ill.

Having had lunch and washed up, I pull out my portfolio of current illustrations from the plan chest. I have to stare for a while, as what I'm looking at does not compute. A red wine glass ring is across the top half of my latest picture. I shake my head. No. That can't be right. I never, ever, *ever* make mistakes like that. I'm always so careful, *beyond careful*. How could this be? I rack my brain trying to remember when I had my work out when there was a drink around. The only time was when Alice and Rose were here that first evening. I never drink while paint-ing, especially if it is a paid commission. It just doesn't work well. Yes, the image of Rose cockling her wine glass on my desk – hang on, no, that doesn't make sense either. I hadn't started this particular illustration then. I was on the one before, which I now have to check, but it is okay.

I rub my hands across my face. What the actual *fuck*? Now I need to check all my images to ensure no others are marred. You can't paint over watercolour the same as you can with oils. You can do damage limitation of sorts, but it's not great. I always scan each image after they are completed. I check the scan, and there is no mark. How has this happened? It takes me all afternoon of careful erasing and painting to get back to where I was. If you weren't aware of it, you wouldn't be able to tell, although the thing is, *I know. And let's not mention that bowl...*

Chapter Fifteen

I'M TRYING to get into the festive spirit, though it's hard, as the wine glass stain is irritating the heck out of me. The thought of it is pecking at the back of my head. I must focus on the *now* or risk ruining the evening. The living room looks pretty good, so at least that's one thing off the list. Delicious, meaty smells waft from the oven. I'll put the rice on once Alice and Rose arrive and get comfortable.

It's freezing when I open the downstairs front door. 'Quick, come in and get warm.' We gallop up the stairs and into the warmth of the flat.

'Wow!' says Alice. 'Very festive. Especially as I felt a couple of flakes of snow outside. Brr, bloody cold.' She hangs her jacket up, and I note she is finally in leggings. *Hurrah!*

I welcome her and Rose into my flat. 'I'm not usually into all the Christmas decorating lark, but I thought I'd make an effort. I can't believe it's December 18th already. Only seems last week when we met you, Rose, after my book launch, not a whole month.'

'I know. I can't believe it either.' She looks about her. 'It all looks beautiful, Lily.'

Garlands of glittery white lights are spun about a fake Christmas tree sitting in the corner of the living room, decorated with brightly hued hanging baubles and twines of tinsel. I have another set of coloured fairy lights draped along the curtain rail, and there are all sorts of Christmassy things dangling from paintings or tucked into nooks around the room. Tasteful? Possibly not. Fun, definitely.

'Is that mulled wine?' Alice sniffs. 'Ooh, yummy.' She heads into the kitchen, and I hear clanking and sloshing noises.

'Remember not to burn your lip like you did a couple of years back.'

Rose has hung her jacket on the rack and is unwinding a long scarf. Her freckles are burning. 'It really is cold out there. I wonder if it'll snow for Christmas?'

'Some part of me would love that, but afterwards, you get dirty slush and skiddy pathways.' I stop. 'I think I sounded like my dad then. Oh, God! Have I turned into a grumpy old man?'

'Not quite yet,' laughs Rose.

I indicate the kitchen. 'Fancy a mulled wine? Did you drive over? Because I should warn you it's got quite a bit of brandy in it.'

'Always. And no, I caught the bus, so all good here.'

It occurs to me I still have no idea where Rose lives.

'What is that fantastic smell? You been cooking, Miss Lily?' Alice dances back into the living room, waving her glass, and I refrain from asking her to be careful, or my moniker of grumpy old man might stick. 'Want something, Rose?'

I say, 'Catalan pork with coriander seeds and soy sauce, with basmati rice and French beans.' I wait for the offer of a wine, too, but Alice reappears with only one for Rose.

'So,' laughs Rose as she takes her drink, 'Spanish, Chinese, Indian and French all in one dish?'

'That sounds like something Harry would make,' says Alice, and then I can see her swivel her eyes at Rose, who luckily doesn't seem to have noticed. Alice and I tactically decided not to mention Harry again in front of Rose in case she has a melt-down. Not that I want to be reminded of him any more than I am currently. Which is to say, a lot!

A hot dinner and mulled wine are just what we all need on such a night as this.

'This is bloody scrumptious,' says Alice. 'Are there seconds?'

I wave at the kitchen. 'Help yourself.'

'Have you always been able to cook?' Rose shakes her head. 'I mean, did you learn at home or school... or...?'

'I think *or* springs to mind,' says Alice. 'I remember the days when Lily's culinary offering was Heinz spaghetti on toast with melted cheese on top.' There are times I wish Alice would think before she reveals stuff. When she tells people details like this about me, I feel humiliated. These were things from the past and I'm not like that now.

Alice has necked a fair deal of wine, and I will her not to blurt out who taught me to cook. I urge, 'Go and get some more, Alice.'

'Don't need to be asked twice.' She takes her plate into the kitchen.

'So, you're a self-taught cook, then?' Rose pins me with one of her laser stares.

'Nah!' Alice stops in the doorway, waving a serving spoon. 'Harry taught her. He tried teaching me, but I'm crap. I can't be bothered with all the faffy bits. It's so much easier to get a takeaway.'

Bugger! The part about not mentioning Harry has been

wiped from her memory by too many glasses of wine. I pray she doesn't let slip anything else that might set Rose off.

Rose's eyes narrow, although she says nothing. A vein throbs at her temple, the only indication she heard Alice. 'I can't fathom how you can eat so much, Alice,' she nods, 'and still stay so slim.'

'I'm like my mum,' Alice shouts through the hole in the wall, 'so I expect now I've hit thirty, I'll turn into a blimp.'

'Your mum is a blimp,' I call back, 'because she married your dad at thirty and cooks the most amazing Jamaican food for him. If I lived with your mum, I'd be topping twenty stone by now.'

'Your mum isn't twenty stone, is she?' says Rose, her fork poised in shock. 'Not that I'm judging.'

'No way, she's just a bit round.'

'I'm going for a top-up of wine,' I say. 'Rose? Alice?'

'Yes, please.' Rose holds up her glass. 'So *your* Harry taught you to cook?'

I wish Alice hadn't mentioned Harry, although I can do nothing about it now. I top up our glasses.

'He was pretty good. Had a knack, and he cooked for me, well, us, all the time.' I wave at Alice, who butts in.

'He was bloody brilliant. Cooked all manner of things, didn't he, Lily?'

'That's an unusual trait in men.' Rose's mouth is pursed. 'Usually, they expect us to wait on them hand and foot.'

'Not always,' I counter. I want to get off this line of thought. 'I need to ask if Jack can cook.'

'That'd be great,' slurs Alice. 'If he can, he can cook for all of us, then.'

'Maybe we should ask him first?' Rose raises a perfectly plucked eyebrow.

'Well,' I say, 'I'm seeing him tomorrow, so I can ask him.'

That's all it takes to steer us onto less problematic ground.

Back on the sofa, I have to fend off the next set of questions about Jack from both of them.

Is he nice?

Is he kind?

Does he make me laugh?

Does he wash up/put the toilet seat down/make the bed...?

How many times can I say 'yes, yes, yes, yes, yes'? And still keep a straight face.

Then the final one from Alice. *Is he good in bed?* Then she and Rose look at each other and giggle. Like schoolgirls. Like best mates...

This makes me flounce to the toilet. Sometimes I think a line should be drawn, and I'm unsure if Alice knows where that is. I know it's all a joke, but my bad mood is betraying me. Maybe it's the wine, because I'm beginning to worry again about the painting. Did Rose do it? Alice picks up on it. She collars me when Rose nips to the toilet.

'I'm sorry, did I go too far? You know it was just a bit of banter.'

'I know, um...'

Alice frowns and edges closer. She whispers, 'What's the matter? I can tell there's something wrong!'

I tug her into the kitchen. 'It's bizarre. You know I keep all my work safe in the plan chest? I mean, I'm always so careful with it. I got them all out on Tuesday, as I have to take the illustrations to Mary this Monday, and one of them has a red wine ring across it. Jesus wept! You know me, Alice. I wouldn't ever do anything that stupid.'

Alice's face shows she understands. Sometimes I feel she knows me better than I know myself. 'That's awful. You're always ultra-careful. How the hell did this happen, then? If you didn't do it, who did?'

'Well,' I glance down the corridor. 'I noticed a couple a few weeks ago when Rose was here, she—'

'You think Rose might have done it and not told you?' She's frowning heavily at me. 'She wouldn't do that, Lily. She's not that sort of person. She'd admit it and say sorry. I'm sure of it.'

'Yes, but—' I hear the toilet being flushed. I pull away from Alice, and we start a random conversation. Alice is astute enough to understand I don't want to continue this in front of Rose. I will have to finish this head-to-head with her later. I don't want to accuse anyone, but I have to look at two possibilities here. The first is that I am going mad, not watching what I was doing, and I put my wine glass without thinking onto my illustration and wasn't aware, not even when I cleared up the glass. The conundrum being I never drink while I'm painting. Or, and this is equally disturbing to me, someone else did it and covered it up. I can understand if something happens and it's an accident. It can only be Rose, as Alice would have owned up to it and grovelled like hell afterwards. I know I disregarded Rose, yet I can't think of anything else to account for it. I can feel both Alice and Rose sensing my mood, and even though I try to hide it, I know I am a little sharp.

'Lily,' says Rose quietly. 'Have I done anything to upset you?'

'Why should you think that?' Probably by the frosty tone of my voice?

'If I have done something, please tell me. I can't bear it if you're angry with me, and I don't know why.'

'I'm sure it's nothing to do with you,' says Alice, giving me the evil-eye.

I close my eyes. 'It's, well...' I shake my head. I have no proof, and what if I did it myself? Been so focused on Jack I damaged my own illustration without even noticing? I remember the date on the scan. It was days after Rose and Alice came round that night. It couldn't have been her. Then I have a disturbing thought. What if it was *Jack*? We were drinking wine, weren't we? Had I left that painting out when he was here? I remember getting them out to show him, but did I forget to put them away afterwards? Oh, shite! I'm about to accuse Rose of something she could not have done.

'It's nothing, Rose. I'm sorry, I think I'm a little nervous about seeing Jack tomorrow.' I laugh lightly to shrug it off.

'New relationships are like that.' Rose smiles. 'I'd nearly forgotten what it's like.'

Alice pours three more glasses of a superb Cabernet Sauvignon she brought with her and rummages through her enormous Mary Poppins bag. She whips out a packet of cigarettes.

'Alice? I thought you gave up last year. What the hell are you doing?'

'Ask me how Matt is.' Oh, no! This can only be bad tidings. She goes to the window and wrenches it open a crack. Cold air whooshes in as she exhales smoke out into the night.

'How's Matt?' I ask, swallowing a mouthful of wine. I think I know what's coming. I wonder if we take turns being happy with a bloke. When she's happy, I'm not and vice versa.

'Well, the answer to that is, how the bloody hell should I know? I haven't seen him for five days.' Alice's voice rises an octave. 'Do you know what he *did*? He came into the bar with a bunch of flowers, and I said, "Are those for me then?" And he said, "No. I didn't know you had a shift today." I was *so* embarrassed as there were other people in the bar too, and there was this awful silence.'

'Oh, I know this one,' says Rose, 'where everyone is looking away but listening really hard.'

'Yeah, exactly that.'

'Well, what did he expect?' I say. 'He walks into his girlfriend's bar with flowers. Most of us would put two and two together and come up with four.'

'I don't know what he expected. He left without saying anything, and I went out the back, feeling like a berk!'

'Didn't he leave the flowers?'

'No!'

I wave my hands around. 'Then who did he bring the flowers for?'

'Another one of the waitresses. I couldn't believe it!' Alice wipes under her eyes. 'As he said, he didn't think I had a shift that day, so he wasn't expecting me to be there.'

'*What?*' I think I shout this. 'No! I can't believe it. He wouldn't do something like that!'

'He bloody well did!'

Rose jolts and knocks her wine off the arm of the sofa, where it spreads slowly like a pool of blood across my sand-coloured carpet. When I get enough money, I will bloody well get a red wine-coloured carpet laid in here.

'Oh my God.' Rose leaps up. 'I'm so sorry. Where is a cloth so I can mop it up?'

'No worries,' I say, resigned to a wine spill at least once a month. I grab the floorcloth from under the sink and kneel to sponge it up.

Rose also kneels and tries to grab the cloth. 'Please let me do it, as it's my fault. I'll pay for any cleaning that needs to be done.'

I shake my head. 'As I said, it doesn't matter. Me and Alice have knocked over enough glasses in our time, haven't we?'

'Yep,' says Alice. She looks utterly forlorn.

'Okay. Thank you.' Rose sits back on the sofa and looks over to Alice. 'I'm also sorry, Alice, to hear your news. I know I haven't met him, but he sounds like a complete and utter dolt.'

'Turns out he is.' Alice rubs her face, and I'm not sure if she's going to cry. I fling the sodden cloth into the sink.

'I know you're not all right but are you kind of all right?' I pull her into a hug. 'Bloody men, eh. Who needs them?'

We stare at each other.

'Fuck!' I say. 'I think we all need a gin and tonic, eh?'

'Damn right,' says Alice.

'I am so sorry, Alice,' I tell her again and hand her a very laden G&T. 'This'll either make you feel better or make you throw up. And you're more than welcome to stay here until you get your head around it all.'

'I know. Thanks.' She makes a face when she sips her drink. 'Dearest God! Lily, did you put any tonic in this, or is it neat gin?'

'A slosh. Didn't want to overdo it.'

'Well, chin-chin.' Alice takes a hefty swig. 'Feel better already.'

The clock hands have whizzed round and round, and now it's nearly one.

'Okay,' Alice says. 'Perhaps we should leave in a bit, as you probably need to get some rest?' She waggles her eyebrows saucily at me. Her make-up is tear-stained, but I'm glad to see she's perked up, although that might be due to the second gin. 'Somebody needs to be getting some action.' She sniffs noisily.

I grin. 'Here's hoping.' From the corner of my eye, I can swear I see Rose twitch and her face changes. Oh, shite! Am I rubbing her face in it? It's not my fault I'm happy. And getting some!

Suddenly, I have a flashback. Two years ago. Matt was visiting his parents in France for a week. They had a French provincial house with a pool. And a tennis court. For whatever reason, he didn't invite Alice. I gathered he had issues to sort with his parents and needed privacy, but she was still miffed. In fact, she was so angry about it, she brought a strange man home from a nightclub while he was away. I'd stumbled out of my room early in the morning and bumped into a man wearing only his boxer shorts exiting the bathroom. As it was only Alice and me living there, and I had never clapped eyes on this bloke in my life, I assumed he was with Alice. He nodded a greeting and bounced into Alice's bedroom. Judging by the giggling and crashing coming from there, I guessed he wasn't there to read the electricity meter. The matter was never mentioned and maybe she didn't realise that I knew about it. So, even though I have sympathy, it's a bit tricky when the pot is calling the kettle black... or whatever that stupid saying is.

Outside it is icy, and I watch them hug each other as they go their separate ways. Some part of me fears Alice will start to like Rose more than me. That I will lose my 'bestie' to another woman. Jealous claws rake at me. Could that ever happen? Would Alice forsake me? Am I now boring? What is the matter with me? Alice has stood by me through every experience of my life so far, and I have stood by her. What is it about Rose that makes me feel so insecure?

My mind slips back in time to when our art course finished, and a new life beckoned. How could I ever be prepared for the shit-storm coming my way?

When the work for my show was finally on the walls of my cubicle, I stepped back. Three years on a few square metres of white wall. A biography and a photo. My life was encapsulated right here. Three years of my life and a student loan a weight around my neck. But then, look at what I'd gained. A fantastic boyfriend, great friends, and a sense of self I'd never had before. Life was sweet!

My family came up to London for the opening of the degree show, and I booked them into a cheap hotel nearby. I took them for lunch to a Greek restaurant down one of the back streets that didn't need a bank loan to pay for it. Food cooked 'like Mama used to make' was their slogan. Their moussaka was to die for, and I ordered a bottle of retsina.

'Can't believe you're graduating,' said my mum. 'We're so proud of you, Lily.'

'Can't believe,' said my dad, 'we're drinking stuff that tastes like turpentine!'

'Give it time,' I grinned. 'It works well with the food. And as to graduating, I can't believe it either.' We'd already been given our grades, and to say I was happy was an understatement of gigantic proportions. I was bloody ecstatic. Harry had a grade below mine, and I wasn't sure if he was pissed off by that. I wasn't about to ask. I did know the grade didn't really count and that it was the work that got you a job or not. Except a good mark could undoubtedly open doors.

Standing in front of my show, my family couldn't contain their excitement.

'It all looks wonderful, Lily,' said my mum. 'The quality of your work is amazing.' She dabbed at her eyes. 'One moment you were scribbling pictures with your crayons on the dining room table, and the next, you're doing all this.'

'Please don't cry on me, Mum.' I pulled her into a hug. 'You know you'll set me off.'

'This is stunning,' said Sophie. 'When you're famous, don't forget us, eh?'

'Shut it, Soph!'

'She's right. I expect you'll do very well,' said my dad. 'I didn't realise how talented you are. Like your mum, I knew you were good, but not this good.' He put his arm around my shoulder. 'Maybe you can move out of that horrible little bedsit after this?'

'That horrible little bedsit has done me proud, although I have news.' I grinned at them. 'Harry has asked me to move in with him. We're trying to find a place so we can move after the show.'

Sophie chimed in. 'In that case, I'd like to have that horrible little bedsit in the centre of London. When Lily moves out, can I move in? That would be *so cool*!'

'Oh, please,' said my mum, 'not yet.'

'Where's Harry's work?' Dad peered about him.

'Over there.' I pointed. 'I'm glad our styles are completely different. I don't want to be competing against him for work.'

'Of course you don't,' said my mum. 'That might put a terrible strain on your relationship.'

I hadn't thought of that.

'Let's go and say hello,' said Sophie. She bounded across the gap, and I saw Harry hug her. Sophie had been up a couple of times to visit us, and Harry and I had slogged across London, taking her to museums, art galleries and craft markets. She'd taken to London like the proverbial duck to water. We followed Sophie across the room.

Harry's parents had caught the train down from Sheffield, and this would be the first time I'd met them. Harry was the spit of his dad, peas in a pod, as they say, but his mum was tall, slender and very blonde. She looked like a Swedish model, and I expected her to have a Nordic accent, so I was non-plussed when she spoke with a broad Yorkshire brogue.

'So nice to finally meet you, Lily love,' she said as she kissed me. 'We've been waiting for *his nibs* to bring you up to ours for ages.'

'Er, we've been kind of busy trying to get a degree?' Harry rolled his eyes affectionately at her.

'I know, love. Hey? Maybe you can both come up for Christmas?' She turned to me. 'It's right beautiful where we live, Lily. The village will be decked out, and there will more than likely be snow. Not a sprinkling, mind, but proper Christmassy snow.'

'Can I come too?' said Sophie. 'Sounds wonderful.'

'Good grief, Sophie,' huffed my mum. 'You can't go around inviting yourself to places. I'm so sorry—'

Harry's mum's face lit up. 'Why don't you all come? There's more than enough space at ours—'

'Hold your horses,' said Harry's dad. 'Not so fast now, pet. Give them time to actually meet us. Then we can sort out Christmas.'

The show was a success. The students are meant to sit by their exhibition area while the show is open to the public in case a prospective client comes. Day after day, the place was packed, and interested parties shuffled from stall to stall, sucked on their teeth, twiddled their beards and moustaches, adjusted glasses and then walked away. We all decided to go for a pint in The Enterprise on the final day. Just the one, for old times' sake. It felt like a watched kettle never boils, so a watched stall does not get you a job. When I returned, I found a note scrawled in my notebook, asking me to call a number to speak to a Mary Southerland from New Renaissance Books. I gazed at the message for quite a while.

'You're dribbling,' said Harry. 'What's happened?'

'I just got a message from a publisher. They want to talk to me.'

'What? *Who?*' He snatched the note and read it. 'Bloody hell, Lily. New Renaissance Books? Aren't they the lot who did the Herbert the Bear series?'

'Yep.'

'The illustrator made it big after that, didn't she?'

'Yep, I think so.'

'Then bloody well call them!'

I phoned Mary of New Renaissance Books, and after an extensive chat, I was called in for an interview. Clutching an A2 portfolio of my best work, I caught a taxi to their company building, where, looking up, I had an impression of hundreds of shiny windows. I walked through the revolving doors to the main desk, introduced myself, and was directed to the seventh floor. There was a sturdy desk with a sturdy secretary sitting behind it.

'Sit down, dear. They'll call you when they're ready.'

I nodded my thanks and then sat, trying not to let my nerves get the upper hand as one leg jiggled uncontrollably.

Eventually, I was shown into a swanky office, where a slim but sharp-looking woman was sitting at a large mahogany desk. Two men with granite faces sat at each shoulder. It felt more like an interrogation than an interview.

'I'm Mary Southerland, and I was pleasantly surprised by your work in the show. This is Mr Baker and Mr Stratoni.' She nodded left and right. 'Please?' She indicated the portfolio. I supposed if she'd been 'unpleasantly' surprised, I wouldn't be here.

Heaving it onto the table, I opened it and let them finger their way through it. They made noises, and I wasn't sure if they were approving sounds or negative ones. There seemed to be a lot more sucking of the teeth. I was hard-pressed to stop fidgeting.

'Can you give us a moment, please, Lily?'

I stood outside the office, trying to hear what was being said but not wanting to appear to be eavesdropping. The door sprang open, and Mr Baker ushered me back in.

Mary indicated a chair. 'We have a new writer, Johnathan Elliot, who has recently joined the company, and we believe your illustration style would fit perfectly with his work. We would like to offer you a contract to illustrate his first book, with the proviso you continue to work with him for future books.'

Mary gazed at me expectantly, but I'm sure my chin was on the floor.

'How does that sound to you, Lily?' Tilting her head to one side, she reminded me of a small bird. She also didn't appear to blink.

'That sounds perfect,' I managed to croak.

'Good.' She smiled. 'We shall introduce you to Johnathan, and if we all agree, we shall draw up a contract.'

A contract? Had I been asked to illustrate a book? A whole book?

'You can either drop it back to us signed or sign it at home and send us a scanned copy. Please ensure you read every sentence on the contract. There should be no nasty surprises, yet it's astonishing how many people sign on the dotted line without reading it first.'

'Thanks. I will.' We shook hands, and I left, my legs now jelly. I had to clutch at the railing in the lift. I couldn't phone Harry and Alice fast enough.

'A real, proper book? I'll get the champers in,' said Harry. 'I think we've been upgraded.'

I was beyond ecstatic the day when Mary offered me that illustration job. And every day since, I am grateful to be so lucky my day job is the thing I love to do more than anything in the world. But I'm scared of losing it, worried that one small trip up and it all might come crashing down. A fragile House of Cards. I now don't like change. Anything that might wobble my status-quo. Is that what the problem is with Rose? That I'm not up for sharing my closeness with Alice instead of being happy that we have another wonderful friend? I used to think I was an open book, although now I'm not sure. And the incident with the wine glass stain has left me disorientated. I'm looking for someone else to blame, but maybe that should start at home? Have I done this to myself somehow?

Chapter Sixteen

SATURDAY, 19 DECEMBER - WHAT IS MY REALITY?

I'VE BEEN in bed for a couple of hours, although sleep is eluding me, and no number of sheep can fix it. There is a sound that is remarkably like the door to my roof terrace being clicked shut. My hair stands on end, and, for a moment I freeze, unable to move. What the hell? Maybe that second gin wasn't such a good idea now. My head is thick and fuzzy, and I'm sure there's a dead vole in my mouth.

I drag on a sweater hanging over the chair in the bedroom and slink down the hall. Everything appears normal. The key is hanging off the nail where it always is. It's not moving. My hands are shaking as I unlock and open the door. Flicking the hall light switch, the terrace is illuminated. There is no one – no shadows, no fleeing figures. I tiptoe outside and hang over the rail to peer into my neighbour's gardens. Still nothing. The roof is shined with a heavy frost, and ice crystals crunch between my toes. They are going numb.

So, I must have either imagined it or misheard something and interpreted it as my back door. I let my breath trickle out of me. Wow! I seem to have a surge of adrenalin, as my heart is thumping. The thought of another person, *a stranger* in my house, uninvited, makes me feel nauseous. But it's okay. There was no one in here. I close the door and lock it again. I'll buy a bolt, just to make sure.

Then I have a thought. Hands shaking, I re-open the door and creep out. Yes, I can see the imprints of my feet, the toes prominent as I was on tiptoe. Can I see anything that shouldn't be there? The breath freezes in my throat. Scuff marks go down the side of the fence. I peer closer. There aren't any discernible footprints, but I can't rule it out. If I can climb up to here from the garden below, anyone can. A couple of cats caterwaul in the neighbour's veg patch, and I jump as if I've been poked with a cattle prod. I clutch at my chest. Again, I bend down and follow the marks. There are cat paw prints all over, so that must be it. I can feel I'm shaking, and it's not only due to the cold, even though I'm only wearing a T-shirt and knickers under the sweater. I know the cats have often used my terrace to fight over territory or potential mates. I will accept this, and now I must forget about it because the alternative is too horrible to contemplate.

I scuttle back to my bedroom and pull the duvet over my head. The early dawn light comes gradually through my gauzy curtains. I've had one of those nights where you're not quite asleep and wake feeling as though you haven't slept at all. Although I know I have slept because I can recall snippets of fevered dreams.

Oh, God! Jack will be here in a few hours. Why on earth did I invite Alice and Rose over the day before seeing Jack? I should have known we'd all drink too much. It's no good trying to get back to sleep. I will probably miss my alarm or wake up with a thumping headache. Hauling on leggings, I make a coffee and have toast and marmite. If Jack is one of those people who doesn't like marmite, he can bloody well sod off... Oh dear. I think this must be the stress radiating out from last night. I haven't forgotten it, merely shoved it underground, where it rises in bouts of biliousness and bad temper.

A hot shower and fixing my face for the day make me feel marginally better. I do appear tired, though, and no amount of foundation can change that. Do I tell him what I feared? Or wait until he asks why I look so knackered? Or shrug it off, as he might put me down as neurotic and unstable? Should I tell Alice? Though what, exactly, would I tell her?

It's not as if I'm watching the clock or anything, but when I hear the downstairs buzzer go, I hurtle down to open the door. Jack has his hands behind his back and a sly smile.

'Happy nearly Christmas,' he shouts, whipping out a big bouquet of flowers. They are my colours, pinks and oranges, purples and lilacs.

'Oh, Jack! They are gorgeous!' I rise on tiptoes and kiss his cheek. He pulls me close, gathers me into his arms and kisses me deeply. It's warm and slow and very sensual. Then an icy blast of air whistles past us.

'Sorry,' he calls gaily. 'Too cold for this here.' Hooking the door with his foot, it slams behind him. He has his holdall in his other hand.

'Come on in, then.' I grab his hand, and we race up the stairs. He rips off his coat and hangs it up, kicking the holdall down the side of the sofa.

'Oh, wow!' He nods around the room. 'This all looks great. Very Christmassy.'

'I tried, although I'm not really a Christmassy person. I'll get a vase for these.' The only thing I can find that will fit them is a large green glass juice jug. It's the one I use for the roses, so part of me doesn't want to use it, but it's all I have. They look beautiful, but as I place it on the table, Jack grabs me, and I nearly upend the whole lot onto the floor.

'I've been waiting all week for this.' He nuzzles into my neck. 'I'm so sorry I had to rush off last Sunday. Trust me, it won't happen again. I kind of messed up my own idiom there, didn't I?'

I look up into his face.

'I said I worked to live, not lived to work.'

'Yes, you did. I had all sorts of plans for us, though I guess we'll just have to do them this weekend instead?'

'Hmm, fancy a little...?' He glances towards the bedroom.

'Don't mind if I do.' I flutter my eyelashes, glad I've put the central heating on early.

Practice makes perfect. There's less clashing of teeth, and bumping of knees, and elbows in the ribs, so we must be doing something right. Lying in the crook of Jack's shoulder, I lightly trace my fingers across his chest. The sky is still a pewter grey, edged with a soft yellow. The colours of impending snow? I hope so.

Jack stirs. 'I know you had plans I ruined last week, so what have you got lined up for us this week?' He turns his head, and our noses touch.

'I have lots of plans. It's what I do. How about something simple to start with? A walk along the beach?'

'That sounds great.'

'I hope you have your winter warmers with you. It can get pretty chilly down there.'

'After I forgot my gloves last week, I've brought a stack of woolly things with me. Not going to get caught out again.'

We dress, glancing shyly at each other. I find my gloves and scarf, and he does his coat up to the neck and rummages for a beanie-style hat. As we head out, something cold and wet is on my cheek, a tiny, icy kiss. Light snowflakes are swirling around us, and even though traffic is crawling past us, there's a silence you only get with falling snow. It doesn't take us long to get to the beach. The pebbles are limned in frost and glisten. I must be careful not to slip and fall over. The waves rolling in are practically the same hue as the sky, though the sounds are soft and muffled.

'How beautiful is this?' I breathe in, filling my lungs to capacity before I let the air whoosh out. 'Aren't negative ions good for your mental state?'

'Isn't your mental state good right now? Mine is. And, yes, you are beautiful.' He pulls me to him, and we kiss, unaware of anyone else around us. Not that there are many people about by now. The snow is thicker, and vision is limited as the beach disappears into a white haze.

'My mental state is brilliant, thanks.' I grin up at him. 'But I think my bodily state is pretty cold.'

'No kidding,' he laughs.

'Fancy a coffee?' I link arms with him. 'There's a cute little café up ahead.'

'Can you find it in all this? I can barely see my hand in front of my face.'

'Well, if we get wet feet, we're heading in the wrong direction.' I shouldn't joke, as visibility is low now. The wind is behind us, making it slightly more manageable, though it takes us time to find the main path, and then the café lit up with all its Christmas fairy lights. Pushing through the door, we shake ourselves like wet dogs on the mat. There's one other couple in there, who glance up as we fall in but then return to their conversation. We choose a small round table at the far end.

'What a cute place,' says Jack.

It is painted Brighton colours, all the sea greens and turquoises, the candy floss pinks and burning oranges. The furniture and artwork on the wall are mismatched, which is probably why I like it here. I spot a domed glass jar of chocolate muffins the size of hamsters.

'What can I get you?' An elderly lady, in a crisp green apron, with round pink cheeks and rosebud lips, is standing with a little pad and a pencil.

'I'll have a cappuccino and one of those chocolate muffins.' I point.

Jack looks across at the counter. 'Are they homemade?'

'Absolutely, dear,' says the waitress. 'Everything in here is. No shop-bought in our establishment, I can assure you.'

'Then I'll have the same.'

'Coming right up.' She ambles off.

How nice it is to be far from the hustle and bustle of the city, with the snow falling steadily outside.

'You have to be prepared,' said Jack, 'that our wonderful British Rail might stop dead in its tracks because of this... Literally, I mean. You know what the trains are like here.'

'That's fine by me. I have enough food to feed the five thousand at home, and you're welcome to stay.'

'Good to know.' The cups of coffee and muffins are placed on the table. 'These are seriously yummy muffins.' Jack licks his fingers.

'Listen, I think strolling along the beach might be off the list now, but I was hoping to impress you with my culinary prowess tonight and cook you a meal? Are you up for that?'

'You can cook? I love anyone who can cook, as I'm particularly rubbish at it.'

Ah! Then that's one question answered.

'I kind of fell into it gradually.' This isn't the time to say I cooked with Harry, that he guided and taught me. My repertoire went from tomato soup with cheese in it and a side of bread roll (as Alice would say, that was on a good day) to authentic Chinese, Indian and Moroccan dishes using all the correct ingredients sourced from the local supermarkets. It had been a magical time for me. Something we shared and valued. *Bastard!* Oh no! Please stop thinking about Harry!

There's another sharp tinkling sound, and two men pile through the door. 'Good grief,' one of them says. 'It's cold out there.'

'I hope they've got hot chocolate,' says the other.

'Can I recommend the chocolate muffins?' I call across the space. 'They are out of this world.'

'Got to have one of those, then. It feels like a chocolate day all around.'

Jack and I finish our coffee and cakes.

'Is it letting up yet?' Jack walks to the main window and peers through. 'Looks like a scene from Scott of the Antarctic!'

'Should we stay here and have lunch, or do you want to brave it now?'

Jack turns to the people in the café. 'Sorry, has anyone got a correct weather forecast?'

The man with the chocolate muffin looks at his phone. 'It says it's snowing.'

'Wow!' I laugh. 'So accurate, it's uncanny!'

'It also says it will be heavy for about the next hour and then ease off.'

'Lunch it is then.'

'I concur,' says the man. 'Menus for everyone.'

Glancing up and down the menu, I choose a lamb hotpot with a side of green beans. Jack has two eggs and chips.

'No one can mess with egg and chips,' he says, with a knowing wink. 'Not that I'm saying anything here. I do love eggs and chips.'

Not sure what he's alluding to, I raise an eyebrow.

'My gran used to work in catering, and she would only ever eat egg and chips when out. She said all sorts of vile things happen in the kitchens. Things that would make your hair go curly... or fall out.'

'Yuck!' I look over at the counter. 'Maybe I should change my order?'

'Nah. You're fine in a place like this. I'm sure they'd give us a tour of their kitchen if we asked.'

'I'd like that.'

The food is piping hot and delicious when placed in front of us. 'Maybe I don't need to cook tonight, after all?'

'No, I'm sure we'll be hungry again soon. Especially if we get lost in the snow for hours.'

I see the snow easing off as we finish, so we might make it home safely. After paying, we thank the elderly waitress and wish her a 'Happy Christmas', and then, hauling on coats and scarves again, we brave the outside. The seascape has changed dramatically. Snow carpets the beach and softens hard outlines as if the whole place has had a soft, white blanket tossed over it. Only a few stubborn flakes are falling out of a metal-hued sky.

I skid on the pavement. Jack catches me. 'We should take it slowly, as we don't want to break a leg or ankle just before Christmas.'

I stop and face the sea. The salt wind caresses my cheek. 'You know, most people want to be buried when they die, but I think I'd find that claustrophobic.' I shiver. 'To be surrounded by so much darkness and mud.'

'Er, I think by then, you wouldn't be bothered?'

'Maybe?' I shrug. 'Maybe not.'

'So, cremation? And this is a weird conversation but do go on.'

'No. Not cremation, although that's pretty final.' I nod out. 'I'd like to be dropped into the middle of the sea and sink slowly down, to see the light fade through the water, and maybe at the bottom, I'd still be able to see the sun and moon come up. See their light above me.'

I turn to see Jack gazing across the water. There's a strange expression on his face.

'Have I freaked you out?'

'Not at all. I found it interesting. You should write a story like that. A fairy tale.'

'I've probably read too many mermaid books for my own good.' I laugh. 'As to writing my own story, maybe one day. Come on. Back to reality.'

Inching our way up a slope by gripping the icy rail, huddled together, we walk back past the Old Steine Gardens, now a winter wonderland. On past The Level, now silent of skateboards and shouting kids, until we are opening my front door. The central heating has been chuffing away since we left, and the wall of heat is a shock after the temperature outside. Stripping off coats and sweaters, we fall in a heap on the sofa.

'I fancy a glass of wine.' Jack gets up and retrieves a bottle from his holdall. An image of a wine glass stain leaps into my mind. 'Want one?' He doesn't wait for an answer and heads into the kitchen to find the opener. He returns with two glasses and the opened bottle.

'Not much time to breathe but never mind!' He pours two glasses carefully. 'Thanks for today. It's been great.'

'My pleasure.' I accept the glass and take a sip. 'Nice. What is it?'

'A Rioja. I like my wines a bit rough and slightly oaky. I thought you'd like it too.' He rubs his shoulder as he sits next to me.

'Your old war wound?'

'Yep.' He rolls his eyes. 'So, I know you like Adele, but what other stuff?'

'I'll surprise you.' I go to the shelving units on the wall, switch on a tiny Anker speaker that has twice the power of similar bigger products and sift through my iPod. 'Ah, here we go.' I scroll around until I find a JohnOOFleming album. 'This is an artist recommended by my sister Sophie. I don't know who got her into it, but this guy makes great ambient dance music. He's been going for years, and his stuff is brilliant.'

The music drifts across the room. I put on the fairy lights but leave the main ones off. We sit on the sofa with the curtains open, listening quietly and watching the colours outside the window change. At some point, I realise the room is in shadow. I wonder if Jack is asleep. I can hear soft breathing, and all I can see is streetlight from outside thrown onto his face in planes of light and dark. His fringe has flopped over his forehead, and he appears very young. I leave him and sneak to the bathroom for a wee. When I creep back in, he is awake and twiddling the iPod.

I ask, 'Had enough of JohnOO on loop?'

'Nah, I enjoyed it, though I need something different now.' He nods. 'Here we go. A bit of Amy.'

The first song on the album *Back to Black* slides out of the speakers.

'Ready for some supper? I'm doing Chinese tonight.'

'Brilliant. I'll pour us another glass of red. We only had the one glass before we were nodding on the sofa.'

In the kitchen, I find all the ingredients and get them prepared.

'I use Chinese rice wine. It's similar to Japanese sake, except you're only meant to cook with it.' I peep out of my kitchen porthole. 'Of course, when you're told that, you have to try it.'

'There's a challenge I have to take on, then.' Jack comes into the kitchen, and I pour about a tablespoon into a shot glass.

'Is that it?' He takes the glass.

'Trust me, you'll thank me.'

Jack knocks it back and makes a scrunched face. 'Yummy,'

he croaks. 'And thank you for not giving me more. I expect it doesn't grow on you? Like drinking sake or retsina? Have you tried any of that?'

'Yeah, I used to go to an authentic Greek restaurant in London when I lived there. The original owner, well into his eighties, always sat in the corner and smiled at everyone who came in. Maybe you've been there? George's? It's in a basement in Frith Street in Soho.' I heat the oil in my wok and toss in the ingredients. The water in the kettle has just boiled, and the rice has been washed.

'I've heard of the place but haven't been there yet. I will now.' Jack is watching what I do. 'I never realised it would be so fast.'

'That's the whole point.' I serve the food straight from the wok onto the plates. 'I hope you like it, but I will not be offended if you don't. We can easily get a takeaway.'

Perched on the sofa, we eat, stuffing the food down as if we are starving. Jack appears to enjoy the dish, as he asks for more. I'm a happy bunny.

Chapter Seventeen

CONFUSION?

A SET OF SOFT, glowing fairy lights draped over the mirror in my bedroom is the only illumination. Because we are at the back of the house, we can't hear the road. Added to that is the snow deadening all noise. It's as if we are in a bubble where the passing of time and the pressures of responsibilities have no place. I should keep quiet, and by saying something now, I will break this spell, but I have to. Lying in bed with him, his arm lazily across me, our heads are close together. I ask *the* question.

'Do you have plans for Christmas? I mean,' I should qualify this, 'I'm thinking of going to my family in Bristol, though I haven't decided yet.'

I wait. Jack sighs and shifts position.

'I've made tentative arrangements to spend the day with my uncle Seamus and my cousins, Finn and Evie. They're the only family I've got left.' He makes a sound. 'God! How melodramatic is that?'

'Where are they?' I realise I may sound nosy. 'Sorry, just wondered, as their names sound Irish?' And I register that I won't be spending Christmas with him and feel a little deflated, but what was I expecting?

He puts on a broad Irish brogue. 'Oh, what? The name Jack Kelly didn't give it away? Yes, the family moved from Belfast at the start of "the troubles", as they call it. We've been based in Cheshire ever since. Hence the loss of the accent, although I think that was intentional.'

'I obviously can't hear my own accent, but I love accents. I'd hate everyone to get homogenised and all sound the same.'

'At least the newscasters have finally been allowed to sound like normal people.'

'I agree.'

He kisses me gently on the cheek. 'Sorry, I need to get some shut-eye. So, goodnight, Miss Lily and sweet dreams.' He rolls from me and turns over. I can see the gleam of light on the puckered scar on his shoulder. It's pretty bad, as it appears that something went right through him. That must have been a dreadful accident.

I remember there were good times with Harry. Moments when we lived together amicably, but the cracks were beginning to show, although we shored over them like consummate builders. Things might have been different if I hadn't accepted that invitation to go to Sheffield to spend Christmas with Harry's parents. If I'd never met Jo. Who knows? Hindsight is a wonderful thing.

Alice saved us. Well, for a while, at least.

'Listen,' she said a few days after our graduation. 'What if we got a house together? I know you intended to get your own place, so I understand and will not be offended if you don't want to. I thought we could all have a room and then see if we can pay a bit extra for a shared studio—'

'Oh God, *yes!*' I practically screamed, and Alice took a step back. 'Yes, please, let us move in with you. What do you think, Harry?' My reaction might have shocked them both, but it was an excellent way to break ourselves in gently to the idea of living together.

Alice snorted. 'And it would just be us three. No finding people doing drugs in your kitchen…'

I added, 'No wondering if the police might turn up for the dope plants—'

'Tomato plants, you mean,' said Harry. 'I kind of feel we've already been there, considering Alice and I are already in a shared house—'

Alice twiddled her fingers at him. 'But shared houses are always cheaper, and as I said, we wouldn't have the crazy flat-mates to contend with.'

Harry nodded. 'I reckon it would work.'

I couldn't tell if Harry was disappointed or grateful.

'Quite frankly,' I said, winking at him, 'if you'd said "no", Harry, I'd probably move in with Alice without you.' It was meant as a joke.

'Cheers!' He nodded. 'I expect you would.'

The most pertinent fact here was that I was relieved. Alice's presence would be a bulwark between us and the spectre of engagement, marriage and kids. Because that's what comes next, isn't it? Everyone expected it. I wasn't sure that I was ready for this step yet.

Stoke Newington was still the cheapest area, and it was relatively safe to wander around at night. More to the point, we already knew the area. Realising we could afford a house, we found one near Ridley Road market. A fully furnished four-bedroom property with a large living room and ample kitchen. It even had a garden with a small lawn, shrubs and rose bushes.

Harry and I decided to keep a room each, as we felt we needed to have some privacy on occasion. We could invite each other to our rooms but also have the option of shutting the door and having time alone in our own space. It felt grown-up. Or maybe it was more to do with safety? Personal and mental sanctuary. We all shared the largest bedroom as a studio, each having a set amount of space.

With all my worldly belongings in two suitcases and three black plastic bags in the back of a London taxi, I moved from my bedsit to the new house. It was here I discovered that Harry loved to cook, as we now had a kitchen we weren't terrified of entering. Not sharing with others meant it was clean, the rubbish was put into recycling bins, and the gas hob and oven were wiped down and spotless. We even had a tea towel.

Every Sunday morning, I woke to the smell of freshly baked sourdough bread. Alice and I would race down in our pyjamas and dressing gowns and settle at the table. Harry would slice the bread, still steaming, and we would slather it with butter and jam.

Was this what being an adult was? Inviting our friends around to 'our place' and never being embarrassed by the state of the kitchen or if there might be a bloke passed out, dead drunk on the sofa? Or worse, as Alice said, strangers doing drugs over the gas ring? Harry would cook something amazing from a foreign land, poring over a cookbook picked up in a second-hand shop. We would sit at a real table in the living room, drink red wine with fancy French names and discuss art, politics and religion.

Now, he rarely came into the studio. It had been months

since I had seen him paint or draw anything. Ostensibly, Harry was applying for jobs in design studios and sending his work off to every agent and publisher that accepted his style of work, though as yet no one had bitten. His desk remained clear. And let's not mention Alice's. She didn't even bother to come into the studio anymore.

Like Alice, Harry had started full-time work as a waiter in a Mexican restaurant in the centre of town and was now getting to grips with Tequila. Any money he brought back was barely enough, especially as he spent more time with new friends, drinking his wages away before they even had time to come home with him. I didn't know what to make of this. And there were twinges of uncertainty. Who were these new friends? Why weren't these people my friends as well?

'This is just a stop-gap, isn't it?' Not wanting to sound as if I was pushing him, I found it difficult to broach the subject. 'You are still sending your work out, aren't you?' So many questions, and it was apparent he didn't want to answer them.

'Sure,' he said, but he never quite met my eye.

I started to feel a pang of insidious guilt when I picked up my paintbrush, as though I was somehow betraying him, yet I knew you didn't get somewhere you wanted to be if you stopped moving. I had my first commission to complete, which was my main priority. This was where my source of income was, and I couldn't blow it.

Alice's shifts in the bar were regular, though often she was out until gone two or three. She slept in late, and it was like we had to make an appointment to catch up with her.

One morning, when she was in the kitchen. I asked, 'Alice, are you applying for *any* graphic design jobs now? I've kind of noticed you're not in the studio much.'

'Nope.' She slathered a piece of toast with butter. 'You know what? I like working in a bar. It took a while to realise I hate deadlines, I hate stress, and I loathe being told exactly what to do.'

'Like I am now,' I said pointedly. 'I seem to be the only one of us utilising the studio. It's beginning to feel as if it's my own personal space.'

'I'm not talking about you. You can handle it all, take it in your stride. I crash and burn at the slightest setback. Anyhow, I love the buzz of the bar. It may not be the most salubrious venue, but it feels like it's mine.' She shrugged. 'And it's great you are using the studio. I don't begrudge you that one bit.'

'Thanks. I appreciate you saying this. Do you know if Harry has abandoned looking for jobs too?'

Alice stopped and stared at me. 'Don't you?'

'He hasn't told me anything for a while now. I don't know if the fact I got work straight from art school has upset him—'

'Why on earth would you think that? He was so chuffed when you got the book deal. We both were. Listen, one of us has to make it.'

'Why can't we all make it?' I knew I sounded petulant.

'Because the world doesn't work like that. One out of three ain't bad, baby!'

It was two weeks before Christmas. Harry had just come off the phone. 'Mum has invited you and yours to ours for Christmas.' He shook his head. 'She's like a Pitbull with a small kiddie in its jaws about you lot!'

'That's a ghastly analogy, Harry!' I shunted over on the sofa. 'Who, exactly, has she invited?'

'You, your mum and dad and Sophie.' His face clouded. 'If they all want to come, that's fine by me, but I don't want your family to feel pressured into coming up.'

'Will Alice be there too?'

'My aunt and uncle live on the other side of the city, but I imagine they'll all be coming over for Christmas day, or at least Alice will, especially if you're there.' He raised an eyebrow. 'Will your lot be scared shitless to come to mine?'

'I can only ask?' I tugged my phone out of my back pocket. 'I'll call them now.'

'I'll make us a coffee.'

When he returned, I grinned at him. 'Mum and Dad have already made plans to be with my Aunt Sally and Uncle Bob. Sophie says she'd love to come. If that's okay with you?'

'I'd be great to have Sophie. At least my mum will be happy now and get off my back, especially as my brother Mark can't make it this year.'

'He's still in New Zealand then?'

'Yeah. He'll be on a beach somewhere, topping up his tan and drinking Tequila Sunrises, while we'll be slogging through ten feet of snow.' Harry shook his head. 'She gets so disappointed when he doesn't come home for Christmas, but it must cost him the earth in travel costs.'

'Well, I know it's not the same, but she'll have us this year instead.'

A snowy day on the beach, with a cosy flat to return to. Who could ask for more? It's been a perfect day. Except I feel like my timelines are twisting together as if they are strands of DNA. My old life with Harry meshing with my new life with Jack. Seven years ago, I was preparing to go to Harry's family's place in Sheffield for Christmas with my sister Sophie. What's going to happen this year? Hopefully, not the car crash I experienced at that time with her. *With Jo.*

Chapter Eighteen

SUNDAY, 20 DECEMBER – CHECK AND DOUBLE CHECK

IT'S NOT light enough to see clearly yet, as dawn is only beginning to scrabble under the curtain. Jack is still sleeping like the proverbial log. Tiptoeing to the bathroom, I lock the door and stand staring at my reflection. Is that a sparkle in my eyes? Ooh, I wonder why! I shower and climb quietly into clean clothes.

Opening the back door, I marvel at the amount of snow that has fallen in the night. Bird claw shapes and cat prints are the only things to mark the fresh snow. I breathe in deeply. Closing the door, I pass the bedroom and peep in. Jack is still snoring, one arm flung out across the duvet. I switch on the heating and then make a mug of tea. Sitting at my table, I'm watching the street outside my window come to life. People are trudging on regardless, the cars creeping up the road that hasn't been salted yet. Why does anyone feel the need to go out in conditions such as this? It's Sunday. Can't they let things go for a bit?

A hand on my shoulder makes me flinch so hard I slop tea down myself.

'Woah!' Jack laughs. 'I didn't mean to make you jump. I thought you'd heard me get up?'

I had, in fact, forgotten he was here, not that I would say anything. 'I was too absorbed in the goings-on outside.' I uncurl from my seat. 'Tea? Coffee?'

'Tea, for the moment.' Pulling me to him, he nuzzles my neck. 'Good morning, Miss Lily.'

'Good morning, Jack.' We stay like that for a few moments, entwined, and I can feel his heartbeat through his sweatshirt. I breathe in deeply, breathe in his scent, his warmth. 'Right. Tea, then.' I kiss his cheek, a soft brush of my lips.

He watches as I bustle about in the kitchen. 'I think I might miss having breakfast outside today. If you don't mind?' Jack is resting his head against the doorjamb. 'It might be a bit cold.' He indicates towards me. 'Feel free to freeze outside if you want to, though.'

I hand him his tea. 'I'll give it a miss this morning, although I might have coffee on the terrace later?'

'Knock yourself out!'

Nestled together on the sofa, a blanket pulled over our knees, with a fresh mug of tea and a plate of toast and marmalade, we sit and observe the sky. Fat snowflakes drift down, spiralling when caught in a gust of wind, flurrying when the wind gets a little stronger. We have yet to broach the subject of what we will do if we get snowed in.

'I think my plans might have changed for the rest of today.' I tug the blanket up higher. 'As it mostly involved being outside.'

'I get that.' Jack appears worried. 'Listen, Lily. I know I said I wouldn't abandon you this weekend the way I did last,' he rubs the bridge of his nose and nods out the window, 'but I might have to. You know what British Rail is like. Stops running at the slightest problem.'

'I understand, except we're not having much luck, are we?'

'I disagree.' He snuggles under the blanket. 'I think we are graced by a vast amount of good luck.' He bobs up to kiss the end of my nose. 'Do you think we can meet up after Christmas? Say, the day after Boxing Day?'

'I think we have a date.' I pull him towards me and kiss him fully on the mouth. We are making plans for the future, and though I might not see him over the festive period, we are meeting up soon after. It's enough for me. A win.

We make it back to bed after lunch. A last 'quickie' before Jack has to go. I think we're getting the hang of this sex malarky! Eventually, we have to stir as the light is fading. There might be more snow, meaning he won't be able to return to London. It's not that I don't want him to be here for longer. It's more that I'm not used to having another person in my space for this amount of time. I need to break myself in gently. Six years of solitude and self-reliance can't be undone in a couple of weeks. I shouldn't rush into it and blow it by freaking out. I believe I can have a future with Jack, which is enough to make goosebumps pop out over my skin. I want this so badly, it practically hurts.

Jack nods at the kitchen. 'Did I see cream in your fridge? How about I make us an Irish coffee? As neither one of us is driving. You have a whisky in the cupboard, and if you've got brown sugar, then that's perfect?'

'I have all that. Anything else?'

'A grating of nutmeg?'

'Possibly at the bottom of my spice box, but I can find it.'

Jack puts a coffee on to percolate while I rummage for the spice. It's beginning to feel a lot like Christmas...

.   .   .

'I'll call you Christmas Day if that's all right?' Jack leans down to give me a final, lingering kiss. 'It's been a great weekend, Lily. I enjoyed it no end. I wish... Well, I wish.' He laughs. I detect an uncertain sound to it, and I wonder if his wish included me. Did he wish he could be here for Christmas? Or maybe I could join him at his uncle's? There is still time, but I will never bring the subject up. Christmas is always a touchy subject for me and something I never push for. It is a wonder I managed to get into the Christmas spirit enough to put the decorations up, although it was mainly for Alice and Rose.

'Listen.' He's hauling on his gloves. 'You've got a big day tomorrow. The weather is against you. Make sure you have everything where you want it. Don't leave anything to the last minute, eh?' He stops, as he must have seen the look on my face.

'I never leave anything to the last minute. I have lists about my lists about what I need to do.'

He grins. 'Okay, I meant like me. I'm notoriously bad at getting organised and then run around like a bleedin' headless chicken to get sorted.' He kisses my forehead. 'Enough with the preaching. As I said, good luck tomorrow, and I shall see you the day after Boxing Day.'

'Thanks. Looking forward to it. Now,' I glance at my watch, 'not wanting to shove you out, but you have a train to catch, and it's pretty hairy out there.' I guide him to the door.

'I'll be very careful.'

'Let me know if they have cancelled the train and come back. Okay?' The air outside is chilly as he steps out into the communal corridor.

'Don't worry, I will. I'm not sleeping out in the park in this weather.'

. . .

Jack's call comes through about half an hour later to say the trains are skeleton, though some are still running. He will catch one that will get him back to London by early evening if it all goes to plan.

I'm starting to feel as if a strobe light has been put on in my head. I decide to lie down and take a nap. I don't feel guilty, as it's Sunday, and I've had a busy weekend. Setting the alarm, it's only moments from when I put my head down on my pillow to jolting upright, woken by its strident beeping. Peering at the clock, I can see two hours have whizzed past. It's close to seven, and it's black outside my window. Shaking myself awake, I have a shower, hoping it will invigorate me. There are so many things I must do; I need to figure out where to start. What was the last thing Jack said to me? Ah, yes. I should check all my stuff is ready for tomorrow.

My list is pinned to a corkboard on my desk. I go through it: bag packed, *check*. Phone charged, *check*. Smart clothes and clean underwear, *check*. Scarf and gloves on the hook with my warm coat, *check*. Umbrella, along with winter boots. No slipping and falling trying to impress in heels. *Check*. Oh, and the most important part, my portfolio of paintings. I unzip it and get all the work out to examine again. Lifting the sheet of thin tissue paper off each one, I feel pride. This is all mine. I have made these from nothing. Placing them carefully back into the portfolio, I re-zip it and leave it on the table.

My head still thumping, I crawl back to bed. I pray I'm not going down with anything, as I feel as though I am nailed to the bed. I'm so tired.

Chapter Nineteen

MONDAY, 21 DECEMBER - LOSING MY MIND?

I MUST HAVE SLEPT like the dead, as the alarm goes through two cycles to wake me. I've given myself a lot of time in case I need it. Clambering groggily out of bed, I rush my shower and breakfast, which makes me feel as though I'm not adequately prepared for the coming day. I don't normally have to hand over work this close to Christmas, but the publishing company had to put the date back for some reason.

It's an arduous journey. Checking on the internet, I see trains are delayed, so I ensure I arrive early at Brighton Station to assess the situation. There is a train that will get me into Victoria at a reasonable time, as long as there are no delays or dramas anywhere en route. I phone Mary to update her, not that there is anything I can do except cancel, and this is not an option. I get the impression she's not had an easy time getting into work either. I'm wondering why her phone hasn't melted, the amount of vitriol she is spewing about public transport, the infrastructure of London and the *bloody* government. She lives in Kensington, and I know from experience the city shuts down as easily as the trains. It used to be faster to walk somewhere in the snow in London than crawl along in a bus or car.

Getting a taxi from Victoria to the New Renaissance offices is also an ordeal. Too many people are hailing not enough taxis, although I eventually manage to grab one. It is beginning to snow as I slog up to the building, feet, fingers and nose frozen, battling gusts of icy wind, and with my portfolio acting as a sail, I'm already exhausted. Heads are lowered, and I get the sense people want to be home for Christmas *now*. These last few days are pointless. It'll be Christmas Eve on Thursday, and everyone, including me, wishes we could all slink off home this very minute.

I'm ushered in and offered a coffee, although we don't get that far.

Mary is in her big office, and my portfolio is open on her large, shiny, mahogany desk. We are both staring at it.

'I don't understand,' she says. 'What, exactly, is this, Lily?'

My breathing is erratic, and I need to place both hands on the table to stop myself from falling over. My legs are like rubber. I'm sure I will collapse right here in front of her.

'I don't know—' I put my hand across my mouth. Is that to catch the scream threatening to come roaring out? 'I don't know how this has happened.' I feel tears prickle at the corners of my eyes. 'Mary! I don't know what's going on—'

'I think,' says Mary, 'we need to calm down and talk this through.' She doesn't sound calm.

'*Talk what through?*' I know I sound hysterical. Who wouldn't be in these circumstances? 'All my sodding work is gone, and I don't know where it is!' True, the backing card and the protecting sheet are still there, but the paintings are conspicuously missing.

'I can quite plainly see it is not there.' Mary sits in her oversized, comfy computer chair, although she looks far from comfortable. 'What we have to ascertain then is where *the fuck* is it?'

Mary never jokes, and she never, ever swears. Sweat dribbles down my ribs.

I try to control my breathing. 'That's it. I checked it all last night—'

'Then you must have forgotten to put them back into the portfolio?' She looks like a condemned man offered a lifeline, but I dash it.

'No. I remember putting them all back in and then leaving the portfolio on the table. Mary! You know me. I don't make mistakes like this.'

'Agreed, except you seem to have made one now.' Mary frowns and taps the table with a beautifully manicured nail. It is bright red, and I get the impression she has dipped all her nails in fresh blood. Maybe she's thinking she'll get a second coat this morning? 'Was there anyone else in your flat? Anyone who might have, um, say, moved them without your knowledge?'

'My boyfriend Jack was with me all weekend—'

'A new boyfriend? And why haven't I heard about him until now?' She points at me. 'Could he have had anything to do with this?'

'What? No. In fact, as he left, he told me to check everything was where it should be. I know it was all there after he left.' I nod stupidly. 'Because I checked.'

'Then, Lily, my dear, we have a problem.'

'What the hell do I do?'

'You either find them or replace them. Have you scans of them?'

'Yes, I always scan them, just in case...' I look at her. 'Can you use the scans?'

'I will need to see them, see how you've cropped them—'

'I don't crop. I have the whole thing, the edges and all.'

'I also need to know the resolution you scanned them at. If we are lucky, we might be able to use them. If not, well, I gave you the options.'

'Bollocks!' I hold my hands over my face.

'Ditto!' says Mary.

I long to *shriek* out of the train window all the way home. Am I losing my mind? How could this have happened? But that's not the only thing, is it? Last Tuesday, I found that used bowl in my sink when I returned from the supermarket and then the damaged painting. I don't ever want to go down this line of thought. Has there been someone else in my flat? Add to that the strange noise in the night and the scuff marks on my roof terrace. *What the hell is going on?*

Ripping off my coat and flinging it on the floor, I stand in the middle of my living room, fists clenched and sweating profusely. Think, now. *Think!* Where could they be? I take a deep breath and stare about me. Starting at one corner of the living room, I search in all the obvious places, then I search in the not-so-obvious places, and then I have to look in the most ridiculous places. I do the same in the kitchen, and when I open the freezer, I have the most terrible shock. As expected, the top two drawers are frozen lasagnes and packets of peas, then the third one makes me stumble back. They are all in there. I take them out, crisp and cold. The colours have melted and run as if water has been dribbled all over them. Every single one is ruined. My breath catches in my throat, and I crumple to the floor. I am blinded by my tears. I know they were all in the portfolio when Jack left. So that only leaves me, doesn't it? Did I do this? To myself? The phone ringing makes me jump. Mary. I let it slide from my hand onto the lino. A message pings through. She wants, no, needs to know if I've found the paintings. I have to laugh. Yes, indeedy, I have found them. And to all intents and purposes, I am going utterly mad!

Perhaps a nice cup of sweet tea will make this all better? Make this nightmare go away? No, better than that. A bottle of wine will do the trick.

The only person I trust to call is Alice. She arrives like she's been beamed over. I'm eyeing the second bottle of wine as she takes off her jacket and gloves. 'Fancy a glass?' Am I slurring? I bloody well hope so.

'You look smashed,' she starts. 'But yeah, I'll have one.'

'Smashed? No shit!' I nod and grin at her. 'Alice? Can I ask you a personal question?' I think for a moment. 'I mean, a personal question *about me*?'

'What?'

'Am I mad?' I chew on my bottom lip, tugging at a piece of skin. I make it bleed. 'You know? Crazy-arse bonkers?'

Alice sits on the sofa and pats the space next to her. 'You need to explain what the heck is going on!'

'Yes, I do, and yet, unfortunately, I don't have a blinking' clue!' I hand her a very full glass of wine.

'Lily?' She is talking to me in that particular tone people reserve for frightened children. 'What happened today? Is this to do with Jack—'

'No, no, no. Me an' Jack are fine.'

'Then it's to do with Mary? And your book?'

'Oh yeah. Just a little bit.' I refill my glass, but most of it sloshes over the rim. 'Oopsy.'

'*Lily!*'

'Okay, okay. It's like this.' I close my eyes. 'When I got to the publishing house and opened my portfolio, guess what?'

I watch her face change. 'Oh no. *What?*'

'No, go on. Guess.'

'You know I can't. Just tell me.'

'It was bloody empty. Nothing inside. Nada. Rien. Fuckin' zilch!'

Her hand flies to her mouth. 'You are joking, aren't you?'

'Ha, ha, ha! I wish.' Wine slops down my chin and seeps into my top. 'You know, you've gone so pale you look almost white!'

'God forbid! Listen? Did you leave them behind—'

'Let me stop you there.' I hold up my hand and totter to the table, sloshing wine as I go. 'Here they are! I bet you can't guess where they were? No? Give up? They were in the freezer, all covered in water as if they'd been run under the tap. Isn't that nice?' I fall back onto the sofa.

'This isn't right.' Alice stands and starts to pace around the living room. 'First, the red wine stain on your artwork and then the whole bloody lot is destroyed?'

'Exactamundo.' I wag a finger at her. 'And the only suspect is liddle old me.'

'No, Lily. I know you, and you don't do stuff like this. There has to be another explanation.'

'I think the explanation is staring you in the face.' I point at myself. 'I've gone mad.'

Alice sighs. 'What you need to do now is drink some water and get into bed. I'll be back to check on you before my shift. Are your spare keys still on the hook?'

'Yep.'

Alice helps me to bed after forcing a couple of glasses of water into me. 'I'll work this out. Don't you worry.' She kisses my forehead gently. 'There's something wrong here, Miss Lily the Pink, and I'm going to get to the bottom of it.'

Why the hell did I agree to go to Harry's parents that year for Christmas? Maybe it was because my sister Sophie was so excited to be coming with us? I should have stayed home with my parents, as although we didn't know it then, it was the last Christmas my mum was alive. But we did go, and the consequences blindsided us all.

The day before Christmas Eve, we all stood in St Pancras, having met Sophie off an earlier train, wondering if we would be able to get to Harry's parents for Christmas. Alice had bar work and aimed to catch the last train home that night. I worried she might not make it.

'She'll be cutting it fine,' I confided to Harry.

'It's her decision, and if the worst comes to the worst, she'll stay in the house and come up when she can.'

Sophie made a face. 'On her own? That'd be really miserable.'

Sophie, at eighteen, was four years younger than me and yet, somehow, a lot older. Was this the bane of the elder child? That we used machetes to clear the way, and our younger siblings blithely hopped, skipped and jumped in their designer trainers or stilettos at our heels? Seemingly so. She was smaller and rounder than me, with short-cropped, bleached blonde hair, but we both had hazel-coloured eyes, the same as our mum.

We'd booked tickets for the 8.33 am train, though that wasn't going to happen any time soon. Snow on the tracks meant every train was either delayed or cancelled. Clutching our rucksacks and bags of presents, muffled in scarves, hats and gloves, we stood watching the announcement board with everyone else, our breath huffing in the air. Finally, the train we needed to see rolled in, the passengers disembarked, and when the announcement came, we all rushed up the platform to get seats. We were lucky and found three together. I sat next to Sophie, and Harry faced us.

'Fingers crossed, there will be no more delays.' Harry hauled off his coat but left his woolly scarf on. 'I'll call Dad to come and pick us up when we are within spitting distance. Snow is snow, after all.'

A bulky man thumped into the seat beside him. I saw Harry roll his eyes as the man spread across his seat and started to inch Harry up against the window. Harry jostled back, and the man grunted and frowned. I was glad I had Sophie next to me, as I could elbow her in the ribs with impunity. A few stragglers leapt for the train as the doors slid shut. A sharp jolt meant the train was beginning to move.

'At last,' sighed Sophie. 'How long does the journey take?'

'About two hours,' said Harry, 'but as I said, that's when conditions are perfect.'

Chugging past Camden Town, we pointed out all the places we knew to Sophie. Light snow was fluttering down, and though Sophie and I thought it was magical, I could see Harry was worried.

'If it's snowing here, that probably means it's like blizzard conditions back in Sheffield.'

'Then that's even better.' Sophie clapped her hands together. 'We'll have a proper white Christmas.'

'Not if we're stuck in a cheap, nasty little hotel in Welling-borough over the holidays.'

Sophie looked aghast. 'That's not going to happen, is it, Harry?'

'I hope not.' Harry shrugged. 'I'm looking forward to my mum's Yorkshire pudding and Christmas cake. Not stale cheese and onion crisps and a Crunchie!'

'Don't tease me.' Sophie turned to me. 'He is joking, isn't he?'

'I certainly hope so.' Thinking about it, though, I also felt anxious when we passed by St Albans and then Luton with the snow deepening on either side.

'These are the Chiltern Hills,' said Harry, indicating out of the left-hand window. 'In summer, they are rolling hills of green countryside. Now you can see why I'm concerned we might not make it?'

The rolling hills had been replaced by white. The hedgerows were bumps in the white, the trees poked up, laden with white, and the villages we shot past were heaped with white. It looked as if the whole place had been covered in icing, and we were crossing a gigantic Christmas cake.

There was movement further up the train. The snacks trolley was being wheeled down the aisle.

'Listen,' I said. 'As we had breakfast so long ago in the mists of time, shall we order something now?'

'Okay.' Sophie eyed the contents. 'Is there anything remotely edible? Ooh! Don't they have any alcoholic drinks? We can start celebrating early.'

'Wow!' Harry nodded at me. 'You can see whose sister she is.'

'I may have been first out, but I do believe she has over-taken me.' I rummaged in my bag to find my purse. When the trolley arrived, we got three coffees that were not particularly coffee-like and three limp sandwiches. Harry tweaked out a note and got a packet of Porky Scratchings and three Mars Bars.

'We might need these later.' He winked.

'You mean,' I said, 'when we're stuck in seven feet of snow on the line, the electricity has gone out, and we're all starving?'

Harry grinned. 'It'll be like an episode of *The Walking Dead* in here.'

'Oh, shut it!' Sophie put her headphones on and scrunched her eyes shut. 'Sometimes, I hate you guys.'

One scare later, when we stopped somewhere between Wellingborough and Nottingham and didn't move for ages, we finally got into Sheffield. During the wait, there was the same announcement on a loop that told us nothing. There was a lot of shifting about, general grumblings and people hurrying to the train loos. We were only an hour late, and Harry's dad was waiting outside the station in the car, the windscreen wipers going as fast as they could, though it didn't make much of a dent in the snow gathering on the windscreen. Brushing the snow from our clothes, we shook hands and hugged.

'Wasn't sure if you were going to make it,' he said as we dropped our rucksacks and packages in the boot and climbed thankfully into the car. 'Thought I might have to do an emergency dash cross country to find you all.'

Once we were inside, the heating was switched on, and the smell of damp clothing wafted noisomely around us. Neither Sophie nor I had ever driven through such deep snow. All those jokes about an inch in the south and everything ground to a standstill, but up north, even in a foot, they would only be contemplating getting their winter coats on. That now seemed undeniable. Harry's dad drove us with consummate care along some of the scariest lanes imaginable. The edges were lost in the drifts, hiding hedgerows and gullies. Trees, their branches weighed down with snow, overhung us, at any moment ready to dump their load on us. Under these arches, the gloom deepened, and it felt like we were underwater. It was magical.

Creeping over a humped back bridge, the windscreen wipers squeaking, Harry's dad said, 'Normally, you'd be able to see the dry-stone walling we're famous for.' He indicated out the window. 'But as you can see, the snow has covered it all. Which is a pity.'

'Nearly there,' said Harry, as we drove into a small village, past a pub festooned with twinkling fairy lights, then up the main road with the butcher's, baker's and probably candlestick maker's! The lights were blazing in the quaint tearoom and gift shop, and we could see fuzzy shapes through the misted windows. The post office had a small queue, and I hoped it was to pick presents up, not send them, as it was far too late for anything to arrive in time now. People were scurrying around, pink-cheeked and purposeful, some calling 'hello' and waving to others across the street. Most of the buildings were buff-coloured sandstone and steep-roofed, sections of grey slate visible where the snow had been too laden and slipped off. A tall steepled church was set back, deep tyre marks overlapping along the lane that led up to it. Smoke dribbled from chimneys into a leaden sky. I wondered if Harry's family had a real fire at home. I hoped so.

'There's the cricket pitch,' said Harry, pointing through the trees. 'Got great memories of playing there.'

'We have, lad,' smiled his dad.

Tall stone-clad houses came into sight, and Harry's dad drove up a tiny side street. As he parked, he called over his shoulder, 'Now, none of this Mr Bryson malarky. I want you to call me Ben.' He turned to Harry. 'Not you though, I'm still *sir* to you!' he chuckled throatily.

'Yes, sir,' said Harry, tugging on his fringe.

'Right. Girls? Get your stuff out of the boot, and Harry can get you in. I've got a few things to sort out first. No rest for the wicked.'

Dragging our rucksacks and paraphernalia out, we slipped and slid after Harry as he led us through a small front garden and up five large steps to the door, which had a wreath made from holly with bright red berries hanging on it. His mum must have been watching out for us, as the door was yanked open before we pressed the buzzer.

'Welcome in, you lot. Quick now, get into the warmth with you.' She smiled as she practically hauled us in. 'It's so lovely to see you all again. *Even you, Harry.*' She winked.

'Hi, Mum.' Harry was enveloped in a big hug. 'It's good to be home.'

'Shame your brother couldn't make it.'

'It's quite a hop from Auckland to here. I'm sure he'll make it back at some point.'

'Well, I miss him, that's all.'

Harry patted his mum's back gently. 'We all do, Mum.'

'Get your coats hung up here.' She indicated the coat stand. We stripped off our outer gear and kicked off our boots. The heat was a smack in the face after the cold from outside.

'Leave all your stuff here,' said Harry, 'and we'll get it upstairs in a mo.'

Jostling and bumping, we left our packs under the coat stand, now lilting at an angle from the weight of so many coats and jackets.

'Wow, it's hot!' said Sophie, her cheeks reddening. I could feel my own face heating up and my nose tingled.

'Here we go.' Harry's mum ushered us into the living room.

'You've got a real fire. It's amazing,' I groaned in delight. Logs were piled high in the grate, glowing red and crackling, and more were set ready on the large stone hearth. Christmas decorations and tinsel were wound along the main lintel, which was covered in knick-knacks. Rattan snowflakes hung from wall lamps, and all the cards the family had been sent were hung on a line pinned above the fireplace, held by tiny red pegs.

'Oh, it's so lovely and Christmassy in here!' Sophie gazed around, entranced.

In the corner furthest from the door was a Christmas tree that grazed the ceiling. Fairy lights twined around the branches, and glittery baubles and gold-embellished ornaments twinkled and shone. There were wooden reindeer, snowmen and robins peeping out, and silver tinsel spiralled round and round the tree. On top was a rather lopsided fairy holding a wand with the tiniest bit of glitz still on it. Although she'd seen better days, she was smiling. How old was she? Had she always graced the tree from when Harry's parents were kids? Placed under the tree were presents wrapped in bright paper and golden bows. LED candles glimmered on every surface. Had we stepped into the pages of a Dickens novel?

Harry's mum flapped at us. 'Sit down, you lot, and I'll get the kettle on. Everyone for a brew?'

'Yes, please.'

As she swung into the kitchen, she said over her shoulder, 'Please call me Shirley. I don't want to be called Mrs Bryson. I think Ben might have mentioned this—'

'He did, Mum,' Harry grinned, 'but I have to call him *sir*. So that means I must have to call you *ma'am* then?'

Shirley laughed. 'No, love. Mum is fine by me.'

Cups of tea and slices of homemade Bakewell tart in hand, we sat on the sofa, warmed by the fire. Ben bundled in with plastic bags loaded with stuff he whisked into the kitchen.

'Looks as if you're feeding the five thousand,' said Harry through a mouthful of cake.

'Well, truth be,' said Shirley, 'the aunts are coming tomorrow, and we need to be prepared.'

'Are they still alive?' Harry looked shocked. 'I mean, how old are they? They must be at least a *hundred*?'

'Maybe I should explain.' Shirley grinned. 'We have two great aunts—'

'Or are they great, great aunts?' queried Ben. 'I can never remember.'

'Very, very old aunts,' laughed Harry.

Shirley tutted. 'Anyway, they're coming for tea tomorrow. They're twins and have been inseparable even though they married. They come to us on every alternate Christmas Eve and then spend Christmas Day with one of their grandsons, who lives in Sheffield. They are teeny-tiny dots of things that eat like ravening wolves!'

Ben said, 'then straight down to the pub on Boxing Day, and no, I'm not joking.'

'Every time I see them,' said Harry, 'I tell them to write their memoirs, but they tell me they're too busy having fun. The stories they've told us over the years are incredible.'

'They lived through the war,' continued Ben, 'and they went out with the army lads, though they never let on there were two of them. They wore those young men out.'

'They were so naughty,' smiled Shirley. 'I think the war years made them realise nothing lasts and to make the most of each and every moment you have.'

'Good motto,' said Sophie. 'We should all live that way.'

We sat and chatted, warmed by the fire, until we moved into the kitchen for a late lunch.

'Shirley?' I said, 'Did you cook all this yourself?' I waved my hand across the table.

'Every last scrap.' Shirley nodded.

'Then I can see where Harry gets his culinary prowess from.'

'That's a lovely compliment, Lily love.' Shirley smiled at

Harry. 'We made sure both our boys could fend for themselves. I know Harry's had his moments of eating Pot Noodles, but at least we know he can cook a good spread if needs be.'

'Harry's a fabulous cook,' I said.

We chatted, idling the hours away, sitting comfortably in the living room, until Ben ordered a supper of take-away Chinese, which we followed with a few games of scrabble. There was no TV, iPad or computer, and we didn't dare get our mobiles out. It again felt as if we'd stepped back in time. The radio had the volume on low, and muted Christmas music slid out. When we started to yawn, we were shown to our rooms.

'So sorry to be lightweights,' I said, 'but it's been a long day.'

Harry had already taken our packs and presents upstairs, and he sheepishly told me Sophie and I would be sharing the spare room, which had twin beds. Which meant I would not be sharing with him.

'Ah!' I grinned. 'It's okay. I understand.'

'Mmm,' he rolled his eyes. 'They didn't want to assume, so they plumped for safe, not sorry... and embarrassed.'

'What time are we expected up?'

'I'm sure I'm allowed to bring in a cup of tea for you both. It won't be before eight-thirty.'

As I kissed Harry goodnight, I could see Sophie making lewd faces out of the corner of my eye.

That was the Christmas to end all Christmases. It started off so well, but how were we to know how it would end? My fateful meeting with *Psycho Jo*. The fact both Sophie and I missed the last Christmas with our mum. And the other thing that shattered both mine and Harry's hearts to the point where we couldn't glue it all back together again. The point where I must have lost him.

And now, in the present, I am still trying to figure out how my illustrations ended up wet and spoiled in my freezer. This experience is not something I will bounce back from lightly. There are too many connotations here, and some of them are frightening. Should I speak to Sophie? No, she's dealing with her own stuff and taking on Dad's as well. She has a husband and a little kid to look after, so even though I know she would try to help me, I believe it's too much for her. Isn't Rose something to do with mental health? Should I ask her opinion?

Alice is stumped. She has gone through every iteration of what could have happened, and none are good.

'Is there anyone who... I don't know how to put this—'

'Say it, Alice.'

'Well, anyone you might have pissed off? Anyone who might want to harm your career?'

'I don't think so. And if I have, do you think they would advertise their hate or whatever on a bloody big billboard?' I sigh. 'Sorry, did not mean to take it out on you.'

'We're missing something that's right in front of us.'

'Like what?'

'I have no idea, though we've got to get to the bottom of this, Lily, in case they try again.'

'Oh, thanks, Alice. That was one thing I hadn't even contemplated, and now it's like a big beacon shining in my mind!'

'Sorry. I didn't mean to upset you, but we should consider all the options. Even the difficult ones.'

'Have I got an enemy? Only one person hates me, and I have

no idea what happened to her. *Do you?*' I close my eyes. I can see her face that day. *Gloating*. 'It's been years. Why would she suddenly pop out of the woodwork now? It doesn't make sense.'

'No, but maybe it's time to find out?'

'Can we do this after Christmas? It's too much for me right now.'

'Sure. We'll have a lovely Crimbo and then get back on it afterwards. Okay?'

Chapter Twenty

WEDNESDAY, 23 DECEMBER - BUSES IN A ROW

MY PHONE RINGS. 'Hiya. It's me,' says Alice.

I am sitting at my desk, slogging through some last-minute details for Mary.

'I know it's you because your name pops up when you call. You okay?' I haven't exactly recovered from my shock, but as I didn't know what to do about it, I put it to the back of my mind. To work through later, or it would drive me bonkers. The main thing is, Mary has accepted the scans of my illustrations, just about, with minimal grumbling. In other words, saved my bacon. If I'd messed it up, I would have had to start again, and the time-line would have been messed up, and then *everything would have been messed up*. Let alone the thought it might put my whole career in jeopardy. I'm relying on that money to pay the mortgage and all the mounting Christmas bills. Getting a bank loan would snowball. Funny how you can spend so much and have very little of worth to show for it. I promised myself I would never get into borrowing from Peter to pay Paul. I know too many people who have gone down that route.

'Listen,' continues Alice. 'You know I said I wasn't sure

what to do about Christmas? Well, my lot have decided to go on a cruise. Without inviting me, I might add—'

'Would you have wanted to go?'

'Course not!' The scorn in her voice is palpable. 'What do you take me for?'

'They probably knew that, and more to the point, I gather you haven't told them about Matt yet?'

'Not exactly, no.'

'Then they've also assumed you'd be spending Christmas with him?'

There's a hesitation. 'He moved out last night. Gone to stay with a mate, so he said.'

'It might be for the best. Give the both of you a breathing space?'

'Maybe. Anyway, what I'm trying to say is, would you like to have Christmas with me? I don't know if you've finalised any plans yet, and I thought – hey – I can but ask?'

The relief of not screwing up my mortgage and ending up a homeless person on the street, scavenging through other people's wheelie bins, makes me a bit euphoric. 'Hell yeah. I went to Sophie's last year, so I'm sure they won't miss me.' That might be a lie, though some part of me wants to not have to bother; no catching unreliable trains, no dragging mountains of bags and packages, no having to meet Dad's possible new fling... no missing Mum...

'Okay. Then we need to plan—'

'Don't be daft. You have never planned anything in your life. You're such a wing and a prayer girl, whereas I have lists and am organised. I have got most of what we need already in.' I stop for a moment. 'Sorry, did you want to come here or go to yours?'

'I think in my current mood, I'd rather be anywhere than here right now.'

'Here it is, then. Goody! We're going to have such fun!'

When the phone rings again, I assume it's Alice calling back.

'What have you forgotten now?'

'Um,' says Jack, 'not sure, really.'

'Oh, sorry, Jack. I thought you were Alice. I mean, she's just called, so I assumed – Oh, never mind. How are you?'

'I'm fine. You know I said I was going to be at my uncle's place for Christmas?'

'Okay... yes...'

There's silence for a moment.

'Oh, right.' Jack clears his throat. 'What I'm trying to say is, he has cancelled due to the family now having a godawful flu. So...' He clears his throat again. 'Well, what I'm trying to ask is whether you'd like to spend Christmas with me?'

There is another silence as I'm somewhat stupefied.

'Lily? Are you still there?'

'Yes, I, er—'

'If you don't want to, I will not be upset. We've only met recently and—'

'No, no. It's just Alice, you remember Alice? My best friend? She rang a moment ago and asked if I'd like to spend Christmas with *her*. Buses, you know? Either none or three in a row.'

Jack makes a strange sound. 'Right. Okay. Why isn't she with her boyfriend? I remember you saying he'd moved in with her after you moved out?'

I sigh. 'They split up recently.'

'Sorry to hear that. Bummer at Christmas time.'

I close my eyes. Is this too weird to ask him? Nothing ventured, nothing gained. 'Could we spend it together? You, me and Alice? Her family are going on a cruise, so she's got nowhere else to be. I'd feel bad if I blew her out now.'

'Bros over hos, or whatever that saying is?' He sniggers. 'Or is it sisters over misters?'

'That's it, kind of.'

'What if we invite a fourth person? Balance the numbers and make it less like Alice is a gooseberry?'

'I can ask her. Who else do we invite?'

'I could invite one of my mates—'

'A bloke? No, that wouldn't work as she'd think we were trying to set her up.'

'All right. What about any of your friends? Someone she won't worry about. Someone she's okay with?'

'Well, we could see if Rose is here over Christmas?'

'Rose?'

'A new friend we've just met. I mean, she's lovely, and she doesn't know many people here yet. Shall I run it past Alice first? See if she's in, and then see if Rose can come?'

'I'll leave it with you. Whatever the outcome, it's fine by me.'

'I'll get back to you asap, Jack.'

I can hear the doubt in Alice's voice. 'Are you sure you want me and Rose there? At your first Crimbo with Mr Perfect? Won't that cramp your style?'

'Not at all. In a way, I'd prefer that. It takes the onus off me. I don't have to try so hard. You know what I'm like!'

'Oh, unfortunately, I do.'

'So, am I calling Rose?'

'Go for it.'

. . .

I return Jack's call. 'Alice and Rose say they'd love to come. Am I presuming we're having it at mine? I'm pretty prepared for a nuclear winter, so a Christmas do is easy-peasy.'

'Nuclear winter? You really are one of a kind, Lily.'

'That I am.'

He pauses. 'Sorry, it's remiss of me not to ask how Monday went?'

My head spins for a moment, and I say nothing.

'Lily? Is everything all right?'

'Yeah, it is now.'

'What does that mean?'

'I had a bad day on Monday, but I don't want to talk about it. I need to concentrate on getting Christmas sorted and make sure I haven't missed out the obvious.'

'Like turkey? Are we having turkey?'

'I expect so. If that's what everyone wants. I'm happy with any meat.'

'I'm just happy...'

I smile. 'Good to hear.'

'I'm aiming for Christmas Eve late afternoon or evening, depending on the bloody trains. I'll call you when I get in.'

'I'll be here.'

I have so much still to do. Having spoken to the group, I get the feeling no one is particularly fond of turkey, so I go straight out this afternoon and ask in my local butchers if they have anything special. The butcher produces a fat leg of something.

'Wild boar,' he says, pride in his voice. 'Organic and certified.'

'How do I cook that? Is it the same as pork?'

'Because it's a wild creature, it's got less fat and can be tougher, so you have to salt it first for a few hours and then marinate it for a good thirty hours or so in wine and other stuff. Look up a recipe online as there are loads.'

'I'll have it, thanks.'

Red wine – whole bottle; juniper berries – thankfully I rummage in my spice box and find an old bottle; orange juice; bay leaves; thyme – should be fresh, except I've only got dried; cloves, but not too many of them; peppercorns – got loads of those; carrots; onions; stock; red currant jelly – need to find a jar in Sainsbury's. Sorted and ready to go. If this isn't one helluva delicious dinner, I don't know what is!

Chapter Twenty-One

THURSDAY, 24 DECEMBER

CHRISTMAS EVE, the call from Jack comes through about six.

'I'll be at yours by about half six. The shops are still open, so is there anything else you'd like me to pick up? I have brought bits and bobs with me, though I wondered if there was something you'd missed?'

'Thanks, but I think I've got way too much as it is. Just concentrate on getting here. Can't wait to see you.'

I'm re-packing one of my cupboards when the doorbell downstairs rings. I race down and tug the door open.

'Happy Christmas, gorgeous.' Jack is like a panting dog as he comes into the communal hallway. He's bundled in a winter greatcoat with the collar up, a soft scarf and black fingerless gloves. His head is bare, and I notice his ears are pink. As I gather him into my arms, I can feel the chill on him from outside.

'Come in and get warm.' We take the stairs two at a time, sniggering like kids. I kick my flat door shut. 'God, it's cold out there.'

Dropping his holdall and myriad bags onto the floor, he

shrugs off his coat and then pulls me back into his arms. Our kiss is long and deep.

'Bloody trains,' he says as we pull apart. 'I aimed to get here earlier, but not with British Rail at the helm.'

'You're here now, and that's all that matters.' I gesture at all the bags. 'What's in all these, then?'

'Now, now.' He wags his finger and makes tutting sounds. 'I'll go through these, as there are things you don't need to see. Yet!' He winks saucily at me. 'There are other things we need to get out.' He rummages and out come boxes of After Eight, Turkish Delight, dates, bags of cashew nuts, walnuts, peanuts, a slab of Brie and a box of Camembert, two bottles of red wine, and last but not least, a good quality bottle of Champagne.

'Good God! You've got a Mary Poppins bag!'

'Yep.' He rubs at his shoulder and waves the bottle of Champers. 'Got any space for this, as it's for us and not for sharing?'

'If I haven't, I will have.' In the kitchen, I turf out a carton of orange juice and slide in the bottle.

'It's already cold,' says Jack, 'so it won't take long.' He picks up the rest of his stuff and takes it into the bedroom. He's at home here, and that makes me glad. No standing on ceremony.

A simple supper is pre-prepared, so we tuck in, opening one of the bottles, a deeply red Cabernet Sauvignon.

I don't want to mention work, not his and especially not mine, so we chat about inconsequential things, although it has to be broached at some time. As I'm washing up, Jack is drying.

'So what happened on Monday? You sounded upset.'

I stop washing and groan. 'I don't even know where to begin. I'm not sure I want to unload on you, as it is Christmas Eve, after all.' I tilt my head to stare up at him. 'And if I get going, I will unload, and you'll be sorry you asked.'

'Isn't that what partners are for?'

I register the word 'partner', and my heart does a somersault.

'Okay. I checked everything, as you advised, on Sunday night, but by the time I got to my publishers, when I looked in my portfolio, all my work was missing. All of it.'

The look on his face says it all. 'Oh my God! How the hell did that happen? You're telling me it was all there when you checked on Sunday?'

I nod.

'But it had gone on the Monday? That doesn't make sense. *At all.*'

'No. It doesn't and I still can't get my head around what happened—'

'Have you found them? I mean, were they here when you got back?'

'Yep.' I turn from him, as I don't want him to see my face.

'Well, where were they? Did you get them out to check them and then somehow leave them on the table or whatever?'

'Not quite.'

'What does that mean? Lily? Talk to me.' He pulls my face around so he can look into my eyes. 'Where did you find them?'

'In the freezer drawer. Third from the top. They were all water damaged.' I drag in a deep breath. 'And completely unusable.'

'*No way!*' Jack shakes his head. 'There's no way that could happen.'

'Well, it did.'

'How?'

I close my eyes to stop the tears. 'As I was the only one in here, I suppose it must have been me.'

'That doesn't make sense, either. Why would you destroy your own work?'

'I have no idea. Maybe I'm going mad.' I maintain eye contact to see his reaction. He appears shocked, all right. Maybe

I shouldn't have told him, although if I was in his shoes, I might need a heads up I was dating a crazy person.

'How have you left it with your publisher? Oh, what's her name now?'

'Mary. She graciously said I could use my backup scans. I don't know what I'd have done if they'd been useless... Likely lost my contract with them. Maybe even lost my career altogether.'

'You had back-up scans?' He glances at the computer.

'Yeah, thank God, or I'd probably have reneged on my mortgage and lost the flat, along with my career.'

'Oh, Lily! I'm so sorry, but it turned out all right in the end. That's the main thing here.'

'Yep.' I finish washing the dishes. *I rather think the main point might be that I'm losing my mind.* 'I'd prefer if we don't talk about this again? I want a nice time with you, not to be the downer in the room.'

'Of course. Whatever you want.' He kisses the end of my nose gently. 'How about a glass of that fizzly-pop in the fridge? Must be cold enough by now?'

'I will never turn down a glass of fizzly-pop.'

Tonight, I am naughty. Jack is dead to the world when I creep to the loo. The bedroom curtains are pulled open, and the moonlight is streaming through the window onto his face. He is beautiful, and I want to catch it forever. On the way back, I grab my phone and take a photo of him sleeping. He stirs but doesn't wake. I have a picture of my angel boy.

This memory is hard to look at. The juxtaposition between this Christmas Eve with Jack and the one Sophie and I experienced that year in Sheffield with Harry. As I said before, hindsight is a wonderful thing, and it's no good wishing we'd stayed at home. Wishing will never change what happened.

After a delicious cooked breakfast, Shirley drove to pick up the aunts. I was astounded how no one seemed to worry about the snow piled up that would have generally crippled the south.

'We have salt trucks,' said Harry, 'and we're prepared. All you softie southerners freak out at a couple of snowflakes. In fact, you are snowflakes... get it?'

Both Sophie and I stared at him, stony-faced.

The ancient aunties were finally ensconced in the living room, chatting and catching up. They might have been a hundred or so, yet they acted like children, squabbling over the best seat, nagging about who'd forgotten to pick up what, their eyes twinkling in merriment. I'd never seen anyone as wrinkly and frail looking as these two old ladies, as they scrabbled into the living room and bickered light-heartedly over everything.

After helping them get settled, Harry whispered, 'I need to pop out to check something. I'll be back in a bit. Okay?'

'Yeah, sure. We're fine.'

The thing for Sophie and me was that the windows in the living room were locked shut, the door was pulled closed to stop any drafts, and both aunties had lit up a cigarette the moment they came through and had chain-smoked since that point. Lilac smoke curled towards the ceiling until we couldn't see the fairy on top of the tree. Shirley was in the kitchen, and wonderful smells wafted out every time the door opened. She'd given all of us a small glass of sherry, but while the aunties sipped, Sophie and I drank ours almost immediately.

'Poor old Madge,' said one auntie before proceeding to cough for a couple of minutes.

'What about her?' said the other, lighting her fag from the glowing tip of the last one.

'She's had her leg amputated.'

'Again?'

'Eh?'

'I thought she'd already had one lopped off?'

'No, that was Mildred.'

'Oh. Right. So, Madge? How is she?'

'Eh? She's had her leg amputated, so I expect she's not feeling that bright right now.'

'I suppose not,' nodded the other one. 'Like Glenda, she got throat cancer. Now talking through some dreadful thingummy stuck in her throat. She sounds like an old man now.'

'She always did.'

I glanced at Sophie, who was staring at the old ladies with her mouth open. I wondered if she was horrified or lapping it up, as if watching a social documentary. I could never tell with her. Sophie has asthma, and this environment couldn't be doing her any good. Anyway, where was Harry? He'd been gone for quite a while now. In fact, where were any of the men?

'Soph? I just need to look into something. Try not to stay in here too long, eh?'

She nodded; but I noticed her eyes were a little glazed.

Shirley was beavering in the kitchen, taking trays out of the oven using Christmassy oven mitts, and the smell of freshly baked cakes made my mouth water. She turned to me, 'You all right, love?'

'Yeah, fine. I wondered where Harry is. I haven't seen him for a while.'

'Oh, him and his dad are down the pub. They like to have a jar in the afternoon before tea.'

'What? They're down the pub?' I held out my hands. 'Why weren't Sophie and I invited?'

Shirley paused from cutting and spreading butter icing on tiny fairy cakes. 'It's always been a tradition the women sit in and have a sherry, and the men clutter off down the pub to stop getting underneath our feet. Never thought you two might wish to go...' She frowned. 'But why wouldn't you? Tell you what, get going now, and you'll be in time for a couple before teatime.'

'Where is the pub?'

'Straight down the road to the left, past all the shops. You can't miss it. It's the only one in the village. You must have seen it as you came in with Dad... I mean Ben.'

Sophie pushed into the kitchen and coughed. 'Sorry, I had to get a breath of air.'

'Okay, I know where it is.' I half turned towards Sophie. 'We're off down the pub, Soph.'

'Great.' She coughed again.

'Thanks, Shirley.' I pointed at Sophie. 'It's just Sophie has asthma, and I don't think she should be in all that smoke. I don't mean to be rude or anything.'

'Dearest Lord.' Shirley shook her head. 'Those two have smoked a pack of ciggies every day since they were girls in the war. Never stopped. Not for a day. They also drink a couple of whiskys even now, and they're hitting a hundred. Goes to show the doctors are not always right about stuff.'

'That's incredible,' said Sophie. 'I hope I'm like them when I'm their age.'

'Not sure I'll even make it to their age. Come on,' I tugged Sophie out. 'See you in a bit, Shirley.'

'Wrap up warm,' shouted Shirley, 'and make sure the menfolk come back on time. It's never happened before, so I doubt it will this time.' She sighed. 'I can but hope!'

· · ·

Slogging through the snow, I looked about me. Rolling hills blanketed in white could be seen at the ends of twisting little lanes. We seemed to be nestled in a valley. Most of the houses and cottages had smoke coiling out of their chimneys, and we could smell wood smoke in the wind. The sky was a sullen grey, but at least it wasn't snowing now.

'Isn't it pretty here?' I breathed in a lungful of air. 'And it's so fresh. Way nicer than London.'

'You're not going to come and live up here with Harry? Are you?' Sophie looked horrified at the thought.

'God! Where did that come from? Highly unlikely, as I know Harry was desperate to move away—'

'Why? As you said, it's lovely here.'

'I know, although I think if you've lived here, or a place like this, all your life, then it can become boring or jaded or whatever. London is the antithesis to here, isn't it?'

'Yeah, I suppose so. Perhaps you have to go away for long enough to be able to come back and appreciate what you left behind.'

'Wow! That's deep, Soph.'

'Yeah. I'm right philosophical, me! Look, there it is.' Sophie nudged me.

The pub was beamed and craggy looking, with angles slightly askew. Piles of snow encased the deeply sloping roof. A wooden sign, creaking in the slight wind, showed a magnificently antlered stag.

'Called The Stag, then, is it?' Sophie grinned at me.

'Funny that.' I pushed through the heavy wooden front door into a dim interior. It took a moment for my eyesight to adjust. A fire crackled and spat in a massive hearth. Whoever had done the decorations must have bought the whole Christmas decorations store. Sparkly things were hanging everywhere, with entwined lights and garlands of twisted tinsel. It smelt of wood smoke, beer and damp clothes. A traditional pub with burgundy flock wallpaper, a large dark wood bar and mirrored shelving showing glittery bottles of the hard stuff. The lights were muted, and there were, thankfully, no pool table or fruit machines plink-plonking in the background.

The sturdy tables and heavy chairs were filled with people. I thought the women were meant to be back home cooking and grumbling? Slugging back the sherry, thankful their men had got out of the house for a bit and left them in peace? But they all seemed to be here, not stuck in the nineteen fifties. I scanned for Harry and his dad, although it was easy to spot them. There seemed to be some sort of shouting match at the bar.

Alice and Harry were standing at the counter. Ben was next to Harry. A girl, who had her back to me, stood in front of them all. The surrounding lights lit up her hair a deep red and orange, where it cascaded down her back as if it was on fire. I couldn't catch the words, though she sounded angry. I was as surprised as all of them when she threw her drink into Alice's face.

'*Fuck you, you meddling bitch!*' Well, I certainly heard that!

'*Jesus wept!* What is the matter with you, you *psycho*?' Alice spat onto the floor and headed across the room. She looked mad as hell.

'Oy!' shouted the barman. 'We'll have none of that here.'

'*Alice?*' I hurried to catch up with her. 'Are you okay?'

Alice raised an eyebrow. 'I'm dripping with someone else's drink, so maybe not.' She wiped her face with her sleeve. 'I need to wash this off. Give me a moment, and I'll be out. Harry's over there,' she indicated the bar, 'but be aware, he's not a happy bunny either.'

'What the hell is going on?'

'I'll leave him to tell you.' She paused. 'Merry bloody Christmas, Lily.'

I turned just in time to see the figure, who had her back to me, slap Harry hard. He stumbled, but his dad caught him.

'Now then, young lady!' His dad waved his finger at her. 'That's enough now!'

'Serves him right, the *prick*.' She turned, and at the same time, she pulled a hoodie up over her head. With her face lowered, she barged past me, bumping hard into my shoulder. She pulled the door shut behind her so forcefully, the windows rattled.

I searched for Sophie, who had sidled up behind me. 'Good. There you are. Well, this is a cracking Christmas Eve, isn't it? Who the hell was that?'

'I'm hoping Harry will tell us.' Sophie's eyes were wide.

'Lily. Sophie.' Harry beckoned us over. 'Sorry you had to witness that.'

'Whatever that was, it looked serious?' I reached for his face, but he pulled away from me. 'Are you all right?'

'Sure. Listen, half the pub is watching, so can I get you two a drink and then we can sit down, and I'll explain?'

'No call for that sort of behaviour,' grumbled Ben.

'I'll give her that one for free,' said Harry, eyes cast down.

Ben smiled ruefully. 'It's not always as colourful as this. What can I get you?'

'I'll get these, Dad.' Harry held up his hand. He looked a bit shaken. I needed to know who this woman was and why she'd slapped him one. And why he'd given her a free pass?

'Next one, son, eh?' Ben shook his head. 'Girls? What would you like?'

'Er, a pint of lager for the both of us?' I looked at Sophie, and she nodded. 'Whatever you've got here. Thanks, Ben.'

'No worries.' He flagged the barman down and ordered five more pints. 'Need a pick-me-up after so much drama.'

Shuffling to an empty table, away from most of the people

still staring at us, we sat down. Alice charged out of the toilet and joined us.

'What an absolute *clusterfuck!*'

'*Alice!*' Ben huffed. 'Language.'

'True, though.' She sat down with a thump.

'That's as maybe. But it's Christmas Eve, and we should have forgiveness in our hearts.'

Alice snorted. 'You do whatever makes you happy, but if I see her again soon, I'll thump her one!'

'Who is she?' I looked at everyone around the table. 'Why is she so angry?'

'She,' said Harry, 'is my ex-girlfriend—'

'His childhood sweetheart...' Alice ground the words out.

Harry glared at Alice. 'And as you might have gathered, we didn't break up amicably.'

'No shit!' said Sophie. 'Oops, sorry, Ben.'

It hit me. She must be the ex-girlfriend Alice had told me about. The one who Harry broke up with by sending her a text. Well, she was obviously still mad at him. I'd probably still be pretty narked, but I wasn't sure if I'd go so far as whacking him one in front of everyone down the local pub. And hadn't it been years ago? Obviously, she could hold a grudge. Or maybe it was something else entirely. I needed to find out.

Ben rolled his eyes and took a swig of his pint.

Sophie stared at Alice. 'Why is she so angry at *you*?'

'That'll be because she thinks I broke her and Harry up.'

'Did you?' I asked. Then I recalled what Alice had told me. That Alice thought she was a nutter and had her claws in him in a way you wouldn't believe. What did she say? That she was like a rabid stalker.'

'Absolutely!

'Wow!' I said. 'What did she do?'

'Argh! Harry rubbed his hands across his face. 'What *didn't* she do! She didn't want me to have any female friends, including Alice. I mean, Alice is my cousin, for crying out loud!'

'She was jealous to the nth degree and back again.' Alice shook her head.

Harry continued. 'She would check my phone for messages, delete stuff she didn't like the sound of, so I missed loads of things because I didn't know about any of it.'

'She even rang some of us back,' said Ben, 'and told us what she thought of us.'

'She also followed him,' said Alice, 'when he came home from his job.'

Harry nodded. 'I worked in the tea-shop at weekends and summer holidays—'

'And she'd pop up if he ever dared to meet me.'

A muscle twitched in Harry's jaw. 'Screaming mad shit – sorry, Dad – but she was crazy.'

'I know, lad.' Ben nodded. 'As I said, she even had a go at me and Shirley. Imagine that! Your mother's a sweetheart and was very upset. The names she called this family.' His glance slid to Alice.

'All she wanted,' said Harry, 'was for me to spend all my time with her and her family. It was as if they owned me or something.'

'Yeah,' said Alice, 'like you were their pet dog.'

'They were all an unpleasant bunch,' said Ben. 'Never had much time for the lot of them.'

Harry wiped his sleeve across his mouth. 'It wasn't all her fault though, was it? She didn't stand a chance with her family.'

'We all have a choice, Harry.' Alice gulped her drink. 'No matter what our background is.' Turning to me, she said, 'Best keep you out of her way, or she'll probably rip your face off.'

'Does she know about me? That I'm Harry's girlfriend?'

'If she doesn't, she will do.' Ben motioned across the pub.

'It's a small village, and everyone knows everyone and everything that is going on.'

'Dad?' inquired Harry. 'Did you tell anyone that I was bringing Lily up here for Christmas?'

Ben sank into his pint, and we leaned forward for his answer.

'*Dad?*'

'Might have mentioned it to a couple of friends.'

'Then everyone knows,' said Alice. 'Gossip is like wildfire in places like this. We'll have to be careful and not let Lily and Sophie out of our sight.'

'That sounds pretty scary,' said Sophie. 'And could I point out I'm not Harry's new squeeze? I should be left out of this.'

'New squeeze? Thanks for that, Sophie.' I poked her. 'May *I* point out that no one knows which one of us is Harry's new squeeze. So, you're in the line of fire too.'

'Don't joke about this, Lily.' Harry closed his eyes for a moment. 'When we broke up, she took it badly.' At least he had the grace to look sheepish, even if he wasn't forthcoming with why she might have taken it badly. 'You have no idea what she's capable of.'

'Okay. But I kind of wish you'd warned us about her.'

'I know. I'm sorry. Someone said she was still in Edinburgh, where she trained to be a teacher. She must have done the same as me. Come back home after graduating.' Flexing his fingers, he said, 'If I'd known she'd be here at the same time, I wouldn't have come.'

'Hey!' Ben gave Harry a disapproving look. 'We can't and won't let ourselves be bullied into doing stuff. Or not doing stuff. Otherwise, what we're saying is this young slip-of-a-thing can control our lives.'

'Happy Christmas to us all.' I raised my glass. 'And here's to not being scared off by nutters?'

'Hear, hear,' said Ben. We all clinked glasses.

'Sorry,' said Alice, turning to me. 'I bumped into Harry and Ben earlier, and we were about to call you to come down when it all kicked off with Jo—'

'Jo? That's her name?'

'Yeah.' Harry sniggered. 'I didn't mean to leave you both with the aunties. We wanted to do a quick recce first and a good thing too.'

'Luckily,' said Alice, 'Harry had a bad feeling and wanted to check if she was here before bringing you both down to the pub.'

'It's all fun and games up north,' said Sophie, putting on a horrible Yorkshire accent.

'Not cool,' said Harry.

'Sorry.'

Two pints later, we rolled back to Harry's house. Alice's mum came to pick her up, and as she clambered into the car, she waved and shouted, 'I'll pop by tomorrow morning before Christmas dinner.'

It seemed a longer walk back, what with all the slipping, skidding and laughing.

'Not bad timing,' said Shirley. 'Well done, you girls. Normally, they stumble in after I've driven the aunties home—'

'They're still here?' said Ben. There was such a layering of despondency in his voice I nearly laughed.

'Don't be mean, Ben Bryson!' Shirley's fists were on her hips.

'I only meant it's tricky to sit through all their tales of death and embrocation.' He held his hand over his face. 'Makes me feel icky, you know? Especially if we have blancmange!'

'Come on, now,' chided Shirley. 'The table is set, and the aunties are nearly done. You can all wash up, and then, while I drive them home, you can be the second serving.' She chuckled. 'That's if they've left you anything.'

'Thanks, love.' Ben grinned at her. 'I appreciate that.'

We took it in turns to pop upstairs to the bathroom to freshen up. By then, the ancient aunties had finished their tea and were being helped into their coats.

'One for the road?' cackled one of them.

'Be gone with you,' laughed Shirley. 'What are you two like?' She shooshed them out of the front door as if they were a couple of chickens, with Harry and Ben helping them down the steps and to the car. There was a honk of the horn, and Shirley slewed out onto the road.

As tea was set up, we sat down at the table and tucked in.

'Did Shirley make all this?' Sophie gestured at the spread on the table.

'She surely did.' Ben winked at us. 'Get it? Surely? Shirley?'

'Good grief, Dad!' Harry shook his head..

'She's a fantastic cook.' I nodded. 'Can I have that last fairy cake?'

'Go for it,' said Harry.

Having taken one bite, I was startled when there was a noise at the back door. Shattered glass sprayed across the lino as a large rock crashed through the window.

'Harry?' The voice outside in the garden was strident. *'Yer a fucking, lying bastard!'*

'Oh, no!' Harry rose so fast his chair fell back. 'Not *her* again.'

'What the heck does she think she's doing?' Ben had also risen, and he was squeezing around the table. He looked mad, fists balled, and a grimace across his face changed him completely.

Harry yanked the door open, just as the girl we'd seen in the pub shoved her way in.

'Which one of these slags is she?' She poked at Sophie, who reared back. '*You*, you fucking bitch?'

'Me!' I stood and faced her. 'If you have a problem, it's with me.' In the light of the kitchen, I could see her eyes were a vivid, luminous blue lined in kohl, black lines streaking down her cheeks, and her pretty face was a mask of hate and anger. Her red hair tumbled down her back, and again, she gave the impression of being on fire.

'Oh, I've got a problem, all right.' Lunging, she tried to smack me in my face. I saw it coming and dodged but I stumbled backwards and cracked my elbow on the windowsill behind me. She gobbed a big blob of spittle at me, which landed on my dress. 'Harry's mine. He'll always be mine—'

Sophie cried out. 'You're disgusting.'

'Fuck off, Jo!' Harry pulled her around and yelled into her face. 'Get it through your thick skull I was never yours and will never, ever be yours. *Ever!*'

'Yer a chicken, Harry. You loved me but you dumped me like a coward. A fuckin' text message, for God's sake! I know you didn't mean it. It was her, that bitch, Alice. She set you against me—'

Harry stepped back, face white and his jaw grinding. 'I did love you but that was before I knew what kind of person you were. All the horrible stuff you did. Now get out before we call the police on your scrawny little arse!'

'You promised me—'

Harry grabbed her and started to propel her towards the door. 'I should call the police. You've smashed our window and attacked my girlfriend—'

'Attacked her?' It was a shriek. 'She ain't seen nothing yet.'

'Go home.' I'd never seen Harry so angry, his face leached of colour, his lips thin.

Struggling against him, she cried, 'You promised me we'd be together forever and you'd never leave me!'

'I was twelve, for God's sake!' Harry stopped and let her go. 'You can't hold a kid to a promise he made half his life ago. I don't know how many times I have to say this, Jo. I don't love you. I will never be with you, and you have to understand that now. No more of this.'

Jo turned to me. 'He'll never be yours. You're nothing but a thieving bitch.'

'And you're a psycho!' I was shaking and clung to Sophie, who stood defiantly in front of me as protection. I hated showing how frightened I was of her, of her sheer hate and fury.

'Get out of my house,' Ben pointed to the back door, 'or so help me, I will call the police.'

Jo spun and stomped out, screaming, *'I'll get you in the end. All of you. That bitch Alice too.'* The back door slammed behind her.

Standing like statues, it took a minute for us to come alive.

'We *should* call the police.' Harry spun from his dad to me.

'No, please don't call the police on my account.' I sat down, my legs quivering. It was incredible how shaky I felt, and pain was ricocheting up my elbow to my shoulder. I clutched my arm tight to me.

Sophie reached out to me. 'You're hurt, Lily.'

'I whacked my elbow trying to get out of her way.'

'I'll get some ice.' Harry delved in the freezer and held out a packet of peas. I wrapped the bag around the bit that was throbbing. 'She's in a right state. It's like she's a stuck record. But,' and he looked shamefaced, 'I have to admit I didn't help the situation. She's right. I did end our relationship with a text message.'

'I know.' I held out my hand to him. 'Alice told me.'

'Ah!' he closed his eyes for a second. 'So, I presume she told you what I did next?'

'Yep.'

Sophie piped up, 'What did you do, Harry?'

I wagged a finger at her. 'It's all in the past and nothing to do with you, Miss Nosey-Parker!'

'I am *so sorry*,' said Ben, alternately patting my hand and turning back towards the door. The cold air was whistling through the hole in the window. Sophie had searched for a dustpan and brush and was sweeping up the broken glass. Ben nodded. 'I need to board that up. Now, we can still call the police. She's had a go at you, Lily and smashed our window.'

'She's a very ill young woman,' I said. 'Would calling the police on her help her? Or make it worse?'

Harry groaned. 'I don't want to know what else she's capable of.'

'Then leave it.'

'What the heck,' said Shirley as she came into the kitchen, 'has gone on here?'

'Jo!' we all chorused.

'*Oh!*' said Shirley. 'I see.'

Christmas Eve, both past and present. A world of hurt and fear in between. One reason why I have no special affinity towards the Christmas period. The memories of Jo always sneak into my psyche at this time of year. That first time she crashed into my life, raging and wild-eyed. I should have called the police, but I was trying to be understanding, to acknowledge her pain. *Stupid me.*

But I have Jack in my life. He's here with me now. My 'partner'. My friend and lover.

Chapter Twenty-Two

FRIDAY, 25 DECEMBER - WILD BOAR AND WILD TIMES

'HAPPY CHRISTMAS.' Jack hands me a present wrapped in pretty paper and tied up with a big gold bow. 'I had no idea what to get you, but I tried.'

We are drinking our first coffee sitting at the Moroccan table in the living room, having had croissants for breakfast. Even though it's not even nine yet, we don't want to stuff too much, as the main event will be the roast boar for dinner. I must remember to put it on, or that will be a complete disaster.

I carefully pull off the bow and paper, and inside is a box and inside the box is the prettiest jumper I've ever seen.

'Oh, Jack! It's perfect. I love it.' I slip it on, and it fits like it was made for me.

'I didn't want to go down the route of sexy underwear. I thought that might be a bit crass and so much of a cliché.'

'I don't know many men who can get clothes right, but job done, Mister.' I kiss him on his stubbly cheek. 'Let me get you yours. I tried my best too.'

Ripping off the paper, he holds the sweater I spent ages

choosing for him. It's a rich blue-green, round-necked and made from Merino wool. I hope he likes it as much as I adore this top.

'Great minds think alike,' he grins. 'I love it, and I'm glad you didn't get me any slinky boxers with *I love Santa* on them.'

'Nearly.'

Alice arrives early, ostensibly to help me prepare, loaded with bags packed with Christmassy stuff: crackers, mince pies and a bottle of Baileys, which I am tempted to hide.

Jack is still in the shower. It's *that early.*

'Where is he?' Alice is hissing.

'In the bathroom,' I hiss back.

Decanting it all into the kitchen, we look around. There's no available space. Anywhere. And barely any floor space left, either.

'Did you, by any chance,' says Alice, 'go completely mad? I mean,' she gestures around her, 'you've got everything, including the kitchen sink. Did I miss a memo somewhere? Have you invited another fifty people for Christmas?' She winks at me. 'Please tell me you didn't ask the ancient aunties over? Now that would explain it!'

'Yeah, well,' I make a face at her, 'I only wanted it to be nice for all of us.' I wave around us. 'And Jack arrived with a mountain of goodies too.'

'Whatever is in the oven smells divine!'

'Wild boar.'

'*Boar?*' She practically shrieks. 'You mean one of those big piggy things with huge tusks?'

'Yep. I've marinated it in a bottle of red with juniper berries and loads of other stuff. I found a bottle of quince sauce to go with it—'

'What the hell is quince?'

'Similar to apples except more fragrant. I looked up what went with wild boar, and there it was. I found a bottle in the supermarket. Couldn't believe my luck.'

'Can't wait. You may have noticed I'm not in my finery, so direct me to what you want me to do. We can get changed later.'

I think for a moment. 'Could you peel the spuds while I do the parsnips?'

'Sure thing, boss.'

'Fancy a cup of Colombian coffee while we work?'

'Do bears shit in the woods?' She laughs. 'Or should I say boars?'

Jack strolls into the kitchen as I'm putting the pot onto percolate. He's wearing the new sweater, and I try not to salivate. He's in soft jeans that ride low on his hips. His hair is damp from the shower. I resist the urge to grab him and snog him. That wouldn't be cool in front of Alice. She pre-empts me.

'I'm Alice. It's great to meet you, Jack.' She extends a hand, and he shakes it.

'Nice to meet you too, Alice.' He smiles shyly. 'If you're allocating jobs, Lily, what am I expected to do?'

I peer about and then go into the living room. 'Can you clear the stuff off the table so we can actually eat dinner on it? Maybe put it all in the corner over there?' I point to the opposite side from the Christmas tree. 'Then we can hide them behind the curtain and not trip over them.'

'Right. I'll get on it now.'

'Fancy another coffee? I'm putting one on to give us that extra oomph.'

'I'd love one, thanks.'

Cups by our elbows, we all start on our various chores. As our hands are wet, when the doorbell chimes, Jack volunteers to open the door for Rose. I hear him thump down the stairs and the burble of voices coming back up. Rose comes in, face flushed and, again, loaded with bags.

'Let me help you,' says Jack as she struggles through the door.

'Thanks, er, Jack. I got a taxi here,' Rose slips off her jacket and hangs it, takes a deep breath and sighs loudly, 'but what a palaver!' She shakes her head as she comes to greet us in the kitchen. 'I need to say again how stoked I am you invited me for Christmas. I was Billy-no-Mates for a bit there. I had resigned myself to a ham sandwich and a Swiss roll for Christmas dinner today.' She sniffs. 'What is that incredible smell? I hope that's dinner?'

'Wild boar.' I nod at the oven. 'Never done anything like it before, so don't knock the ham sandwiches yet.'

'I've brought a selection of things, including homemade stuffing. It's my mum's recipe. It should go well with boar as it's got nuts and apricots in it.'

'That's brilliant. Tell me when to put it in the oven.' I indicate Jack. 'And I presume you've both introduced yourselves?'

'She's Rose,' says Jack, 'and I'm Jack. Job done.'

'Very nice to meet you at last.' Rose smiles up at him. She places trays and bottles and bags and boxes on the table until Jack enlightens her that he's just about to clear it. The stuffing is put on the kitchen counter, ready to be popped in the oven, and all the rest is tucked behind the curtain. She is in a beautiful dress that suits her colouring. A necklace and bracelets reflect the fairy lights as though she is sparkling. Her makeup is immaculate, and she's in a gorgeous pair of high-heeled shoes.

'Coffee, Rose? You look fabulous, by the way.'

'Thanks. I did my best. And don't mind if I do.' She nods around her. 'I see you all have jobs, so what can I help with?'

'How about getting some music on. You know where it all is?'

'Who wants some nuts?' Alice upends a bag of cashews and a bag of walnuts into bowls. Even with the prospect of a colossal meal pending, we all scoop handfuls as we work.

At some point, Alice and I have to change and get into our festive clothes. I let Alice nip in the bathroom first. She emerges looking radiant.

'What's that wonderful smell?' I sniff her.

'Probably the dinner?' She laughs. 'Found this new perfume. John Smith's *Rose*. I love it, and it's my new best thing.' She squints along the corridor to where Rose is chatting with Jack. 'I've got a bottle for the actual Rose in the group.'

'I'm a Rose too, remember?' I don't know how to feel about this. Alice, *my best friend Alice*, has forked out for an expensive bottle of perfume for Rose. If I get a couple of pairs of socks I'm going to be annoyed. No, I will feel betrayed.

'Well, you're actually a Lily. And I thought if I got you a bottle of Lily of the Valley, or whatever, it would be like me saying you're an old lady. You know what I mean?'

'I suppose so.' I can't keep the disappointment out of my voice.

'You can have a squirt if you'd like? When you get out of the shower?'

'Will do.' *Thanks for that, Alice.*

I swap what I was going to put on to make sure I'm wearing Jack's top. I team it with black trousers to set it off. Hovering over my shoes, I realise I'm not out to impress. I don't need my stilettos; anyway, I'd probably trip over at some point. Finishing my makeup, I stare at my face in the mirror.

'Looking good there, lady,' I whisper to her. She winks back.

We open our first bottle of red, and Jack turns to all of us.

'Here's to a wonderful Christmas with new friends.'

'And old ones.' I chink my glass against Alice's.

When we open the gifts we have brought for each other, I

am mollified, as Alice has given me Freida McFadden's three latest books, an Alice in Wonderland bookmark, with the most adorable pen and ink illustration, and a pretty scarf. That'll do, even though I wince when Rose is ecstatic about her perfume. Everyone seems happy, and that's all I can ask for.

Eventually, we get a slap-up roast boar Christmas dinner on the table. The vegetables are not overdone, the roasts are crunchy, the stuffing hot, and the gravy delicious, as it is made from all the juices and wine from the boar roasting tin. Jars of condiments litter the table. Our plates overflow with food, and there is the contented chink-chink of cutlery on china. Soft music is in the background.

'I think I can categorically say that was one of the best Crissy dinners I've ever had.' Jack undoes his jeans' top button, exposing a slice of flank. 'If not the best. Compliments to the chef or chefess?' He blows a kiss across the table to me.

'Thanks.' I raise my glass. 'I couldn't have done it without my sous-chefs. So, thanks to them too.'

'God, I'm stuffed.' Alice lolls back in her chair. 'Please don't tell me we have to eat more?'

'Christmas pudding and brandy butter are coming out in ten, along with trifle and ice cream for those who don't like pudding.'

'Can we have both?' Alice grimaces. 'I couldn't possibly choose.'

'I thought you were stuffed?'

'Second separate stomach for puddings. You know the score.'

'Yes.' I stand to clear the plates off the table. 'I was joking. I think we should have the desserts in a bit, or do you all need something sweet now?'

'Later,' mumbles Rose, 'please!' She eyes the room. 'Bagsy that armchair?'

'It's yours.' I take plates and cockled bowls into the kitchen, putting leftovers into plastic pots. At least there's space in the fridge, as we've made a hefty dent in eating its contents.

I fill the sink with soapy water and start to wash up. Jack appears at my shoulder and kisses my neck. 'Need help there?'

'No, I'm fine. Go and entertain our guests. I can sort this.' I swivel and kiss his cheek. 'Thanks for being here, Jack.'

'My pleasure, Lily.'

I turn slightly to see him land with an 'oof' next to Alice on the sofa.

I have no idea how, but we force down a variety of desserts late afternoon, all covered with cream.

'Is it all right to make a coffee?' Jack yawns and stretches. 'Otherwise, I might nod off where I'm sitting.'

'Please do.' Yawning is contagious.

'We have two options, as I see it... no, I mean three.' Rose is trying to stifle a yawn but fails. 'We can curl up where we are and have a nap. Or we can play a game or go for a walk?'

'No naps for me,' I say, 'or I'll wake up and the day will be over.'

'Not sure about the walking outside bit,' says Alice, 'so I vote for games.'

'What games have you got?' Jack stirs again, and I note he's now in the other armchair next to Rose. 'I think I'm far too warm and cosy to go and get a blast of freezing air. The furthest I'm willing to go is the roof terrace.' He heaves himself out of the chair and heads to the kitchen. 'Getting that coffee on now.'

'Okay.' Hauling myself to my feet, I totter to the cabinet and slide the doors back. Boxes are piled there. 'I have Pictionary, Scrabble or...' I reach in, 'Balderdash.'

'Balderdash. I love that one,' says Jack, poking his head through the hole in the wall.

'Remind us of the rules,' says Rose, 'as I'm not sure if I've played it.'

I précis the instructions. 'It's all to do with real words that, supposedly, most people have never heard of. One player reads out a question to the others. They each write down a made-up but believable answer and hand it to the person who read the question. This person then reads out the actual answer and all the made-up answers in random order. The others must guess which is correct.' I pause. 'How does that sound?'

'Great,' says Alice.

As we are sorting ourselves out, Jack returns with the coffees.

Gathering around the table, as I am the host, I begin.

The game has progressed. Surprisingly, you can start to determine whose answer is whose. Alice always writes a sarky little off-the-wall interpretation, Rose is pithy, and Jack's answers are astute and so believable. What are mine, I wonder? I think I might be losing, but what the hell! We are all laughing so hard, I can't imagine a better way to lose a game.

'Is anyone keeping score?' Alice is filling our glasses, and again, I vow to buy a red wine-coloured carpet. The table is sticky with red wine glass stains. An image of my illustration pings into my head. How did that happen? How did I end up with my entire *fucking* book in the freezer? Damaged beyond repair? I need to stop myself. I must not go down this route. My friends and my boyfriend are here. Let it go for now.

'Are we meant to be keeping score?' Rose is a bit unsteady as she clambers upright. 'Need the little ladies' room.'

We laugh.

'If no one is keeping the score, then who is winning?' Alice digs into the bowl of nuts Jack has put on the table between us.

'None of us?' Jack scratches his nose. 'Or maybe all of us?'

'Who is hungry?' I wave around me. 'I can put a little spread out?'

'Who could ever be hungry after what we've all gobbled?' Alice pats her stomach. 'Mind you, a bit of paté on toast sounds good.'

'Coming right up.'

We eat more. It must be a World Record of gluttony.

'I feel like I'm a tortoise on my back,' I groan. 'If I fell over now, I'd never be able to get up.'

'Same here.' Jack makes a face. 'If I undo anything more on my jeans, they will fall down.'

'Do you mind if I put another coffee on to brew?' says Alice. 'It's way past my bedtime, and I should think about going home.'

'Me too,' says Rose, 'or you might find me in the morning still on your sofa.'

'Rose?' says Alice. 'Can we share a taxi?'

'Yeah, sure.' She nods. 'I can drop you off first, as I'm further out.' How does Rose know that? Has she been to Alice's place without me?

'I'll help with the coffee,' says Jack, 'as I need to stretch my legs. Mugs or cups?'

'Cup for me,' I say.

'And me,' Rose yawns. 'Although maybe it should be a jug!'

I plead, 'Please take some of the stuff you brought with you home. Please, please, please do not leave it with me. I have no willpower, and I will eat it all.'

'Are you sure? I might take some mince pies back,' says Alice.

'Take what you want,' I smile.

———

Christmas Day in Sheffield, seven years ago, is the main reason I can't bear Christmas.

When I woke after a restless night, it felt like someone had whacked me with a cricket bat on my elbow. I vowed to ask for a painkiller as soon as possible to dull the intense throbbing.

'God!' Sophie rolled over and stared at me, her eyes round. 'You look dreadful.'

'Thanks for the vote of confidence, Soph!' I grimaced. 'I didn't sleep very well.'

'No, I meant it as sympathy.' Sitting on the bed opposite me, she held out her hand. 'You haven't broken it, have you? Should we get you checked out?'

'It's Christmas Day, so no. I'm not spending today hanging about a hospital with a skeleton crew on the off chance there might be something more amiss.'

'I've got tea for you both.' Harry tapped on the bedroom door. 'Are you decent?'

'Yep,' shouted Sophie back, 'but be prepared. Lily's elbow is playing her up.'

'It's okay.' I shrugged as Harry pushed through the door. 'I feel sorry for her. I mean, she's angry and desperate. That's horrible, and I wouldn't wish that on my enemy.'

'Saint Lily!' Sophie made her most angelic face. 'If I were you, I'd prefer to punch her one back.'

'No, Lily is right.' Harry shook his head as he handed us our mugs. 'I know Alice loathes her, but Jo hasn't had the sort of family we've all had. It's easy for us to be judgemental, but her family are nutters. And I don't think we know the half of it.'

'So, we should feel sorry for her?' Sophie slurped at her tea. 'Is that what you're saying?'

Harry blew out of the side of his mouth. 'What I'm trying to say is that if we'd experienced what she has, maybe we might be a bit unhinged as well. Her family are violent and unstable.'

'More violence just makes people more violent.' I stood and slipped on the dressing gown Harry had lent me. 'Or something like that. Is that bacon I can smell downstairs? Come on. I'm starving.'

'I don't know how you do it, Lily,' said Harry. 'To be so forgiving, and that's why I love you.'

'Oh,' Sophie rolled her eyes and made retching noises. 'So bloody slushy it's nauseating! And, is it okay to go down in our jammies?'

'Of course.' Harry nodded. 'No one gets dressed until at least midday.'

Ben was bent over the hob in the kitchen, cracking eggs into a large frying pan with a big pile of bacon. In another pan, mushrooms and tomatoes sizzled. A plate cockled with toast.

Harry got in first. 'Lily's elbow is giving her jip.'

As he looked up, Ben's face fell. 'Dearest Lord! I'm so sorry this happened to you, Lily, love!'

'It's fine,' I said. 'You should worry more about your window.' I nodded at the scrap of cardboard that covered the hole.

'No. It's not fine. That bloody girl has to be stopped. I regret not calling the police yesterday—'

'Please. We all need to move on. For starters, I'm looking forward to that yummy breakfast.'

'You're a good lass, Lily.' Ben tutted and dished the food out onto plates. 'Here, Harry. Start laying out the cutlery and sauces.'

Shirley bustled in. 'Oh, Lily, love.' She shook her head. 'That girl has been the bane of our lives.'

'What, exactly, is her story?' I sat down at the table, as far from the shattered window as possible.

Shirley eyed Harry. 'Her family were, oh, how do I put this? They were the family all the neighbourhood was terrified of—'

'Like the local gangster family,' interrupted Ben, 'with sticky fingers in all the dodgy pies. The whole lot of them. You didn't cross them for fear of reprisals.'

Shirley nodded. 'Jo and Harry went to the same primary school and were best friends for years. We tried to dissuade their friendship, but the more we tried, the more Harry here dug his heels in.'

'Joined at the hip, as they say,' said Ben, placing a butter dish and pot of marmalade on the table.

'Then,' continued Shirley, 'when they moved to different senior schools, she wouldn't leave him alone.'

'She basically stalked me,' said Harry, placing plates on the table. 'Never let up. Some part of me thought that was what love was all about.' He motioned. 'Come on, don't let it go cold.'

The others sat down at the kitchen table, and although they tried not to, I knew they were all watching how I fared.

'Give it here.' Harry took my plate and cut up my food.

'I feel like a baby,' I said.

'I'm just trying to help.'

'Sorry.' I waved at Shirley. 'You were telling us about Jo.'

'You were childhood sweethearts, weren't you, Harry?' said

Shirley. 'But as he got older, I think we all realised this wasn't a good relationship, as she was so controlling.'

Harry nodded. 'Alice got involved and warned me off her. She told me stuff about what the family did and what Jo did, but I was kind of caught up in it all and really confused. Initially, I didn't believe what she was saying as she'd never met the rest of the family and was going on hearsay—'

'Like what?' Sophie's eyes were wide.

Harry frowned. 'Oh, you know, extortion, getting local businesses to pay them so they'd be left alone—'

'Lots of intimidation,' said Ben, 'if they didn't get their way...'

Shirley nodded. 'People got hurt, and we didn't want Harry to get on their bad side.'

Harry continued, 'I reacted against Alice until I saw for myself what Jo was like. She was threatening a friend from school. It was sickening and made it that much worse when I finally broke up with her. I was seventeen, for God's sake. A kid.'

'So,' I said slowly, 'she thought Alice had managed to break you two up?'

'Yeah. She kind of blamed Alice for everything. I also think she couldn't work out that Alice was my cousin because she didn't look the same as me. She saw Alice as a threat—'

'Especially', said Ben, 'as you were so close to her. More like a sister than a cousin. That Jo didn't get it.'

Sophie put her cutlery on the side of her plate. 'How can she be a teacher if she's this unstable?'

Ben frowned. 'She may be unstable, but she and her whole family are not stupid by a long chalk. Bright as buttons, the lot of them.'

'And twice as crazy,' said Harry. 'Listen. I don't want our Christmas to be dominated by talking about her.'

'I agree,' said Ben. 'She's already had too much of our air.'

The doorbell rang, and for a moment, I worried it was Jo, back for a second bout. But it was Alice, hidden behind brightly wrapped presents.

'Mum's just dropped me off. She'll pop by to pick me up before Chrissy dinner.' She peeked over the packages. 'Can one of you lot take these while I get my boots off?'

Harry scooped them off her. 'Don't worry about taking your gear off. We were just out for a walk.'

With the turkey crisping in the oven, we donned all our warm outdoor wear and slogged out as a family to do a round of the village before our Christmas dinner. This felt nice. To be with them, to feel accepted, loved even. A proper family *do*.

We traipsed down the High Street, passing the shops now closed for the break, lights off and slumbering as if they were hibernating creatures. Skirting the pub, as no one wanted a repeat performance of the day before, we wandered down an alley. Past cottages set back in time, wood smoke redolent in the air, peering into tiny gardens blanketed in snow, watching our breath curl into the biting air. At the end of the alley, the vista opened up to sprawling hills dotted with groves of trees and the humps in the snow that must mean a hedge or a wall.

'If I lived here, I'd never leave,' said Sophie.

I saw Harry's mum glance at his dad. It must be so hard when your children move a long way from you. Okay, Harry was only in London, while his brother was in New Zealand, though neither one was easily accessible.

'We'll walk across here', said Ben, 'and pick up the pathway again over there.' He pointed.

Untainted snow. Who doesn't love to kick and thrash and send it whirling into the sky? We were all like children, laughing and throwing snowballs that made our fingers ache and filled hoods with melting slush that trickled down the back of our necks.

Back on the path, we linked arms. I took Alice's arm, and Harry took Sophie's. His mum and dad trudged on ahead. We should have been paying attention, but it was such a glorious morning, it was as if we'd already pushed all thoughts of Jo from our minds. She came at us from the doorway of the Post Office. She must have been hunkering down there, as none of us spotted her until it was too late.

Her cry was incoherent as she lunged from the shadows. An animal sound of rage and loss. Bowling Alice and me over, she tried to lash out at the both of us. Rolling and twisting, we got out of her way, but I heard her words.

'I hate you. I hate you, and I'm gonna kill you. I'll make you suffer, just you wait...'

She lashed out at Alice, who yelped. 'I'll get you too, you bitch!'

'Get off them.' Hands were reaching to pull me out of the way, and someone had their arms around Jo, and it wasn't an embrace.

Ben picked Jo up bodily and threw her away from us. *'That's enough!'* he roared. Blood beat at his temples, and his face was contorted. *'Call the police, Shirley! Do it now!'*

Ben had to pull Alice back, hanging onto her arm, as she looked as if she wanted to throttle Jo. I hoped he'd lose his grip and let her. I could hear Shirley's breathless voice talking into her phone.

'There's a police car on its way,' she said.

It was satisfying to see this crazy girl bundled into the back of a police car and driven away. We all gave our statements to a young officer.

'We'll be in touch,' he said. 'For now, we'll put a restraining order on her. Go home now and enjoy the rest of your Christmas.'

To say that Christmas was subdued was an understatement. Alice's parents came to pick her up but stayed for quite a while as we discussed what had happened. Alice had quite a nasty bruise on her leg. Harry took photos.

'She's a wrong'un, that's for sure,' said Alice's mum. 'Thought we'd seen the last of her when she went up to Edinburgh.'

'Especially,' said her dad, 'as we haven't heard much about the family for a while. We hoped they'd all calmed down a bit.'

'Well,' said Ben, 'I never thought I'd say this, but maybe it's a good thing you all live in London now. Keep a bit of distance between you lot and her.'

'Does anyone know if she's got a job offer yet?' Alice sounded thoughtful. 'I mean, is she staying up north?'

'You mean,' Alice's mum nodded, 'is there a possibility she might have secured a job down south? Near to you?'

'I really hope not.' I felt my hands bunch. 'That would be awful.'

'I heard,' said Alice's dad, 'that she'd got a job teaching in a small village school just outside Sheffield. But don't quote me on that.'

'Here's hoping,' I said.

Alice hugged me tightly when they left, a pile of presents for her from us in her arms. 'Don't give her another thought. I hope she's spending Christmas Day banged up in a cell in Sheffield police station.'

'Yeah,' said Sophie, leaning in for a hug. 'Being fed gruel and dry crackers.'

Alice sniggered. 'I love where you're coming from, Sophie.'

We waved them off, clumped together on the front step.

'Well,' huffed Shirley, 'I'm not letting that girl Jo ruin our Christmas. Who wants a sherry?'

'Me,' shouted Sophie.

'All right then.' Shirley bustled into the kitchen and returned with a tray of tiny glasses. 'We are going to have a lovely time and not think about her. She's a sad and sick individual, and that's all I will say on the matter.'

'Hear, hear,' nodded Ben.

'I'll get the table laid,' said Harry. 'I'm starving.'

We sat down, and it was lovely, except I kept re-running Jo's words through my head. '*I hate you. I hate you, and I'm gonna kill you. I'll make you suffer, just you wait...*'

After dinner, the presents under the tree were hauled out and opened amid a great deal of laughter and exclamations, but the words still rolled around in my head, and I couldn't shake them out. All I wanted to do was get as far away as possible from wherever Jo might be. I longed to be home, safe in my own house. I'm not saying it wasn't a nice Christmas. Ben and Shirley made it as special as they could, but I felt a shadow lunging over us, darkening what should have been bright and sparkly. I'd never encountered such spite in my life. She wanted us to suffer... so what was she capable of? It was easy to find out where people lived. Would she follow us? Stalk us? Hurt us?

Ben drove us to the station the day after Boxing Day, apologetic and downcast.

'It's not your fault,' I told him for the umpteenth time. 'I had a great time—'

Harry butted in. 'Except you didn't expect to have to deal with my psycho ex-girlfriend.'

'No,' I raised an eyebrow at him. 'Listen, we'll all look back on this in years to come and have a good laugh about it.' At least, I hoped we would.

I'm so thankful this Christmas has gone so well. It's not rocket science, as they say, to work out why Christmas might be a bit tricky for me. I know it's stupid, but at this time of year, I look over my shoulder, watching for shadows and listening for sounds that shouldn't be there.

Oh! That doesn't bode well, now does it...?

Chapter Twenty-Three

BETRAYAL

WHEN ALICE HANDS me my cup of coffee, there's a look on her face I find disconcerting.

'I'll call a taxi now,' she practically snarls and then plops down in one of the armchairs. She avoids my eye as we drink.

After an hour's wait, the taxi arrives. That's not too bad for Christmas Day, or is it Boxing Day now? Although a little blurry, my watch tells me it's gone two. In fact, closer to three. Alice has become monosyllabic and leaves with a grunted *goodbye*. I have no idea what is wrong with her. Perhaps the booze has caught up, and she's feeling a bit of, oh, what do they call it? A mix of a hangover and anxiety. Hangxiety?

Jack and I wave from the window as Alice and Rose totter to the taxi, arm in arm. They wave back, and Rose blows kisses. It may have been a wonderful day, but I'm tired and glad they've gone, especially if Alice is a bit crabby. All I want is my bed.

'Baileys nightcap?' Jack makes a rueful face. 'Or is that a step too far?'

'Much as I love Baileys, I might be violently ill afterwards. I think I will clean my teeth and fall into bed.' I put my arms around him and rest my forehead on his chest. 'You do what you want. I'm shattered and maybe a little drunk.' I look up into his face. 'Thanks again for a magical day, Jack.'

'I didn't do anything.' A strange expression flits across his face.

'What? Is something wrong?'

'No... well, listen. We'll talk in the morning. I don't want to ruin such a fantastic day.'

I pull back from him. 'You can't say something like that and not follow through. It's not fair. Now I'll be awake the rest of the night worrying about what might be wrong, and trust me, I can come up with loads of stuff.'

'Okay, we'll talk in bed. Go and clean your teeth and get into your jim-jams.'

Tiny bolts of pain are shooting at the corners of my eyes and around my skull. I don't get migraines often, but when I do, they are blinding. As I scrub at my teeth, I wonder what it could be. Have I done something wrong? Hang on, is it always going to be about me? The woman in the mirror now looks tired and worried. '*Fuck it!*' I nod at her and spit.

In bed, Jack pulls me onto his shoulder. 'I don't ever want to hurt you, Lily, but—'

My heart physically lurches, and I jerk from him. 'What's happened?'

'I don't know how to tell you this—'

'Then just tell me and get it over with.' Don't cry. Hear him out.

'Okay. When you were in the kitchen washing up... well... Alice kind of came onto me—'

This was not what I was expecting. 'She what? I'm sorry, what did you say?'

'We were sitting on the sofa. She told me about splitting up with her boyfriend, Matt. She said they'd been together for years and how angry and upset she was... and then... it was strange... she started to kind of snuggle into me, kept running her hand up and down my chest—'

'No, no! Alice wouldn't do that—'

'I'm sorry, Lily. She did. You can ask Rose. She looked pretty freaked out about it too.' He grimaces. 'She then said if I ever got bored of you, I knew where to come to.' Jack runs his fingers through his hair. 'I got up and went to the loo, then sat in one of the armchairs to get away from her.'

I think back. When I was in the kitchen, Jack had been sitting by Alice, but when I popped back out to clear more stuff up, he'd moved to the chair. It made sense, except I couldn't make sense of it. Or could I? Last time Matt pissed Alice off, what did she do? No, I cannot let myself go down this route.

Jack continues, 'Listen, we'd all drunk far too much, and if she's feeling all maudlin about her bloke, then we can excuse it, can't we? I only mentioned it because I don't want any misunderstandings, nothing that can get out of hand. There. I've told you. Please don't say anything to Alice, as I don't want to embarrass her.'

'Embarrass her? *I'm going to fucking kill her!*' How could my best friend do something like that to me?

'Oh shit! Perhaps I shouldn't have told you. You might not trust me if Rose said something and I hadn't spoken about it. Does that make sense?'

'Of course it does. You know I've got trust issues, and I'm a bit paranoid. The thing is, I never in a million years expected it to come from Alice.' I wipe my eyes. 'Sorry, I seem to be leaking.' *Never in a million years?* An image of that strange man bounding into Alice's bedroom pops into my mind. I know for a fact that she can do something like this. She slept with another man when she was with Matt to get him back for not taking her to France. Is it possible she could be doing the same here and I am simply collateral damage?

'You can cry, Lily. It wasn't a cool thing to do. I promise you we can laugh this off in the morning.'

'I'm not so sure I will.' *Fuck!* Harry and Alice. Does infidelity and sheer lack of empathy run in their bloody family, then?

'I don't want to drive a wedge between you and your bestie. She was just drunk—'

'I've heard that before. I don't want to hear it again.'

'Let's sleep on it, and as I said, the morning will be better. I'm sorry if I've upset you, Lily. I thought I should be truthful.'

'Thank you, Jack. Yes, we'll talk more in the morning.' I switch off the light but lie awake for a long time, running it through my mind. Maybe her pique at the end of the night was to do with Jack turning her down?

Boxing Day is a blur. I go through the motions, eat and drink far too much, as is required at these festive times, smile at Jack's jokes, and be the perfect girlfriend. Although inside, I am seething. He tries to gloss over what he divulged last night, and I wave it off.

'Everything's fine,' I lie. But it's not, is it?

By the time I kiss him at the door, wish him 'bon voyage' or whatever, I am ready to explode.

'Don't do anything you might regret,' he advises as I close my door. I say nothing. At the living room window, I wave as he climbs into the taxi. He does an elegant bow and blows me a kiss. When the taxi has receded up the road so far I can no longer see it, I return to the sofa to think. Jack said Rose could confirm what he said. The thing is, do I let it go, put it to the back of my mind in a box marked 'not to be opened', or do I call Rose and ask her outright if she saw Alice making moves on Jack? I put the kettle on for a mug of tea and ping the lid off the posh biscuit tin. My favourites are still there. Good. I unwrap a chocolate-covered coffee biccy and munch my way through it. By the time I come back to myself, there is a pile of shiny wrappers in front of me, and my tea has cooled. Bunging it in the microwave, I resist the temptation to eat more. I am heading towards 'blimpdom', and whose fault will that be? Bloody Alice's. I could show some respect and call her, talk one-on-one, instead of including someone else, practically a stranger.

Why would Jack lie about this? There's no rhyme or reason. He told me he wanted to start with trust and no subterfuge. This is what it looks like.

The question is burning in my mind as if it's on fire. Do I call Rose, embroil her, maybe make her take sides? Do I trust our friendship enough? In fact, do I trust *her*? That bloody word again. My finger hesitates on the call button under her name. Do I head down a path I might not be able to get back from? It certainly looks like it!

'Hi, Rose? Can I ask you something?'

That Christmas in Sheffield might have been, in Alice's favourite vernacular, a *clusterfuck*, but it was about to get worse. Much worse.

· · ·

No one can prepare you. As a family, we didn't notice at first. Mum, never a complainer, started to feel tired. *Then stop working so hard*, we said, *put your feet up every so often, and pamper yourself*. When she began to lose weight, we girls at least congratulated her on her new look and asked what her secret was. Dad didn't look so happy. Perhaps he already had an inkling things weren't right. We all began to take note when she continued to lose weight, lost her appetite and was nauseous. We weren't worried when she went to the doctor for a mammogram. It's what we all did. Nothing scary in that. Why should we be concerned? Mum was young and fit as a fiddle.

At fifty-two, Mum was diagnosed with an aggressive form of breast cancer. The doctors tried chemo and drugs, and we looked up every alternative therapy and hippy-dippy crack-pot idea, begged her to take this vitamin or that... then they removed her right breast. It would be okay, we thought. They'd stopped it in time. How wrong could we be? It had spread into her organs. Metastasised. No, no, no! There must be something we could do? Do something! *Please do something! Anything!* They talk about the seven stages of grief, and hell yeah, we were living them.

Standing at her bedside, she lay as though she was only sleeping. All the tubes and paraphernalia had been removed, and they'd put some frilly weird shit nightie on her. We stared at her face. She couldn't be gone. There was no way. It didn't matter that she was as still as a statue, her skin was leached of its pink, or that her hands were folded on the bed and her eyes were closed. She couldn't, I mean, absolutely couldn't be dead. *No way.*

'Mum?' I croaked. 'Mum, please don't do this. Please don't leave us.'

Sophie bent over the bed and kissed Mum on her cheek. 'She's so cold,' she whispered.

'I know, love,' said Dad. 'She's gone now. That's just her shell. She's somewhere looking down on us, and she'll be shouting at us to buck up. Come on now, girls. Say your good-byes, and then can you leave me with her for a moment?'

Dad looked half the man he used to be, as if he'd shrunk in on himself. Is this what grief does to you?

'Love you, Mum.' I also bent down and kissed her, stifling a sob as I didn't want to upset Sophie. 'Come on, Soph. Let Dad have his goodbyes too.'

'Love you so much, Mum.' Sophie held out her hand, and I led her out of the room as if she was blind.

I don't know what Dad said to her, could barely imagine the pain that he was feeling, but he stumbled out of that hospital room a broken man.

I returned to London to Harry and Alice waiting with ready shoulders to cry on, though I don't think they were prepared for the times I knelt in my room, arms around myself, sobbing my fucking guts out. I wanted to howl, a wounded animal, kick anything within reach, and scratch at my arms to stop this pain. Had I been a crap daughter? Had I driven her mad over the years? Was I selfish and arrogant, not listening to her advice, thinking I knew it all? What was the last thing I ever said to her? I knew that. I told her I loved her. At least I had that. I kept returning to how many times I hadn't been home for Sunday lunch with the family and spent a birthday and a Christmas elsewhere, always believing I would have time to settle down and be the perfect daughter. That I would have time. What a joke!

'Lily?' Harry would try to help me. 'I can never begin to understand what you're feeling. I can't even contemplate losing my mum or dad. I just need you to know I'm there for you. Me and Alice are there for you.'

'Thanks, and I know that, Harry.'

Having believed I'd hit rock bottom, the metaphorical floor caved in under my feet and swallowed me whole. I did the test and there was no mistake. I was pregnant.

'This is perfect, Lily.' Harry cradled me in his arms after I'd shown him the test. 'One life ends and another begins.'

'I don't think I can cope with a baby.' It was a whisper, but I knew he'd heard when his body stiffened.

'What are you saying?' He shifted so he could look into my eyes. 'Please tell me you want this baby? I mean, you're not contemplating...' He swallowed.

'No, of course not.' I shook my head. But was I? Even the tiny, day-to-day tasks were practically beyond me. I had to push through them, as if I was wading through deep water against the tide. How on earth would I cope with a newborn? And, as I was still the main bread winner, how could I continue with my work?

As the first few weeks crawled past, we muddled through, starting to roll baby names around our mouths to test them out. Both of us tentatively embracing the idea that this new person would be entering our lives.

My dad was ecstatic. 'Best news ever, Lily.' He must have been seeing a part of Mum coming back to us. Sophie spent her time searching for baby clothes online and telling us all the weird things she'd discovered about how to care for babies.

Harry's parents were 'over the moon'. And Alice was always by my side. Maybe she grasped more than she let on.

I can see now how it might have come across to Harry. Just

after my first trimester, I lost the baby. That awful, impersonal word. Miscarriage.

'You never wanted the baby!' Harry could barely look me in the eye.

I couldn't believe it. 'Are you saying *I* did this? I lost the baby on purpose?'

He shook his head but didn't answer.

'If sheer willpower can get rid of an unwanted baby,' I could barely keep the howl out of my voice, 'women would never have the need for abortions. Something happened in my body, like so many millions of other women, and it rejected it. Maybe there was something wrong with the baby. I don't know, but *I didn't do this, Harry.*'

'Okay,' he said. It was far from okay.

It wasn't that I was depressed. I know that now, although, from the outside, it must have appeared as if I was. Harry and Alice did their best, but it took a long time for me to climb out of the feeling of emptiness and self-hate. Did my mixed feelings about the baby cause the miscarriage? Was it even possible I'd killed... no, murdered our unborn baby? Harry disappeared sometime in that period of mourning. Both of us physically here but mentally absent. Both of us devastated and bereaved. Perhaps he did blame me. I was mourning both my mum and this nameless, faceless child. Great, isn't it. Having lost them, I was about to lose another person who meant the world to me.

Alice? My chest hurts like it has a vice being tightened and strapped around it. After all she said about Harry, she has the audacity to come onto my bloke? Being drunk is never an excuse. I know she's cut up about Matt, but to try to filch my boyfriend is low indeed.

No! She's my sister from another mother. I know Alice. She wouldn't do this to me. Not after all we've experienced together. We've always been there for each other. What am I to believe? My world is breaking apart.

Chapter Twenty-Four

SUNDAY, 27 DECEMBER - LIES AND MORE LIES

WHEN I SPOKE to her last night, Rose confirmed what Jack told me. Word for word, practically.

'I'm so sorry, Lily,' she said, her voice wavering. 'I didn't know whether to say anything or leave it be. I don't know you both well enough yet, and I really thought I would stick a spanner in the works, so to speak. She was pretty drunk. In fact, we all were, and I hoped it was all a misunderstanding...'

My heartbeat was thumping loudly in my ears. 'Did you hear what Alice said to Jack?'

'No. I was over on the other chair. All I can say is he didn't look happy about it. He sort of shrugged her off, said he needed the loo. When he came back, he sat on the other chair next to me.'

'And she was touching him? You know, in a way you shouldn't touch your best mate's boyfriend?' There was silence for a bit. 'Please tell me, Rose. I need to know.'

'Yes.' I heard her sigh. 'I was naturally horrified, but I didn't think it was my business to say something. Perhaps I should have? Oh, I don't know. I'm sorry if I let you down,

Lily. I really didn't know what to do. And...' Her voice trailed off.

'What?' I shook my head, even though I knew she couldn't see me. 'What aren't you telling me?'

'Well... when Alice came round to my place the other day, she sort of let slip she had a crush on Jack...'

I registered 'came round to my place' before her other words sank in.

'A crush?'

'Yes.' Her voice was small as if she didn't want me to hear. 'She said she wouldn't throw him out of bed for dropping biscuit crumbs!'

I could practically hear Alice saying something like that. My heart lurched and I had trouble breathing. Alice was not only around Rose's, but she confided to her that she'd happily shag my boyfriend. I had to swallow down the bile rising up my throat.

'I'm so sorry, Lily.'

'No, you're fine. Thanks, Rose, for telling me.'

'What are you going to do?'

'I have to think about it. If I speak to Alice now, I think I will say things I might regret. I need to have a cool head for this.'

'You're a better woman than me, then. If I was you, I'd have gone round to her place and ripped her fucking head off!'

I'm pacing back and forth in my living room this morning when the phone rings. I make a grab for it, expecting either Jack or Rose.

'It's me,' says Alice. 'I need to talk to you. Face to face.'

'Hell yeah, we do.'

I can't believe she has pre-empted me on this. Is she calling to apologise? To throw mindless excuses at me as if I'm stupid?

What's weird is that *she* sounds angry. Why should *she* be angry? 'Come round whenever you can. I'm here.' I slam the phone down. I don't want to have another coffee as I'm already jittery. Perhaps a herb tea? I have a pot of lemon verbena growing on my roof terrace. It may be winter scrawny, but it still does the trick. The snow outside my back door has frozen into crusts, which crunch underfoot. Then I see something I find unnerving. A footprint of a shoe, a trainer. It's on the edge as if someone had taken a step onto my terrace and then stopped. It's not one of mine, and it's too small to be one of Jack's. Has someone cut across my neighbour's garden and climbed onto my terrace? I stand staring at the route I take to get into his garden and there are scuff marks and disturbed snow. Were they intending to get to the terrace next door and then realised their mistake? Then why come sneaking around the back? Perhaps whoever it was forgot their key and has a spare under their flowerpot? I don't like this one bit but can't wrap my head around it. I close and lock the back door. I still haven't got around to picking up a bolt. Maybe I should.

I make a mug of tea. Whose is that footprint? It's someone quite small, so maybe a kid? I reach for the last of the After Eights as my head floats off towards the ceiling. I'm brought back to earth with a jolt when the doorbell rings stridently. It must be Alice with her finger glued to the buzzer.

'*Shut up, Alice. I'm coming.*' Stomping down the wooden staircase, I make sure she can hear me. Flinging open the door, an angry faced Alice pushes in and stabs a finger at me.

'How could you think that? *How could you ever believe I would do that to you?*'

I'm taken aback, although I don't mind having this out here, in the communal hallway. I'm ready for a fight.

'Maybe because I have two witnesses. And speaking of belief? *I can't* believe that you would do that to me.'

'Two witnesses? How the hell have you got two witnesses when you didn't have a clue? In fact, neither of us had a clue how it happened?'

'There were two people who saw you do it. One was the person you did it to.' I stab a finger back at her. 'And it's not like the first time you've done something like this, is it?'

'What are you talking about? I did what to whom? And what's not the first time? Last time we spoke about this, you were completely in the dark, and now you think *I did it*?'

'What do you mean I was in the dark? I was in the bloody kitchen. That's where I was!'

'The kitchen? *What?*'

'I was washing up in the kitchen when you made a move on Jack!'

'*I did what?*' This comes out as a screech.

'Isn't that what we're talking about? That you tried it on with Jack—'

'Hell, no! I'm talking about you accusing me of destroying your artwork. You told Jack you believed it was me who stuck them in the freezer!'

'I never said that...' I stop. What the hell is going on? 'Come on.' Grabbing hold of her, I drag her upstairs.

'What's this all about, Lily?' She wipes her hand across her face. 'And what did you mean by it's not the first time?'

'Right,' I say. 'Okay.' We stand and stare at each other as I slowly shut the door. 'We need to say what we've been told and then what we think actually happened. How does that sound?'

'Got any drink with alcohol in it? I could use something around about now.'

'Wine?'

'That'll do.' Alice hangs her coat and goes to sit on the sofa. I wince.

'Can we sit in the armchairs?' I pop the cork on a bottle of

red and pour two hefty glasses Alice would be proud of. 'Here
you go.'

Alice takes a gulp. 'Who wants to start? You?'

I nod and take a deep breath. 'After you and Rose left on
Christmas Day, well, Boxing Day by then, Jack told me...' I have
to take a swig of my drink.

'What did Jack tell you?' Alice looks puzzled and definitely
not shifty.

'He told me you tried it on with him. That you touched him
and told him that if he grew bored with me, you'd be up for it.' I
shake my head. 'Or something along those lines.'

'When the fuck did that supposedly happen?' Alice's mouth
is a perfect 'O'.

'When I was in the kitchen. You and Jack were on the sofa.
He said you'd told him about Matt, about how upset you were.'

'I never said a word about Matt. We were discussing our
favourite films on Netflix. I remember he got up to go to the loo
and then sat in the chair next to Rose and started chatting to
her—'

'None of this makes sense. What were they talking about
then?'

'I don't know. They were kind of whispering. It sounded like
a conversation I wasn't included in.' Alice frowns. 'Jack told you
this? About me?'

'Both him and... Rose—'

'*You asked Rose?*' Alice looks as if she might bite me. 'So, let
me get this right. Instead of coming straight to me, you called
someone we barely know and asked her?'

'I was confused and upset. Jack told me Rose had seen it
all... She described exactly what Jack had said. She revealed,' I
can barely get the words past my throat, 'that when you were
around her place, you told her you wouldn't kick him out of bed
for dropping biscuit crumbs! How do I explain that, Alice?

And... and, you shagged that bloke when Matt sodded off to France.'

'Oh!' Alice bites down on her lip. 'You knew about that?'

'Yep. I bumped into him going back into your bedroom wearing practically only a smile.'

'That was the only time I've done something like that. Swear to God! Why didn't you say something to me?'

'Probably because you didn't say anything to me, either?'

Alice frowns. 'Hang on. What do you mean? When I was at her place? I've never visited Rose and I have no idea where she lives!'

'What? *Really?*' I shake my head. 'What the hell is going on?'

'Okay, well, how about this?' Alice shunts forward on her seat and stares me in the eyes. 'Jack told me you believed I was the one who put your illustrations in the freezer.' She waves her hands around in agitation. 'So, tell me about *that?*'

'I never said that. Not ever.' The ground is shifting under my feet. 'When did he tell you this?'

'When I made us all coffee. He came into the kitchen and told me he thought I should know that you were convinced I'd done it to you. On purpose, because I was jealous. He said he didn't want to cause a rift, but he thought you were behaving a bit unpredictably, you know, like you were acting neurotic. He said he believed you'd destroyed your work yourself.' Alice drained her glass. 'In fact, he said he thought you needed help.'

'I what? You mean he said I was going mad?'

'That's about the crux of it. I was so shocked. More because of what he said about me. You know, I'm selfish like that. But I was still worried.'

'Okay.' I hold my hands out in front of me. 'Let's work this through. Jack tells *me* something he knows will get me worked up into a froth. Rose confirms it. Jack tells *you* something different with the same end result. What does that tell us?'

'That Jack's a liar?'

'And?'

Alice looks as though she might be sick. 'That Rose is part of it?'

I know I'm ripping the skin off my bottom lip, but it feels good.

'Don't do that. Your lip is bleeding.' Alice pours more wine into our glasses. 'I hate to say this, Lily. Who chose Jack from that OkCupid site?'

'Oh shite! Rose did.' I suddenly jerk, slopping wine as a memory hits me.

'What?'

'On our first date, I didn't tell either of you where we were going, but I could have sworn I saw Rose in the shadows outside the restaurant. I dismissed it at the time, though maybe it was her?'

'You think Jack told her? Then they must know each other.' Alice looked about her. 'Is there any way Jack could have destroyed your work?'

'He had already left when I checked they were there. Something happened between him going and my arriving at New Renaissance.'

'Could he have come back in between and snuck into your flat?'

'It was locked.'

'Could he have got hold of a key?'

'No, I don't think so... except...' A croissant pops into my mind. 'Hang on. I gave him my key to go and get croissants when he stayed over that first time. He was gone a long time—'

'Long enough to get a key cut?'

'Possibly.' I close my eyes. 'The supermarket up the road

has a little booth for key cutting. It would have been open Sunday morning.' I shake my head. 'It would have taken much longer to get a key cut and then have to queue for the croissants—'

'Unless there were two of you?'

'Rose?'

'Rose... or whoever she might be. I tried to find her on Facebook but couldn't.'

I nod. 'So did I. I presumed it was because she didn't want to be bogged down with it like the rest of us, or maybe it's because Rose Briar doesn't exist.' I think for a moment. 'Do you think they were the ones sending the bloody roses? You know, to intimidate me—'

'Oh God!' Alice puts her head in her hands. 'The roses are from Harry—'

'*Do what?*'

'He's sent them for every launch to... you know, show his support...'

'His support? He's scared the shit out of me.' Then it hits me. 'You knew it was him all along and never said a word!'

'I'm sorry.' Alice groans. 'I told him to stop this last time when I realised that you weren't taking it in the way he was hoping—'

'Well, if he was aiming to creep me out, that worked a treat!'

'He knows that now and I'm sure he's sorry. It's just he never stopped loving you, Lily.'

'Loving me?' I have to push these words away. They hurt too much. 'I can't cope with this right now, Alice.'

Alice bobs her head. 'Okay. I understand. What we need to concentrate on is who is Rose?'

I nod, 'And more to the point, who is Jack, and why are they doing this to me?'

'I have no idea.' Alice appears grey, as if all her colour has leached away. I wonder if I look the same. 'Have you got any photos of Jack?'

I colour a bit as I find my phone. 'I took a photo of him when he was sleeping. It's not brilliant, though you can see his features well.' I stare at the face in the photo and wonder who that man is. Had I been falling in love with Jack? He'd been so perfect, and perhaps that was the point.

'I'm so stupid.' I hold my head in my hands and let the sobs and tears trickle between my fingers.

'You're not stupid.' Alice pulls me into a tight hug. 'You've been played. We need to find out who these bastards are. Now, I know you don't want to hear this, but I think they are targeting me too? And if that's the case, what is the only link between us?'

I wipe my nose on my sleeve. There's only ever been that one link. 'Harry?'

'Harry. And who threatened us all? Threatened to get us all?'

'Jo.' I turn to Alice. 'What has any of this got to do with Psycho Jo?'

Alice suddenly slaps her face. 'God! I'm so dumb! Jo. Jo-anna. Joanna. Her name is Joanna.'

'*What?*' I think I might have squealed this.

'Everyone called her Jo, but her name was Joanna. That inscription in your book. The one you wrote for Rose. For Mama Anna and baby Lara? What if Anna is Jo? Listen, we need to contact Harry. Right now. We need to send him your photo of Jack to see if he recognises him.'

We send Harry the photo, and then we have to wait. Harry is seven hours ahead, or is it behind? If it's three or so in the morning, it doesn't matter. It might take him a while to see it. We've left a not so cryptic message: 'URGENT! Do you know who this is?'

'Fancy a snack? I've still got loads of food left over.' I motion at the kitchen. I think it's more that we need food to counter the wine. I know we both drink too much and should stop, but now is not that time.

'Sure. Stress eating is always a winner.' She holds out her glass for a top-up as she trails me into the kitchen. 'What do we know for certain about either of them?'

'That's it, isn't it? How do we know any of what they said is true?' I pause and nearly pour all the wine over Alice. 'Oh, for God's sake! We're such numpties! What was the first thing Rose said to us about *her* Harry?'

Alice stares at the ceiling for a moment. 'That if he fell off a cliff, she'd clap.'

'I remember she said 'we' because I wondered at the time who else she was talking about.'

'Rose Briar? We fell for that one. Should have known. Are you okay?' Alice rubs her hands over her face. 'I know you're not, obviously, but are you hanging on in there?'

'I don't know. I think I'm still in shock. One thing's for sure – I am never, ever going to trust a man ever, *ever* again.' I stuff a piece of Turkish Delight into my mouth but can't swallow it and start to choke. I spit a chocolatey mouthful into the sink and begin to cry.

Alice hugs me again. 'I'm so sorry, Lily. Did you love him?'

I sniff loudly. 'Do you know what? I think I knew there was something off, except I didn't want to explore it, as I believed it'd come back to me and my trust issues. I liked the Jack I'd met. He was funny and caring and sweet, but that's not the man he is. That's a lie, a projection. He was an actor. So no, I don't love him. In fact, I'm afraid of him. And of her.'

'Come to think of it, so am I. What are we doing here if we

think they have access to your flat? Can we bolt your front door from the inside?'

We both rush to the front door and double lock it, leaving the key in the lock. Wedging a chair under the handle, we stare at it for a few minutes.

'Should we call the police?' I ask.

'And say what, exactly? We have no proof.' Alice rolls her eyes. 'In reality, we have no idea what is going on. Can you imagine the call?'

'Yeah, I suppose you're right, though this is nerve wracking.' I glance at my phone sitting on the table. 'I hope Harry gets our message soon.'

———

And then the fall. I don't want to go where my mind is leading. This memory has always been buried deep and for a very good reason.

Surprises, eh? Well, even though the surprise was meant for Harry, I was the one who got the biggest surprise. I'd not arranged anything, but I thought I'd pop into the Mexican restaurant where Harry worked. I was waiting for my next commission and had time to spare. A rarity by then, as I'd thrown myself into my work. I'd recognised I'd not been easy to live with. Six months after my mum passed away, I finally felt as if I could raise my head. I thought I owed it to Harry to now make an effort to live and be alive.

I was halfway through the main doors when I spotted him. He had his arms around one of the waitress's waists, and there was body language that spoke of more than *just friends*. She had her back to me, and I could see piled deep burgundy hair and lots of silver bangles on her thin arms. A flash of memory seared into my mind: my twenty-first birthday. That so-called drunken *misunderstanding*. Could I be mistaken? I darted back outside, aware of heat spreading up my neck and cheeks. I had to slow my breathing. What should I do? Run in, shouting accusations and making a complete *arse* of myself if nothing was untoward between them? All trust would be totally broken. Wait until later and ask him outright if he was seeing someone else as well as me? How would I word that?

'Hey, Harry? You shagging that waitress I saw you with then?' Lead balloon sprang to mind.

I was startled by a customer pushing past me with an, 'excuse me'. I followed him in, stepping out from behind him as I neared the bar. The waitress was nowhere to be seen. Harry looked momentarily shocked, and then he came round the bar to give me a kiss.

'Wasn't expecting to see you here, Lily.'

I stopped myself from retorting, 'I bet!' and simply said, 'Surprise!' I stared up at him. 'I know your shift ends in a little bit, and I wondered if you'd like to go for supper with me?' I wanted to saw the top of his head off and have a look inside for dirty little secrets. But then, whose fault was that? Mine?

'Yeah, sure. I'll be off in ten. Do you want a beer while you wait?'

I nodded. A beer was placed in front of me with a small bowl of nachos. I couldn't believe how cool he was, how unutterably unshaken, so much so I believed I had imagined the whole thing. While gazing around the bar, I caught Harry frowning towards the door, and he had a weird look on his face. He made a slight motion with his head. It looked as though he said 'no' to someone. I turned quickly but not fast enough. A figure was already pushing out of the door. I saw the glint of silver. Had I misread that too? Now, all I wanted to do was run after whoever she was and demand an explanation, or more like, throttle the truth out of her.

Harry acted as if nothing was wrong as we walked, arm-in-arm. Skirting Covent Garden, we headed down Henrietta Street towards our favourite Italian restaurant, Ave Mario. It was packed with skinny young things with money to burn. Did I have money to burn? Harry didn't, and if he did, it was the first I'd heard of it. I would be paying, of course. The place had a funky vibe and was kitted out like a peacock of colour and glitter, with splashes of blood red and dark stripes as you slid into your individual booth. There were so many glowing bottles of liquors on the shelves around the curved bar and arrayed down one wall, the colours practically hurt your eyes. The staff were accommodating and friendly. The year before, they had even let us bring our own birthday cake for Harry's birthday and gave us free shots of tequila. They know how to lure a customer back.

The food was delicious, as it always was, but I could hardly taste it. Who was that girl? Why couldn't I ask him? Was I so terrified I could break what we had with a question? That our relationship was so fragile? The answer was obviously, yes.

By the time we got back to the house, it was as it had always been. We laughed and talked and mucked about. That may have been due to the amount of wine and shots we'd had, though it didn't matter. We made love for the first time in ages, and it felt so good. How could I ever have doubted him? How indeed?

It was inevitable, I suppose. There's only so long before a secret is outed.

I'd arranged to go into the centre of town with Alice to visit Tate Modern. Sometimes you just need to get a bit of outside inspiration. Alice and I intended to spend the day roving around, submerged in art and culture, waffling utter pretentious shite at each other, and then go for a late lunch somewhere snazzy nearby. We weren't expected back until the evening. Of course, Harry knew this. And made good use of this time. *Oh yes!*

It started off well. Blackfriars underground was busy, but we navigated through, walking the half a mile towards the iconic building. As we entered each section we were excited about the exhibits, and I wanted to go home and start painting something bold and intriguing no one would understand, that would make people *think* they understood. So, in a way, I was quite pleased when Alice turned to me and said, 'I need to go home.'

'Okay,' I said jauntily, and then I saw her face, a pasty off green with a side helping of sweat. Oh dear, she didn't look good. At all.

'I feel quite ill.' Alice paused in a doorway, clutching at the frame as people pushed past us, chattering or silent in awe. '*Oh, bollocks!* Lily? Which way are the loos?'

I got my bearings fast, and we practically ran to the women's toilets. Alice charged in ahead and luckily managed to find an empty cubicle. As I entered, I could hear her loudly throwing up.

I tapped on the door. 'Alice? Have you eaten something, or, God forbid, you're not pregnant, are you?'

'I had a take-away with my mate last night—' There was another bout of ghastly noises. I could hear women tutting from other cubicles and while washing their hands behind me. In the mirrors, I could see a great deal of waggling eyebrows and snotty looks. *Sod the lot of them!*

Alice continued, 'There was something that tasted wrong, really—' I cringed at the sounds. 'One bit tasted really sulphurous, but by then, I'd swallowed it.'

'Food poisoning? Oh, Alice. Right, I'll call a taxi, and we'll get you home as fast as possible and hope you don't hew all over the back seat.'

'Okay. Just give me a moment. I don't think there's much left in my stomach, but we'd better be quick.'

I've never run out of a building the way we did that day. It's a wonder no one called the police. We must have looked as if we'd robbed the place. A little something worth millions stuffed under our sweaters.

Alice held a bag under her chin throughout the whole taxi ride.

'Oy,' said the taxi driver, 'she's not gonna be sick, is she? 'Cos, if she is, you'll have to pay to have the cab cleaned.'

'She's all right,' I lied. 'Just a bit queasy. Morning sickness, you know. You wouldn't refuse to take a pregnant woman home, now, would you?'

The look the taxi driver gave me in his mirror should have turned me to stone, but he was caught. You know, rock and hard place. Alice made it home and legged it to the front door while I paid. I was following her up the stairs when Harry emerged from his room.

'*What the...?*' He turned quickly, and half shut the door, so I couldn't see in, although I'd seen enough. He was in his boxers, and there was a mound in the bed that was person-shaped... no... woman shaped. It was a drip-feed, drip, drip, drip. I was expected to be away from home for most of the day. Drip. Harry was home in the middle of the day wearing only his boxer shorts. Drip. There was a shape in his bed that shouldn't *in any scenario* be there.

'Harry?' I felt my legs buckle, as I grabbed at the wall to keep me up. I remember shaking my head. This did not compute. At all. Oh, yes, it did, didn't it? That girl in the bar? The one he had his arms around. As I pushed into his room, he tried to block me, and then I saw who was in his bed. Jo. *Jo?* His bat-shit crazy ex-girlfriend?

She rose out from under his duvet like the Queen of fucking Sheba! Naked breasts pert. Her beautiful face was no longer marred by anger and hate. Now she wore a beatific smile, a triumphant smile.

'Hello, Lily,' she grinned. 'I said Harry was mine, didn't I?'

'Shut up, Jo,' snarled Harry. 'God! Lily, I never—'

I said it very quietly, 'Fuck you, Harry.' Then I turned and walked down the stairs, grabbed my bag, dropped only moments before yet seemingly a million years ago, and walked out of the front door.

'Lily! Lily, wait...'

But I didn't wait. What would I be waiting for? An excuse. It was all a misunderstanding like last time. I'd been mistaken. Been jealous. Been silly...

Christ-on-a-bike! He was shagging Jo? Mad as a hatter Jo? There was no world where this should be happening. All those things he'd told me about her, how scared he'd been of her, how unpredictable, how aggressive she was. And the fact she'd frightened me so badly. Me. His actual girlfriend. All of it meant nothing, then?

How long had this been going on? Did it start when my mum died? Did the bastard jump between the sheets with her because I was off selfishly grieving? No, it must have been after I'd lost the baby. Was my head going to explode?

I suppose it was automatic pilot, but I found myself in Clissold Park, weaving through the ancient gravestones towards the old church. This was a place that scared the Bejesus out of some of my friends, yet I'd always found it restful. Funny how the last time I'd felt terrible about Harry, I'd ended up here. The inscriptions on the headstones, weathered and sometimes indecipherable, were testament to the passing of time, which was what I needed right then. That time would pass, and it would be sometime in the future, and this pain I felt as a vice across my chest would be transmuted to a dull ache. Although I couldn't face it, I had to. Harry, *my beloved Harry*, was not only shagging another girl, but *that girl was Jo*. The breath juddered out of me, and I think I howled. It was a sound to scare away any spirit who might still haunt this place. Wasn't I just so dumb? So trusting. Well, that was going to change now.

With my back against the same tomb as the last time, I let my emotions wash over me. When I eventually focused on what was in front of me, I knew it was getting late. Dusk was fast approaching, and the light was trickling from the sky. A figure stumbled through the trees.

'Fuck!' said Alice, landing in a heap next to me. 'I would have been here earlier, except I was too busy turning inside out.' She grabbed me and pulled me into a tight hug that bordered on painful. 'I'm so sorry, Lily. I have no idea what to say.'

'You don't have to say anything, Alice.' I pulled apart from her grip. 'You didn't know about...' I swallowed, except the spit stuck in my throat.

'Of course not. I'd have told you...' She was shaking.

'But he's also your cousin?'

'Blood may be thicker than water or whatever that stupid quote is, but when your *blood* is a dumb-arse dickwad, then that's a different matter.'

'Thanks. I like the sound of dumb-arse dickwad. It has a ring to it.'

'Sorry... I need to—' Alice lunged sideways, and I heard her dry retch. 'I caught a glimpse of her. Please tell me she wasn't Psycho Jo?'

'Yep. *She* who he'd never touch with a bargepole.'

'*What the actual fuck!*' She retched again.

'You don't need to be here, Alice. You need to be home in bed. I can't tell you how much I appreciate you coming to find me, considering how ill you are.' The tears were streaming down my face, though I didn't care.

'No problem. I would say any time, except I never want to be here with you like this ever again.' Her hand trembled as she wiped her mouth. 'Maybe we should swear off men? How does that sound?'

'Like a bloody good idea.' I hugged my arms around myself. 'I don't want to go home. It's just I don't know where else to go. I can't face him. I don't want to see him.' I started to sob. 'And I really, really don't want to see her. You should have seen her face. Gloating!'

'She said she'd get her own back on us all. What a *clusterfuck!*'

'I wish I still had my bedsit.'

'Can you go home to your dad and Sophie?'

'Oh, I don't know. I don't want to burden them.'

'That's kind of what they do?' Alice's smile was sad. 'They are always there to pick us up. We're their family, and they will be there for us no matter what happens. Think about it, eh?'

'Yeah. At least I can go to my own room and shut the door in his face. Come on.' I stood and hauled Alice to her feet. 'Let's get home.' She did look spectacularly green, with purple bands around her eyes, and she was shivering. 'Do I need to call a doctor?'

'No. It's only food poisoning. You don't die of food poisoning.' She looked at me. 'Do you?'

'No. Never,' I lied.

Harry was gone by the time we got home.

. . .

Grovelling. Shouting. Pleading. Accusations. Anger.

'I get it, Harry. It was my fault you accidentally fell and slipped your dick into the woman you professed to hate?' I ground my teeth. 'Well, *sorry* for that.'

'I didn't mean it like that.' He deflated. 'She tracked me down and got the job at the bar.'

'I thought she was a teacher in Edinburgh?'

'She was, but she told me she'd taken a few months off and gone travelling.' His words were rushed, breathless. 'She told me she'd gone to some sort of retreat, an Ashram or whatever in India, to sort out her head—'

'Good for her, but what's that got to do with this? With us?'

He was squirming. 'She said she'd got over her childhood trauma—'

'You mean you dumping her by text and within minutes, snogging her mate? That childhood trauma?'

'All of it. All the shitty stuff she'd done. Her godawful family. She said she'd put it all behind her.'

'*So what, Harry?*'

'I tried my best to avoid her, and then you were kind of absent after... after...' He swallowed loudly. 'She kept telling me she'd changed and she said you weren't acting as my girlfriend should—'

'Sorry, my mum's and the baby's deaths got in the way—'

'I couldn't handle it, Lily. I couldn't cope with losing the baby. You were in such a state, and I felt useless. It was as if you weren't here anymore. I mean here with me.'

'Do you not understand what grief means? It's not something you click your fingers at, and it disappears. I needed you to be there for me. It's what partners do for each other. I needed you to have a bit of patience. I needed you to look it up on the internet, so you had a clue what I might be going through!'

'I know that now. I was hurting and confused—'

'And I wasn't? I know you thought I'd lost the baby on purpose. How do you think that made me feel? That you could even contemplate I could do something like that?'

'I know that now.'

'And how could you think the best way to deal with this was to shack up with a woman who'd made your life and the life of your family hell for years? A woman who'd tried to attack me twice? You thought *that* was a good idea, Harry?'

'It only happened that once, Lily. She said for old time's sake. I just wanted someone to be there for me. I needed to feel wanted, loved... I've told her I don't want to see her again. Please give me a second chance—'

'Don't you mean third chance? Remember Amy?'

'I only kissed her.' His voice was sullen. 'It didn't go any further than that.'

'Bully for you. Was that because your girlfriend was sitting next to you? Do you think?'

'I'll make it up to you—'

'I can't do this. You've broken everything we had. Smashed it all to pieces. I can't put it back together again. Not now.' I faced him. 'I've been talking to Alice. We've decided to get a flat in Brighton. I can work from anywhere, and she'll find a bar job down there. We've started making arrangements. We've already given the landlord a month's notice.'

'No, no, no!' Harry took hold of my shoulder. 'Please, Lily. We can talk this through, work it out. I've never stopped loving you—'

I shook him off. 'It's far too late, now.'

It might say a lot about my boyfriend that he was a fickle, cheating prick! Though what did it say about me? That I wasn't worth being faithful to and there must be something wrong with me? Was there? Is there still?

Psycho Jo. Is she haunting me? Haunting us? Anna. Jo-Anna?

'And what about Jack? Rose?' I gesture wildly at Alice. 'If they're connected to Jo, why haven't you recognised them? Are they members of her family?'

'I never met the rest of them and quite frankly, from everything I knew about them, I never wanted to. They kept themselves to themselves. I only ever met Jo and and I wished I'd never met her either.'

'But could they be?'

Alice bites down on her lip. 'I know she has an older brother and a younger sister.' Her words hang in the air between us. 'Then that would make them the same ages as Jack and Rose.'

Is this all a complete fabrication? A farce, and Alice and I are playing the fools in it? Is my relationship with Jack a work of fiction, where Jack will take a bow at the end and walk off stage? Then, where does that leave me?

Chapter Twenty-Five

THE TRUTH COMES OUT AT LAST

WE'VE SAT for a couple more hours, and the light is dimming outside. Every so often, one of us sneaks to the window and peers surreptitiously out. Do we expect Jack to be standing outside wearing a Michael Myers mask? I have no idea what we are expecting, but the beep from the phone makes us both jump.

'You go and look,' says Alice. 'I'm going to draw the curtains, as I feel as if we're in a goldfish bowl lit up for anyone to see.'

A message has come through. It's from Harry. *Are you there?*

Alice clicks on the Messenger button, and we see Harry's worried face appear on the screen. It's a shock to see him.

There's no preamble. 'Why the hell have you got a photo of *him?*'

I respond as Alice hangs over my shoulder. 'Harry? Do you know who he is?'

'He's Jo's older brother Nathan. What the hell is going on?'

'Listen, Harry,' says Alice, 'this is important. Did Jo's sister look a little like her. Reddish hair and very pretty?'

'Yes. Their younger sister Angela. They're all nutters. Keep away from them.'

'It's too late for that,' I say. 'They are in our lives. Why should we be afraid of them?'

'Because the whole family are wack-jobs. Trust me, you don't want to get involved with any of them. Hang on, how can they be in your lives?'

'Long story. Do you know who baby Lara is?'

'No idea. What's going on?'

I shrug. 'Where do we start?'

There's a sound that shouldn't be. I freeze, and I know Alice has heard it too. 'Alice?' Strange noises in the night? Scuffled marks on the roof terrace? A footprint?

Dread snags me, and I can barely talk. 'I think they might have a backdoor key as well as a front. Can you still hear me, Harry? Can you record what happens? I think things are going south—'

'Lily?' There's fear in Harry's voice. *'What the hell is happening?'*

'I need you to stay quiet, no matter what you hear. If we get into trouble, call someone, anyone... Can you do that, Harry?'

'Lily? Alice?'

'Shut up, Harry,' hisses Alice.

We both jump as we hear noises outside the front door. Someone is trying to get a key in the lock. There is a soft thump at the end of the hallway. I put the phone on the bookshelf, where it's not noticeable.

'Help us, Harry,' I whisper. 'Alice? They're coming through both doors. We need to run, and I mean now.' Grabbing hold of Alice, I propel her along the corridor, but now I can see Rose blocking the back door. She lazily raises her arm. She's holding a huge knife that seems to enlarge as we get closer. It's a cleaver. Light glints off its edge. I can hear the front door creaking and groaning as someone, I presume Jack, tries to kick it in.

'Hello, ladies,' says Rose, smiling at us. 'It's marvellous to see you both again.' How we couldn't have noticed it before is anyone's guess. That's the trouble with hindsight. Her eyes may be green and her red colouring different enough not to raise our suspicions, but now, faced with her, I can see the resemblance. I duck into the bathroom and grab a towel, which I throw at her, wrapping it around the cleaver as I barrel into her. We both sprawl, and I hear the front door splintering. Why aren't my neighbours out investigating what this awful racket is? Because they're either away for Christmas or hard of hearing. It might have been a blessing when I was playing my music a little too loudly but now it's gone against us. It's unlikely anyone here is going to call the police. There will be no cavalry galloping up the stairs to save us.

'Run.' I can feel something sharp in my side. *'Run, Alice! Get help!'*

'Fuck, fuck, fuck, fuck!' Alice dodges past Rose onto the terrace. She's nimble, but I hope she doesn't fall or crick an ankle. The front door crashes in, the chair topples, and I can hear heavy footsteps pound towards us. I stick out my foot, and Jack stumbles, although it barely slows him down. He leaps past us and onto the terrace. I see something shiny and sharp in his hand. He also has a knife!

'Come back, you fucking bitch!' He's roaring now. *'I'm going to fucking skin you alive.'*

I struggle with Rose, but she seems to have her arm around my neck, and the pain in my side worsens. Oh, God! Did I fall on her bloody great big cleaver? Has Alice made it? I can't hear much except the rush of blood beating at my temples. I twist and grapple until I pull from her.

'Help! Please help us!' I scream and hope Harry has heard. There may be the cavalry, after all.

Stumbling back up the hallway, I reach for the doorframe and try to force my way past the smashed door. And then there's a blinding flash of white and searing pain, and it goes dark.

Chapter Twenty-Six

DEAD OR ALIVE?

BUBBLES OF VOICES. Where am I? Floating somewhere in the dark. They sound excited or maybe angry. Who am I to tell? I don't particularly care, as I'm cosy down here. It's like being underwater. Is that where I am? Should I take a breath? Maybe I'll drown? The voices get closer, clearer. No! I don't want to, yet I rise up to meet them. The dark becomes light, seeping through my closed eyelids.

'You nearly fucking killed her.' There's reproach in Jack's voice. Or should I call him Nathan? No, I'll get all muddled up, and anyway, my head aches.

'She was getting away. What was I supposed to do? Ask her nicely to stay?'

'You didn't need to brain her with that cleaver—'

'It was only the handle. You're lucky it wasn't the actual blade. Now that would have been a pretty sight to come back to.'

'That would have made me very angry, Angie. You know we vowed to do it together.'

'Did she twitch?' Rose's voice creeps nearer. 'Coo-ee? Are

you listening to us, Miss Lily the Pink?' She tries to open my eyes, so I roll my head to the side. 'There she is.'

'Hey, babe!' Jack smiles down at me. 'Glad my kid sister didn't kill you. I would have been extremely disappointed. As I said, we vowed to do it together. You know, a family affair.'

'Vowed to do what?' I mumble. I know, of course I do. It's just I can't believe it.

'Why, kill you. You and Harry and Alice killed Anna and her baby, so we are going to return the favour.'

Water is leaking from my eyes, although I don't want to give them the satisfaction of seeing me cry. And I won't beg. I do have to know, though. 'Where's Alice?' I wriggle my fingers and toes. Yes, they are still working, though they seem to be bound. It's pretty loose. Perhaps they don't want marks on me?

'Oh, she won't be bothering anyone any time soon. Dear, sweet Alice is dead in a ditch, where she belongs.'

My heart nearly stops beating. Alice is dead? 'No—' I say, but Jack mimics me.

'*No, no, no,*' he squeaks. 'Yes, yes, yes,' he growls.

This must be a nightmare, mustn't it? I'm going to wake up any minute now and laugh it off. Just a horrible, terrifying dream. *Please wake up!*

'Jack—'

'My name is Nathan—'

'Okay, Nathan. I don't believe you. Alice isn't dead.' I need to know where she is.

'Oh yes, she is.' His voice is sing-song. 'She's in your next-door neighbour's garden. Such a perfect place to hide a body. You've been such a bad girl, Lily. Fancy killing your bestie in a fit of jealous rage!'

Is she dead? I can't bear it. Has Harry heard this? Help us, please help us. Alice can't be dead... *Stop!* I mustn't think about her now. I try to slow my breathing and quieten my mind. I will return to Alice when, or if, I'm no longer in danger. If I can't help myself, how can I help her?

'So all of that, with me, was a show? None of it was real?' Can I get him to feel pity?

'A pantomime. I think I deserve an Oscar for that performance.' He leers. 'I got some free sex out of it, although it was hard to block out your repulsive, ugly little face.'

I try not to show how hurt and shocked I feel by those words. 'You felt *nothing* for me?'

Jack grimaces. 'Of course, babe. I felt utter loathing and disgust, but I'm a consummate actor. And you fell for it hook, line and sinker. Didn't you?'

I clench my jaw and crush the feelings rising up. I must not cry.

'Smile for the camera!' Rose is filming.

'You got a spare key cut when you went to get the croissants—'

'Worked it out then?' He shakes his head and tuts. 'Bit late though, eh?'

'You put that wine glass stain on my painting—'

'What a treat it was. Got you rattled, didn't it?'

'And you were the one who destroyed my illustrations—'

'Why, no,' smiles Rose, 'that was me. It felt so good, Lily. Washing water over all your work. I mean, how long had it taken you?' She shook her head. 'And then when I put it in the freezer. Such a shame.' She gazes adoringly at Jack. 'Nathan watched over you, to make sure, although you were dead to the world—'

'Like you're gonna be soon.' Jack sniggers and winks at Rose. 'Properly dead. Good one, Angie.'

'Backfired though, didn't it?' I smile back at her, although all I want to do is claw her beautiful green eyes out of her face.

She looks put out. 'I admit it didn't quite go to plan. We didn't know you'd scanned them, but no matter. It caused a rift between you and Alice, and more importantly, it made you look stupid in front of your publisher. Job done.'

'We would have loved to have been there,' says Jack, 'when you opened your portfolio and, oh no!' He makes a little girly gesture. 'It's empty. Old Mary must have thought you'd lost your marbles, as there was no one to blame except you.'

'And the back door key?' Is Harry catching all this? I've seen enough crime shows to know people who do stuff like this love to crow about how clever they've been. Let them crow. Every minute or even second I can keep them occupied might give me a chance.

'Nipped back in after you'd gone to London. Easy-peasy. Got the back door key copied and was home before you'd even made it to the station.'

A thought occurs. 'What? Have you both been camping outside my flat?'

'Oh, darling Lily,' says Rose. 'We rented a flat above the doctors up the street. I must admit I was crushed when you invited Alice over and not me that time. How terribly mean.'

Have they been watching me? Fuck! That's how they knew to come here now. They saw Alice arrive.

'It was you that night. I heard you, didn't I? Closing my terrace door.' Why do that? Risk that?

'Needed to know if you'd wake up. And you did. And do you know what the funny thing was? I was standing in your bathroom. You walked right past me, and you didn't know. So, I put a little something in your drink before I left you that last Sunday. Just to make sure I'd knocked you out.'

'That coffee... Ah! So that's why I felt so groggy.' I blink. Don't react, I scold myself, although I want to scream and scream.

'And I presume you don't work in engineering?'

'Ugh! Not a chance. I'm a chippie, although I'm currently on holiday, and I must say, I'm having a great time so far.'

I nod. Yes, Jack's hands are rough. I should have realised he does manual work, but I didn't know if engineering was hands-on or not. Silly me.

'And it looks as if it's only going to get better,' says Rose, clapping her hands like a small child at Christmas. And I'm her present, aren't I? Gift wrapped in a shiny bow.

'You chose that top for me.' It's a statement.

'I knew exactly what you'd like.' She simpers. 'Never rely on men to get you clothes. What do they know?' She makes a sad face at Jack. 'Sorry, Nathan.'

'No worries.'

I say, 'You won't get away with this.'

Jack laughs. 'Oh, I think we will. In fact, I rather think we have.' His laugh makes my insides coil in horror. 'We have a plan, you see. You didn't think we'd do all this and not be prepared, charging in half-cocked, so to speak? No, no, no.' He leans down and kisses my temple gently. I twist from his touch. 'Now, don't be like that. Don't be a nasty little girl.'

'Why are you doing this? I had nothing to do with Jo.'

'You had everything to do with her,' says Rose, 'and she was called Anna, not Jo. We know what you lot called her. *Psycho Jo.* And you're going to pay for that.' She smacks the side of my face hard. I yelp.

'I didn't even know her. She's the one who attacked me!'

Jack grunts. 'And she had every right to. She should have cut your throat, but she graciously let you live—'

Rose's face lunges into my view. 'And how did you repay her kindness?' She tuts. 'You stole what wasn't yours.'

'You can't steal a person!' I can feel the fear bubbling up. How do you reason with unreasonable people? 'Why can't you understand that? Harry left Jo... Anna for me. Then he left me for her. It's called life. We were all kids, so why can't you get over it?'

'Because Harry got Anna pregnant, and when he split after you found them together, and wouldn't return her calls or listen to her, she slit her wrists. She was four months pregnant.' Jack sighs. 'When I found her, I thought we'd lost the both of them, but they survived.'

Oh my God! Jo tried to kill herself? And the baby, little Lara, was Harry's kid? 'Then that's good, isn't it? I thought you said she died, that Anna died?'

'Not that night.' Jack shakes his head. 'She was at home with us when her waters broke, and she started to have contractions. She said the baby was coming, so I got her in the back seat of the car to take her to the local hospital. There was a terrible storm that night. Mum and Dad were in the front. She was screaming so loudly, and the rain was beating down. Dad turned to see how she was, and then – *bam* – we hit a vehicle coming the opposite way. Man, oh, man! I saw the lights too late. I shouted, but it was too late.' He struggles with the words. Is he seeing that time and place?

'Then it was all shrieking and yelling, the car was spinning and spinning, and then it buckled in.' He focuses back on me. 'Mum died instantly. I could see her neck was snapped. Dad and Anna clung on. I was hurt bad. Do you remember my scar? Because I'd been holding onto Anna, her body bore the brunt of the accident. She basically saved my life. A piece of metal went through her and the baby first and then through me. Baby Lara was speared alive in her mother's womb.' Jack sways and looks as if he might be sick. I don't want to hear more.

Rose continues. 'Dad died two days later, but Anna was strong. She fought until we had to tell her the baby had died. She was going to call her Lara. Little baby Lara. Well, after-wards, she lost the will to live. She faded, and eventually, she died about two months later. *Bam, bam, bam, bam.* All four of them dead.'

'And me undergoing surgery for a couple of years.' Jack raises an eyebrow. 'Otherwise, we would have got to you sooner. And that's when I discovered the pain meds didn't work. Even upping the dose couldn't touch how much it hurt.'

'I'm so sorry—'

'Nah,' says Jack, wagging his forefinger at me, 'remember what we said? No saying sorry.'

Rose continues. 'It was when we saw an advert for your book we started to plan.' Her voice is dreamy again, like when she spoke about Harry. 'I knew I could get to meet you and Alice, get under your defences. And I also knew my brother Nathan would be just up your street,' she chuckles throatily, 'after a few tweaks. It helps to know what will lure a prospective prey in.'

'Prey?' I swallow. 'You see me as prey?'

'We're going to kill you, so yeah.' Jack nods.

'Then fucking get it over with, you cowardly pricks!' My emotions are see-sawing. I need to get a handle on them.

'Now, now,' Rose hushes, 'it's not going to be that easy. First, we need you to write your suicide note. We have your best watercolour paper here and some of your black markers. We think that's fitting for Lily Maye's farewell message.' She continues to film me.

'I won't do it.'

Jack squats beside me and sticks his thumb into my side. I scream. The pain washes over me, and my vision dulls for a few moments. 'We can make this as hard or as easy as you'd like.'

'Okay.' I need to be as clear-headed as I can be if I have any chance of getting free from them. I also have no idea how badly I am hurt. How deep the wound is or if it has cut into anything important.

Hauling me upright, they undo my bonds and dictate my suicide note from a script on one of their phones. I write the words blindly. It seems I am heartbroken after breaking up with my boyfriend, Jack. I can't continue any more, *yada, yada, yada.*

'How will you explain this wound in my side?'

'We can add,' says Rose enthusiastically, 'that you've just found out your best friend Alice was sleeping with your boyfriend behind your back. After what's happened before, you can't bear to endure all this anguish again. That you are crushed beyond repair.'

'That sounds great,' smiles Jack. 'I think you've caught her tone spot on.'

'And you had to kill her, the cheating bitch! But she got you back. There, I think we have adequately explained your cut.' Rose smiles warmly at me. 'Come on, chop-chop. We're on a time limit here.'

I write it all down and sign it. Except it's my literary signature, not my real one. Anyone who knows me should be able to see the difference right away. It might be all I have to trap them, to let the authorities know I didn't do this by choice, that I was forced. My mind threatens to black out, but I breathe it out. Focus on the now, this second. How will I escape from them? I don't know what they are planning, how they will kill me. If it must resemble suicide, there are only so many options. I will not think about them, or my heart will fail, and I will die from fear. Is Harry still listening? Can he hear all this? Can he help us? *Help me?*

'They'll find you on OkCupid. They'll have your photo—'

'I removed it a few days ago. There's nothing to link me, Nathan, to you.'

'We don't exist.' Rose moves her phone in close to my face. 'And as I said, neither will you in a short while.'

'What are you going to do to me?' I have to be prepared.

'We're going to run a lovely, warm bath for you,' says Jack. 'Just like Anna did.'

'Oooh.' Rose ambles into the kitchen. 'We need to find a nice sharp knife. We want it to be clean now, don't we? We don't want it to look as if you tried to saw your arm off.'

'How will you explain that?' I nod over my shoulder at the wrecked door.

'That will be when someone comes gallantly to your rescue.' Jack smiles gently. 'We have a friend, well, not so much a friend as an acquaintance, who we can call on to help out. He'll say he got a call from me, as the worried boyfriend. I thought something might be wrong, and as he was closer, I asked him to check on you. He'll say he thought he heard a distressed cry from inside your flat and felt he had to break the door down.'

'As we said,' Rose comes back into the living room with my paring knife, 'we've got it all worked out. How poetic,' she laughs. 'Remember the story of the Little Goose Girl? When the false princess tells of her own fate? You've always been the false princess, and you sealed your fate that day when Anna tried to take her own life.' She winks. 'Aren't we just the best?' Her voice is joyful, as if she has told me we're going out for a surprise picnic. She walks to the bathroom, and I can hear the bath filling. I think she is humming.

'Strip,' says Jack. Come on now, it's not like we haven't seen it all before.' He laughs, and it has a malicious sound to it.

I start to undress but stop when I get to my underwear.

'I said strip. All of it off now.'

My clothes lie in a heap on the carpet. What's that? I twist to see the open wound under my ribs on my left flank and dark stuff smeared and thickly dribbling. It's where I was injured by the cleaver. I need to try one last time. 'Please don't do this. What happened to Anna and your parents was a terrible tragedy, but none of that was my fault.'

'Yeah, yeah, yeah.' He frowns. 'No. It was. Yours and Alice. She stopped Harry from seeing Anna when they were kids. They were meant for each other, so she got what was coming to her—'

Alice? Oh God, I'm so sorry for everything! My heart constricts at the thought of Alice. I shove her from my mind. *Later*, I promise her.

'As to you,' he runs his finger down my cheek, and I flinch from him as if he burns me, 'you took him away from her. She was pregnant with his child, was going to be a mama to his baby, but you fucked that up for her—'

Rage bubbles up. 'According to Harry, he'd only been with her that one time. She was manipulating him again. Like she'd always done. If he had wanted to be with her, he'd have been with her. *She* was with *my* boyfriend, you know. I was with him for years, so your beloved Anna was a cheating, *crazy psycho!*'

'*What did you say?*' He raises his fist then stops. I get it. They won't risk marks on me that can't be accounted for. Otherwise, it might look like I'd had help killing myself. And they can't have that, now, can they? Although I'm not sure the gash in my side will be explained so easily.

It hits me, then. The full realisation that they are going to kill me. Here and now. I hold up my hands as if in supplication and then knee Jack as hard as I can in the balls. He doubles over with a grunt, and I try to punch him in the head, but he is faster. He turns and grabs me around my waist, and we barrel across the room, smashing into the table. Air is forced out of my lungs, and the pain threatens to overwhelm me. He lands on his bad shoulder, and I hear him gasp in what I hope is a vast amount of agony. Flailing my elbows, I clip his jaw.

Footsteps are running up the hallway, and then Rose has her arm around my neck, and I feel a burning pain as she tears open the wound in my side. I howl.

'Get off him, you bitch!'

I don't know how to fight, although I know I don't want to die. Now I have the two of them on me. Jack kicks me in my stomach; I fall to the floor, retching, and Rose is now beneath me. She still has her arm around my neck, and I fling my head back and hear a satisfying crunch. She's squealing.

'I'll kill you for that!' Jack no longer has to disguise himself. This is his true form, eyes wide and a grin practically ripping his face in half. A Halloween mask is gazing in rapture down at me. I kick out at him and thrash like a fish on a hook.

'Get her, Nathan. *Kill the bitch.*' Rose has shoved me off and is now standing. I see her face over Jack's shoulder, in a rictus. She is a snarling beast. Blood is gushing out of her nose and down her shirt. Yet she is still holding her phone up. She wants to film my death at all costs. *I fucking hate her!*

He's orgasmic, his face expressing such pleasure. The monsters in our nightmares are real. And they are human. White lights are spiralling at the edge of my vision. I'm getting weaker, and my mind is foggy. His weight is bearing down on me, his hand clamped around my throat. I have so little left, though I still stare into his eyes. I want him to see me, to take on the enormity of what he's doing.

Sirens blare in the distance as I go limp. There are jubilant voices. They are celebrating my death gleefully. How vile they are. But then their voices change. I can hear worry and then panic.

'What the *fuck*?' says Jack. 'Angie! We have to get out of here—'

'Why would they be here for us?' Rose's voice is above me. Is she still filming me? 'They don't know we're here. How could they?'

'We can't risk it. We need to get back to your flat, and then we're out of here.'

'Then we go out across the terrace and over the gardens?'

The sirens are now closer. I can see flashing lights reflected across the ceiling.

'Just got to make sure,' says Jack.

There is a burning sensation in my side, and then pain floods through me. It goes dark again.

Chapter Twenty-Seven

MONDAY, 28 DECEMBER - DELIVERANCE

WAKING in a strange place is disorientating. Then it hits me. I'm awake, so that must mean I'm still alive. Everything is muted, but I can hear peculiar whirring sounds, clicks and beeps. I sniff. There's a distinctive smell I recognise. It's the same as when I stood beside Mum's bed while she was dying. I can only be in a hospital. Opening my eyes, I heave in a breath. There's a drip attached to my arm, and I'm tied to a monitor, which shows I still have a heartbeat. The blinds on the windows are closed, and I can't see out. Which hospital am I in? I try to remember what happened. It comes in shards of memory, bright and piercing, and it's painful.

'Oh,' says a voice, 'you're awake.' A nurse has come in on soft feet. She is smiling at me, but I jerk from her as she reaches for me. Some part of me wonders if she's a friend of Jack and Rose. Will she lull me into a false sense of security, and then they'll strike? 'Gotcha', they'll laugh, and then they'll kill me for real?

'It's okay,' she soothes. 'You're okay now.'

'Am I?' My eyes prickle, and my cheeks are slicked wet. 'Am I really? They're not going to kill me again, are they?'

The nurse looks disconcerted. 'You are safe here.' She nods over her shoulder. 'The police have an officer outside.' Patting my hand, she gestures at her name tag. 'I'm Nurse Reynolds. The doctor will be in to check on you in a few minutes. You've been through a lot, Lily, but you're safe now. Trust me.'

Those two words. *Trust me.* I need to get out of here.

As I start to try to claw out the drip, a doctor in a white coat comes into the room. 'Good morning, Lily.' She steps forward and lowers my hands. I'm too weak to fight her. 'I'm Doctor Marsh. It's good to see you awake. Now, I'm unsure what Nurse Reynolds told you, so I shall recap for you. You had a serious wound on your side and have undergone an operation. You were also suffering from being half-strangled, but you are now stable. In fact, doing extremely well, all things considered.' She turns to the nurse. 'And I'm sure Nurse Reynolds has told you that you are safe.'

'I'm okay?' I bite down on my lip, 'Is this an act? Are you part of this?' I wipe the tears and snot from my face. 'Are they coming to finish me?' I start to sob. I can't hold it in anymore. 'I don't want to die!'

Nurse Reynolds comes to the bed. 'You're going to be fine, Lily.'

'How do you know my name? You're with them, aren't you?'

The doctor intervenes. 'We know your name because your friend Harry told the police who you are.' She pauses. 'And Alice.'

'Alice?' I can't say it. 'Has anyone—'

'Alice is in a room down the hall—'

'*What?*' I scream. 'She's alive?'

'Yes, she is. She's in the ICU. She was severely injured and has been on the operating table for many hours.' She's got one of those expressions doctors reserve for when they are about to tell you *the dreadful news*. I tense. 'The next few hours are critical. We can but wait and hope.'

'And pray,' says Nurse Reynolds.

'If that helps, then by all means,' nods Doctor Marsh.

Alice is alive? Can I believe this? My heart pounds in my chest with sheer joy. 'How was she found?'

'It seems your friend Harry alerted the police here. I'll let them elaborate when they come to interview you.'

'Harry told them?'

'Yes.' She turns to leave. 'By all accounts, Lily, you're a fortunate and courageous young woman. Now, please try to rest.'

An officer in uniform is ushered in. 'Are you up for a few questions?'

I nod and shift to a more comfortable position.

He opens a notepad and lays his phone on the swing table. 'Do you mind if I record this, so I can get an exact transcript?'

'No, fine.'

'Please tell me everything you can remember.'

I tell him. Then I need to ask, 'How were we found?'

'Harry Bryson recorded the conversation between yourself, Alice Bryson and the two assailants, Nathan and Angela McCready. He contacted the police here in Brighton and sent them the recording. He told them where you lived and where we would find Alice. An ambulance was dispatched immediately. We got to the crime scene and found you. Alice was discovered to be alive, although severely injured. She was rushed to the hospital.'

I shake my head. 'Have you found them yet?'

'They are in the holding cells in Brighton Police station. Mr Bryson told the police where Miss McCready's flat is. They were apprehended within minutes. Officers are examining their phones as we speak. If, as you say, they were filming you, then all the evidence is there.'

'Oh, they were filming all right.' I turn my head from him. 'What kind of people do that? Film someone dying for the fun of it?'

'Terrible people.' He taps his notebook. 'With all the evidence we have so far, they will be in prison for the rest of their lives.'

'Is that a promise? And please don't say "trust me". I'm having trouble trusting anyone right now.'

He nods and says nothing. At the door, he stops. 'You did the best thing you could by keeping them talking, else I think you wouldn't be here now. Think on that, Lily Maye.'

'It wasn't me. It was Harry.' I choke and turn my face away. At the last, he came through for us.

'I'll let you get some rest.' I hear his footsteps recede.

I doze, but when I wake, Dad and Sophie are sitting in the bucket seats that are in every hospital. Maybe they are made to be so uncomfortable that visitors leave before they outstay their welcome?

'Oh, God! *Lily!*' Dad obviously doesn't know which part to hug, so he fumbles around and manages to plant a kiss somewhere on my forehead.

'What the hell?' Sophie looks manic, as if she might thump me one. Her hands are balled on her hips, and then she stumbles towards me and pulls me into a tight hug.

'*Ouch!*'

'Sorry, sorry, but you scared the crap out of us!' She rubs the tears from her face. 'What the hell happened?'

'I don't know where to start. Do you know how Alice is?'

'They're still waiting to see, though they seem hopeful.' Dad's face is grey. 'We thought we'd lost you—' He turns from me, and I can see he's hiding the fact he is crying.

'Cut it out, you two. If you set me off and it splits my stitches, I'll get mad, and you don't like me when I'm mad.'

'Get as mad as you want,' says Sophie, pulling a seat closer and clutching my hand.

'How much do you know?' I ask.

Dad also pulls up a seat and leans in. 'The police called and told us you were here, that you were injured but stable. We came as fast as we could—' He swallows loudly. 'I couldn't bear it if...'

Sophie pats his shoulder and continues. 'Left Mike with Bob and just drove until we got here. They told us you'd been interviewed by a police officer, and now you were resting. You were asleep when we arrived. We were so thankful to see you.'

'What the hell happened?' Dad's hands are held wide.

'Apart from the fact that I now hate Christmas with a vengeance.' I point to the door. 'Better go and get some coffee and cakes in. It's a long story.'

'Oh, by the way,' Sophie looks at Dad, 'we got a call from Harry. He's coming on the next available flight.'

'By all accounts,' says Dad, 'he was terrified. He believed both you and Alice were dead.'

'He wasn't the only one,' I say.

'He wants to see you.' Dad nods. 'If that's all right with you?'

'Harry's coming here?' I close my eyes and swallow. My throat is parched. 'He saved our lives. We'd both be dead if he hadn't done what he did. Of course I want to see him.' Harry. *My Harry.*

Epilogue

THIS MAY BE my ninth book launch, but I'll tell you, there are no more nerves, just plain astonishment at how my life has panned out.

It's been about a year since my last launch, where I glimpsed Angela McCready in the audience, and I often wonder what would have happened if I'd ignored her at the bar that evening. I'm sure both she and Nathan (I can't bear to use the names I knew them by) would have modified their plans to get to Alice and me. That was a given. And maybe if that had happened, the ending would have been different, the ending they both craved. Our deaths. I still, sometimes, look over my shoulder or jump at sudden sounds I can't identify, but I am trying to live in the 'now'. To enjoy my life to the maximum.

Today, fifty fold-up chairs are spread across the area in front of the table, piled with my latest creation. Another Johnathan Elliot story. We are making quite a team. I adore his stories, and he is neither a mother nor a primary school teacher. Not everyone fits the norm.

Mary is settling herself beside me, and on my other side is

Johnathan. He also finds book launches stressful, though we will hold each other up. It took me a while to get back into my work, but there is something about my new work, and many have noted it, that has people fascinated. It is grimmer, wilder. As if my near-death experience left a dark smudge on my soul that leaches out into my paintings.

I glance across the room. People are coming in quietly, hands in front of mouths as they whisper. They all know me, as I was front page news, complete with photos and interviews from anyone who thought they knew us. The story of how Alice and I ended up in hospital had the makings of a great thriller. Except it wasn't a tale in a story, it was real, and it happened to us. The knife wounds not only marked our flesh but tore parts of us that have taken a long time to heal. I understand some may be here to simply gawp. Let them. Maybe they might buy a book out of sympathy. (Please insert a laughing emoji here!).

The front row has been reserved for my family. My dad is beaming, the pride in every movement palpable. I wish my mum could be here with us too. Maybe she is? I don't know. I feel a comforting presence here, as if she's leaning over my shoulder to wish me good luck. Next to him is Sophie, little Mike, who is not so little anymore, wanting to get away from his mother so he can explore this amazing bookshop (or cause havoc, which is more likely), and Sophie's husband Bob, who is looking decidedly harassed. He would be, because Sophie's bump is showing now, and soon there will be another addition to our family. The gender is unknown, but I'm betting on a girl.

I nod at Alice, who is sitting next to my dad. She grins back at me and winks. Although I am concerned about how hard her recovery has been and how she has battled with what that monster Nathan did to her, I worry more about her mental scars. She hides it well, but I can see that a little bit of light has gone out from behind her eyes. She is not so gregarious. She watches more, talks less and is not the extrovert she once was. This has been cut from her. I suspect she believes the same of me, but we dare not broach the subject. Not yet at least. We are both haunted, but we stay away from the shadows. I am so thankful she is here with me today. I love her so much. My other sister.

Nathan and Angela McCready received life sentences with no parole. In the film Angela took of me, her hateful words are engraved across my poor battered soul. I heard that the jury members who watched it were shocked to their core, and some needed counselling afterwards. Can a person bounce back from such experiences? To have willingly given your heart to another human, to discover that all they wanted was to plunge a knife into it. And twist it.

I rub at my own stomach. I'm not as far along as Sophie. I will be giving my dad his third grandchild about four months after Sophie. He's going to have his hands full, and he's going to love it.

Harry's mum mouths something at me, which I can't hear, but I know it is encouraging. Ben is sitting one seat up from her. He does a thumbs-up and bobs his head. Between them sits Harry. My Harry. My husband and the father of my child.

And twelve long-stemmed red roses look stunning in my green glass juice jug.

Acknowledgments

I would like to thank my publishers, Hobeck Books and their dedicated team, for believing in me and my work. So, thanks to Rebecca and Adrian, and thanks to my hard-working editor, Sue, who has been brilliant and caught those inconsistencies. And thanks to Jayne for her fabulous cover.

My thanks are extended to my amazing beta readers, who include Pam Newman, who has read all my work and is perhaps my Number One Fan (but not in an Annie Wilkes sort of way), Fi Primarolo, Sarah Bohannon, Julie Urquhart, Dee Groocock, Theresa Terry Hetherington, Jan Gibbs, and last, but by no means least, Ted Jonsson. Thanks for all your invaluable insights.

Thanks to my partner Malk, always so supportive, who also lives and works in his own box (he's a musician), while I live and work in mine. We meet for coffee in the garden.

Thanks also to Cornerstones Literary Consultancy, who have critiqued my work and taught me invaluable lessons along the way.

So again, thanks to everyone who has helped me on my journey to here.

HILLY BARMBY

About the Author

Hilly attended Rochester College of Art to experience an excellent Foundation Course, which led to a degree course in Graphic Design at Central School of Art and Design in London. Here, she led a colourful life, which she has woven into many of her stories.

After her degree course, she went on a woodworking course to make furniture. Combining her art and woodworking skills, she got a stall at Covent Garden Craft Market to sell hand-made chess and backgammon sets.

She moved to Brighton, a fabulous city and this is where Best Served Cold is set. After teaching Design Technology for fifteen years, she gave it all up to relocate to Órgiva in southern Spain. She has been here for the last seven years, living happily in an old farmhouse on an organic fruit farm in the mountains, with her partner and two rescue dogs.

Hilly is also part of Artists' Network Alpujarra (ANA), a community of artists who have exhibited extensively in the region of the Alpujarra. She also makes ceramics, jewellery, and up-cycles anything not nailed down.

To connect with Hilly you can find her on a variety of platforms.

Website: www.hillybarmbyauthor.com
Instagram: https://www.instagram.com/hillyollie

Twitter: https://twitter.com/Hilly_Barmby
TikTok: https://www.tiktok.com/@hillybarmby387
Facebook: https://www.facebook.com/HillyOllieBarmby
BlueSky: https://bsky.app/profile/hilliebillie.bsky.social

Hobeck Books - the home of great stories

We hope you've enjoyed reading this novel by Hilly Barmby. To keep up to date on Hilly's fiction writing please do follow her on Twitter.

Hobeck Books offers a number of short stories and novellas, free for subscribers in the compilation *Crime Bites*.

- *Echo Rock* by Robert Daws

- *Old Dogs, Old Tricks* by AB Morgan
- *The Silence of the Rabbit* by Wendy Turbin
- *Never Mind the Baubles: An Anthology of Twisted Winter Tales* by the Hobeck Team (including many of the Hobeck authors and Hobeck's two publishers)
- *The Clarice Cliff Vase* by Linda Huber
- *Here She Lies* by Kerena Swan
- *The Macnab Principle* by R.D. Nixon
- *Fatal Beginnings* by Brian Price
- *A Defining Moment* by Lin Le Versha
- *Saviour* by Jennie Ensor
- *You Can't Trust Anyone These Days* by Maureen Myant

Also please visit the Hobeck Books website for details of our other superb authors and their books, and if you would like to get in touch, we would love to hear from you.

Hobeck Books also presents a weekly podcast, the Hobcast, where founders Adrian Hobart and Rebecca Collins discuss all things book related, key issues from each week, including the ups and downs of running a creative business. Each episode includes an interview with one of the people who make Hobeck possible: the editors, the authors, the cover designers. These are the people who help Hobeck bring great stories to life. Without them, Hobeck wouldn't exist. The Hobcast can be listened to from all the usual platforms but it can also be found on the Hobeck website: **www.hobeck.net/hobcast**.

Other Hobeck Books to Explore

Silenced

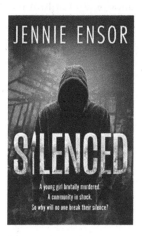

A teenage girl is murdered on her way home from school, stabbed through the heart. Her North London community is shocked, but no-one has the courage to help the police, not even her mother. DI Callum Waverley, in his first job as senior investigating officer, tries to break through the code of silence that shrouds the case.

This is a world where the notorious Skull Crew rules through fear. Everyone knows you keep your mouth shut or you'll be silenced – permanently.

This is Luke's world. Reeling from the loss of his mother to cancer, his step-father distant at best, violent at worst, he slides into the Skull Crew's grip.

This is Jez's world too. Her alcoholic mother neither knows nor cares that her 16-year-old daughter is being exploited by V, all-powerful leader of the gang.

Luke and Jez form a bond. Can Callum win their trust, or will his own demons sabotage his investigation? And can anyone stop the Skull Crew ensuring all witnesses are silenced?

Pact of Silence

A fresh start for a new life

Newly pregnant, Emma is startled when her husband Luke announces they're swapping homes with his parents, but the rural idyll where Luke grew up is a great place to start their family. Yet Luke's manner suggests something odd is afoot, something that Emma can't quite fathom.

Too many secrets, not enough truths

Emma works hard to settle into her new life in the Yorkshire countryside, but a chance discovery increases her suspicions. She decides to dig a little deeper...

Be careful what you uncover

Will Emma find out why the locals are behaving so oddly? Can she discover the truth behind Luke's disturbing behaviour? Will the pact of silence ever be broken?

Blood Notes

Winner of a 2022 Chill With A Book Premier Reader's Award!

'A wonderful, witty, colourful, debut 'Whodunnit', with a gripping modern twist set in the dark shadows of a Suffolk town.' EMMA FREUD

Edmund Fitzgerald is different.

Sheltered by an over-protective mother, he's a musical prodigy.

Now, against his mother's wishes, he's about to enter formal education for the first time aged sixteen.

Everything is alien to Edmund: teenage style, language and relationships are impossible to understand.

Then there's the searing jealousy his talent inspires, especially when the sixth form college's Head of Music, turns her back on her other students and begins to teach Edmund exclusively.

Observing events is Steph, a former police detective who is rebuilding her life following a bereavement as the college's receptionist. When a student is found dead in the music block, Steph's sleuthing skills help to unravel the dark events engulfing the college community.

Also by Hilly Barmby

From My Cold Dead Hands (Bloodhound Books)

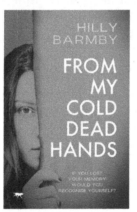

Little by little, Cassie, an amnesiac, pieces together the truth about her Southern family, her old life, and a friend's murder, in this engrossing novel of suspense.
https://geni.us/ColdDeadHands

The Pact (Bloodhound Books)

A get-together reveals dark secrets that tie old friends together—
and tear them apart—in a twisting new thriller.
A group of old friends caught up in a terrible tragedy.
https://geni.us/ThePactCover

Hilly also publishes Young Adult fiction. She has four books
with SpellBound Books under the pen name of **Billie Hill**.

Eazee Life Trilogy

Eazee Life (Spellbound Books)

What is it that makes you human?
The ability to pass your genes on into the future?
Or maybe it's how *rich* you are.
Could it be the fact that you were born and have the right to a soul? But what about Benedict? A clone. Not born but grown in a tank to fulfil a purpose not his own? Is it his capacity to care, to *love* that will make him human?
https://amzn.eu/d/aHax9Tv

Glimpse (coming soon)

Milton Keynes UK
Ingram Content Group UK Ltd.
UKHW041333251123
433126UK00005B/49

9 781915 817266